PICKLED PUNK

PICKLED PUNK

by
Chris Minnick

Secret Gallery Publishing
Astoria, OR

The Secret Gallery
160 10th Street
Astoria, Oregon 97103
https://thesecret.gallery
email: info@thesecret.gallery

Printed in the United States of America

First Edition
ISBN: 978-0-578-61358-1

Part 1
Get your throw right . . .

CHAPTER 1

In which Mike becomes a clown

At 14, Mike's job was to clean up after the animals and clowns. Sometimes, he'd pick up a set of juggling balls and try to imitate the casual juggling he saw the other performers do when they were standing around smoking and talking. They made it look so easy, but even with just two balls, Mike couldn't keep them moving and catch them.

Lucy, the cook and former clown, saw him practicing one day and gave him some pointers.

"You're doing it wrong," she said. "Don't look at your damn hands, and stop moving them all over the place. Get your throw right and your catch will take care of itself."

Mike tried to not look at his hands and he dropped both balls.

Lucy kicked him hard in the shin. "You're not gonna forget that," she said, while he was bent over holding his shin and holding back tears. "Now try again, but with three."

Mike picked up another ball and tried to juggle the three. He dropped two after the first throw and Lucy's hiking boot slammed into his right shin. "Stop dropping the goddamn balls, motherfucker!"

Mike limped away fast, rubbing his shin and sniffling.

"Get back over here, pussy ass!" Lucy yelled as she ran after him, a cigarette hanging out between her lips and her hairnet still on. Mike picked up the pace, and Lucy gave up after a hundred feet.

That night, as Mike was falling asleep in his tent, he heard a rustle on the path outside. The door flap of his tent opened, and Lucy stepped in. She stood over him with three wooden balls in her left hand, which she threw at his head, one at a time. Then, for good measure, she kicked him in the shin.

"You need to be practicing right now, pussy face."

The other tents erupted into laughter. Within a week, Mike could juggle three balls.

It was that same summer that Mike had his first taste of alcohol. It was July, and the first night of the circus's stay in Cleveland. The day had gone well, they had a good crowd, and the clowns and dwarfs sat around a campfire, some of them with smudges of makeup still on, playing guitars, ukuleles, toy wind instruments, and makeshift drums. A bottle of booze made its way around the fire.

Mike's big sister, Pauline, drank with the rest of the clowns. Mike refused, because he thought Pauline would be disappointed if he drank. On this night, Pauline and Steve the Trapeze Artist ran off into the woods, and Leo the Dwarf insisted that Mike take a swig. Mike took a small sip, his lips only opening enough to let a couple drops pass. He felt a warm, clean sensation on his tongue and his heart sped up at the thought of how bad he was to be drinking.

He lowered the bottle from his lips and smiled. "You fakin' us, son?" Leo scolded. "You didn't even take half a sip—much less a real circus swig. Are you a man or your sister's puppet?"

Mike took a deep breath, closed his eyes, and tilted the bottle up to his mouth and drank until he almost choked, dropping the bottle and coughing with his eyes watering and his throat burning. The clowns and dwarfs burst into a raucous laughter like only drunken circus performers can do.

From that night on, Mike would partake in the nightly fireside booze ritual. At first, he hid it from Pauline. It was his secret, shared with the dwarfs and clowns. Over time, he grew more relaxed and Pauline found out. She didn't care.

Pauline was a loose clown. When she slipped into the woods with acrobats or animal trainers, the other clowns would look at each other and wink or make a comment that Mike didn't understand.

One Saturday, Pauline was joking around with the other clowns and preparing for a performance when Mike passed by and repeated what he thought were words of encouragement he had heard a clown say about his sister.

"Go get 'em, Pauline! Tonight's the night you'll blow the whole big top!"

Pauline looked aghast and her face flushed under her makeup. "What did you say?"

"Blow the whole big top, Pauline! You can do it!"

Pauline slapped Mike across his face and turned to the head clown, Tiny.

"Where the fuck did he get that?"

Tiny shrugged and smirked. With his sad face makeup on, the mixed-up expression on his face looked sinister. Pauline stormed off and Tiny took Mike aside.

"Look, Mikey," he said, "The things we say around the fire when it's just guys are just for guys. You don't repeat them to anyone, and especially not to your sister. There's a dwarf-clown-man secret pact in the circus, and if you're going to be part of this group, you need to follow the rules. You understand?"

CHAPTER 2

In which we meet Princess

At twenty-two, Princess was the youngest of the dwarfs. She had long blond hair, blue eyes, and, biologically speaking, she was a midget because she had normal body proportions. In the circus, she was an acrobatic dwarf—two specialties that guaranteed her work for as long as she was able-bodied.

She flirted with Mike in a joking way when they were both drunk, but Mike was afraid to take things further—both because he was a big person and because he was a minor.

Leo the Dwarf suggested to Mike that he would need to make the first move. "Princess is ripe," he said, "but you need to do the pickin'."

Mike thought Leo was just joking, and he laughed it off. Two days later, Leo checked back in. "Hey Mikey! You start the pickin' yet?" He puckered his lips and thrust his groin several times while slapping his own ass.

The next night, Mike sat next to Princess at the fire. After the vodka had gone around the fire a few times, Mike passed it to Princess and left his hand on the bottle as she grabbed it from him. Their fingers overlapped for a moment and it excited him. On the next turn around the fire, they both lingered, and the same on the following time around. Mike became aroused and he could see by the looks that Princess was giving him that she was too. How would the other dwarfs react? How would the big people react? What would Pauline say? If anything happened, they would need to keep it a secret. But how do you keep a secret when you live in a traveling circus camp?

Later, Mike and Princess sat facing each other in her tent. Mike's armpits and palms were damp. Princess was experienced. She was experienced with every dwarf he had ever known. But who was he to feel jealous or uncomfortable? He knew nothing. He was an imposter in this world. He wasn't even sure he enjoyed being around Princess. Was he just here trying to make Leo proud of him?

He looked into Princess's eyes and tried to keep his gaze fixed on hers and not blink. He stared until his eyes watered and he couldn't stand to stare any longer. As he was about to blink, Princess said, "What?"

"What do you mean?"

"You're staring at me like a creep. Is that something that someone told you to do or is that how you are?"

"I don't know. I guess I thought it was important to look in your eyes."

"Look me in the eyes, yes. Staring like you're a dog who hasn't eaten in a week and will bite my face off at the first sign of weakness—not ok."

"Sorry."

"And don't say sorry. You're just a kid. I can't believe I'm doing this. OK. Give me your hands."

Mike put both of his hands into hers. She pressed them against her breasts so that his hands were cupping them. After a moment, she let go of his hands and he let go of her breasts.

"What are you doing? Leave them there. Here, give me."

He gave her back his hands, and she put them back on her breasts. She gave them a squeeze and let go. She tilted her head back and looked up at the roof of the tent and closed her eyes.

Mike didn't know whether he should move his hands. Was he supposed to squeeze or rub or what? He tried squeezing.

"What are you doing? Stop that. Be still with them."

Mike sat still. Princess sat still too, but with her head tilted and her mouth open slightly. They sat silent like this for several minutes. He felt his penis growing and wanted to touch it, or for her to touch it. He didn't dare let go.

Princess smiled and tilted her head down to look at Mike, glancing for a moment at the bulge in his pants. She removed his hands from her breasts and put them on his lap.

"OK. I'll see you tomorrow," she said.

Mike stood up, his stiff penis making it uncomfortable. She noticed and smiled.

CHAPTER 3

In which Pauline loves France

Pauline saved her clown wages in a stocking in the bottom of her backpack. A benefit of being a loose clown was that she never had to pay for anything. Anything she wanted or needed was given to her by one of her lovers or by someone who was afraid of what she knew about them.

She had big plans for what she'd do with the money she saved up from clowning—she wanted to go to France. When she was drunk, Pauline talked about France in a fake French / Michigan accent. She'd accomplish this feat of bilingual hackery by inserting French-sounding syllables, such as 'le' into sentences that all took a surprise turn into a nasal, stretched-out question.

"In France(?)," she'd say, "Le Clowns are treated with the respect they deserve. A French clown is more than just something to laugh at. In France, there are over fifty different words for 'clown', depending on what le clown is doing and where she is doing it. Now, I say 'she,' because most, if not all, French clowns are women."

"In France, le clowns, or zouvarvre, are respected and looked upon in the same way that we respect famous movie stars. They are recognized on the street, sometimes even when they aren't in makeup, and the paparazzi chase them. In fact, paparazé is a French word for 'clown chaser.'"

Pauline had a knack for putting on airs and talking for hours about a subject she knew nothing about but talking how she imagined that the world's foremost authority would talk about their passion. She was an excellent liar, or else she was misinformed and naïve.

Pauline became a Master Clown the year Mike left the circus for college.

For her Master Clown performance exam—which lasted four hours and was just her and her props and tools—Pauline focused first on the magic component. All the other skills she used and showed were in a beautiful orbital dance around the magical show. Clown magic seldom rises to the level of magic as done by a professional magician, but when Pauline performed, it was like watching a great magician, rolled in flour and dressed like a tropical bird.

Pauline moved with grace and ease, and even her pantomimed falls and gags where she pretended to botch the trick were beautiful. She had a French style—although she had never been to France.

Pauline owed her sudden rise in the clowning world to her apprenticeship in Indianapolis with M. Claude de Boom. M. Claude took advantage of his status in the clown world to get VIP seats at every circus that came through town. He'd meet the clowns backstage before and after the performance to sign autographs and to promote his clown seminars and his private lessons.

Claude took a special interest in Pauline, and he offered to take her on as his only student for a period of three months at what he said was only a third of his normal rate. Pauline had been saving her money to go to France, but Claude convinced her it would be better spent on her education.

Two weeks into her three-month training program with Claude, Pauline had fallen in love in the worst kind of way. Pauline loved his avant-garde performance art and his approach to clowning—and she loved that he spoke with a French accent. She loved his older, wrinkled, face and she loved the serious grin he made while he applied his makeup. She couldn't stand to be apart from him. She needed to see his face at all hours. She felt nervous and insecure when they weren't together.

Pauline wasn't sure that Claude knew her name, but he called her René, and so she called herself René when he was around.

She came to his trailer thirty minutes early one Monday morning with the intention and the need tell him how she felt—to become closer to him, to stroke his wild hair as she had imagined so many times as he manipulated her body like a puppet.

She knocked on his door. After a minute, he opened the door, looking surprised to see René arriving early.

"Bon jour, René. You are early zis morning. Would you like to join me for un Croissant un cafe'?" he said.

She smiled. He was a perfect gentleman. So open. So generous.

"Oui, Master," she cooed.

René had never called Claude "Master" before, and he had never asked her to. He was a little taken aback at first—he had never heard any Master Clown called "Master" in the way you might call a professor "Professor" or a doctor "Doctor", but he sort of liked it. Other Master Clowns might think it ridiculous that his pupil calls him Master, however, so he wouldn't encourage this behavior.

"Just Claude is fine, ma petit," he said.

René felt a rush of blood to her genitals and her face flushed when he called her his petit. She knew little French, but when she heard the word petit she always imagined a small pet—my little pet. When he said it—when Master said it—she felt safe and controlled—taken care of and loved. She felt a loyalty and love for Master Claude that she had never felt for a man before.

She climbed up into his trailer. Claude had two croissants and a French press full of coffee on the table. His bed was made, and the trailer—his home—was decorated in a foreign way.

Claude motioned for René to have a seat at the table, while he opened the bread drawer in the kitchen and retrieved another croissant, placing it on a plate, and then placing the plate on a serving tray. René practiced her French in her head as he did each task.

"Le man placée le croissant un de serviette."

She knew it wasn't perfect, but she felt good about her immersion language learning ability and she was determined to become fluent in French. Mastery of French was a key to earning Claude's respect—Master's respect.

Claude got out a cup from the counter and placed it on the tray with the plate and croissant. Then, he pulled a fresh and colorful napkin out of a drawer and folded it next to the plate. He brought the tray to the table and placed it in front of René.

"Merci," said René.

M. Claude smiled. Her French was horrible and not getting better. She was cute, though, and she showed a talent for clowning. She has that "jee nee says quoy", as she might say.

Claude was an eighty-year old man now. He looked younger because he had always been active, and he laughed often and ate only French food—never the corn dogs or cotton candy that the rest of the clowns in America seem to gorge on daily.

Claude could tell that René was passionate about clowning, and she was passionate about him. He knew this trailer visit.

He'd seen it many times with young clowns over his years as a clown mentor. The trick, he'd found, was to act surprised when they get around to what they're thinking. They'll always say something innocent-ish that one could interpret in several ways, or they'll make a physical move that one could interpret as an accident, even though there's no chance that it is.

M. Claude sat down across from René at the trailer table. His first croissant was half-eaten, and his second one was waiting. Two croissants in the morning, no lunch, and a light supper at 8:00. This was the secret. Also, a liter of brandy per day and only twelve cigarettes, along with as much strong coffee and tea as he wanted. This was his sustenance for over fifty years as a clown and he wouldn't change a thing. He thought he would die if he did.

René wasn't touching her croissant.

"Is zere somezing wrong wiz my croissant?" Claude asked.

"Oh no, M. Claude de Boom, Master. The croissant looks delicious. I don't know how I can possibly thank you for everything you've shown me, and for this croissant and for taking me on as your pupil. You have been so kind and such a gentleman. How can I show you how thankful I am?" she asked.

Claude smiled a good-hearted elder clown smile and placed his elder clowns hand on top of hers, which was resting palm-down in an innocent student expressing gratitude pose.

"Shh, ma petit," he said. "I am a teacher. I teach. You are a student—a very promising student, it's true. I can show you much more if you're willing. My zanks is ze alive feeling I get from watching you develop and mature as an arteest. You show your gratitude when you do your best and hold nozing back. A wiser clown than I once told me 'live like ze tiger: fast and hard.' You live ze life of ze tiger and I will give you all I have of myself to see you excited and blooming as a clown.

René wiped tears from her eyes. This was Claude's favorite part. The magical moment where innuendo and innocent expressions of gratitude take the turn. The dance of the student-teacher love affair he had been rehearsing and had mastered over the years.

"That's so sexy, Master," René said.

She was a bold one, Claude thought. Good move. He knew where to take it from here.

"L'Art is sexy. We live for ze sexy art, we get wet for ze sexy art. We feel more, we have passions and desires and loves zat are larger zan life. We show the world what ze life of exaggerated, ecstatic, wild untamed emotion and pure feelings feels like. Only we can express zis joy, zis pleasure, zis love of ze pleasure and ze pain, ze orgasm of ze arts of ze clown."

René licked her lips and pushed her leg between Claude's legs and pressed outwards—to connect her knee with the inside of Claude's thigh in the unmistakable gesture of moving it forward.

M. Claude continued, "To teach you—to be your Master, as you say, zis is my greatest joy—my pleasure."

René pressed harder on his inner thigh. "I would like to give you other pleasures, Master."

M. Claude said, "I am an old man, but I am not yet dead, and I am still a man. You are beautiful, René, and I would like zis very much."

René slid around to M. Claude's side of the table. She kept her eyes locked on his as she moved, and she smiled a tiny, sexy smile. M. Claude looked into her eyes as an experienced teacher guiding a young, virginal student through her first time. René was not young—twenty-two was old to be learning clowning with this much intensity—and she was not virginal. This was the dance.

She offered her hand to M Claude and she arrived on his side of the table. With his other hand, he touched her cheek—establishing control, then slid his fingers back and tugged her hair—establishing his desire.

René placed her hand on M. Claude's cock and felt it stiffen as she traced its outline through his thin pajama pants. She unzipped his pants and, looking M. Claude in the eyes, lowered her head to his lap.

CHAPTER 4

In which René gets beat up

As the only Master Clown in the Great Western Circus of the Americas, René (Pauline) believed that she could boss around the other clowns. She returned from her summer with M. Claude de Boom and called a meeting of the circus's clowns, where she, using her new fake French accent, told them that they were going to start applying make-up in the French style and that there would be other changes in the circus to conform more closely to the traditional French clown ways.

She got beat up that very first night.

It happened while she was walking from her tent to the bathrooms after she left the camp fire. She was carrying her flashlight, her toothbrush, her towel, her hairbrush, and a plastic bag containing a bar of soap, a tube of toothpaste, and her makeup remover.

Lucy the Cook's daughter, Rita, was hiding in the bushes near the bathroom. As Pauline approached, Rita stuck out her foot onto the path and tripped Pauline. With her hands full, she couldn't catch herself and she landed face-down on the gravel path. Rita stood over her, with her legs on either side and kicked her several times on each side before running back into the woods. Pauline never saw who beat her up, and she never suspected that the reason they did it was that the other clowns were angry that Pauline, who had only been in the circus for three years, came back from her summer with M. Claude de Boom acting as if she were better than them.

Most clowns who weren't Master Clowns and who had been clowns for any length of time knew that the Master Clown certification had become nothing more than a money-making scheme. But, they profited from the benefits that it allowed the Court of International Clowns to give its members— the pension and the (meager, but better than nothing) health insurance. So, most clowns didn't say anything negative about the Master Clown certification or about clowns who paid to become Master Clowns.

Other Master Clowns understood that any clout the title gave them was only for marketing yourself to non-clowns. It was fine to list your Master Clown certification in the yellow pages or to brag about being a Master Clown to a potential birthday party client, but any clown who tried to assert authority over another clown based on his status as a Master Clown was asking to be beat up.

Rita had spent twenty years in the circus—her whole life. She was the daughter of Lucy, who, for a time, had been the boss of the circus. No one was sure who Rita's father was, and paternity wasn't all that important in the circus, where everyone took care of everyone. There were rumors (and rumors are quite often true in the circus) that her father was Mr. Schmid, the circus's producer and financial backer. Mr. Schmid liked to encourage rumors about his being the father by never denying them and always raising his eyebrows as if he were surprised whenever someone would suggest it.

After she was beaten up and Rita ran back into the woods, Pauline gathered up her toiletries, now covered with dirt, and stumbled into the bathroom. Her face was untouched by Rita, but she had some scrapes on it from falling on the path. Her sides hurt, but it didn't seem that bad, and Pauline was in great shape and could withstand a couple kicks. She had never been beaten up before and she was frightened. Her hands shook, and she cried as she washed off her makeup and brushed the leaves out of her hair. After she removed her makeup, she sat on the floor of the bathroom, in the brightest part, until she heard someone outside the bathroom. She stood up and increased the volume of her crying and inspected the scrapes on her face in the mirror just as Princess the Dwarf came in.

"Oh my god!" screamed Princess when she saw Pauline's scratched up face and the way she was examining herself in the mirror. "What happened?"

Pauline cried harder. She didn't cry so much because of the pain in her sides or the scratches on her face, but because she had had a tough day. M. Claude de Boom respected her and treated her like an artist. She missed him. The clowns in the circus knew their craft, but they weren't artists in the way that she was. She wanted to leave the circus and go back to M. Claude.

Princess put out her arms to hug Pauline, and Pauline sat down on the bathroom floor so that she could. She wrapped her arms around Princess and buried her head in Princess's hair and wept.

"I was walking to the bathroom," she said, between sniffles and frightened gasps for air, "and I was attacked. Someone knocked me to the ground and started punching and kicking me."

"Do you know who it was?" asked Princess.

"No. They were very strong. It was horrible. I don't even know if it was a person. It may have been an animal," Pauline gasped in horror and covered her face with her hands at the thought that she may have been mauled by an escaped animal or a bear or a drugged-out wild wolf-man.

Princess knew that any number of people in the circus wanted to beat up Pauline. She knew that the "trip and kick" was a familiar and old circus clown trick. She knew that wild animal attacks were rare. She also knew that Pauline tended to exaggerate to make herself look good. She knew that Pauline was not smart, but Princess found it hard to believe that Pauline didn't seem to suspect that someone was trying to send her a message. But, when someone is sitting on a bathroom floor, injured and crying, it's no time to contradict them.

"This is horrible. We need to find out if any animals have escaped or if anyone has seen anything. But, we need to get you to safety first," said Princess.

Princess held out her hand for Pauline, who took it. Princess pulled as hard as she could to help Pauline stand up. Pauline was one of the tallest women in the circus. She had the figure and height of a model, and she could have been one except that she fell in love with clowning when she was in high school. Princess was the shortest person in the circus. As they walked out of the bathroom and towards Mr. Schmid's trailer, Pauline leaned to the side to use Princess's shoulder for support.

They arrived at the business trailer and Princess knocked hard on the door. Mr. Schmid opened the door in his red velvet Chinese robe and holding his pipe in his hand.

"What can I help you ladies with?" he asked, but then seeing Pauline's face, the tone of his voice changed. "Goddamn! You look like hell, Pauline. Come in."

Pauline was intimidated by Mr. Schmid, so she didn't say anything at first. Princess told him what happened.

"Pauline was attacked on her way to the bathroom," she started.

"Goddamn." Mr. Schmid was bad at consoling people. He wished they'd gone to Lucy's tent—she's better at it. But Schmid knew that Princess had brought Pauline to him because Lucy wasn't likely to be sympathetic in this case.

"First things first," said Schmid, "is anything broken?"

"No," said Pauline. She knew nothing was broken, but she didn't want to give away future rights to exploit her injury, so she added, "I don't think so."

"Well, that's good. Next—do we need to get the police involved?"

"No," she said, "I don't think so. What do you think?"

"Well, I don't know," said Schmid, "why do you think someone did this?"

"I think it may have been a wild animal," said Pauline.

"Now, you know there's no way for an animal to escape one of our cages without the handlers knowing, and if they knew, they'd wake up the whole damn camp," he said, "and wild animals stay away from the smell of lions. So, I find it implausible that it was an animal."

Schmid knew that the culprit was another clown in the circus who wanted to send Pauline a message. He hoped that she knew that too and that she wouldn't decide later to get the police involved. Getting the police involved was the death blow for a small circus.

Schmid opened his liquor cabinet and gave Pauline and Princess shots of whiskey. While they were sipping that, he brought out his first aid kit from the closet next to his kitchenette. Mr. Schmid dabbed at the scratches on Pauline's face with an alcohol wipe. Pauline pointed out all the places where she thought she might have a wound. She loved Mr. Schmid's smell—booze and cigar and old man—and it was reassuring for him to be touching her and listening to her.

CHAPTER 5

In which we learn about L'Art du Clown

It was illegal to be a clown (or pitre) in France during the Nazi occupation and so the clowns went underground, creating secret societies in every town and city. At first, these were loose groups of plain-clothes clowns who would meet at the bar or cafe or in basements and share news of what was happening to clowns who were captured or who escaped. In the early days of the occupation, the northern clowns called themselves Pitre Occupée, while the clowns in the south called themselves Pitre Libre. When the south was occupied, both groups went by the name Pitre Anonyme.

Because they were forbidden from performing in public by the Nazis, Pitre Anonyme members decided to document and record the ways of clowns and the complete (as much as anything can be complete) art of the clown, as it had been practiced in France for hundreds of years.

The project came to be known as L'Art Du Clown. Pages of L'Art Du Clown were smuggled between cities in the bottoms of pastry boxes as deliveries were made to offices, schools, and shops. Even when paper and pastries became difficult and expensive to obtain, somehow the clown societies always seemed to have an abundance of both. After the war, it was discovered that that the Nazis were secretly diverting funds to the clown groups. Their thinking was that the clowns were so incompetent that making them the richest and most powerful people in their communities ensured complete German control.

With an abundance of paper and pastries, and only an imagined threat of surveillance, a process for writing the book emerged. Each of the thousands of participating clowns would receive some pages each day. These pages would be annotated to note the date they were written, the section and subsection to which they belonged, and the city in which they were written. Each city had its own clowning style, and there were larger macro-styles of clowning, such as the regional styles or the directional styles (east style, south style). To the original members of Pitre Anonyme, it was vital to preserve variations as well as the core knowledge.

When a clown got her pages for the day (most participating clowns were women), she would start by checking for any pages that she had already seen and updating her copy of them. She'd then make another copy of all the pages in the delivery, including her additions and corrections to the material. She would hand this second copy to the pastry delivery boy the next morning.

No clown was to keep a copy of the changes they made to a page. In this way, the authors believed the book could better represent a consensus because no one would have any changes that multiple other clowns hadn't read and approved.

Since it was believed that most of the copies of the book would be destroyed by the Nazis, this was just one of the precautions taken to ensure that the official L'Art du Clown wasn't just the opinion of one maniac clown.

Part 1, Section 1 of L'Art du Clown specified the process for writing and updating the book. After that, parts were written about clown makeup, clown dress, clown training, clown history, and the seven clowning arts. Prior to the war, much of the knowledge that was to be recorded in L'Art du Clown was guarded by a small number of elite clowns. The result of L'Art du Clown's urgent mission was that clown secrets became public knowledge—at first just within the secret society network, but later, after the war, among everyone in France. The result was the clown ban of the 1950s, which was far worse than the Nazi clown ban, because France did it to herself, and she knew where to find and how to root out the rebel clowns.

Because of the scattered way in which it was written and the secretive nature of the project, and the differing writing abilities of clowns, the L'Art du Clown is a mess. It's between 1,500 and 1,700 pages long, depending on which authoritative edition you have, and it contains 600 illustrations, each one copied several times by people who may have had no experience or knowledge in the subject of the illustrations. One illustration, which would later be introduced as evidence during the debate over whether to ban clowns in the 1950s, is Figure 6-24, in the section on mentoring and apprenticeship. It features two clown-like shapes, one inverted head over foot, facing each other, with giant shoes and giant penises. In the air between them are six juggling balls. The caption of the figure is "Le Petit Oui Oui."

Clowns and clown scholars have given up on trying to understand the meaning of Figure 6-24, although it appears in every edition and copy of L'Art du Clown known to exist. This would indicate that it may have been one of the first illustrations contributed to the book.

The differences between the one hundred or so editions of L'Art du Clown are not large, but they are important to certain groups—important enough to warrant an edition—and they are irreconcilable in their nature. For example—the Paris

Edition states that mimes may break character when threatened. The Lyon Edition, however, holds that it's honorable to defend yourself only as much as your character would do so.

When France banned clowning, escaping clowns brought their editions to the United States and Canada and they created new editions of L'Art du Clown for the regions of North America. Some of these, such as the Minneapolis Edition, kept the French name. Others, such as the Central Texas Edition, took on a new title that was thought to be close to the original intent of L'Art du Clown: Let's Do the Clown Art.

With so many different editions, no one could keep them all straight. In the 1970s, a so-called standardized version was compiled and translated into Esperanto. But, that project failed, and the rules and practices of clowns, as well as the rules of clowning and the requirements for membership into clowning guilds became even more splintered. They remain so to this day.

Several organizations claim to be the official and sanctioned officiators of clown culture and clown law. But, their powers and reach are limited to regions and clowns who share the same or similar editions of L'Art du Clown.

Of these International Clown Associations, the largest is La Cour Internationale des Clowns, or the International Clown Court, as it's known in the English-speaking world, or La Cour, as it's known in clown circles. La Cour was founded in Paris in 1960, after the clown ban was lifted. The first action of La Cour was to pardon M. Claude de Boom, France's most popular anarchist clown prior to the war and public clown enemy number one after the war. M. Claude de Boom claimed to know the true meaning behind Figure 6-24 in L'Art du Clown. His lewd and violent performance of it in a basement bar in Paris was, more than anything, the catalyst of the clown hatred that led to the clown ban. M. Claude de Boom went into exile in Indiana and spent more than more than a decade pretending to be a mechanic.

When he learned that he'd been pardoned, he came out of hiding but refused to go back to France, even for the unveiling of his statue and the plaque in the lobby of La Cour bearing his famous words from his trial, which I've translated and included here.

"What is a clown? A clown is an entertainer, yes. But a clown is so much more. A clown is the soul of man. A clown is the extremes—the extreme of love, the extreme of passion, the extreme of happy, the extreme of fear, the extreme of sadness, the extreme of loud, the extreme of quiet. For a clown, there is no normal baguette. A clown has a giant baguette or a miniature baguette. So, it is true that a clown may incite panic, but a clown may also incite laughter in a child. What is the value of a clown? The value of a clown is no more and no less than the value of our best memories and our worst. The value of a clown is the value of every tear, every smile, every gasp, every failure, and every success a society has. You want to control a clown? You want to put a number or a sentence or a wall on a clown? You may not. No. It is possible to wall off a country, or to wall off the atom bomb, but not a clown. A clown shall forever be free, because a clown is everything."

The speech was convincing enough get the judge to allow M. Claude de Boom to leave France rather than be sentenced to life in prison. However, no country would accept him. Desperate to get out, he disguised himself by removing his makeup and he took a job as a dishwasher on a ship headed for New Jersey.

When he emerged from hiding in Indiana, he was more famous than he had ever been in France. He was still an anarchist clown at heart, and any actual clown skills he used to have before the war had atrophied. Both the Paris Cour Internationale des Clowns and the U.S. affiliate, The Court of

International Clowns, granted him the title of Grand Fromage Master Clown, which entitled him to train Master Clowns and to serve as a judge for trials in Clown Court cases involving master clowns.

As the Grand Fromage Master Clown, M. Claude de Boom used his power to train and certify hundreds of Master clowns who all had the same hardline ideas about clowns that he did. He believed that clowns needed to militarize and weaponize if they were going to survive in the age of television.

All it took to become a Master Clown during M. Claude de Boom's reign as Grand Fromage was a sizable contribution to the Clown Court. Actual skill in the seven clowning arts was secondary.

Before Claude, the process for becoming a Master Clown was rigorous. A clown would train for decades and would gain recognition as a clown of superior talent from his or her peers. The candidate clown would then be nominated for consideration by another Master clown. The nomination required a letter, several testimonials and references, and some evidence of the candidate's superior skills in clowning. Prior to the writing of L'Art Du Clown and the formation of Le Cour, this application would be passed around between Master Clowns as they had time. If the application was found to be worthy, an audition would be scheduled for a time and place that was convenient to a panel of at least three Master Clowns.

At the audition, the panel of three Master Clowns would ask the candidate to perform as they like and would quiz the candidate on fundamental clown history knowledge. Because the odds of an application ever reaching the audition phase were so small and relied on the motivation of a big enough group of Master Clowns to schedule a way to get together in the same place at a certain time, the actual audition itself was little more than a formality. The candidate had already been judged to be a great clown—the audition was a chance for

Master Clowns to enjoy a personal performance, which they felt was their privilege as Master Clowns. They would then make a declaration and bestow the title of Master Clown upon the candidate.

When M. Claude de Boom took over as the Grand Fromage, he insisted on writing down the Master Clown application process and making it formal. He instituted a ten-dollar application fee to cover copying and distribution costs. By 1980, the fee had gone up to $2000. If you were willing to pay the fee, you were guaranteed to become a Master Clown unless there was something terribly wrong with your clown act or your application. The fee was non-refundable. M. Claude de Boom ran a full-page ad every month in Clowning World Magazine, which encouraged people to apply to become Master Clowns. The ad had a coupon that you could cut out and send with a self-addressed stamped envelope to a P.O. Box in Minnesota. Once you did, you would get a package in the mail within three to five weeks. This package contained a brochure detailing the application process and offering to accept payment using Mastercard or Visa in convenient monthly payments. The package also held a sheet of testimonials from people who had become Master Clowns, talking about all the new fame and fortune that they enjoyed and the many benefits that being a Master Clown had bestowed upon them.

The fees and the applications would come to the Court of International Clowns, and half of each fee would go towards advertising, printing, and managing the Master Clown program. The other half went into a special fund for the "betterment of clownhood." This phrase, "betterment of clownhood", has been the subject of much debate in the clown world. Different interpretations of the phrase were used to justify everything from the founding of the Clown Pension System (CPS), to the purchase of underground bunkers, to the custom-tailored orange suits that M. Claude de Boom wore during his reign as Grand Fromage.

After M. Claude de Boom's reformation, regional Master Clown organizations conducted auditions in high school auditoriums. The judge panel would be comprised of whatever Master Clowns were available. Every Master clown had a responsibility to sit as a judge for auditions at least once a year.

During the auditions, sometimes as many as ten clowns would take the stage and perform for the judges. The rule was that they would, in ten minutes or less, demonstrate "sufficient mastery of at least two of the seven clowning arts."

The seven clowning arts were magic, humor, miming, physical, and a couple other things that changed from town to town and as people could remember them.

In rare cases, M. Claude de Boom would allow a clown to skip the application fee or pay a smaller fee. He also had the power to call a special audition for clowns that he thought were worthy of special consideration. M. Claude de Boom often wielded this power to seduce young clowns. This was how Mike's sister, Pauline, became a Master Clown after only three years in the circus.

CHAPTER 10

In which we learn about the clown court

For several decades after the war, the secret societies of clowns kept their activities concealed from the public. They did so by co-opting veteran's clubs, Rotary clubs, and chambers of commerce in small midwestern towns—the kinds of organizations that most people avoided becoming part of, but that were important enough components of the communities that no one asked any questions.

Sure, there are always rumors about what the Masons are up to, and everyone knows that the VFW hall has an illegal slot machine, and that the parties at the Elk's Lodge sometimes feature strippers, and that all of them are in flagrant violation of the fire code, that the kitchens aren't up to snuff, that minors drink at the annual Strawberry Festival and leukemia fundraiser, and that the president of the chamber of commerce has a problem with prescription painkillers.

When clowns showed up at city hall meetings, and when the local Moose Lodge marched in the parade in clown costumes, people thought it was a little odd, but the Shriners wore costumes and had little cars, and they seemed to be doing well. Success breeds success or something. "As long as I don't have to join the Toastmasters' club or speak in front of a group, I don't care much whether they want to wear clown costumes or not," was how the thinking went.

This is the story of how clowns infiltrated small town USA. It's also the story of how clowning went from being a female profession to one dominated by male enthusiasts who were in it for the comradery and the power.

In 1973, an article appeared in Parade Magazine, that, had anyone read it, would have been mistaken for a short story. The article described, for the first time, the secret clown underworld and their system of laws and justice that was infiltrating small towns throughout the U.S. Here's how it begins.

I'm a Victim of the Secret Clown Society

by A Former Clown

I had heard of the secretive international court of clowns, but I didn't believe in it. Those were just stories told by clown-phobes. Then I got mixed up in it. It turns out that the International Clown Court, or La Cour Internationale des Clowns, does exist, and the things I've discovered about its practices and power should frighten every person—whether clown or norm—on this planet. Perhaps on other planets too.

The following information is everything—as complete as is possible—that I found out about La Cour Internationale des Clowns, during my decade-long "trial" and subsequent punishment, and during the investigations that I've done for the years since while constantly moving and attempting to stay one step ahead of them.

Today, I find myself out of options, and unable to escape. I'm writing this letter so that some unfortunate person who finds themselves in the situation I was in twenty years ago will perhaps have an easier time or find a weakness in the clown systems.

CHAPTER 11

*In which we learn about the no clowns
allowed movement*

Times haven't always been easy for clowns. After World War II, however, they were at the height of their popularity and power in the U.S., and they were once again accepted and allowed to practice their craft in Europe.

But, as has happened time and time again with clowns, when they were at the height of their power, they overreached. In the late 1950s, clowns had it all. A clown could walk into any bar in any city in the U.S. and drink for free. They could cut to the front of the line at the grocery store. They got upgraded to first class on planes. In the still-segregated areas of the south, they took their choices of bathrooms or drinking fountains, and everyone would give them room and respect.

It was no small thing for normal people to accommodate clowns. Clown costumes take up more space, clown hair gets everywhere and has to be cleaned up, and clown behavior can be disruptive at times. When the clowns saw it as their right to special treatment, their behavior became much worse. It wasn't uncommon for a small group of clowns to enter a bar and take the best tables near the windows. Other clowns, seeing the clown party, would follow. Soon the bar would be packed past their fire marshal limit with clowns, all dressed in full costume and makeup. Before the war, clowns were respectful guests and they provided free entertainment for any venue they decided to visit. After the war, clowns were bad tippers when they paid their bill at all, and a visit by two clowns always escalated until clowns were packed shoulder to shoulder.

Because clowns were making it so hard for them to stay in business, bars were the first to hang "No Clowns Allowed" signs in the front window. Movie theaters, bowling alleys, and restaurants soon followed suit. In New York City, there were entire neighborhoods where it was impossible for clowns to get a drink, a meal, or a pack of cigarettes. Clowns were relegated to going about their day-to-day business without makeup on or to living only in the few clown-friendly cities that remained.

CHAPTER 12

In which Mike returns from College and goes for a walk

When he was seventeen, Mike quit the circus to go to college. When he left for college, circus life continued, with one less introspective and quiet clown. He vowed to return after he graduated. Mick the Stick Man said he was gonna track him down and bring him back if he didn't keep his word. But, most everyone knew Mike was a bad fit for the circus and it was better for Mike, and for the circus, if he went away.

Mike applied every lesson to the problem of making the circus relevant to the modern audience. He understood the problems and the challenges better than anyone—but this was his passion and he was determined.

The summer after he graduated with a degree in marketing, Mike was back with the circus. As the only college graduate, he was put in charge of the circus's business affairs. He intended from the day he left to return to the circus and make it great, and viable, again—like he had heard about circuses being during the heyday of the traveling circus. At college, his professors and fellow students mocked his interest in the circus and tried to dissuade him from what they saw as a near-certain failure.

His first day back, they threw him a great party and Lucy made a cake in the shape of an elephant. They had balloons and balloon animals, music and dancing, and drinking, of course. For most of the crew, this was the first time they'd seen Mike in four years. They had gotten updates from Mike's sister on how he was doing. But, no one expected that Mike would return and that he would be an actual man when he did. The party was everything it could be. But, there was also sadness. Mike was returning to a circus that was on its heels, and that had spent more than it could afford to put on a party for the man who was to save them. But, everyone knew the mission was doomed. The ones who cared most about Mike told him as much over the noise of the accordions and tambourines. Mike nodded and pretended to listen while taking on the air of the wise man and scholar who had come down from the mountain to use logic and science to save the village.

"How are you going to save us?"

"People don't need the circus anymore. They have TV, they have video games."

"How can a traveling circus—an independent goddamn circus that's not part of the giantest show on earth—make it?"

Mike had written papers and proposals on this topic for the last four years.

Here he was at 4:30 am, awake, five days after his triumphant return to the circus where he learned how to do the things a man does, and he's a man of whom things were expected and to whom real people had entrusted their lives and their careers. The responsibility struck him hard that morning, and he felt a pain in his chest and a panic in the back of his head as if he had been told he was terminally ill.

This time, it was different. It was real this time. He couldn't shake it off or put it off or delay action any longer.

The patient was going to die. He was going to die. Something had to be done, and it had to be done right away. At 4:35 A.M. he put on his shorts and his shoes and headed out into the world outside his tent to forge a plan to save the circus.

Mike walked towards town. It was ten miles, but he figured a cafe would be open when he got there. As he walked towards town, Mike's first realization was that he was no longer a performer. He would have to separate himself. This realization—so basic, but so important—hurt him. The performers were his friends. They were his mentors, and they had raised him and given him wisdom and booze before he had earned or deserved either. Now he would elevate himself above them all?

He had to. He thought about the elephant cake. They'd put their faith in him and didn't want to be let down.

Mike stopped at the intersection of the dirt road leading up to the camp and the main highway leading to town. He could see the glow of the lights of the town in the distance— ten miles down that road. He could see the last embers in the fire pit from last night's fire as they glowed and crackled in the middle of camp.

He took a cigarette out of his pack and lit it. Taking a deep drag and a deep breath, and tilting his head back to exhale and spot the stars—he took a step towards town, and then shook his head.

The road was a two-lane state highway with gravel shoulders. It ran straight as a farm boundary from town. It was unlit, but the moon provided enough light to walk by and the sun would come up soon at this time of year—mid-June. A truck passed him on the other side of the road. Small animals scurried into the woods as he walked. Twigs broke under his feet.

In his time away from the circus he had learned so much. He had changed. In circus time, four seasons had gone by, but it was the same. Or was it? Had tremendous changes happened in the circus too and he didn't see them because he was so self-absorbed? Or, was time different depending on the amount of change? Was this stream of thought somehow the answer to the problem of preserving the old ways for the modern times? Or was he in over his head and full of shit?

The circus, when you strip away everything else, is a business. The people come, they pay money for tickets, and they get a show that aims to be good enough for them to return next time.

No one taught Mike the history of the circus when he was part of the circus. They taught him how to do certain tasks. They taught him how to tie and store ropes, the way to pitch a circus tent, the way to do a safety check on a tightrope. The oral history of the circus starts with the skills that make it entertaining and the processes that make it safe. There were also traditions and processes for how to run the money side. They specified how much to charge for tickets, how much different performers earned, and how much to spend on supplies and food. No one ever wrote down these rules. They were passed down by the elders in the circus through stories. The eldest member of the circus was Lucy the cook, and she would tell a story every night around the campfire. Most had heard all her stories numerous times, but everyone paid attention. If they were lucky, they would tell the stories someday.

Prior to college, Mike didn't know anything about how to run a circus. But, he knew this circus had a tradition of paying the lion tamer 1.6 times the clown rate, which was 1.2 times the dwarf rate. This tradition went back to the 1870s when the circus bought its first lion from a zoo in Spain for $200.

Ticket prices in the 1870s were ten cents. The lion, therefore, represented 1000 customers, or between ten and twenty total shows if they had no other expenses. To pay for the lion investment, the circus performers did ten shows without pay. This was the simple business sense of the circus, and this naive yet responsible sense of taking care of debts and checking ropes while taking massive risks is what kept the tradition of the circus going for so many seasons.

The lion tamer earned 1.6 times clown rate because the first lion tamer at the circus demanded that his wages should be based on how much more he could drink than the drunkest clown. Three days into the competition, Randy the drunk clown gave up and the lion tamer had drunk 1.6 quarts of wine for every quart Randy drank.

The rate of 1.6 clowns worked fine in the 1800s and early 1900s, but in the modern circus, the lion tamer doesn't just need to be brave and hearty. He also needs to be a certified animal medical technician, submit to frequent drug testing, stick to a grueling daily schedule that's based on the sleep patterns and needs of the lions (they had four) and prepare food and medications for the lions per standards and laws of each state in which they performed.

Clowns' responsibilities, on the other hand, included goofing off not much else. They didn't make much money, but they didn't mind because they had few responsibilities.

Even at such a low wage, they somehow still always managed to find a lion tamer—but there was always a catch. The current lion tamer, Rosco, lived for danger. This is an admirable quality in a lion tamer—to a point. When the desire for danger outweighs the will to live and the welfare of the lions, however, it's a dangerous situation for the whole circus.

Rosco took risks no other lion tamer would take. He'd put himself in dangerous positions between the lions and their food. He'd put his head in the lion's mouth and leave it there past the point where the lion's jaw got tired. He'd turn his back on two lions—something that every lion tamer will tell you is the most dangerous thing to do. Rosco may have been suicidal, and most circuses would have fired him. But, he worked for cheap, so they kept him on despite the risks.

When Mike thought about how he wanted the circus to remain true to the old ways, he exempted the old ways of doing business. But, he knew, these old ways of business wouldn't be easy to change. You can't change how much the lion tamer earns without changing everything else.

In the old days, they understood this. They didn't have old ways and lore then. They made it up as it suited their needs. Mike needed to somehow return the circus to this version of the old ways—the old ways before there were old ways.

Mike took a stick of jerky out of his jacket's inner pocket and took a bite. He had reached a high point on the road and he could see the town in the distance and nothing but road in the other direction. The sun was coming up, and Lucy would start on breakfast soon.

CHAPTER 14

In which the circus breakfast is prepared

Lucy filled the five-gallon bucket with water from a hose. She then put in 3 cups of coffee grounds and lifted the bucket onto the propane burner. She opened the valve on the propane tank, turned the knob on the burner to light and used her lighter to ignite the coffee maker.

Lucy kept a neat kitchen. She had plastic tubs, all labeled in neat handwriting on blue masking tape and packed with pots and pans, foil, spices, and oil. She stacked the tubs according to how and when she used them in the mess tent. She kept the perishables in the refrigerated truck and organized them in other plastic tubs, with similar labels and in similar stacks to the ones that didn't require refrigeration.

After putting on the coffee, Lucy's next task was to get the eggs and biscuit mix from the truck. She had portioned out today's eggs—360 of them—the previous day and had made the thick mix she was famous for—her buttermilk and pepper biscuits. These were both waiting in the back of the truck in a bin, labeled "Today's Breakfast", that she lifted and carried to her kitchen in the mess tent.

Lucy had three assistants at any one time—the dish, the bus, and the sous. These jobs, like most jobs in the circus camp, were rotating—with clowns and midgets filling different roles depending on the day of the week, the meal, and their relative status in the circus hierarchy. The clown with the most years in the circus got bus on Sunday, for example. Sunday was the easiest day to bus because a good number of the crew would go to the pancake breakfast at whatever church was local. This turned Sunday into the day that you didn't want to eat at the camp because the sous would be the bearded lady.

Today, being Saturday, was the busiest breakfast. Lucy's helpers on this day were Pancake the Sober Clown (who loved to cook breakfast and didn't mind waking up early on Saturday to sous), Lil' Lazy on dish, and Applesauce on bus.

Saturday's breakfast was run by the pros who had all had kitchen experience outside of the circus and who loved what they did, and you knew it would be good. Lucy insisted on starting her prep work thirty minutes before the other kitchen help arrived. She liked to put things in order and have time to plan by herself. On Saturday, however, she cut her prep to fifteen minutes and Applesauce showed up early to help with the "Stir n' Scrape".

The Stir n' Scrape was the name given to the series of tasks to be completed after the "Boil n' Tow". The coffee and batter had to be tended and stirred, the grill had to be prepped, and the juice had to be mixed from the concentrate bucket. Applesauce did the Stir n' Scrape while Lucy started cracking eggs.

Lucy's jobs didn't have names because she was the only one who did them. The egg cracking used to be a rotating job ("The Crack"), but too many shells got into the eggs when the smaller people, who couldn't see over the edge of the mixing bowl, were doing it.

Lucy enjoyed cracking the eggs, and the way she did it could have been a circus act. Both her hands were always in motion. The left hand picked up and palmed the first egg, then picked up and tossed another egg straight across to her right hand which would crack it. She'd throw the palmed egg in a tall arc that would reach her right hand just after it tossed the empty shell. The pattern would then repeat in a mechanical rhythm.

Pick pick throw throw crack toss crack toss.

A few minutes later, the eggs would all be cracked and Pancake and Lil' Lizzy would show up and the breakfast prep would be in full swing. Pancake would add the salt and pepper to the eggs and beat them while singing Beat It.

Lil' Lizzy would start moving dishes—the first thing she'd move was the pan of empty shells, then she'd inspect the work of the night dishwasher. This was known as the "Shell n' Sniff". After the Stir n' Scrape, Applesauce's highest priority was to make sure there was no clutter—the kitchen was small, and everyone had to move fast to get everyone fed. Clutter was not only slowing, it could be dangerous. The grill got hot, and the biscuits started flying. Pancake would ladle out a half-cup of batter and toss it to precisely the right spot on the griddle to fit the maximum number of biscuits. Lucy poured the first batch of eggs into the large pan and started scrambling. The acrobats would be the first to arrive for breakfast, and this first batch of eggs would be ready just as they walked through the door.

Mike's return from college had thrown the morning routine off balance. He'd show up at an unpredictable time—sometimes half an hour early—and ask for coffee. The coffee wouldn't be ready for twenty minutes, and whoever he asked had other things on their minds—the Stir n' Scrape, the eggs. No one would deny a man his coffee, though, so whoever was the dish learned to ladle a cup from the big coffee bucket into a small pot and heat it for Mike, then clean up and get back to the usual order.

Mike had been part of the kitchen crew years before and he should have known better than to interrupt the system. Who did he think he was to come back here and demand special treatment in the kitchen? Did he deserve it? Only time would tell.

Lucy was expecting Mike to come into the tent at any moment. Fifteen minutes later, however, Mike hadn't shown up, and the acrobats started to enter the tent and the biscuits, eggs, juice, and coffee were moving through their turns, loops and the shuffles of feet in the food line.

CHAPTER 15

In which Mick the Stick tells a joke at breakfast

Breakfast was in full swing at the circus camp. Several people in the line asked Lucy if she'd seen Mike. Her response, as she piled eggs onto their plates was "Nope. Maybe he ran away from the circus."

This got some big laughs from the members of the crew suspected Mike wasn't one of them, and expressions of mild concern from those who were on Mike's side.

"Nah, he probably just went for a walk is all," Lucy would say to the latter group.

"Off to join the corporate world!" she'd howl to the former.

Circus breakfast wasn't as lively as circus dinner, but given the crew, it never failed to be amusing. Per circus tradition, the first to finish eating would provide entertainment for the rest of the group. This rule kept breakfast moving, since everyone wanted to be the entertainment. Today, it was Mick the Stick who finished first.

The truth was, Mick was so fast because he didn't eat. He was having a tough time maintaining his weight of sixty-five pounds as he got older, so he started skipping more meals.

You would expect that someone as skinny as Mick would have little energy or be sickly, but Mick was just as enthusiastic a performer as the best of them. His skills were limited, however, to the things that only an exceptionally thin person can do.

Mick would do a dance in which he slid his way through smaller and smaller hoops and he'd play a trombone and do a bit where his arm seemed to disappear inside the horn as he hit low notes.

At this breakfast, however, Mick was working on his standup comedy routine.

"What do you get when you combine Lucy's biscuits with Lucy's eggs?"

He paused, and the midgets drummed on the table to build the suspense.

"Fat!"

"What do you get when you take the winter off and do nothing but watch football and drink?"

"Fat!"

"What do you get when you quit the circus, take a job at Wal-Mart, and get married?"

Mick pointed to the audience to respond.

"Fat!" they shouted half-heartedly, not sure whether this was going anywhere or was just the worst stand-up comedy ever.

"What do you get when you lift up Matilda the Snake Lady's blouse and push your face between her tits?"

"Fat!" the crowd responded.

"No, Bit!" yelled Mick.

The audience laughed and applauded.

CHAPTER 16

In which Mike talks with a townie at the gas station

Mike arrived on the edge of town ready for some coffee. He stopped at a gas station. The dual-warmer had the usual coffee and decaf pots—the decaf full and the coffee half full.

Mike nodded to the woman behind the counter.

"Morning, ma'am," he said.

"Good morning, sir," she replied.

Mike poured his coffee into the largest paper coffee cup size, and then put on the paper sleeve and the lid.

"Looks like it's gonna be a hot one," he said as he picked up his coffee and brought it to the counter.

"Yup. Sure is," she said. "What brings you to these parts?" she asked. "I noticed your accent."

"We're performing at the fairgrounds."

"Are you with the circus? One of my regulars came through last night and said he saw you setting up camp down the road," she laughed. "He said it was the strangest damn thing he ever saw."

"He did, huh? Well, pardon me, ma'am, but it's not so strange to me."

"Ya, sorry. I suppose not," she said. "Do you just do that for the summer?"

"No."

The woman started to ring up his coffee and then stopped with her hands on the counter.

"You know, sometimes, as a girl, I thought about running off and joining the circus. Such a cliché, right? But, I really did. I wanted to be an acrobat. I'd practice flips and cartwheels and balancing. Then I forgot about it as I grew up and learned to live with my older brother a little better. What did your family think?"

"My family was in the circus," Mike said. It was a little bit of a stretch, but he'd go with it.

"Oh, so you didn't actually run away to the circus?"

"Not exactly," Mike said, even though that's exactly what happened. He didn't consider himself a circus runaway and he didn't like to encourage the stereotype. Also, he wanted to drink his coffee and move on to breakfast somewhere where he could sit down alone and collect his thoughts.

"I wonder," the woman said, "where do people who grew up in the circus dream of running away to?"

"A quiet place where they can read a book and take a nap," Mike said.

"Ha, that's fresh," she said. "I imagined they'd want to run off to a job with the post office or to a desk job."

"No, I can't say I've ever met a circus person who aspired to have an office job and a stable life. Seems like such a person would never think to get involved with the circus in the first place."

Mike hadn't paid yet and was getting impatient. He picked up the coffee and took a sip, then reached into his pocket and pulled out a wad of ones.

"What do I owe you?"

"Just take me with you is all!" she joked.

Mike had heard it a million times, but he laughed and then issued the challenge he always did, but that no one ever accepted. "Fine. Come on."

"Haha. I was joking," she said. "I couldn't do that. The boss would kill me! That'll be two bucks."

Mike handed her two dollars and picked up his coffee to leave.

"Well, at least come down and see the show tonight. My name is Mike. Ask for me and I'll give you a tour."

"What do you do in the circus, Mike?"

"I run the office."

CHAPTER 17

*In which Mike eats breakfast and thinks
about townies*

Mike found a diner called Jack's Diner not far from the gas station. He sat at the counter and ordered two eggs over easy, bacon, hash browns, and wheat toast. It was 7:00 A.M. and the restaurant was full of people.

In the circus, everyone had a superlative. Everyone was special and worked hard, or they had a genetic misfire that made them different. At Jack's Diner, the differences and the special-ness was more difficult to see. Understanding these people was the key, he thought, to understanding how to save the circus. But, Mike was getting nowhere. It seemed that the real world was maddeningly boring unless you dug deeper.

There were two other solo diners at the counter. One may have been a driver of some kind. The other was an elderly regular. The driver was making some notes on a clipboard and the regular was chatting with the waitress whenever she came behind the counter. Their conversation was the same as a million customer/waitress conversations at diners across the country. It was a well-worn path that never surprised anyone.

Mike observed and moved his focus around the room, noticing everyone, but he was hoping they didn't notice him.

Alice brought out his breakfast. "Are you looking for someone, love?" she asked.

"Ah, no. Just thinking."

"You gotta be careful with that," the driver chimed in.

"What's that?"

"The thinking. That stuff'll get you into trouble," he said.

Mike wondered what it would be like to have a normal life with normal conversations and normal concerns. School was the closest he ever came to such a thing—but even then, he was far from normal.

School life for Mike was pure intellect. He did almost nothing except read and write. Normal daily life, as he imagined it, was pure action. People go to work to make the money to pay the bills and buy the food that they cook to feed the kids to make them bigger, so they can get the job that makes the money that pays the bills to feed their family and make it bigger.

The circus was also pure action. People move from place to place and do things that people in each place think are remarkable for long enough to not outstay their welcome and to not become commonplace in any one place.

Circus life relied on being strangers. If normal people knew just how ordinary most circus people were, it would all be over for the circus. But, like in the normal world, if anyone looked deeper, you'd find the dark and awful truths hidden underneath. Mike, like everyone, didn't care to explore that. But, he thought, this could be the only way to keep the circus afloat. The circus, rather than showcasing extraordinary feats and people, could be a mirror that would show people themselves. This has been the key to the fortuneteller's success and the best storytellers' success for generations.

People love to hear a good story, but they love it even more if it's about them. The circus was already a metaphor, but perhaps it could be made more explicit. Mike imagined a circus poster that read:

Can your powers of persuasion tame the lion? Find out at the circus.

Or

Are your management skills up to the job of running an actual circus?

Or

You've tried balancing your budget and balancing your work / home life. But, have you tried balancing a thirty-foot pole with a basket full of knives on top of it?

Mike thought about how an audience might react to a circus that asked them to get involved. Traditional circuses work because people feel safe to stare. No matter what they say or how much they express their fear, repulsion, or love for an act, they know that the performer won't acknowledge them individually. In the diner, it was a whole different thing. Looking at any one person for any length of time might not get you thrown out, but it certainly would cause discomfort and it was widely known to be unacceptable behavior. You can get away with staring at people in the diner, but you should have a plausible excuse. They look familiar, for example. Or you're reading the sign above them.

CHAPTER 18

In which Mike learns about whiskey from Mr. Schmid

When Mike returned to the camp just after noon, preparations for the show had begun. The circus camp was set up on the other side of town from the county fairgrounds. The county wouldn't let them sleep on the grounds, but the circus-friendly landowners in the area would let them camp in exchange for tickets.

As Mike walked into camp, Rosco the lion tamer was leading one of the lions onto the truck. Because Rosco couldn't stay on the grounds, he repeated the process of moving the lions before each show.

"Mike! We thought we'd lost ya!" yelled Rosco.

"Nope, you're stuck with me!" replied Mike.

At this point, Mike was unsure of his position in the circus. He was supposed to be the business manager, but he most certainly wasn't in charge. The people in charge were the Ringleader, Jasper (the Great), and Mr. Schmid, the producer. After rehearsal season, Jasper only showed up on show days, and he preferred to travel by plane. Mr. Schmid rarely left the business trailer or his RV. His role, after approving the show at the beginning of the season, was to make sure that his investments were paying off, or, more commonly, to put more money into the show when needed. To the average circus performer, Mike was now "the man." It was starting to occur to Mike that maybe no one else wanted the job, which is why he got it.

Mike headed towards the business trailer, saying "Hi" to everyone he passed as they loaded equipment and costumes onto trucks.

When Mike entered the business trailer, Misty, the bookkeeper, was at her desk, making tidy notes in her ledger with several different-colored pens and a ruler. Mr. Schmid was in his office with the door closed. On the door hung an engraved wooden sign that read "IN" on one side and "OUT" on the other. Unless you saw him enter or leave, or heard him arguing on the phone, this sign was the only way to know whether Mr. Schmid was in or out.

Mike's desk was across from Misty's, so that if he sat down at it his head would be about five feet from Misty's. Mike hadn't yet sat at his desk, and on this day, he learned that he couldn't if he wanted to, because there was no chair behind his desk. Mike stood behind his desk and pretended to be typing and filing papers while standing there. Misty laughed.

"Ya, Mr. Schmid took your chair," she said.

"Well, I'll just have to get it back," he said.

Misty was thirty-five, which made her thirteen years older than Mike. She had watched him and his sister growing up in the circus and she knew as much about him as anyone did. One thing she knew was that he wasn't a tough guy who would walk into the boss's office and demand his chair back, as he was implying he was about to do. Misty pursed her lips as if to say "ooo, you tough guy", and Mike smiled and walked the eight feet to Mr. Schmid's office door. He knocked.

"Come on in!" said Mr. Schmid.

Mike opened the door. Mr. Schmid was sitting back in his own chair, with his feet up on Mike's chair.

"Ah, Mikey! How's it going?

"Not bad. I've got some ideas and plans I want to write up and talk to you about next week."

"Excellent, son," said Mr. Schmid, "what can I do for you today?" Everyone knew that you don't just bother Mr. Schmid unless you have a good reason.

"I'm here to work, but I don't have a chair."

"Oh yes. I guess this would be yours. I didn't think we'd see you in here. Which is fine—if you produce results, I'm not picky about where you work. But, you'd best let people know when you take off like you did this morning, at least until folks get used to you not being a kid. K, Mikey?"

"Yes, sir."

"You want a drink?" Mr. Schmid asked.

"Yes, sure."

Mr. Schmid got up from his desk and walked behind the elaborate cherry wood cabinet in the corner of his office. The cabinet was about the size and shape of a half-height book-shelf, but with sturdy legs on the bottom to bring it up to the correct height for Mr. Schmid to mix drinks. The back of the cabinet had two doors that folded out. Two hinged pieces on the top of the cabinet folded out over each of the opened doors to form a four-foot long bar with a copper and wood top. The front side had a brass rail at the bottom and padded leather with a juggling clown embedded in it.

Mike stood in front of the bar with one foot placed comfortably on the brass rail and he watched Mr. Schmid take out two crystal old-fashioned glasses, drop an ice cube into each, and pour two simple but generous bourbons.

"If you're working in here," Schmid said, "you're going to learn to drink."

"Cheers." said Mike.

The first bourbon went down fast, with Mike following Mr. Schmid's lead. The whiskey was hot and cold, sweet and bitter, harsh but smooth. Just the suggestion that Mike would be learning to drink, rather than just drinking, was enough to put him in a contemplative mood. The drinks and the moment sealed the deal that they had made, without either of them speaking a word. Mike was going to become a responsible and vital piece of the business, and Mr. Schmid would treat him with respect and teach him what he knew.

The second whisky, a different one, Mr. Schmid poured into different glasses. These were more bulbous, and without ice—just a drop of water in each, which Schmid poured from a fresh bottle he opened just for this drink.

"Have you ever had single malt Scotch?" Schmid asked.

"No."

"If anything in this world is special and precious, it's this," Schmid said. He swirled his glass and brought it close to his face to catch the smells coming up from the amber liquor.

Mike did likewise.

Schmid continued, "What you have here is the purest connection between the untamed earth and the most refined of refined human achievements. Wine can be flexible. You can quaff it or sip it, it goes with food, and you can live on it if you have some bread too. Single malt Scotch hates food. It's still part way buried in the earth and it resents you for taking it out of Scotland. It calls for home, wants to return, can't return, and it expresses everything it knows how about the place it's from. It wants to pass on the feel of its special isle or bog, the taste and smell of the air. It's from a place you'll never see. Most people won't see it. It's a place that doesn't fit well into our world. But, if this special place can cause this whisky to express itself so boldly, to the exclusion of all other concerns, then this place and the values it holds, and the history and culture that are so artfully captured in this very peculiar and particular bottle of whisky, are worth our consideration and full attention. You don't ever fuck up a glass of good Scotch with ice, soda, food, or people who don't deserve it."

Mike took a tiny sip from the much less generous pour of the Scotch. The taste was much more complex than the first whiskey and it evoked a sense of an old leather couch or wallet, in a shack in a swamp, where the mud and the air are saturated to the point of becoming one. The moss on the roof of the old place traps the warmth inside and the fire burns and dries the wet wood slowly in the cast iron stove.

Mike stood at the bar in a trailer in the middle of America, with a general feeling of dread and apprehension about the journey he was about to embark upon and the responsibility that had landed on his shoulders. But in that sip, he was somewhere else entirely, with universal concerns, a connection to history and place, and a sense that no matter what, we're all going to return to where we started and the best we can do is to find a true way to express our values and passions and where we've been.

Mr. Schmid was silent for several minutes as they both drank the whisky and thought their private thoughts, then he brought the meeting back to the business trailer.

"Do you see that poster?" Schmid said, nodding to the most prominently positioned poster in the room, just behind the bar. "That was the love of my life," he said, "I was fourteen, and the circus was the family business. This was the year that both of my parents, and three other members of the circus family died. Crushed and trapped when the big top collapsed during a rehearsal. The woman in that poster, Lovely Lucy the Loon, took charge. She told us that the best way to honor our dead was to be the best living people we can be and to put on the best damn show we knew how. She put away her clown makeup and made damn sure that the circus never missed a beat, despite how devastated we all were. For the next thirty-five years, she ran this operation like the inspired and magical thing that a circus should be. We had no accidents during those years and we developed into the tightest family there's ever been, and we had all the ingredients for success. But the world changed underneath us as it does. Lucy got older and couldn't keep up with the stress of the changes that she needed to make. She resigned from running the show to focus on just the kitchen. The job she created fell to me, and I did it as best I could for the next twenty years. But, I couldn't help thinking it was a lost cause, or I may just not be up to the task or have enough smarts or enough distance from the problem to see it clearly.

Maintaining an artifact such as the circus—an expensive and dangerous artifact—against the wishes of most of the population that would be happier to watch TV, is strenuous. I'm not going to lie. This is now your job. Your primary job is to keep things running smoothly. When they run smoothly, no one gets hurt. Your secondary job is to preserve the traditions."

Mike listened and agreed with what Mr. Schmid was saying. He understood safety, order, and continuity. He thought he understood tradition.

But he also had a secret plan. Mike was going to ensure safety and preserve the traditions, but he would also do what no one believed was possible.

It was his time and place to restore the glory of the circus and bring its magic into the new world, just as that bottle of Scotch transported the ancient swamps of Scotland halfway around the world and through the years to this place that no one in the old country could imagine.

CHAPTER 19

In which preparations are made for the show

The first show on Saturday started at 3:00. When Mike left Schmid's office, it was 2:00. The preparation for shows proceeded on its own at this point, and Mike didn't have to do much, other than to show up and watch the crowds watch the show.

Mike went back to his tent and packed a notebook and pen, a change of clothes, and his flask into his messenger bag and headed for the old school bus that most of the cast traveled in. He boarded and found an empty seat next to Princess.

"Hi there," he said to her.

"Hey, boss! How's it going?"

"Not bad. Glad to be back. Have you kept things in order around here while I was away?"

This was the first conversation Mike had had with Princess since his return, and it was going horribly. He had no idea what to say to her and felt they had nothing in common now.

"Of course, boss. You know you can always count on me," she said.

The bus was bustling with the action of fifty performers and their bags boarding. Lucy the Loon took her time finishing her cigarette, and she was, as always, the last one to board.

"OK, cocksuckers! Sit the fuck down and let's roll!" Lucy yelled.

Mike had always known Lucy was an important person in the circus—she made sure everyone was fed. What could be more important than that? But, he had no idea that she was so important and was the main reason the circus still existed.

As the bus started moving, Princess threw a blanket over hers and Mike's legs and put her hand on his lap. Mike thought that maybe it wasn't such a good idea to sit next to her just now. As the bus started moving, Princess fiddled with the zipper on Mike's jeans. Mike slid his hand under hers and squeezed it as a way of telling her that he didn't want a hand job on the bus to the show.

She took her hand and the blanket back and turned to look out the window. She folded her tiny legs underneath her on the bus bench.

The bus drove down the same street Mike walked that morning. He recognized certain mailboxes, but overall it was just like any rural highway in America. There were areas of trees, areas of farmland, and not much of interest.

They passed by the gas station and Mike recognized the woman who had been working that morning. Long day, he thought. She had joked about wanting him to take her along. Someday, someone he meets will say that and then follow through. That will be his soul mate.

Mick the Stick turned around in the seat in front of Mike and Princess and woke Mike from his daydream.

"So, Mikey! You missed my stand-up routine this morning!"

"Oh shoot! Sorry about that. How'd it go?"

"Pretty good. Pretty good. You liked it, right Princess?"

"Ya, totally. Nice work, Mick," she said.

The bus pulled into the fairgrounds and up to the back of the big tent. The ticket line looked good for 30 minutes before show time—good for an average weekend matinee with no school groups and halfway into a week-long run.

Clowns headed for the dressing tent. Acrobats started their stretches and warm-up exercises. Animal handlers rushed over to the cages to ensure that everything was in order.

Mike entered the big tent and found the facilities manager.

"How's everything look, Bob?" he asked.

"Good. Good. Solid turnout. The weather's holding up. The pig show ends in fifteen minutes across the grounds, so I expect a fair number to head here from there. So, you might want to give it a couple minutes before starting."

"Got it. Thanks," Mike said.

Mike took out his notebook and pen and looked around the tent, making a few notes—or pretending to. He wasn't sure yet what kind of notes he'd normally make, but he thought standing with the facilities manager and writing in a notepad gave him an air of authority with any performers who happened to see as he was doing it.

"Anything I can get you, Mike?" asked Bob.

"Nope. Thanks, Bob."

Mike took his seat in the front row and continued to doodle as final preparations for the show ended and the audience filed in.

CHAPTER 20

In which the show begins

Jasper the Great, the ringmaster, was in the tent, and had been there since 5:00 a.m. Jasper had a saying, "If you can't tie every knot, check every knot." And he did. He didn't just check every knot, he also inspected the ropes between the knots and the poles the knots attached the ropes to.

This pre-show routine went far beyond the demands of safety, and was more like meditation for Jasper, Mike believed. He'd seen him do it hundreds of times, and his method, hand and head movements, where he squats down, what he tugs, how he nods and pats lines was always the same. The whole inspection took two hours, after which he would be satisfied that everything was in order with the facilities and hardware, and he would go back to his trailer until it was time for him to dress for the show.

Once dressed, Jasper would check in with each performer. His personnel check-ins varied daily, but he had a system still that allowed him to say "Hello" and ask each performer if they were ready to go. He never missed a person. Once satisfied that his people were ready, and they always were, he'd raise up his arm and start the show.

This week, however, he modified his routine. Jasper walked to where Mike was seated, front and center, and shook his hand.

"Mr. Mike," he said, "is everything ready?"

"Good afternoon, Jasper. You know better than I do," said Mike, "The facilities manager suggested we hold off for a few minutes to give them time to get from the pig show. Is that ok?"

"Yes, certainly boss."

Jasper was a tall man. He wore an oversized cowboy hat and a handlebar mustache. He dressed his part as a ringmaster impeccably in a black tuxedo with tails—every detail as perfect and formal as can be, except for the giant hat, which added an element of humor and levity to his otherwise rigid appearance. The ringmaster is the straight man in the circus, and the touch of exaggerated hubris that the hat represented made any pranks played on him by the clowns even more hilarious.

Jasper glanced at his watch, tapped it with his index finger, pivoted on his heels, and walked back to his spot just off to the side.

Starting a few minutes late was a normal request for Jasper to get just before show time, but it was still irritating. The animals and performers took their positions, all the preparations were done, the torches had been doused with kerosene, the hands of the aerialists had been powdered, the clowns had applied the final additions to their makeup, and the midgets had finished stretching their legs. Each of these preparations has an expiration time—wait too long and the makeup doesn't look as fresh. A few minutes' delay wasn't bad, but it did throw a slight element of unpredictability into the show and schedule, and any unpredictability had the potential to make it less safe. Jasper had once canceled a show because of a venue's last-minute request to delay the start by thirty minutes.

Postponing a show was bad luck, and canceling was preferable. That wouldn't happen here.

Jasper stepped outside, behind the tent. He had just enough time for a smoke and to take leak.

At precisely ten past the hour, Jasper raised and then dropped his right arm. The lights went out, the noise level in the tent dropped in anticipation, and just as it reached its lowest point, the dramatic intro music started.

Spotlights scanned the circus rings, and the announcer's voice boomed over the music:

"Ladies and gentlemen, young and old, tall and short, welcome to our circus!"

A single clown ran across the performance area, appearing lost and out of place. He pulled out a map and studied it for a moment, before looking up, noticing the crowd and looking surprised and delighted. He jumped and ran off the other side of the stage, where several other clowns were waving to him to get off the stage. The clowns laughed, and the audience laughed with them. The announcer's voice came over the sound system again as a single spotlight shown in the center of the ring.

"Presenting your ringmaster and guide through the amazing world of the circus, Jasper the Great!"

A flash of bright light and smoke appeared in the ring. When the smoke cleared, Jasper was standing in the center of the spotlight as the audience roared.

CHAPTER 21

In which the circus does what it does best

Tradition bound the way the circus operated and conducted its daily business, but the circus prided itself on constant innovation when it came to its acts. Larger circuses had the luxury of multiple regional crews that perform the same acts for two years straight, but in different locations. This wasn't the case with the Great Western Circus of the Americas.

The circus had a committee of performers that would discuss each act, review feedback from the audiences, and talk with the creator or creators of the act to determine whether any act needed updating.

The most successful circus acts involve the following components: grandeur, skill, story, and humor. But, truly great acts were rarer than hit songs or bestsellers. When an act hit, the circus would hang on to it for as long as it kept drawing crowds. When an act was anything less than a hit, it was canceled or revised as soon as was possible.

Some of the greatest acts invented at the Great Western Circus were:

Flaming Midget Splashdown

Walking with Bears

Lucy's Clown Cannon Conundrum

Tightrope Train

Lions Leaping Over Lil' Lizzy

Moose Trample

Exploding Midgets

Lion Sawing Lady in Half

While the Great Western Circus of the Americas was one of the oldest circuses in America, it was by no means the largest or most well-funded. What they lacked in big name acts and expensive productions, they made up for in creativity and humor.

While other circuses pushed towards ever greater heights, more lights and sound effects, and more choreographed dance sequences, the Great Western Circus of the Americas worked with the same number of cast members and the same equipment year after year.

The challenge was to find new and interesting ways to combine the same ingredients. It was like Taco Bell, Mike would explain to his business school professors—take the same few things and try every combination until something sticks.

What stuck for the Great Western Circus was incredible acrobatic acts and animal acts with clowns and dwarfs playing key roles rather than just playing their usual role of acting like lunatics. Story sometimes worked too.

One story featured all six dwarfs on stilts and wearing costumes that made them look like giants, standing among the trees (made of plywood) and picking fruit, laughing and having a great time.

In act one, aliens, played by clowns, descend upon this peaceful and happy scene and use a shrink ray on them. The clown aliens want all the fruit for themselves. The shrink ray scene ends with the dwarfs off their stilts and the long arms and legs removed from their costumes. The clowns hover nearby as the dwarfs are jumping up and down at the base of the trees, trying to reach the fruit.

In act two, the evil clowns start to gather up all the fruit using a giant fruit vacuum, and things look grim for the former giants. But, one of the dwarfs goes off alone to his laboratory. He works hard by dim light in the first ring. In the center ring, the aliens continue vacuuming up fruit. In the third ring, the other dwarfs worry and starve. Scene two ends with a musical number involving all three rings, where each of the three main characters or groups of characters sings about what they want.

In the third act, the dwarf emerges from his laboratory with a giraffe! The giraffe starts picking fruit and dropping it into a basket. Then two lions come out and roar at the clown aliens, who run off to their spaceships and blast off. It sounds dumb, but you must see it to appreciate it. Something about those midgets getting tall and short, and then riding the giraffe just makes people happy.

On this day, the weather was humid but not too hot, so it was tolerable. Jasper looked sharp as he introduced the cast members. On hot days, Jasper would sweat through his suit, which Mike thought detracted from the overall effect of his costume and persona. Today, however, Jasper controlled everything, and he swaggered around the ring like John Wayne or a young Marlon Brando.

As he introduced the cast, they flipped, tumbled, swung, vaulted, spun, and even flew out of cannons all around him. When he introduced Rosco the Lion Tamer, Rosco first ran across the stage with all four lions chasing him, then he turned and started chasing them, ending with all of them on the tall platforms where they stood still as he bowed.

Rosco's entrance was the most dangerous part of the whole night. Lions don't like to chase something without catching it and tearing it to shreds.

CHAPTER 22

*In which a post-show rendezvous gets
interrupted and Mike visits the dwarfs*

After the show, Jasper, Mr. Schmid, and Mike met just outside
the big tent to have a smoke and discuss the performances.
Jasper lit his cigarette, kicked at the dirt, and then said to Mr.
Schmid, "I think Sheila's getting too old. She's favoring her
left side, and she's not jumping with as much confidence, and
Rosco won't tell you but she's a little less patient too. I think
it's time we look for a zoo that will take her before something
happens and she or someone else gets hurt."

"Noted," said Mr. Schmid.

Letting go of a lion is a tricky business. You can't just set
them free, of course, and you can't just drop them off at the
nearest zoo. There are large expenses involved with taking on
a lion, and most zoos already have their fill of big cats. Getting
a new lion to replace Sheila would also be a huge undertak-
ing—one that Mr. Schmid wasn't looking forward to funding.

"How long do you think we can stretch her, Jasper?" asked
Mr. Schmid.

"At this point, if we only use her every other show, she
should be fine for a while. Maybe six months. But, we're gonna

have to pay close attention and yank her the minute she starts showing tendencies."

Mike thought this was as good a time as any to show that he was good for something besides having the book learning.

"I heard there's a regional circus out west that's expecting their senior cat to go any day. They might want to take on Sheila as a lookie lion."

A lookie lion's sole job was to sit near the entrance to the circus and roar to attract as much attention to the circus as possible.

"Get in touch," said Mr. Schmid, "maybe we can meet up with them in Oklahoma in the fall."

"Will do," said Mike.

Just then, Pauline appeared from the big tent.

"What's up, lil' bro?" she said to Mike, wrapping her arm over his shoulder.

Mike hadn't had much time to catch up with Pauline since his return, and he had been staying distant for this very reason. She made it more difficult for others to take him seriously, just like Princess, with her hand on his lap. Pauline calling him lil' bro in front of the boss didn't convey the image of a serious and capable adult that Mike wanted to convey to the rest of the cast and crew.

"Hey, Pauline," he said. "Good show today."

Jasper and Mr. Schmid both gave their congratulations and Pauline hugged them both and did an elaborate bow as she sidestepped away.

Like every man in the circus, Jasper and Mr. Schmid couldn't take their eyes off Pauline and they both wore goofy smiles on their faces for a moment after she left.

"Right. So, where were we?" asked Jasper.

"Ah hum." said Mr. Schmid, adjusting his belt and leaning back on his heels.

"Sorry, chap," said Jasper, "I know she's your sister and all, but she does have a way of making a man feel like his life is worth living."

"Wouldn't know," said Mike.

"Well, I'm gonna retire to my trailer for a sip or two before the evening show," said Mr. Schmid, "care to join?"

"I'd love to," said Mike, "but I think I'm going to get right on the Sheila situation."

Jasper, knowing that a sip or two would end up with him too plastered to do the 7:00 show, excused himself as well.

"I'll take a rain check on that one, hoss. These ropes won't check themselves."

Jasper was certain that every rope in the house was in perfect shape, but he kept the ropes in his pocket as a go-to excuse for whenever he needed a rest or had a secret rendezvous with a lady clown. And, if his reading of clowns was right, he was about to have such a rendezvous with Pauline.

Mike excused himself from the group and walked the perimeter of the tent. The last remaining customers were exiting, and the kids of all ages were pretending to be fierce lions or were reenacting their favorite clown bits from the show.

Mike pondered his ideas about how to make the circus profitable again. His first task was to prove himself and earn the respect of the other circus people. But first he'd need to get some things straight with Pauline.

After another lap around the tent, and another smoke, he headed for Pauline's make-up trailer. The door was ajar, so he stepped up and entered.

Inside, Mike saw Pauline with her checkered clown pants around her ankles, leaning over the makeup counter, her wig and makeup half off, and Jasper taking her from behind. Both saw Mike come in. Jasper smiled and winked at Mike. Pauline buried her face in her hands.

"Oh shit," said Mike, "I'm sorry."

He hurried out of the trailer, shutting the door behind himself.

Mike had suffered one too many indignities. Too many situations set him back too many times. He wanted to be in charge, to do his job, to stand up and be a man, but the world seemed to be against him.

Not knowing what to do or where to hide from further embarrassment, he went to the dwarf trailer.

The dwarf trailer was the same size as the other trailers—standard boxcar size—and from the outside it looked much the same as the other cars in the Great Western Circus of America's train. It slept twice as many people, though.

Inside there were six rooms, rather than the normal three. Princess had the first room in the front of the trailer.

Mike pulled himself up into the trailer and knocked on Princess's door, even though it was partially open. Princess yelled for him to come in. Inside, all 6 midgets were talking and drinking beers. They cheered when Mike entered.

"Hip hip hooray for Mike, the tallest little person!" yelled Leo.

They all joined in cheering and toasting Mike.

"Hip hip hooray! Hip hip hooray!"

"Thanks, everyone!" said Mike, "It's good to be back home."

Lil' Rocky, the strongest midget, brought Mike a beer, opening it with his teeth, and Mike squatted down to take it and to pat Rocky on the back.

The furniture in a midget room was all two-thirds size, which made it spacious for the midgets, who were about half size, but for Mike, who was about normal man size (at 5 feet 9 inches), it could be quite uncomfortable. Mike sat down on the edge of Princess's bed. Princess climbed up onto the bed and stood next to him, her hand on his shoulder.

"You know you'll always be one of the little people family to us, Mikey," she said, kissing him on the cheek, "and we're so proud of you."

Mike was relieved that she had forgotten or forgiven his brush-off on the bus earlier in the day.

The other midgets gathered around Mike and Princess, forming a semicircle so they could all hear and see.

Lil' Lizzy spoke next. "The first little person to graduate from college!"

They all laughed, and Mike laughed with them.

Charlie the Midget or "Drunk Chuck" as he was known, pulled another beer out of Princess's cooler, opened it and took a gulp, and then asked Mike, "So, now that you're in charge, can we do something about the unequal pay? I hate to be a downer, but just because we're little shouldn't mean our paychecks are little."

"Chuck, I don't think this is the time, and I don't think Mike is the person to address this," said Princess.

Mike sat up straighter, which had the effect of pushing Princess's hand off his shoulder. "No, I think I can address this, Chuck," he said, "As you well know, pay scales are based on circus rules. Circus rules, as you know, are based on the way we've always done it. We've always done it that way because it's worked for us in the past. The fact is, it's easier and has always been easier to get little people who are willing to work cheap. The circus has to save money where it can, and that's one place where we do."

"These days, I don't think anyone would say it's right, the same as we now know it's not right to pay women or others less just because of their sex, color, or where they were born."

"But, the circus rules are tough to change. It's a complex system of balances and counterbalances that keeps the wheels moving and ensures that there's always a next show. If we raise pay here, we need to cut expenses there. If midget pay, which is two-thirds clown pay, goes up, then do we need to raise clown pay to be equal to animal handler pay? Do we need to raise ticket prices to pay for it? Do we need to spend less on travel? Or, can we get by with fewer people? The circus laws protect us from these decisions by providing strict guides we all agree on, because that's the way it's always been—but how do we adapt circus rules to changing times? That's my job, and I want to do it right for you, for the circus, for the customers, and for the future of the traveling circus and the traveling circus lifestyle we all love."

Mike took a sip of his beer. He was proud of his first real speech as the business guy at the circus, and it seemed to him that the midgets were impressed and satisfied with it as well.

"We certainly do wish you the best, Mikey," said Leo, "I don't envy you, the job you gotta do. You know we've always got your back."

"Or your balls, more like," said Charlie, reaching up and pretending to squeeze something in the air at about the height of a normal man's midsection. The other midgets laughed, and Rocky almost knocked over a vase of flowers when he fell laughing.

"Well, let's give these two some time," said Leo, moving towards the door.

"Yup! See ya round, Mikey," said Charlie.

They all left, except for Princess, who stood next to Mike and put her head on his shoulder.

CHAPTER 23

In which Mike makes a
most grand speech

The rest of the Indiana shows went without a hitch, although they didn't even come close to selling out. They rarely did these days.

Mike was getting into a rhythm and becoming comfortable with his role as circus manager. His goal, as he saw it, was to make the circus work better. To that end, he'd been meeting and talking with each group in the circus, and with each person individually, to hear their gripes and ideas.

The midgets wanted equal pay, the acrobats wanted new equipment, the trainers wanted more animals, the kitchen wanted more staff, the clowns wanted more creative freedom (more attention, thought Mike).

Mike was determined to somehow find a way to make everyone happy. To that end, he decided to get everyone together for a pep talk. He prepared what he thought would be the most moving speech anyone in the circus had ever heard. He polished it for days. He researched, looked up words in his pocket dictionary, remembered things he'd learned in college about how to do a presentation, and used stories from business books he'd read. He typed it out using the word processor in the business trailer and then started practicing it during his sleepless nights and long morning walks.

When he was positive that his speech would have the desired effect of moving and inspiring the entire circus to greater heights and to follow him in addressing their concerns while preserving the traditions, he put out the word (through the dwarfs, those masters of communication) that everyone should meet in the front center seating of the big tent on Monday morning.

When everyone had gathered, he began. He spoke for half an hour. When the speech was over, the circus gave him a polite round of applause, but nothing close to what Mike had imagined. Mr. Schmid came up to the microphone to speak.

"Thank you, Mike, for your thoughtful speech. You raised some interesting points regarding evolving the circus, and I think some of it's things we who have been in the business for a long time don't want to hear, but that doesn't mean we don't need to."

"The fact is," he continued, "we all know damn well that the heyday of the circus is gone. A circus coming to town isn't a huge event the way it used to be before TV and huge events coming to town became normal."

"It's also true that pay and benefits in the circus aren't current with the times. How much can we change without fundamentally changing the nature of the circus? I don't know. I think we need to have this discussion, and I'm glad you've started it, Mike. I'm sure everyone has plenty of questions, but we have a show to get ready for now."

From that moment on, everything was different. The shows still went on, but the feeling inside the cast and crew was altered. The awareness of the struggles and unfairness that was at the heart of the circus was always there, but somehow talking about it the way Mike and Mr. Schmid had done brought it to the top of everyone's mind in a way that it had never been before. The primary thing on the minds of the performers had always been the show. Now, it was the business.

One day, Pancake the Clown complained that her kitchen duties represented unpaid labor that other clowns didn't have to do.

Rosco the Lion Tamer threatened to leave unless he got an assistant who could take care of the lions' feeding and bathing.

Leo the Midget started asking questions and spreading rumors about certain trapeze artists' legal status and lack of work visas.

Mike was spending most of his time in the office reading and listening to questions and complaints from performers.

Mr. Schmid no longer invited anyone else to his office for cocktails after he got a complaint about "favoritism."

CHAPTER 24

In which Mike has taken all the fun out of it

No one blamed Mike for the mood that had overtaken the circus. The feeling was that he had exposed something that had been festering in the background for a long time.

The difference now was that the injustices and resentments the traditional circus system had created were in the open for everyone to see.

Pauline had mixed feelings. She had only been in the circus for seven years—the same as Mike, except that she had been involved the whole time, while he came and went. Pauline knew the traditions, and she understood their purposes, but she didn't understand or know the stories behind the traditions enough to have strong feelings about them.

One tradition she did have strong feelings about was the tradition that the circus doesn't perform on Sunday. In France, she said, Sunday is the day of the clown, when all clowns do kind deeds and perform on the streets for free. M. Claude de Boom himself told her this.

The real reason Pauline liked having Sunday off was that it gave her a chance to recover from her inevitable hangover.

One Sunday morning, several weeks after the speech, it also gave her a chance to catch up with her brother.

Pauline knocked on the door of Mike's trailer and Mike answered.

"Good morning, Pauline!" he said, "To what do I owe the pleasure of seeing you before noon?"

"To Saturday night sucking here now," she said. "The shit's cold out here, can I come in?"

"Ya. Of course." he said.

The inside of Mike's trailer was cramped, sparse, old, and falling apart. It wasn't messy, however, which was its redeeming quality. There was a table that folded down to a bed, a sink inside the curtained-off bathroom area, and that was about it. There was no personalization, and the atmosphere was more like a cell than a home, or even an office.

Mike had notebooks and various papers strewn across the table, which he gathered together and stacked while offering Pauline a seat across from where he had been working. A small electric heater buzzed next to the table and provided all the warmth for the still chilly room.

"Can I get you some coffee?" Mike asked.

"Yes please."

Mike lifted his seat cushion to get to the storage space underneath it where he kept his dishes. He took out a cup and went behind the curtain. Pauline heard him rinse out the cup and pour a cup of coffee. He came out from the bathroom / kitchen with the coffee and placed the cup in front of her before sitting down with his own half full cup in front of him. He took a sip.

"So, how are things?" he asked.

"It's been tense, Mike, you know? It's like most people here have lost their minds and have never thought about these things before and are just going freaking ape shit in every direction. Did you ever expect this when you took this job?"

"No, of course not."

"We're not innocent anymore. When you raised the possibility that the concerns we all privately talked about might be addressable, you opened a whole bag of shit. It used to be that Saturday night we'd drink and talk about ideas and goof around and sing songs. Now we drink and talk about politics. Mikey, it's killing my brain, not to mention my sex life!"

Mike laughed, but he knew it was true.

"I wonder if this happens at other circuses," she continued, "Are we just one in a bigger picture of all circuses becoming less fun, or are we unique?"

"I don't know," said Mike, "I've been thinking about asking around to try and find that out."

"Good," said Pauline, "and let me know if you find the fun circus, because I'm going to go work there."

"Bullshit. You wouldn't do that."

"Don't test me, bro. I can and will. You'd better figure out how to make this shit fun again or I'm out. Hell, I'll do birthday parties and picnics—I don't give a fuck. I just don't want to spend my Saturday nights sitting around a campfire talking about animal rights and human rights.

"These are all important issues to talk about, though, wouldn't you agree?" said Mike.

"For fuck's sake, Mikey. Of course they are, and no one here disagrees with any of it. But can we just get back to singing and screwing around, please? If I wanted to talk about politics, I'd run for the senate!"

Pauline had become tired of her own talk about how she'd become tired of all the political talk, so she changed the subject.

"Speaking of little people—how are you and Princess? Rumor has it she's not too pleased with you."

"There's nothing going on between us," said Mike. "I aim to keep it that way for the sake of us both and for the circus. You know—keep it professional."

"So, you're in her trailer banging out contracts and polling her on the latest financial reports?" said Pauline.

"Ya, something like that," said Mike, trying to hold back a smile. But his red face betrayed him.

"Pauline, I know everything you're saying is true. The circus is supposed to be outside of all this crap. The circus is supposed to be the place where outsiders and those who don't fit in band together in a family and show everyone who ever questioned us or doubted us that we're not nobody."

Mike was becoming more animated and using the phrase "not nobody" triggered in him a character of a New York tough guy mafia boss.

"What we gots to do, see, is keep the family together. We gotta make sure nothin' comes between the family, and that anybody that tries is gonna get a new pair of cement shoes. Believe me, those are not the shoes you want to wear."

Mike cracked up and shrugged at his half-hearted and pathetic, but heartfelt, impersonation.

"That's the speech you should have made, Mikey," said Pauline, "That's the circus we all love. That's the Mikey we all love."

"I know."

CHAPTER 25

In which Mike becomes a connoisseur

As the circus turned into a business around him, and as he tried to manage the change, Mike found comfort in booze.

As a kid, Mike drank beer and cheap wine coolers passed to him by the clowns and midgets around the campfire. When he went to college, he developed a taste for coffee and for good beer. Both were his daily companions, along with cigarettes, as he trudged along towards his marketing degree.

When he returned to the circus as an adult, he no longer had a taste for sweet wine and thin beer.

Good beer was impossible to come by in most of the rural shithole towns where the circus performed, and refrigeration was impossible most of the time. When the show was over, he'd sit on his bed (which could also function as a table when folded out) and drink all six warm beers while listening to local football or hockey games.

Because of the lack of refrigeration and storage space, and urged on by Mr. Schmid, Mike also started to gain an appreciation for hard liquor. Mr. Schmid's elegant bar had inspired him to start collecting the components for his own, and to start learning about the mysterious potions and recipes and names that make up the world of booze.

He would visit second-hand stores when he came across them on his walks and look for striking pieces of bar decor or essential bar tools. He wasn't satisfied with just a basic steel shaker, or a utilitarian long spoon. He would choose the shaker with the most elaborate etchings or with inlaid jewels, trading up or handing down less perfect pieces.

One day, he found a perfect leather and wood box that had a latch and folded out into a miniature travel and picnic bar. Inside, it had room for three bottles, a shaker, a spoon, two crystal lowball glasses, a knife, a strainer, and a jigger.

He kept a bottle of bourbon, a bottle of gin, and a third rotating bottle in the travel bar. The rotating bottle would go from tequila to vodka to dark rum to light rum to scotch and then back to tequila. Since his room, board, food, and travel were all covered, he had little else to spend his pay on, and he found he could keep his bar well-stocked most of the time and he could even buy small bottles of mixers that he couldn't borrow from Mr. Schmid or garnishes and juice ingredients that he couldn't take from the kitchen.

His guide to bartending was a well-worn leather-bound copy of Jerry Thomas's bartending book from the 19th century. He'd found it in an antique store in Cleveland. Its pages and stain on the back cover recalled a time when the book may have seen prohibition-era blowouts and flappers drinking cocktails with names like the Bee's Knees or Gin Rickeys.

Most evenings, he would sit at his table with his bar and make three or four recipes from the book. On some nights, Princess would visit, or Pauline would come by, and he'd make them a drink as well.

Mike's tastes were wide-ranging, and he was always curious about the next drink he was going to make. While he drank one night's drinks, he'd plan what he could make the next night using the ingredients he had. But, because of his space and budget limitations, he often had to be creative.

An unexpected side effect of his cocktail habit was that he had a reason to visit Lucy in the kitchen daily. He'd stop by at some point during the day to ask for ice and the ingredients from the kitchen he'd need for the night's drinks. Occasionally, he'd ask her to buy something that he couldn't find in the liquor stores.

He stopped by the kitchen one hot Midwest Tuesday in July to pay for and pick up such groceries. Lucy had a paper grocery bag half full of mint sitting on the counter in the otherwise neat and organized kitchen. He opened the bag and put his face into it. The smell of the mint seemed to cool him off.

Lucy came back from the refrigerated truck holding a bag of ground beef.

"This is a lot of mint," said Mike.

"Take yours, but not the whole damn thing, and make me a julep too, ya?" said Lucy.

Mike reached his hand into the bag and grabbed a large fistful of the mint leaves and stuffed them into his messenger bag. Thinking of the drinks he wanted to try—not just bourbon juleps, but also rum juleps, brandy juleps, gin juleps, and mojitos—he took a second handful. Lucy was cutting open the bag of beef and had her back to him. She heard the bag ruffle a third time and yelled to Mike, "You'd better be making me two drinks with what you're taking."

"Ya, of course," said Mike.

Mike had become the least social but most dedicated drinker in the circus. When he wasn't working on the financial planning or marketing plan, he thought of nothing but being alone and exploring unfamiliar flavors and liquors.

Normally, Lucy was short with Mike and didn't engage in conversation. Instead, she would go back to her duties after helping him with his mixers. Gradually, though, she warmed up to him and started to act as a mentor to Mike.

"What was the circus like during the heyday, Lucy?"

"It was a hell of a lot more fun than it is now, I'll tell you that," she said.

"Why's that?" asked Mike.

"The crowds were amazed—even if you came out and did a summersault, they'd go ape shit. Starved for entertainment, I guess. But, also not so jaded."

"It would take fifty midgets in a VW Beetle jumping the Grand Canyon while on fire to get the same response today that I used to get for riding a unicycle. Even then, the audience today would be looking for the trick and some snot nose would come up after and say that someone else had done something with eighty-one midgets. Physics has limits, Mikey, and now the laws put limits on too—no way we could even get the permits for the midgets in the bug over the canyon stunt."

"You're talking about this stunt a lot," said Mike. "Is this one that you've thought about before?"

"No. Fuck you piss brain. It's a damn metaphor. Get the fuck out of my kitchen."

Mike went back to his tent with his mint. He picked the leaves off one bunch and put them in a glass with two teaspoons of sugar and a half-ounce of bourbon. He used a bone muddler he'd bought in Minneapolis to pulverize the mixture, then added another ounce and a half of bourbon. He let that sit while he filled his other glass with ice. Then he strained the mint and bourbon over the ice, squeezed a lemon into the glass, and added a sprig of uncrushed mint.

The crushed mint made his entire trailer smell fresh, and he took it out of the strainer and put it back into the first cup and put it on the window sill as an air freshener.

He took a tiny sip of his drink. The sprig of mint pressed on the tip of his nose. He picked up his pencil and notebook and drew the Grand Canyon, or what he thought it might look like, with a car soaring over it.

CHAPTER 26

In which Mike walks again and visits Andy
Pencil

The next day, Mike woke up at 3:30 a.m. He put on jeans, a flannel shirt, and hiking boots and left his trailer and headed for the road. The circus was in Belleville, Michigan for a week, with two shows on Friday and two more shows on Saturday at the fairgrounds.

July in southeast Michigan can be stiflingly hot and humid, but the morning is fine. The humidity kept the air hot all night, but there were periodic short and intense storms that cooled everything down every couple of days.

It was Wednesday morning. Mike walked past the lot where the crew had spread out the canvas for the big top and was pounding stakes into the ground. He straightened a poster for the show as he passed by the restrooms.

The Wayne County fairgrounds is in a semi-urban area, and sits next to I-94, between Detroit and Ann Arbor, next to the Willow Run Airport. Belleville Road, on the east side of the fairgrounds, runs north up to U.S. Route 12, also known as Michigan Avenue in these parts, which used to be the main

Highway from Detroit to Chicago. Beyond Chicago, it continues all the way to Aberdeen, Washington.

Mike had traveled a good part of Route 12 by now, but only through its midwestern beginning and middle. He'd dreamt of taking it all the way to Aberdeen. Route 12 had been a popular route for circuses to travel because of its proximity to the transcontinental railroad and because of the circus-friendly towns it passes through. There was even a popular circus folk song about Route 12 called "Headed for Aberdeen (Cause it's Better than Detroit)".

Mike had grown up singing about Aberdeen, but he only recently found out that it was the birthplace Kurt Cobain. Mike didn't care about Kurt Cobain, but he'd often thought about how his walking and traveling Route 12 formed a connection that he could mention to some of the girls from school to impress them.

Mike reached Michigan Avenue at 4:30 a.m. and started walking west toward Ypsilanti. Ypsilanti, or Ypsi as it's known to locals, was the hometown of three of the circus's dwarfs. This wasn't unusual, considering the history of Ypsilanti.

During World War II, Ford built a massive bomber plant outside of Ypsilanti. Some of the steps in the assembly of the WWII bombers required people who were small and nimble enough to get into tight places. The Fair Labor Standards Act of 1938 made child labor illegal in the U.S., so Ford brought in little people from all over the world to work at the bomber plant. To this day, the descendants of these original Ypsi little people make the area ground zero for circus recruiters. Thus, the purpose of Mike's walk was two-fold: to clear his head of his morning hangover, and to see if he could recruit some new talent.

Mike's destination was the Wolverine Grill in downtown Ypsi. The Wolverine Grill was a greasy restaurant, no wider than a row of booths, a walkway, and a counter. The owners were a Greek father-son team of Greg (known as "Big Greg") and Greg Jr. (known as "Little Greg"). They opened early, made good hash browns, and never refused service to anyone.

The waitresses at the Wolverine Grill were Cathy and Jane, and had always been Cathy and Jane. The restaurant was always the same too, and they always remembered Mike, although Big Greg usually got his name wrong. These days, Big Greg didn't come to the restaurant as often as he used to, which was just fine with Little Greg—and the rest of the staff, for that matter. Big Greg didn't tolerate any slacking off, and the days he came in were twice as difficult for everyone as the days when he didn't.

Besides the friendly staff, Mike's main reason for visiting the Wolverine Grill was the other customers. Like every diner, this one had its regulars. Many of the regulars at the Wolverine were former circus workers and little people. The place was so popular with Ypsi's outsized midget population that they made special accommodations.

The ashtray stand next to the front door was just two feet off the ground—a modification made by Little Greg (who was quite tall) in his metal shop class in high school. The stools at the counter were all adjustable, and a small step stool was available to get on the stools. The restaurant kept extra phone books around for use in the booths, rather than forcing adults to go through the indignity of having to sit on booster seats. The bathrooms had their doorknobs at three feet above the ground. It wasn't too short for normal-height adults, and it wasn't too tall for short people.

When Mike got to the Wolverine, he recognized Andy Pencil standing and smoking by the front door with a disheveled homeless or mentally ill person who he didn't know.

In addition to having more than its share of little people, the Ypsilanti area also had more than its share of insane people, due to the closing of the mental hospital in the 80s. The state released many of the patients onto the streets of Ypsilanti rather than transferring them to another facility.

As Mike approached the restaurant, Andy recognized him and waved. The other man rambled and shouted at Andy, bending over to Andy's height and pointing his finger to make a point.

"You see, it's these power lines everywhere that are interfering with my abilities. I have statements from judges that I'm a certified genius. Do you know what that means? Do you? I'm a brilliant artist, but Caravaggio never had so much interference. Do you see those cones in the road there? Does anything look strange about them? Looks like road construction, right? Have you ever seen anyone working there? Have you ever seen that spot not under construction? They do this to fuck with us. It's called mind control."

"Hey Andy, how's it going?" Mike said.

"Mikey! Me and the boys were wondering when you'd show up!" said Andy.

The homeless man was fidgeting with his watch, then held his cigarette between his lips and looked surprised as he fiddled with the watch on his other wrist.

Andy had never worked in the circus, but he knew all the little people in town and had spent a fair amount of time around the circus and circus people. He was in his late-60s now, and he was the elder of the little people community in Ypsi. He had come to Ypsi when he was 18 to work at the bomber plant, and he was the last of that generation still alive in Ypsi. Andy would tell stories of the wild parties in the giant dormitories that Ford had built at the plant, and these stories made the midget orgies that Mike had witnessed look like pancake breakfasts.

"You going in?" Mike asked Andy.

"For sure, for sure." said Andy.

The homeless man had wandered off without saying good-bye. Mike and Andy entered the restaurant. It was 6:30 a.m. Both Cathy and Jane were already at work. Little Greg was in the kitchen, and he bent down a little to put a plate in the window between the kitchen and the counter. He saw Mike as he was doing so and yelled across the restaurant.

"How's it going, boss?"

The restaurant was quiet—only one of the four booths held a customer, and one customer sat at the counter. Mike and Andy took the stools at the other end of the counter, farthest from the kitchen.

Cathy came over and poured them each a cup of coffee. Cathy was a middle-aged woman, short and thin with curly hair, who called everyone "hon" and loved to talk to her customers. She would often sit down in the booth with them and crack a couple jokes before moving on to the next table. It didn't matter how busy the restaurant was—she would always make time to chat you up.

The other waitress, Jane, was older than Cathy, taller, and heavier. She never said more than a couple of words to anyone. If you were unlucky enough to be at the restaurant when Cathy wasn't working and if the counter was otherwise empty, Jane would tell you about her adult kids, who, Mike thought, were the worst people ever.

Jane's son was in and out of jail on drug and robbery charges, her daughter was always pregnant with the latest in a too-large number of children, all with different men, who would be born and then live with Jane and her husband. Jane's husband retired early years ago after a workplace injury at Ford that left him without the use of his right arm.

Cathy finished pouring Mike and Andy coffee and took out a notepad from her apron.

"Good to see ya, Mike," she said, "Do you know what you want?"

"Two eggs, over easy, bacon, wheat toast. Good to see you too, Cathy."

"The usual for you?" she asked Andy.

"For sure, for sure," said Andy.

Mike took a sip of his coffee and looked around the restaurant. He'd been coming here for years, and he spent a lot of time here during his college years at Eastern, just up the street. While he was deep into his studies, this was his secret place where no other students would go, and where he could keep in touch with the circus and enjoy the camaraderie that only someone who has been through the life of a circus performer can ever experience.

"How's things been out on the road?" asked Andy.

"It's going well," said Mike, "but I feel like the old acts and variations on the old acts won't be enough to keep 'em coming out for much longer. I'm working on something bigger."

"Oh Yaaaa!" said Andy, imitating either the Kool-Aid commercial or the song from Ferris Bueller's Day Off.

"I can't tell you much about it, yet, but what if I told you that I need to recruit eighty little people?"

CHAPTER 27

In which Mike convinces Andy to listen to his plan

Lil' Andy Pencil, the oldest little person in Ypsilanti, leaned back on his stool in the Wolverine Grill as if something heavy was pushing his head. He closed his eyes, then shook his head.

"Mikey, the last time someone said they needed eighty dwarfs was old Mr. Ford, back in '41. Do you know what the bomber we worked on was called? It was the B-24, also known as, aka if you will, The Liberator. For the little people who worked on that plane, it was the enslaver."

"We worked longer hours, in terrible conditions, we were packed four to a bunk and given half the pay, half the food, half the time off, half the booze. Management treated us like machines to push between planes on rolling platforms. We'd tighten the bolts inside the wings, get under the control panel and hook up wires, screw down the seats, fill the fluids that no one else wanted to be anywhere near. We weren't just there to do the work that big people were too big to do; we were there to do the work that big people didn't want to do. We were treated like child laborers with the brains and strength of full-grown adults. For Ford's men, it was perfect. Today, when I hear that someone needs eighty midgets, I get suspicious."

Mike nodded. He hadn't considered this. He thought for a moment about how to frame what he wanted to do in the most exciting and least offensive way.

"I want to create a stunt like no other," said Mike, "something so unique and so amazing that it will go down in history. Not just circus history, but human history. I want your help."

"There's just no way, Mikey," said Andy, "I don't know that many little people. You'd fill this room three times over with that many littles. What in the hells are you thinking and planning?"

"If I tell you, you can't tell anyone else," said Mike.

"You want me to recruit eighty people. Not just people, but my family, my extended family, and everyone they know—for a stunt, but they can't know what it is? Sorry, Mike. That sounds nuts."

"Please hear me out before you say never."

"I'll listen, but only because I'm curious. I'm warning you, Boss, it sounds like you're going down a dangerous road. Even if you only want to break the Guinness world record for most dancing dwarfs, it's still a dangerous road. I gotta drain the worm first. Hang on."

Andy climbed down from his stool and walked to the bathroom.

To Mike, Andy seemed like Yoda. He was wise, old, short, and reluctant. Mike needed Andy's blessing if he was going to pull off the stunt, and he hadn't expected to meet resistance. He knew that it would be incredible, but he also knew that it would be difficult and expensive. If he could get all the midgets in Ypsi to sign on and come to the circus in a show of force, he'd stand a chance of impressing and convincing Mr. Schmid to back the stunt that would save the big tent. The trick would be to get Mr. Schmid to believe that he thought of it. Mike would merely encourage the world's largest show of midget power in one place. Mr. Schmid would connect the dots and realize that it would be an incredibly popular act, and then Mike would be ready with the act to top all acts.

Andy returned from the bathroom and pulled himself up onto his stool.

"OK," he said, "Let's hear what you got, Mike."

Mike took a deep breath. This had to be good, because he knew he only had one shot.

"How would you like to go to the Grand Canyon, Andy?"

"OK. I'm listening. Never been there."

CHAPTER 28

In which Mike's plan sounds fishy

Mike's mention of the Grand Canyon perked up Andy's ears. Andy had only left the Ypsilanti area three times since 1941, when he started working at the bomber plant. The first time he left was by bus, to go to his father's funeral back in Kentucky. That was in 1956. The second was also by bus, to go to his mother's funeral. That was in 1971. The third time was by car, to see Elvis perform in Vegas, in 1974.

He would never forget that week. Some of the guys from the Wolverine saw an article about Elvis in the Detroit Free Press and got it into their heads to go to see him. Big Greg, the owner of the Wolverine, had a cousin in Vegas who was some sort of boss at one of the casinos and said he could get them tickets to the show. Andy had friends working at Circus Circus who got them a comped room. Greg's wife, Helen, stayed behind to run the restaurant. The rest of the Wolverine Vegas crew was Al Lunse and Bill Mustardvich.

Andy was the only little person on the trip, and he sat in the back seat the whole time. It was on this trip that Andy first learned about the Grand Canyon. They drove close enough to it to see signs pointing the way, but they were determined to make it to Vegas before dark and didn't take the detour.

It wasn't that Andy wasn't curious about the world outside of southeast Michigan. He was. It was just much more difficult to get around as a little person. Driving a car is impossible. Affording a plane ticket when no one will give you a decent job is difficult, and riding a bus or train was always risky because you had to venture among strangers. At the least, they would stare. But Andy had also heard stories about people outside of Ypsi taking advantage of little people—robbing them, kidnapping them, making them wear leashes and crawl around a perverted millionaire's mansion like dogs, fetching drinks and towels. No, traveling on his own was not something Andy desired, and the longer he went without going anywhere, the more it seemed like it wasn't even an option. Life in Ypsi was comfortable and predictable. He enjoyed reading about other places and talking with his circus friends about the places and things they saw on the road. That was plenty for him. But, the Grand Canyon was special.

"Tell me more about what your trick has to do with the Grand Canyon, Mike," said Andy.

"OK. The Grand Canyon is huge. It's so wide and long that it can be seen from space."

"Have you been there?" asked Andy.

"To space?" asked Mike.

"No. To the canyon."

"No. But we're about to become very familiar with it. Do you remember Evel Knievel?"

"Ya, of course, Mikey. He's the maniac who does those insane stunts."

"No. He's the showman who does those stunts that seem insane but that are really quite safe. There's no way he'd get insurance or backers for them if they weren't. It's all about the physics. If you have something hit a ramp with a certain angle at a certain speed, you'll fly this far and that's that. There's never any doubt, and all margin of error is calculated, and everything is safer than driving to the store to get some milk. But, they build it up. A great barker could sell out the house for that drive to the store to get that milk. It just has to seem like there's a chance someone could die."

"Right, right. For sure, for sure. But, what does this have to do with eighty littles?"

"I want to create a stunt where eighty dwarfs all gather at the Grand Canyon and jump across it in a rocket-powered bus."

"This is your idea, Mikey?"

"Yeah! What do you think?

"Um. Well, it certainly would be big. That's for sure." Andy stretched out the "sure" to give himself time to think of a polite way to scuttle the idea.

"And, I haven't gone to college," Andy continued, "so I can't speak to the science of it. But, I do know it's going to be impossible to get one little person to get on that bus, much less eighty."

"How about forty dwarfs, a smaller bus, and a leap over a quarry?" asked Mike.

"Not happening."

"How about twenty and a decent-sized river?"

"Why?"

"How about four little people and a little car jumping over a flaming pit?"

"Mike—do you really have an idea?"

"Nah. None at all. But I do need your help, Andy."

"Ha! You son of a bitch! I ought to break your face for leading me on with some damned hairbrained idea and making me think it was either me or you that was off his rocker. Son of a bitch!"

Greg rang the bell in the window and Cathy got up from the booth where she'd been sitting and reading the paper. She picked up Mike and Andy's orders and placed them on the counter, then picked up the coffee pot and warmed up their cups.

"Anything else I can get you two?" she asked.

"Ya," said Andy, "can you tell this guy what happens when you try to pull a prank on a little person?"

"Ooo. Bad news, Mikey!" joked Cathy, "Watch your shins!"

"But seriously," said Mike, "Will you come to the show on Saturday and will you help me spread the word? I'm gonna reserve a whole section of the best seats for Ypsi's little people and call it Little Appreciation Night."

"No stunts?" said Andy.

"No stunts. I promise. It's time that the circus gives something back to Ypsi's littles."

"We'll see you there!"

CHAPTER 29

In which we learn of the animosity between clowns and dwarfs

Mike had known all along that he wanted to do something good for the little people, who had been so mistreated by the circus and by the world at large for so long. He didn't know what it was, though, until he told Andy about Little Appreciation Night and invited all the area's little people. As Mike walked back from the Wolverine Grill to the fairground, he tried to figure out what Little Appreciation Night might be, and how it could start to fix the problems in the circus.

Part of him wanted to impress Princess. He'd heard that all business was personal, and that certainly applied to the circus. But, having grown up with everyone treating him as just Pauline's little brother, and then returning to the circus and seeing it with adult eyes, Mike felt it was his responsibility to start righting the wrongs that had been done by previous generations—and specifically by Lucy the Clown's generation.

During his time as circus manager, Mike spent many evenings drinking and thinking and reading old flyers and reviews of the circus. Princess sometimes joined him, and they'd discuss her early memories. She was seven years older than

Mike and had never known a life outside of the circus. She remembered when Lucy was the circus manager. The accident that nearly destroyed the circus was long before Princess was born, but her mother remembered and would tell Princess that Lucy's cruelty was a direct result of the tent collapse, and the things she had to do to save the circus.

Princess told him how, under Lucy's rule, the dwarfs slept in cages, on straw beds, to save money. Princess was quite young at the time, but she remembered the bug bites they would all get and how they would find and save aloe plants when the circus would get down to the southwest.

The worst part of the dwarf oppression was the role clowns played in it. Prior to Lucy taking over, there had been little people who were also clowns. Little people made good clowns because they could do funny things that big clowns simply couldn't do.

For example, an act that used to be a big hit was the one in which a hobo clown and a business man clown are in a boxing ring and they fight two funny rounds, but then in the third round, when it seems that the hobo clown is losing badly, he's revealed to be a dwarf clown standing on the shoulders of another dwarf clown.

When the two dwarf clown boxers separate, the one on the bottom is already wearing boxing gloves. They go on to fight the other clown using classic dwarf fighting techniques. One of them runs away, which causes the business clown to chase him. The other dwarf clown gets on all fours in the path of the business clown and trips him. Both dwarf clowns then pile on the business clown and each of them pulls one of his arms back to get him into a wrestling hold.

Clown dwarfs were an important part of the circus tradition for centuries. But, the big clowns complained that dwarf clowns had an unfair advantage when it came to clown competitions. They were smaller, and many acrobatic tricks were easier for dwarf clowns. They tended to win competitions more often and many big clowns believed that it was because of sympathy the judges felt towards the plight of the littles. Also, dwarf clowns made more money than big clowns, because circus tradition dictated that they earned money both for being dwarfs as well as for being clowns.

When Lucy the Clown took over the circus, her first act was to ban dwarfs from being both dwarfs and clowns. She claimed that it was for financial reasons, but the effect of her order was that dwarfs had to stop being clowns, since they couldn't stop being dwarfs.

There was nothing the dwarfs could do but accept their fate. They couldn't leave the circus and get jobs elsewhere—the only other places that would hire dwarfs were traveling carnivals. Everyone knows that the carnival treated dwarfs even worse and even went as far as to keep them in cages around the clock for people to gawk at.

The reaction of the clowns when Lucy banned dwarf clowns was to rub it in. In their minds, big clowns competed on an unfair playing field with dwarfs for so long, and now it was time for revenge.

Once word got out that The Great Western Circus had banned dwarf clowns, other circuses also banned them because their best clowns threatened to walk if they didn't. Circus clowns got a taste of the power they had, and they used it to further every selfish and clown-friendly goal they could think up—without regard for the other performers, and worst of all, without regard for the public that came to the circus. More than anything, this is where the myth of the evil clown started.

CHAPTER 30

In which Mike gets the go-ahead

Mike wasn't going to make the mistake of having another general circus meeting or grand plan for reviving the circus. These things were doomed to fail, he'd decided, and the best he could do was to put down the booze, be a leader, and try to right some of the historic wrongs of the circus.

First on his list was to start to make up for the mistreatment of the little people.

He'd missed the circus breakfast while he was having breakfast with Andy Pencil. When he got back to the camp, the normal mid-week circus activities were under way.

A group of clowns was standing under a tree smoking and talking about baseball. The dwarfs were cleaning up the beer cans and garbage around the campfire from the night before. The acrobats were drinking coffee and stretching to prepare for their morning rehearsal. The animals were being fed.

Mike enjoyed watching the elephants and tigers getting fed. When he was younger, he would often help with the feeding duties. But, like everyone who's in the circus for any length of time, the animals become a secondary factor in the day to day life of the touring circus, as they're kept as far from the sleeping and eating tents as possible to cut down on the noise and smell.

The keeping and training of animals for the circus and the ethics of doing so was a battle for another day, Mike thought. His scattered approach to problem solving and life hadn't served him well to date, and as he watched an elephant single-mindedly eat a tremendous amount of hay one bite at a time he decided that he would work through his list one thing at a time.

Mike headed towards business trailer to meet with Mr. Schmid, taking the long way there so that he could sort out his thoughts. He had no idea how Mr. Schmid was going to take this idea. What Mike did know was that Schmid was loyal to Lucy, which is why he kept her on after she started doing more harm than good with her harsh methods. Mike was worried about whether Schmid would get behind his ideas, which were in direct conflict with Lucy's ways.

Mike tried to rehearse what he'd say, but he was coming up blank.

When he got to the business trailer, Misty, the bookkeeper, hadn't yet arrived. No surprise there. She'd been drinking hard the night before. Mr. Schmid was in his office, so Mike took a deep breath and knocked.

"Come in, Mike."

Mike opened the door. Mr. Schmid was on the floor, in the last part of a push up. He got up to his feet with some difficulty and, breathing heavily, sat down in his desk chair. He took a few tissues from the box on his desk and wiped the sweat from his forehead.

"Gotta stay fit, right Mike? Or try. Or some damn thing."

Mike laughed. "Something like that." He took a seat in one of the folding chairs by Mr. Schmid's desk.

Schmid took a long gulp of coffee. "How's it going, Mike? How are things down at the Wolverine?"

"Good. Good. I ran into ol' Andy Pencil."

"I'm always glad to hear that he's still alive and kickin'. Or alive and sitting at the Wolverine, anyway."

"Ya, really. Talking to him got me thinking. We, and every circus I know of, has benefitted from the Ypsi littles, and those old timers, and even the old timers' kids, aren't going to be around much longer. I'd like to do something for them—something like a little's appreciation night."

"I sees," said Schmid, leaning back in his chair, "Have you talked with anyone else about this idea?"

"Not really."

"Lucy's going to throw a fit. What did you have in mind?"

"Nothing crazy. Maybe invite them all to the show on Saturday and have a special section for them. Someone could announce them and thank them."

"Well . . . I don't see how any of that could be too much harm. But, you do know that Lucy's going to throw a fit, right? Are you prepared to deal with that?"

Mr. Schmid had a look on his face of real concern. He was just as afraid of Lucy as everyone else in the circus.

"Yes. I'll deal with the Lucy consequences," said Mike.

Mr. Schmid moved his pen through his fingers, spinning it and flipping it awkwardly and absent-mindedly. It seemed to Mike like the right nervous tick for someone who has worked in and owned a circus but has never performed in one. It was clumsy, but it was still an approximation of a trick or skill.

Schmid was thinking, and Mike knew to not distract him when he was. Mike hoped, of course, that Schmid wouldn't think too hard and would come up with the same idea Mike had just planted—the same idea that, by now, was spreading across the entire little community of southeast Michigan. If he didn't agree, Mike had just fucked up.

"This sounds like a fine idea," said Schmid.

"OK, I'll make it happen," said Mike, "I'll get over to the little trailer and talk to them now."

CHAPTER 31

In which Mike tells the dwarfs too much

When Mike got to the little people trailer, he found them all gathered in Princess's room.

Mike knocked on the open door as he entered. Princess was sitting on the edge of her bed. Leo was playing ukulele and sitting on a small stool. Lil' Rocky was standing shirtless by the cooler of beer and singing "Has Anybody Seen My Gal?" to Lil' Lizzy and Charley, who were sitting on the couch. Leo and Rocky finished their song as Mike was entering. They belted out the last chorus with exaggerated show biz voices.

When they finished, Mike, Lizzy, Princess, and Charlie applauded and whooped. Leo and Rocky both climbed up onto the cooler and bowed.

"So, what do you think?" asked Rocky.

"Sounds great, Rock," said Mike.

"Thanks, we've been rehearsing. We're gonna call the act 'Pint-sized Pickers' and see about doing some shows on the side for beer money."

Mike was still towering over everyone in the room, and he could tell they were uncomfortable, or less comfortable, having to look up at him. He sat down on the edge of the bed, and

Princess stood up so that she could rest her hand on his shoulder.

"It's sure to be a hit, guys!" he said, "You might need to put on a shirt for some of the classier joints, though, Rock."

"Ya, I thought about that too," Rocky said, "Princess is gonna make us matching black shirts like Johnny Cash."

"You've never performed with a shirt on before, Rocky, how do you feel about that?" asked Princess.

"Well, we're gonna see how it goes. Frankly, I expect that the ladies will be begging me to take it off anyway by the end of the show."

Lil' Lizzy and Princess pretended to swoon, while Charlie and Leo guffawed.

Charlie got up and slapped Rocky's child-size shoe to get him off the cooler, and then got another beer for himself. "You want a beer, Mike?" he asked.

"No thanks, Charlie."

"Suit yourself!" said Charlie.

After the fooling around, it was obvious that Mike came for a reason, so he got right into it.

"I want to throw a party for the little people at the show on Saturday, and I want to make it spectacular. I talked to Andy Pencil this morning and told him to invite everyone, and we're going to have a section reserved just for the littles. I was thinking if we have everyone together, we should take the opportunity to show off what you can do. We'll have a real display of little people power."

Rocky, who was prone to excitement, jumped up and made a Superman pose. Lil' Lizzy clapped. Leo and Princess both looked pleased, but like they wanted to hear the rest. Charlie took a swig from his beer, nodding his head.

Princess spoke up. "What do you have in mind?"

"Well, it's gotta be something that will wow 'em, but that we can do without rehearsal, or with just one rehearsal, right?

And it should be something that sends a message that you're powerful, talented, independent people who have been mistreated but that you're back and this is your time."

"I want to have a parade into the big tent before the show starts, with all of the littles, dressed in different costumes—business people, factory workers, animals and clowns—running into the tent and then fooling around doing tricks in the center ring before going out into the stands and doing tricks and interacting with the crowd while the band plays some real dramatic music and the announcer talks about the history and importance of littles to the town of Ypsilanti, to the country, to the circus, and to the world. We can end it with all the littles gathering back in the center to lead the whole big tent in singing Somewhere Over the Rainbow or something else everyone knows, followed by the Star-Spangled Banner."

When Mike finished talking, Leo spoke up first, "Why are you doing all this?"

Mike wasn't expecting to face questions about his motives. Logistics, sure. But, he wasn't prepared for this question. If he were honest, he'd say that he doesn't want to be a failure, and that by helping other people he could make himself feel better about himself and the people who he helps will appreciate and love him, and everyone will recognize his genius and vision and will follow and respect him. Plus, the littles were the only ones in the circus who had always treated him like a full person and a full member of the circus, even when he was just his sister's little brother hanging around. He loved them, and he wanted to impress them and do right by them. But, saying all of this wasn't the right answer to Leo's question.

"It's time that the little people are recognized and that you become full members of the circus and that we restore your reputation as talented contributors, rather than just a sideshow."

Leo put his hand on his head, closed his eyes, and thought for a moment before speaking. "But all of this threatens and pokes a stick in the big clown eye. You know this, right? Have you talked to the clowns about your idea?"

"Yes, I know. No, I haven't talk to them yet."

Then Mike said something he'd regret for the rest of his life.

"The clowns' reign of terror has to stop. They've been the bullies of the circus for too long. They add questionable value but gain positions of power by the force of their personalities and with threats. But, when did you ever hear of a clown making good on a threat? Sure, they make less money than the other performers, but they use that as leverage for power, which is what they're really after. They want to control minds—they talk about making people laugh and how that's the most important thing to them, but what happens when people laugh? They let their guard down. Clowns are masters of manipulating people because they know how to weaken your defenses—whether through humor or fear—it works both ways for them. If you love clowns, you'll let them do anything because they're funny. You take Tiny the Clown, for example. He does children's birthday parties in Florida during the winter, where he makes balloon animals shaped like penises. The parents let him get away with all kinds of inappropriate shit with their kids because he plays innocent and funny. He could be a molester or a burglar and no one would ever catch him because he has the perfect disguise. He plays a child in a man's body and they buy it because his makeup says that's who he is.

"There are people who are afraid of clowns—the clowns have even more power over them. These people avoid clowns, and they'll tell people they think clowns are creepy, but do they ever report them or try to catch them doing creepy things? Do they suspect them of being malicious? No, of course not. They just don't want to be around them. Perfect.

It's as if the police decided to just avoid the criminals rather than trying to stop them or catch them. It gives them a license to do whatever they want and play dumb about it the whole time. They can be the worst people in the world, but they can get away with it."

"What do you think of when I say Charlie Chaplin? You think 'Why there's a lovable scamp!' right? What if I told you that he forced people to work for him for no pay and that he had a torture chamber in the basement of his mansion where he kept his multiple wives and that he was a racist bastard and an alcoholic who beat his kids? Would you believe it? I don't know if any of that is true, but that's the kind of thing clowns get away with all the time because they can. The more famous the clown, and the more loved the clown is, the more they get away with. So, why do this? It's for you. But, do I also want to take the clowns down a notch? Sure."

The room was quiet as they all pondered what Mike had just let out.

Princess spoke first, "Is this about your sister?"

CHAPTER 32

In which the celebration begins

The day of the Little Celebration, as it came to be known, the dwarfs from all over Michigan, Ohio, Indiana, Illinois, and even from Canada started arriving early in the morning. Many came by bus and cab, but others came with their tall friends as drivers. Drivers got in for free too, but they wouldn't be part of the parade or sit in the roped-off section. As more little people arrived, they set up in the parking lot with coolers, barbecues, inflatable and folding furniture, and cases and cases of Mickey's—the favorite malt liquor of little people.

By noon, there were over one hundred little people and their friends partying in the parking lot. The manager of the fairgrounds was pissed, and Mike was sick to his stomach. This could be bigger and drunker than he anticipated. They had all gotten the word that they'd be part of a parade and many of them had already put on costumes or clown makeup, and some had even painted signs.

The signs ranged from mild and funny— "Let's have a 'little' fun!"— to offensive and belligerent— "We may be little, but we're not pussies!" and "Midgets do it with ANYTHING!"

Mike would have to have some discussions about family friendliness. As the new rules and organizational headaches piled up, Mike saw the whole thing getting out of control and he wondered at what point it turned from an event to celebrate the little people and into a freak show and an out of control party. The big tent wouldn't open for four more hours for the 7:30 show, and already there were dwarfs passed out on the grass, standing on cars, boxing and wrestling, juggling bottles and cans, throwing up next to the garbage cans because they were too short to throw up inside them, and urinating and shitting behind the bushes. This was their family reunion and they were making the most of it, dammit.

Meanwhile, there was a clown revolt going on at the circus camp. Lucy had refused to cook for the last two days and no one was happy about it. The clowns warned Mike that the Little Celebration would get out of control and they were gloating that it had happened just as they predicted.

Lucy told Mike he might as well just cancel the show for the night because the clowns sure as shit weren't going to perform with all that mess going on in the stands and everywhere all over the big tent. It was an embarrassment to the circus and to the tradition she had built and saved years ago—she told this to everyone whether they wanted to listen or not.

Mike wasn't going to cancel the show for anything. He would find a way for it to go on, even if it were nothing but littles. Advance ticket sales had been higher for this night than they'd been for any special event all year. He just needed to get things under control.

Mike walked out to the parking lot and told the first group of littles he met that there would be a mandatory preparation meeting in the big tent at 3:30. Word of the meeting jumped from one group of littles to the next, and the pace of drinking sped up as they all tried to squeeze in a couple more before going inside.

CHAPTER 33

In which Mike tries to gain some control of the situation

At 3:30 all the midgets who had been partying in the parking lot at the Wayne County fairgrounds started to file into the big tent, along with their drivers, pets, friends, and hand-painted signs they made when they weren't so drunk.

Mike looked out over the crowd. Princess, who had stayed sober for the event to help Mike manage it, was standing on a chair next to him. Mike picked up a microphone.

"Please, take a seat, everyone. Please sit down. Can I have your attention, please?"

The crowd of more than two hundred dwarfs was uncontrollable. Mike handed Princess the microphone and she yelled into it with her biggest voice, "Everyone! Listen the fuck up!"

The crowd wasn't listening up. They had all made it into the tent at this point but controlling them was a different thing. Mike got Andy Pencils' attention and motioned for him to come down to the ring. Andy ducked under the rail between the stands and the rings and Mike squatted down to talk to him as Princess shouted into the microphone to no effect. The cacophony of two hundred little voices all talking, laughing, singing, and shouting at each other in an enclosed space sounded like a recording of normal crowd, sped up, and playing on a giant cellphone speaker.

"This is some party, hey boss?" said Andy.

"Yes, it certainly is. Listen, Andy, we need to go over a few things with everyone before the show starts. Can you get them to quiet down?"

"Sure thing, boss."

Andy walked to the middle of the ring and pulled one of the stools used for the lion show next to the chair Princess was standing on. He bowed to her, holding out his hand. She held his hand as she climbed down from the chair and gave him the microphone. Andy kissed her on the cheek and climbed onto the chair himself and then onto the stool.

He cleared his throat into the microphone and the room went silent.

"Good afternoon, friends and family!" They responded in kind.

"It's so amazing to see so many familiar faces and new faces. So many littles in one place. This is huge!"

The crowd cheered.

"I think we should thank Mike for making this historic day happen. I know I will never forget what I'm seeing right now."

The crowd cheered again.

"Tonight, we're the stars of the show! But, right now, Mike would like to say a few things, so please give him your attention."

Andy handed the microphone to Mike.

"Thanks, Andy! Hello everyone! In two hours, our audience is going to come in and they're expecting a great show. Are we going to give them a great show or what?"

Cheers.

"Tonight is all about you. But, there are some things we need to do to make sure that it's fun and safe for everyone. How many of you have worked in the circus before?"

Half the audience raised their hands.

"OK, if you have experience, I need you to help others who don't. You know how it works and you'll be my deputies. For those of you who don't have circus experience—the most important thing is to be aware of what's going on around you. There may be acrobats tumbling or an easily spooked animal. Either of these can turn into a major disaster if we're not all careful and aware. Safety first!"

"Tonight, when the lights dim at 7:30, I want all of you to come down onto the floor. You'll be sitting here in the center-front, so you can just file out to the sides and come under the rail once I give the sign from right over there."

"The circus theme music will be playing as you come down and the crowd will be applauding and cheering. When you get down here, wave to the audience and smile. Look excited to be here—which won't be hard to do. This is going to be great!"

Cheers.

"The music will stop, and the cheering will continue as I walk out and introduce you first, followed by Jasper, our ring-master. Jasper will come out and work the crowd, tell a couple jokes, and then he'll say, 'It's time to start the show!'

"That's your cue to go nuts! Get crazy. Do flips, interact with the audience, clown around! The circus theme will be playing again, and the lights will be spinning, and fake cannon blasts will go off and the crowd will go wild! When the music ends, get back in your seats and enjoy the rest of the show. Everyone got it?"

The littles yelled "Ya!" together.

"Great! Just one other thing," said Mike, "If you feel like you've maybe had a little too much to drink today, please take a break, drink some water, eat something, and try to be fresh and sobered up for the show. We want to have fun, but we don't want things to get out of control. Remember—this is a family circus, and there are going to be children here and families out for an evening of clean entertainment with their kids. So, Rocco, keep your pants on."

Everyone laughed.

"OK, meet back here at 7:00, and let's put on the best show this fairground has ever seen!"

Two hundred little people cheered at the same time and it felt like the tent would collapse from the noise.

CHAPTER 34

In which everything goes to shit

The little people celebration was a disaster. By 6:00, all the little people were drunk or sick. Even worse, they had convinced the acrobats to get drunk too.

Acrobats getting drunk prior to a show was rare, but they realized that this would be no normal show and just a little vodka wouldn't hurt. Once the acrobats were drunk, the clowns got sarcastic and starting drinking, smoking weed, and running around the parking lot playing tricks on the dwarfs. They would sneak up behind one and lift him up or put their drinks on top of cars. The clowns were angry.

Mike had never seen clowns behave like this. Even Pauline was taking part in the random tormenting of the little people, who were oblivious to the fun being had at their expense and went along with it in the way that drunks and little people do when they assume that the people around them are just playing.

At 7:00, all the little people were in the bleachers in front and center, and the tent was full of paying customers. Mike and Jasper made the call to try and put on a show.

The lights dimmed, and the little people ran into the ring, screaming and cheering. They didn't even wait for the music before they ran into the stands and knocked hats off heads, screamed in the face of terrified children, grabbed bags, and played catch across the aisles.

Mike tried to get control of the situation or to make it seem like it was on purpose by turning on the music, but that just made it more chaotic. Mike picked up the microphone and started his introduction speech over the noise, as spectators headed for the exits. The clowns and acrobats and animal handlers waiting just outside the tent to make their entrances came inside and stood, mouths open. Mike called the police, and they arrived ten minutes later with two busses that they corralled the little people onto.

The spectators who hadn't left in terror demanded to know who was in charge, and the performers pointed them to Mike, who sat in the ticket booth handing out ticket refunds.

The news stories about the incident increased attendance temporarily, but after the rubberneckers, no one wanted to bring their family or school group to see the circus that might become a riot. The animosity between the clowns and the little people had reached the boiling point, and Mr. Schmid saw no point in continuing things. He fired Mike, and three months later he shut down the circus — selling the equipment, animals, and boxcars to a competitor. A few of the animal handlers could go with the animals. The acrobats went off on their own to start their own touring company. The clowns got on the placement list at the clown society but were all told that prospects looked grim and that they might want to start looking for straight jobs to carry them through until things get better for clowns.

The little people went back home and signed up for welfare. Princess spent three months living in Mike's apartment before taking off for New York.

Mike got a job at a shipping supply store, and he did his best to forget his failure and to stay hidden and drunk.

PART 2
Feathernauts

CHAPTER 35

In which Mike works at a shipping supply store

In his 41 years on Earth, Mike figured he had consumed an average of one pint of beer, one glass of wine, or one shot of liquor a day. This was a rough estimate, but he didn't drink until he was fourteen and there were weeks and weekends where he didn't drink at all, so he thought this was plausible even with his adult average of around three per day.

This one drink per day adds up to 15,000 drinks (or about 70 gallons of pure ethanol) that had entered and passed through his body. A gallon of ethanol weighs 6.6 pounds. He punched it into the shipping calculator one day and figured that, given his weight of around 190 pounds, he had consumed more than twice his weight in ethanol. The most cost-effective way to ship that would be via freight. It would run a couple hundred bucks, depending on the destination and how fast it had to get there.

To ship the total volume of beer, wine, and liquor—water included—would be much more expensive. Now you're talking about an average of around five ounces of water, so around eight pounds per gallon, over 15,000 drinks. That's 586 gallons, or 4688 pounds—two and a quarter ton—of alcoholic beverages. Mike figured he would need to get a container and ship this via rail or boat.

When you're talking about all the different alcoholic beverages—a couple hundred bottles of Bud, two memorable bottles of wine, hundreds of bottles of not memorable wine, the shots of Jaeger that one night in high school—you can't blend them and ship it in a tank. There are bottles, cans, corks, caps, and mixers to consider. What about the ice? That will require a special container.

There's also the matter of taxes, licenses, and fees. A few bottles of wine can slip through the UPS system, but to ship a couple tons of booze and packaging required a distributor license. Or, you could rent a couple vans and drive it there yourself to avoid all the hassle. How far are you going? Some of that ethanol might come in handy to power the vans for a couple hundred miles.

The complexity here is way less than the reality of how a half-lifetime (if you're lucky) of booze arrives at the place where you'll be when you're ready to drink each sip or gulp, an ounce at a time, for 15,000 days.

Mike had done this math before. He was considering whether he should make a spreadsheet when a woman peered through the glass front of the Pack-n-Ship store and made faces with her mouth as she scrutinized each item in the display case.

She was an early middle-aged woman. Mike sized her up and decided that if he had to describe her body, he would say she's "Michigan sexy." She had seen her share of potato-cheese soups, could cook a pot roast, and had blankets on her couch where she liked to read and drink hot chocolate with mini marshmallows.

Her hair was short and dyed black and not arranged in any style. She wore a wool sweater, jeans, and thigh-high boots with substantial heels and looked as if she may have been a punk rocker in her 20s, but she was pushing 40 now and only gave a little bit of a fuck. As she entered the store, she removed her red-framed sunglasses.

The store had its regulars, but she wasn't one of them. Mike sized her up and decided he didn't have a chance with her before asking "Can I help you with anything?"

"Yes, thank you," she replied, "I need to do something."

"We're not hiring," Mike said, "but I'd be happy to take your application."

Mike continued to entertain himself with making up stories about her. She lived in the neighborhood and had tried several ways to make money from home during the day. Her evenings were filled with dinner, soccer, TV, husband on the computer until way after she goes to bed, dogs peeing, and everyone worrying about the next day.

Maybe she likes wine, white and sweet. On a typical October night like this, she might cook tasteless chicken and rice with broccoli and open a bottle of Pinot Grigio that she bought that afternoon because it was on sale at the grocery store. Here's where things get more interesting than she knew. That $10 bottle of wine has roots in Burgundy going back the Middle Ages, but it hasn't been popular there for a couple hundred years. People make wines from this same grape in Italy, Germany, California, Oregon, Australia. Which one is she drinking tonight? Does she just drink, or does she imagine the place named on the label? She loves the places, the accents, the hills or lack thereof, the ruddy-faced winemaker who has never left Alsace dipping the wine thief into the barrel to extract a few ounces to get a taste of how the wine is aging.

"I'm not looking for a job. I want a project, and I don't mean crafts."

This was a first. No one came into Pack-n-Ship looking for a new hobby. Mike nodded his head. "Well—we're a shipping store. Do you want to ship something somewhere? I could help you with that."

The woman perused the shelf of small and medium-sized boxes. She picked up a square 5" box, turned it around in her hands, tossed it to get a feel for its weight, and put it back on the shelf. She did the same with the CD/DVD mailers, the book mailers, and so on through each of the sample assembled boxes on the shelf.

"What could I mail that might turn people's heads?" she asked.

"There are things that are illegal or that require special permits to mail: firearms, explosives, animals, cadavers, alcohol. If you have the right permits, I can help you with that, but if you want to ship something that's illegal to ship, I can't help you with that."

"No, nothing illegal. I want to make a splash though."

CHAPTER 36

In which Mike agrees to have some fun

"I'm not sure what you mean, ma'am."

"Ma'am" wasn't a word that Mike ordinarily used, but in this case, it somehow seemed an appropriate title for the woman who had barged into the store wanting to make her unfulfilling life more satisfactory by mailing a package.

"You just named some things that I can't mail because it's illegal or I'd need a permit. I want to find a loophole and mail something interesting that will cause some sort of ruckus."

"OK. Good luck with that. Tell me when you figure out what that is, and I'll be happy to help you find the appropriate method to ship it," Mike said.

The woman stared at Mike for several seconds too long then said, "I need a drink." She put her sunglasses back on and walked out.

He would have followed her and had a drink with her if the store could run itself.

Mike wondered if she'd be back. Sometimes the crazy ones keep coming back. He couldn't figure out whether this was a crazy one or a bored one with a "nutty" side. She might stroll down the strip mall looking for something fun to do at each store. Or, more likely, she'd get stuck at the bar.

Mike re-shelved the boxes in the right order and lined them up on the shelf. With that done, he glanced at his phone—only 3 more hours.

Whenever something like that happened, he'd tell himself he should keep a journal and write a novel about the people he meets. But, the time in between meeting new people got longer as he got older, and the idea soon vanished, and he never kept a journal.

But how about a novel about people and their drink and how it became their drink or the stories of why a certain person doesn't touch a certain beverage? They range from "Never again!" to "That's for kids!" For him, it was vodka he wouldn't touch. "Why couldn't that damn midget have drunk something less common and that would make me being disgusted by it easier?" he'd think. Even cheap beer would have been better. Not drinking vodka is like not liking the ocean. Half the planet is vodka. Still, he made it his business to know vodka inside and out despite it all.

Two hours later, the woman came back. This time, she was drunk. She left her sunglasses on and meandered to the counter where Mike was standing and doing the crossword.

"What is potato?" she slurred.

"Excuse me?" said Mike.

"I'm helping with that. Answering in the form of a question."

"Oh, I see. Good one." Mike didn't bother to correct or contradict drunks unless they were friends, and even then, he had a policy of going along with it unless someone was a danger to others or themselves or might be. "How can I help you?" he asked.

"You remember what we talked about earlier? I've got an idea, but it's not going to work AT ALL if you don't get drunk with me. So, let's go now."

Mike suspected she was full of shit, but he liked talking to drunk women, and he was curious about what sort of scheme she had cooked up. "Yes of course. That makes sense. I'll meet you outside after I set the alarm."

CHAPTER 37

In which we learn Rita's name, which is Rita

The woman pivoted on her heel and stumbled outside. Mike logged out of the cash register, locked the safe, set the thermostat, set the alarm, and followed her out.

"If we're going to be drinking," he said, "we ought to know each other's names. I'm Mike."

"Well hello there, Mikey darling. I'm Rita. Now, let's get down to business. Shall we go to Friendly's or McDougall's?"

McDougall's was one of Mike's favorite spots. He was often in there alone and he wasn't sure he wanted the staff to see him with Rita. On the other hand, he preferred the ambiance, beer selection, and the general scene at McDougall's. So, McDougall's it was.

"Ya, McDoug's is good. Let's go there."

If you want to get to know a bar, become friends with the bartender, and get the prime spot at the bar, go there at 2 or 3 in the afternoon on a weekday. Most times, the bar will be empty or there will be one customer who has a seat at the corner of the bar where he likes to sit all day and play video poker or make notes in his book or play word seek games.

Today, McDoug's was empty except for the bartender, Jim. The jukebox was silent, and Jim was refilling the juices and stocking the beer. Jim was one of the friendliest bartenders in town. He and Mike had had many good mid-afternoon and after closing-time conversations. Jim was an avid bowler, but he also loved to cook, played guitar, had a wife and two adult kids, and was an upstanding and important member of the community.

Mike hoped Rita wasn't too wasted, but Jim had seen his share of drunk women and could spot the signs. It would be best to come up with a plausible explanation for why he brought in this drunken woman.

"Hey Jim. This is Rita, a colleague of mine. We've got business to discuss."

Mike realized as the words were coming out that this seemed like the most BS explanation ever. "Ah, what the hell?" he thought. He ordered a pilsner. She ordered a gin and tonic. They paid separately and sat at the corner table the farthest away from the bar.

After he sat down, Mike reached in his pocket and found the three dollars change he got from his drink. He stood up, walked over to the jukebox, put the dollars in, and flipped through the songs looking for something that would appeal to both Rita and Jim and that would fit with the mood of what had become an interesting afternoon: mysterious and rebellious, serious but devil-may-care, and good for drinking. Roy Orbison fit the bill to get things started. Only the Lonely.

Mike went back to the corner table where Rita was smiling over her gin and tonic and sat down. They were unequally matched. She was at least three drinks in. He should have gotten something stronger.

"I left my job, which is so interesting and which I love so much to have mid-afternoon drinks with you and to listen to some scheme, the purpose of which I have no idea. So, let me have it already!" Mike said.

"OK. But first, get yourself a real drink."

CHAPTER 38

In which a fire breaks out

Rita took a sip of her drink, then looked around at the bar decor. McDougall's was not that old of a bar, but it looked old. The walls were dark wood, the ceiling had unnecessary beams, the booths had wood benches, and the tables had wooden chairs with distressed wood tops. On the walls hung the usual bar decorations—neon signs, framed Guinness posters, license plates, and plaques commemorating the McDougall's softball team's league championships. There was no real theme, except for something old-world, which the Irish-sounding name of the bar reinforced. The owner's name was not McDougall—it was Frank Papadopoulos.

Mike slammed his beer, and then got up to get a "real" drink. He was the sort of guy who would do whatever a semi-attractive woman said to do. They have magical powers, and there must be wisdom that can be gained by following their orders. He ordered a shot of whiskey and a Rusty Nail. Rusty Nail seemed to be the most appropriately foreign drink for the locale. He drank the shot at the bar while Jim located and poured the Drambuie, and then he went back to the table.

He brought the drinks back to the table and expected Rita to get to the point of what she was thinking. But just then a fire truck passed by outside with its sirens blaring—then another, and another. Mike had his mouth hanging half open, ready to ask for some answers, as the trucks approached, and he kept it that way for the whole time they were approaching, passing, and then stopping just up the street.

When the sirens turned off, he spoke: "I think you have no plan, and that you just wanted someone to drink with. Which is fine."

Mike's phone rang as he was about to suggest that they ought to get wasted and see if they can have a good time together, as long as they were there.

He looked at his ringing phone.

"Fuck, it's the owner of the shop."

He didn't know whether to answer it or ignore it. On one hand, perhaps his boss doesn't know Mike closed the store early. Maybe he's calling with a routine question. Or, maybe he knows and is calling to find out why Mike wasn't at the store. Either way, AC/DC playing in the background wouldn't do much to convince the boss that he's at the store, or that there was a family emergency he needed to deal with. He answered anyway.

"Where the fuck are you, Mike? I got a call from the alarm service, and the store is on fire!"

Mike hung up the phone and ran out of the bar. He didn't even bother getting his car but ran the 2 blocks back to the store. When he arrived, smoke was billowing out of the top of the store, and the firefighters were dousing the flames.

Mike saw Rita swerving down the sidewalk towards him, carrying her shoes.

Meanwhile, the owner was calling again from Arizona. Mike didn't answer. He turned off his phone and watched Rita walk. She didn't look at the burning building, but only at a spot about a foot above Mike's head.

CHAPTER 39

In which Mike and Rita talk to Fireman Paul

By the time the firemen had put out the fire, the interior of the store was a charred mess. Rita hung around and had sobered up enough to not be too annoying. They sat on the curb watching the scene.

A fireman asked Mike, "Are you the owner of the building?"

"No, I work here. Well, used to work here."

"Do you have the owner's phone number?"

"Sure thing."

Mike turned his phone back on so he could get his boss's info. Ten voicemails. He wrote the info for the fireman.

"Do you know how it started?" Mike asked.

"Don't know. Couldn't talk if I did."

"Why not?"

"Could become a crime scene, and that's not my job to get involved or talk about investigations."

"Gotcha. You just put 'em out, right?"

"Bingo."

Mike lit a cigarette, and the fireman asked if he could bum one. Mike laughed, and the fireman said "Seriously." Mike gave him a smoke and lit it for him.

Rita stood up from the curb. "What's your name?" she asked the fireman.

"Paul."

"Hi Paul, I'm Rita. We were having a drink down the street when we heard the sirens. Want to join us?"

Rita was checking out fireman Paul, head to toe and giving him the drunk girl flirt look, with her head tilted to the side, eyes squinted, and lips stuck out. She touched his shoulder as she talked.

"I'd love to, Ma'am, believe me. But, I've got work to do."

"Well, when do you get off?" Rita emphasized "get off."

Fireman Paul looked uncomfortable.

Mike waited a second longer for Paul to answer, then saved him. "Hey Rita, how about we go back to McDoug's and let the man do his job."

Then, to Paul, he said, "Take care and be safe." Mike felt dumb after saying "be safe"—it seemed like something that someone who does something unsafe would say to someone else who does something unsafe. If you do nothing unsafe yourself, do you have a right to say "be safe" to someone else? Even if you do, you don't sound cool saying it in the way that a motorcycle dude can tell a stunt pilot "Be safe, man" right before the pilot takes off.

Mike remembered that he used to do unsafe things. But, not these days. Turning off his phone and not listening to those ten voicemails was about the most unsafe thing he had done in the last 20 years.

CHAPTER 40

In which Mike and Rita get back to drinking

The half-finished drinks were still waiting for Mike and Rita in the booth at McDougal's. They sat down. Mike scrolled through the voicemails and text messages on his phone, but Rita interrupted him by banging another beer on the table.

"Put down the damn phone and drink this."

"What is it?"

"Fuckin' Pabst Blue Ribbon!"

Mike never knew McDoug's had Pabst on tap. He thought for a moment that he'd have to rethink his frequenting of this place, but this was no time to be a snob. He drank half of it in one gulp.

"Thanks?"

"Ya, you better thank me," said Rita, with her arms folded and a half grin on her face.

"Thanks for the beer," said Mike, "I'm a little shaken."

"Not for the beer."

Mike's suspicion of Rita was growing, but there was no way he was going to just come out and ask her if she started the fire.

He took another swig of his beer. Rita put down her drink (is that a Long Island Iced Tea?) and she sat down across from him.

"Well, if I'm not going to listen to my voicemails, and I'm unemployed, and I don't feel like going home, let's drink this place dry. It looks like we're off to a good start with the bad drinks. I'll buy the next round," Mike said.

Mike drank the rest of his beer without talking while Rita did the same. Mike got up and ordered four shots of the well tequila.

They traded buying drinks all night. Rum and Coke. Jack and Coke. Milwaukee's "Beast", White Zinfandel. Mike saw it as a war of cheap tastes made tolerable by the alcohol content. Each time his turn to buy came up, he tried to out-do his last. Rita's choices weren't as studied as his, but they were pure genius in how cliché and corny they were. It was as if she had been practicing making bad drink choices all her life for this moment. Mike thought the Peach Schnapps couldn't be topped, but then she came back with the piña colada-flavored wine coolers.

Rita was way past wasted, and Mike wasn't doing much better. Mike could see the "you're about to get cut off" creeping into Jim's demeanor, and he moved to make a graceful exit.

"Hey, this is getting insane. You wanna go back to my place? I've got some higher-class liquor and we can have a good puke."

"Sounds like a plan," said Rita.

They stumbled out of the bar. Jim offered to call them a cab.

"You're a cab! No, sir. We're walking."

They stumbled outside, turned the corner, and got into Mike's car.

"I can drive," Mike said.

"I didn't doubt it, Mr. sir," said Rita.

Mike drove his usual drunk driving route (suburban side streets and strategic alleys) and pulled into the parking lot of his apartment building.

"That might be the one thing I'm best at in the whole damn world," said Mike.

Rita grabbed his ass while he was leading her up the stairs to his third-floor apartment.

"I totally want some more Bailey's with that ass," she slurred.

CHAPTER 41

In which Rita comes home with Mike and Mike falls in love

"Rita, before I let you into my apartment, I have to know: did you have anything to do with the fire?" Mike asked.

"What? I mean, what?" Rita said.

She was leaning against the handrail about halfway up the stairs. Mike had stopped a few stairs below her to ask the question. He always made sure to follow up the stairs when he was with someone who was drunk. It seemed like the right thing to do, but Mike wasn't sure that he'd be much good if someone did fall backwards down the stairs on top of him— especially considering that he was also trashed whenever he arrived home with someone who was this trashed.

"I mean, did you start the fire that burned down my place of employment this afternoon?" Mike asked.

"Look at me," said Rita.

Mike looked at her. Her head had a fuzzy halo around it, created by the backlight from the bulb at the top of the stairs, combined with Mike's drunken eyes. Rita was swaying a little and had a small smile on her face, not unlike the Mona Lisa's. But, she was a drunken Mona Lisa from North Detroit with an art school punk turned stay at home mom mass of unkempt short black hair.

"I will prove to you, using fucking logic, that I had nothing to do with it. Now, about that another drink," she said, as she turned away and started climbing the stairs again.

That wasn't the answer Mike hoped for, but he'd take it and see what she has in mind for logic once they get upstairs and get another drink.

Rita was climbing fast and singing.

"We didn't start the fire. Blah blah blah! Fucking world is turnin'!"

She swung around on the landing at the second floor and kept going.

"Rita" Mike yelled, in a mountaineer echo voice. "This is my flooooor!"

Rita stopped at the landing between the 2nd and 3rd floors and turned to face Mike, who was standing on the landing below.

"We didn't start the fire!" she sang as she danced with both hands raised above her head, banging her head and kicking her feet like they were covered with snakes.

"OK, come on down, Rita darling, you'll disturb the neighbors." Rita mocked.

She sat down on the top stair, facing Mike, and leaned her head against the wall.

"What if I did do it? You'd owe me big time, buddy boy."

Mike climbed up to her stair and sat down next to her.

"Put your arm around me, Mikey." Rita said.

Mike was happy to oblige. He moved in closer and put his arm around her shoulder. Rita did the same to him.

"Mike. Fuckin. You're good. You've always been good. But, I know you, Mikey. I know you better than you know. I know how that mind works. You think we just fuckin' met but that ain't so. I've been inside your head and I know you. I fuckin' know you."

Mike liked talking with drunk women. They were the most honest and they would tell you things that were sometimes muddled and circuitous, but that were always honest. He thought if he could just remember the things that people tell him when they're drunk and think about those things when dealing with the same people sober, he would understand everyone so much better. But, remembering how a person is when they're drunk is somehow difficult to do when you and the person are both sober. This leads to going out for drinks to recapture the magic conversation and relationship you had with the person. This is how some of the best relationships and friendships of Mike's life were formed. Constantly seek to recapture the drunken honesty and take the relationship to a deeper level of trust through shared wasted talking and sitting on the stairs holding each other up, trying to communicate intuitive feelings that you feel about that person, and trusting that a phrase like "I've been inside your head." won't be taken the wrong way.

"What do you mean by that?" Mike asked.

"You know damn well what I mean. I mean, it's like. You. You're what, 40? Working in a tape and box store. I know why."

"Why do you think?"

"Mikey is sad. You lost something, or someone. Something happened to you between when you learned to have so much fun drinking and when you took that job. Am I right?"

"Something happens to everyone, Rita. We all lose things and people every day. It's all loss."

Rita put on a fake TV fortuneteller voice and placed her fingers on Mike's forehead.

"Yes, but I see something bad and sad in you. You wanna tell me about it, Mikey? Do you want to confess your sins now and apologize to anyone who might have been hurt by your irresponsible behavior?"

Mike laughed, but he was certain at this point that there was something not right about Rita beyond her just being a drunk.

"What do you see?" he asked.

"Hang on. One moment please. I have to clear out all the tape and boxes and huge selection of packing and shipping supplies of every kind," she said. "I see travel and adventure. Parties. Oh, my god! I've got it! You're a washed-up pop star. You had a boy band, groupies, the whole thing. Then one day it all came crashing down. The sex tape leaked. The drugs caught up with you. You found yourself floating in a pool of debt and vomit and ditched it all to live like a normal person and try to get by with crushed dreams and no hope."

"Not bad." Mike said. "But not right."

"OK, so what do you think MY story is?" Rita said.

"I have some ideas about that, but let's go inside."

Rita threw up her hands above her head, while still sitting on the stairs, and then started singing in a drunken mumble. "The night cap is a little old place...where we can get together. Night cap, baby, night cap. Night cap baby!"

Mike helped her stand up and they made their way down the stairs together with Mike holding Rita up and Rita singing.

They got to Mike's apartment on the second floor, and Mike got out his keys and opened the door. Mike lived alone in a one-bedroom apartment. The front door opened into a short hallway where Mike took off his shoes. A closet full of coats was on the left. Past this entryway was the kitchen on the right and the living room on the left.

Mike brought Rita into the kitchen, and she leaned up against the dishwasher. The kitchen had an electric stove, a small white microwave, a refrigerator with some magnets from breweries and wineries on the front, and a bit of counter space to the side of the sink that Mike called the bar.

On the bar, he kept a clean dish rag, a shaker, a small plastic cutting board, a bowl of lime slices covered with plastic wrap, several shot glasses, a long-handled spoon, a corkscrew, and several other mismatched bar accessories.

In the cabinet above the bar, across from where Rita was supporting herself on the handle of the dishwasher, was his liquor. Mike opened the liquor cabinet and took stock while Rita looked on.

Mike took pride in his well-stocked liquor cabinet. He had Scotch, Irish, American, Canadian, macro- and micro-gin, sweet and dry vermouth, light and dark rum, and several different tequilas ranging from silver to reserva. The one thing missing was vodka.

"What'll you have?" Mike asked.

"Gimme a fuckin' Shirley Temple, but with lots of booze!"

Mike cracked up. This was one of the funniest drink orders he'd heard. Rita tried to keep a straight face too, but she started laughing hysterically when Mike couldn't stop.

"OK, ma'am. One Shirley Temple, extra slutty, coming right up."

Mike guessed that a Shirley Temple, extra slutty, would involve vodka, but he substituted rum and layered the grenadine, rum, ginger ale, and orange juice and then garnished it with four cherries on an umbrella, an orange slice, and a lime.

He presented the drink to Rita, who had been watching with rapt attention and providing play-by-play commentary, then he poured himself a generous tumbler of Bourbon.

Rita sat her drink down on the counter and admired it, then she touched Mike's face gently with her fingertips.

"It's perfect, Mikey. Thank you so much."

"Tweren't nothin'," Mike said. He raised his glass with his pinky extended and clinked Rita's glass. "Let's go into the sitting room, shall we?"

"We shall." she said.

They carried their drinks, both filled to the rim, to the living room. Rita spilled a little and let fly a cascade of profanity, but never stopped.

Mike's living room had a couch, an uncomfortable straight-backed leather chair, a long coffee table, and an old TV with stereo and video equipment on the lower level of the table holding the TV.

Rita sat down on the couch and put her feet up on the coffee table. Mike did likewise, just a couple feet away, but just over the crack between the seat cushions.

"Now, tell me what you imagine my story to be," Rita said. Then she pushed the garnishes away from her face and took a sip.

Mike was sure he had her pegged. He'd seen enough drunk women in his time to know how different people act in different circumstances. If there's one good and useful thing that he learned from the circus it was how to read people and how to know which angry clown was joking and which joking clown was angry.

"You grew up drinking Shirley Temples at the country club," Mike began. "You became a hell raiser at 14 and ran away several times. You lived with an older boyfriend from time to time and you stayed out too late. But, you got your schoolwork done. Your dad didn't notice any of this, and your mom and grandma couldn't control you. You pulled yourself together, though, and went to college, where you studied ... let's see ... artifacts."

"Hold on! Artifacts? What the fuck is that? Is that the best you can fuckin' do?" Rita said.

"OK OK. You studied comparative Native American literature."

"Again, is that even a thing?"

"Fine. You studied fuckin' biology."

"OK. Nice. I was a biology bitch. Go on with your crazy tale."

Mike took a long slow drink and looked off into the distance. A thought crossed his mind that he might not want to cross this woman. She was quite possibly insane. And, she was quite drunk. Ah well. What did he have to lose? He continued, "You became sort of a punk in college, and you drank too much coffee. But, you had your wild years a decade before and didn't care much for the party scene. You met a man. He was a chemist and you got married when you were young. You didn't have any kids, and this chemist took off with a ski instructor. You're temporarily living back at your parent's house."

"Fuck, Mike," Rita screamed. "If any of this wasn't spot on, I would have slapped you for thinking that was my life. But you fuckin' nailed it."

"Really?" Mike asked. "I wasn't too sure about some of it. But, I'm pretty good at reading people, I guess."

Rita slapped Mike across his face. "No, you little shit. You've got me all wrong."

"Not even a little right?" he asked.

"Not a smidge. Except for the part about studying artifacts. That was dead on."

"Well, you were wrong about my being in a boy band."

"I guess we're both bad physics, huh, Mikey?"

"Bad physics?" Mike asked.

"I mean bad psychics, but I can never remember how to spell it, so I say physics, which I can spell. Fuckin' psychics. Will you make me another drink? Something not so sweet this time."

"Sure, happy to. I like the way you drink, by the way," Mike said.

"You would," she said.

Mike got up and went to the kitchen to make a drink. He thought he should make something with some water—a gin and tonic maybe? He filled her glass with ice, poured in the gin—a little short—and filled with tonic. He then squeezed a lime slice and dropped it into the glass. He brought the drink out to the living room, and Rita was lying across the couch and snoring. Mike sat her drink down on the coffee table before changing his mind—she's not going to want to see that in the morning.

He brought the drink to the kitchen and dumped it in the sink. Mike got an extra blanket from the hall closet and covered Rita up. He stood over her for a moment—there was something comfortable and familiar about her that he couldn't put his finger on. But, he was drunk, he thought, and lonely, and any company—but especially a quirky drunk woman—was welcome company. He smiled, turned out the lights, and went to bed.

CHAPTER 42

*In which Rita takes a shower and promises
to explain herself*

The next morning, Mike had a slight headache and he was famished. He got out of bed at about 10:00 and remembered that Rita slept on his couch—and that she may have burned down the place where he used to work. He also remembered that he just met her the day before, and she might not have had any idea where she was or how she got there.

Mike would normally walk out into the kitchen in his boxer shorts to make coffee and eggs, but today he put on his pants and checked his hair in the mirror before going out. Rita was up and she was browsing through his bookshelf.

"Morning, Mikey," she said, "You didn't make me another drink last night."

"No, I did, but you were asleep."

"You should have left it on the coffee table," she said.

"Ah . . . next time. How did you sleep?"

"I don't know. I was sleeping."

"Want some coffee?"

"Yes, please, that would be swell."

Rita was still wearing the same clothes that she fell asleep in, minus her shoes and socks. Her hair was more ruffled than it had been the night before, but she was remarkably undamaged by the day and night of drinking.

"Mind if I take a shower?" she yelled to Mike, who was starting to fill the coffee pot with water.

"No, of course not. Go right ahead."

Rita picked up her purse off the couch and walked past Mike, touching his cheek, then patting it. "It's all gonna be ok, Mikey. I'm here," she said.

Mike was stunned for a second at her familiarity, then he continued with making the coffee and she headed to the bathroom. Then it struck him that he should have asked if he could get in there first. Heavy drinking always made him have to shit urgently several times the next morning. But, ladies first. And, he'd go to the gas station next door if it became a real problem.

He was out of smokes, anyway, and so he decided to make the trip. He put on his slippers and left the apartment—locking the door. He wasn't sure whether locking the door was the right thing to do in these circumstances. After considering the pros and cons in his addled brain, he figured it was more important for her safety that the door be locked than for her convenience if she had to leave. Oh, what the hell. He was overthinking from nerves.

When he returned from the gas station and smoking, Rita was sitting on a chair at the table, flipping through one of Mike's books. She was wearing a towel on her head and one wrapped around her body.

"Why do I feel like I know you?" Mike asked.

"Give me some coffee and I'll tell you," she answered.

CHAPTER 43

*In which Rita takes off and promises
to explain herself later*

Rita, still wrapped in towels, sat at Mike's kitchen table, sideways on the chair. Her legs were crossed, and her arm laid sprawled across the top of the table, with the other hooked over the back of the chair. The position emphasized her breasts, which were covered by the largest towel Mike owned—a beach towel he'd had for at least 15 years and had gotten at Marine World.

Mike found himself attracted to Rita, as he would have been to any woman sitting naked and wet in his kitchen. But, she had just offered to explain herself in exchange for some coffee, and Mike aimed to find some things out.

Mike smiled at the dolphin-wrapped Rita, who didn't seem to be hung over and who looked innocent and even cute in the morning.

"Sure, I'll make some coffee," he said.

Mike kept his coffee in the freezer, whole bean, in a glass canister with a metal latch. He pulled out the canister and used his plastic coffee scoop to measure out enough beans for 12 cups of coffee into the grinder.

The sound of the grinder temporarily wrecked the tranquility of morning with a hangover and a naked woman in the kitchen.

Eyes forward, Mike stuck to the job—he ground the coffee, poured it into the reusable filter, filled the coffee pot with water and then poured it into the coffee maker. When he turned on the coffee maker, it sputtered and burped and then started making coffee—slowly at first, but then steadily. Mike needed a shower, but he needed to know why Rita was here even more. But, it could be a long story and Mike felt filthy and had to shit. "I'll be right back, I'm going to take a quick shower. Help yourself to coffee and anything else, and then we'll talk. I'm dying to know how you know me," he said.

"Have a nice one," Rita said.

After Mike got out of the shower and got dressed, he went out to the kitchen and found an empty coffee cup on the table, his two towels that Rita had been wearing slung across the back of his chair, and a note scribbled on a napkin next to the coffee cup.

"Mikey—meet me at McDoug's at 4:00. Kisses"

CHAPTER 44

*In which we meet Jim the Bartender
and Rita has a surprise*

Mike got to McDougal's at 3:30 to start drinking before his 4:00 appointment with Rita. It had only been a day since he met her, the building burned down, he got wasted with her, and she passed out on his couch. He didn't know her, but considering how much she liked to go to McDougal's, he thought it was possible that he had run into her before while he was drunk and that's how she knew so much about him. That was the most likely explanation, he thought. She certainly seemed to think that she knew him. She promised she would tell him. Or did she?

Was she just dragging him along, he wondered? Was this just another odd game she was playing? Her first game ended with Mike out of a job and suspected of arson. Mike wondered whether it was such a good idea to be going along with her this time.

Jim was the bartender again today.

"How's it going, Mike?" asked Jim.

"Eh, you know. Time for a Guinness, I figure."

"Good call. Coming up!"

Jim was the bartender last night and had seen Mike acting like a fool, drunk off his ass, with Rita. A lesser bartender would have made a knowing comment like "Rough night?" or "Looked like you were having a good time last night!" But Jim knew that his job depended on people having the illusion of anonymity and invisibility, or at least permission, when they're drunk. Comments about drunken escapades the next day were quite likely to result in a feeling, no matter how slight, of unease about getting drunk again in that same bar with the same bartender. That's bad for business.

"Here you go, Mike. That'll be four bones."

Mike put a 10 on the bar and left a dollar tip after Jim made change.

Jim snatched up the single, rapped his knuckles on the bar, and stuffed it in his tip jar.

Mike was the only customer in the bar, but Jim knew that he'd be getting busy starting at 4:30. He checked his well bottles, filled his juices, and made sure there were enough Coors Lights in the fridge for the happy hour rush.

Mike sipped his Guinness. The first one after a hard-drinking night was special. It had restorative properties, and Mike could already feel himself becoming more relaxed and his head pounded less after just the first sip. Mike studied the coaster under his pint. It was an ad for a kind of gin Mike never drank. Mike considered whether to try it. The ad made it look cold and classy. The bottle was striking—simple and unusual.

The TV at the end of the bar was showing soccer with the sound off. The TV behind the bar, closest to Mike, was showing a Jeopardy rerun, with the sound on and closed captioning.

Mike enjoyed coming up with Jeopardy answers and questions in his head. "An alcoholic beverage flavored with a variety of herbs, including juniper berries. What is gin?"

The Miller High Life clock above the bar read 3:40. Mike finished his first beer. He thought he should take it easy today, but he certainly needed to relax a bit and think about what he'd say to Rita, what she might know, who she might be, and why she seemed so interested in him.

"Can I get you another, boss?" Jim asked.

"Ya, sure, thanks."

Jim grabbed a clean pint glass and inspected it for chips, smears, and dirt. He held the glass angled as he pulled the Guinness tap. The glass filled with thick foam. Jim let the glass sit as he watched Jeopardy.

"What is hopelessness?" he thought, pondering his wasted youth pouring drinks, his wasted middle age pouring drinks, and now his impending senior years wasted pouring drinks. It wasn't that he didn't still like people and the relative freedom and prestige that his job as a bartender gave him—especially compared to the jobs that his customers described to him. But, he had known little else since his first bar job so many years ago, and even with the occasional interesting opportunity—sexual, travel, or business—that came up because of bartending, he still felt bored and tired of it all.

Jim looked down at the settling Guinness and topped it up again.

"What is restlessness?"

Jim wanted to be doing something adventurous, and he sometimes did, and even more often he pretended that he did. He often thought about the time, eight years ago, when there was that great deal on flights to Iceland, and the beautiful girl at the bar asked if he would ever go there, and he placed the call and bought two round trip tickets that afternoon. Most of the time, however, Jim's life was about as routine as could be, and it never headed in any direction. It was a steady march of days, drinks, and people.

Mike wondered what Jim was thinking about as he stared at the TV. He imagined that Jim knew what the foam on the beer was doing at any point, without having to look. He liked to imagine that Jim was inventing new drinks, planning better ways to run a bar, and estimating the total weight of all the liquor that had passed through his hands over the years. Mike thought that he was good at figuring out other people. But, he was now reconsidering that in light of recent events.

Jim finished pouring the beer and he replaced Mike's now empty glass on the coaster with the gin ad.

"Thanks, Jim."

Mike placed his remaining five dollars on the bar. Jim replaced it with a dollar. Mike pushed the dollar towards Jim's side of the bar. Jim rapped his knuckles and nodded at Mike.

Both Mike and Jim watched Jeopardy in silence for a couple minutes.

"So, Jim, I've been coming here for years, right?" said Mike.

"Ya. You're my favorite customer of course."

"Ha, of course. Thanks," said Mike, "Have you ever seen me with the woman I was in here with yesterday?"

"Ah, nope. I don't think so."

"Have you ever seen her before?" asked Mike.

"Not that I recall. That's not to say that she hasn't been in, but I'd remember her if she were a regular—or so I like to think."

Dead end, thought Mike.

Jim was not one to offer opinions in personal matters. Mike wasn't one to pry or talk much to anyone about anything. Mike knew Jim wouldn't offer anything, but time was getting short and he decided to go for it and try to get something useful out of him.

"Did she seem like a normal person to you?" asked Mike.

"Ah, you can't make up your mind about her, eh?"

"Something like that," said Mike.

"Ya, she seems friendly enough, but with a serious impulsive streak. Reminds me a little of my ex."

"What happened with her?"

"She ran off to a yoga retreat and I never saw her again."

"I'm sorry."

"Nah, I'm better for it."

"Does she seem like she's hiding something?" asked Mike.

"Well—you can tell a lot about a person by how they order a drink, by how they drink, and by how they are when they're drunk. Was she hiding something? I have no idea. She's certainly trying to get over something or make up for something. But, isn't that why everyone's here?"

"Hmm." Mike shrugged, nodded and looked at the TV. "I'm meeting her here soon. Thanks for talking."

Jim was absolutely no help at all, Mike thought.

"Any time," said Jim, and he meant it.

Jim was used to people asking him his opinions about other people, about politics, about what they should do with their lives, on marital problems, on what they should drink, on whether they should have another drink, on what they should say to a girl or boy, on what they should say to their husband or wife when they ask "where are you?" or "where have you been?". Honesty was rarely the best policy, he'd learned. It was better for business, for the customer, and for his own sanity to respond with something close but slightly off from what the customer wanted to hear.

If they said, "My boss wants to know if I can work tomorrow, what should I say?" Jim would respond with his best pseudo-medical / pseudo-psychological advice, such as "You can do this. I'll set you up with a glass of water and a strong ginger ale for each beer you drink from here on out. You'll be fine."

Jim had no interest in most people's questions or problems, except in that he didn't lose good business. Most people, he'd found, are good enough regulators of themselves and it wasn't his business to be cutting anyone off, unless it was his business because they were bad for his business. Jim hoped that Mike and his new girl would be regulars together. It was far better for business to have a couple drinking and having fun than to have another sad man sitting at the bar watching Jeopardy during the afternoon.

Mike was half-finished with his second Guinness when Rita walked in, at 3:50.

Rita waved at him and smiled. Mike was relieved. He expected women to be cold and unfriendly and was always surprised when they seemed happy to see him.

Rita looked stunning. She had clearly put in extra effort in advance of coming here today. Yesterday, it seemed as if she had woken up, put on the first things she could find, dropped the kids off at school, gone to the dentist, and swung by the dollar store to pick up toilet paper before stopping at the shipping supply store to lose her mind.

Today, she gave the impression of a mysterious woman of leisure. She wore a silk scarf over her head and dark sunglasses. Her purse was hanging from her left shoulder, and she was wearing a black dress, dark lipstick, and light powder on her face, with her cheeks pinker than normal skin color. Was it the chill of early October or makeup? Mike wasn't sure.

Rita walked towards Mike, and he didn't know whether to get up and meet her halfway or whether to watch her as she walked, so he focused on finishing the last quarter of his beer as she approached.

"Hey, Mikey!" she said, "slow it down a bit and give a gal a chance to catch up!"

She put her arm over his shoulder and kissed his cheek before sitting on the stool next to him.

Rita looked hard at the bottles behind the bar, then at Jim. As Jim started walking over, she ordered. "G and T, please."

"Any particular gin?" asked Jim.

"This one," said Rita, pointing to the coaster under Mike's empty glass.

"Another for you?" Jim asked Mike.

"Yes, please."

As Jim grabbed Mike's glass, Mike decided he didn't have the patience for waiting for another Guinness right now. "Give me something else for this one," said Mike.

Jim nodded. "I've got one here I think a discerning customer as yourself might like."

"Sounds good."

Jim knew that flattering his customers in front of their dates was always good for business. He made Rita's drink and poured a beer for Mike.

"I've got this," said Rita, tossing a twenty onto the bar. "Keep the change."

Jim couldn't help raising his eyebrows as he rapped his knuckles and nodded.

Mike was about to remind Rita that she promised to explain herself, but then Rita just started in.

"You don't remember me. That's fine. I didn't expect you to. I hoped that you would, but you were self-centered and occupied with other things. I'm the last person you'd expect to find you and you're the only person I've been thinking about for months, or make that for years."

Mike was feeling uneasy. It was starting to become clear to him that, even though he didn't know who Rita was, he knew the makeup she was wearing—and likely the source and brand of it—from the circus days. He had tried to put those days out of his mind for twenty years, but the details were coming back now, starting with the way everything about the makeup was exaggerated but it came in simple and plain packaging.

"My mother told me to give you this," Rita said.

Rita stood up, raised her glass, and took a sip. She motioned for Mike to stand up. As he did, she placed her drink on the bar. Before Mike was ready, she grabbed his head with both hands and kissed him on the lips, then kicked him as hard as she could in the shin. Her facial expression turned to a scowl and she hissed at him, "There you go, pussy-face."

Mike bent over and held his shin to try to ease the pain.

"You're Lucy's daughter," Mike whispered.

"Yes I am, and I intend to make you pay for what you did."

CHAPTER 45

In which Mike and Jim think and drink

Did he still deserve punishment for something that happened twenty years ago? Rita believed so, at least. If she did, there may be others who were still looking for him. Or, she may be the sole messenger for the group. Mike didn't have time to ask, because Rita ran out after slamming her boot into Mike's shin.

"I'm guessing that didn't go as well as you'd planned," said Jim, setting a shot of bourbon in front of Mike.

"Ya, not really," said Mike, "Thanks, Jim."

Mike drank the shot, and then sat down on the stool and looked at the TV, feeling the burn in his throat for a moment before taking a sip of his beer. Remembering he had switched to a beer he didn't want in exchange for not having to wait, he pushed the beer away but then reconsidered and drank it in one giant gulp.

"Can I get another shot, and another Guinness, Jim?"

Jim half hoped or half expected Mike to shake it off, laugh, and chalk the kick up to "who understands women, right?" But, this one fell into a different category. Mike's current re-action was more like "I know I did wrong, honey, please take me back." This one took more drinks—sad drinks, contemplative drinks—after which the man would resolve to do something. Jim would advise him to wait until he sobers up before doing whatever he resolved to do.

The signs of the "sorry loser" as Jim nicknamed this type of patron were all there, but what Jim didn't understand was that Mike's scenario was more complex, even just on its face. This wasn't just about a wronged woman and a kicked and apologetic man who wanted her back.

In Mike's story, as best as Jim could figure, this woman who Mike believes he never met before tracked him down and spent a day getting wasted with him, maybe even going home with him, and then made plans to meet with him the next day so that she could kick him in revenge for something he did to her mother.

By Jim's estimation, that woman's mother would be near his own age, likely older. How had Mike taken advantage of or harmed this older woman? This was clearly a "better not to pry, or even to know, even with the best customer" situation.

Jim finished pouring the Guinness and the shot and put them in front of Mike, taking away his empty glass. He then picked up a bar towel and wiped up the area around where Rita's drink sat and picked up the drink to towel under it. He paused briefly before taking it away just in case Mike wanted it.

Jim wouldn't charge Mike for this one or the beer he didn't want. Not charging for an occasional drink in the right situations was always a good policy and good for business.

Jim dumped out the gin and tonic, then placed the glass in the bus tub under the bar. That gin sucks anyway, he thought.

Jim walked to the end of the bar and turned up the TV, which was now showing golf. Jim didn't care for golf, but the TV at the other end of the bar was the place to go when a customer needed some alone time.

Also at the end of the bar was an old-fashioned phone with a bell ringer, and a coin slot that didn't work, and a rotary dial. The phone was an antique. Jim had bought it when he opened the bar. It was one of the items he got from local antique shops to give the place more of an established and historic feel. When he bought the phone, he imagined it ringing during the performance of a great jazz band, like happens in the greatest jazz recording ever—Thelonious Monk: Live at the It Club. The phone and background talking on I'm Getting Sentimental Over You add a dimension to that song that make it much more than an excellent rendition of a standard, and put it firmly into the realm of a great scene, spontaneously created, by pure chance encounters of conversation, someone calling the bar, and an improvised drum solo. Why was someone calling at that moment?

Any other ring sound—such as any electronic ringer from the last 30 years or so—would have ruined the recording. If the band had been recorded through the board, rather than through the air, that ringer also wouldn't have been picked up. But it's that antique bell sound—the only ring sound that phones made at the time—that makes the song.

Why was it so important that someone reach the bar at that hour? Why did no one pick it up? Did the band hear the phone ring? Jim wasn't an expert on jazz, or even on music, but he'd heard the recording with the phone ringing many years ago and it had stuck in his mind vaguely, but he didn't know who or what it was until he had a chance meeting while working bar at Trackside across town. A jazz musician was performing, and after hours he and the musician sat at the bar and talked. Jim described his recollection of the song and the telephone and the musician knew what it was.

When he started McDougall's, Jim envisioned his bar being the type of place where a song, a phone, a drum solo, and the right people might all come together by chance at the right moment to create moments that they'd never forget and that were far more than the sum of their parts.

This old phone, with the sign taped to it that read, "If you're sitting here, you answer it" was the soul of chance and the most important thing in the bar to Jim. It was the lifeline to the outside world. It was the connector to the past. It was the starter and enabler of conversations and business. It was the hailer of transport for the soused.

It was at that moment, while Mike was drinking his baby please beer and a shot and Jim was thinking about how cool his antique phone was, that the antique phone rang. Strange coincidence, thought Jim. He muted the TV and picked up the phone. "McDougal's Pub, Jim speaking."

Mike looked over at Jim as if he was expecting the call to be for him. There was no sound on the other end, so Jim hung up. The phone rang again, and Jim picked it up. Again, there was no sound.

"Damn thing goes haywire sometimes," said Jim, although that wasn't true. The phone rang a third time. Jim answered and said "Hello!" in a loud and clear voice. There was no answer. He hung up and picked it up again. Just a dial tone.

Jim shrugged and took the TV off mute.

Mike, meanwhile, had a feeling that Rita wasn't done, and that the phone ringing was a message of some sort. But, he wasn't going to live in fear. He had fucked up, it's true, but he was just a kid, and he had to do something, and it was terrible how it turned out, but he couldn't have known. He thought he had left that all behind, that he was better off forgetting and moving away, and they were better off forgiving and moving on.

Rita, at least, thought otherwise. Mike considered whether it would be better if he moved again, and whether there was any hope of him finding a place where they wouldn't find him—maybe Aberdeen, he thought.

CHAPTER 46

In which things don't go so great for Mike at the bar

Mike had nothing. His job had gone up in flames. The girl he met yesterday was hell-bent on revenge for his past. He was broke. He didn't know how he'd afford the beer in front of him. Running away to Aberdeen had always been an option he'd considered, but without money, it was just a dream.

Aberdeen—the end of Route 12. It was the place clowns don't go. There's no sense in hitting a dead-end for a circus, and business is far better in the Midwest. Crossing the Rockies with a train full of animals was risky. Taking them to a small coastal town, with nothing but thousands of miles of water to the west, was unheard of.

Aberdeen—where the welcome sign says, "Come as you are." Even if you're a suicidal junky. Even if you come and all you want is to get the hell out to somewhere like Seattle where you can sing in a band and shoot up. Come as you are for how long you need, or else.

When he left the circus, Pauline told him to lay low. Joining another circus—if there was one that would have him—would only infuriate the ones who were already furious but who were holding back out of respect for his clown back-ground and family. Mike had been laying low. He hadn't even so much as thought about the circus, much less gone near one or tried to reach out to anyone from the old days since he left. He'd even lost touch with his sister after his parents both passed away five years ago. What had changed that made Rita come after him? Mike thought back on everything Rita said. She said she was delivering a message from Lucy. Why didn't Lucy deliver it? Lucy wasn't the type to hold back or send oth-ers to do her work. Lucy was old, even at the time, or so it seemed to Mike. But, older people have a way of not seeming so old once you reach the age where they seemed old. She must have been at least seventy, though, just based on the sto-ries Mr. Schmid told him of when Lucy was a clown in the '50s. That would make her at least ninety today.

It was likely that she was no longer alive. Mike thought he could search for her obituary. There would be one in the paper in her hometown. But what was Lucy's hometown?

If Lucy had passed away, that would explain Rita's mission. Lucy had been holding off the clowns from exacting revenge on Mike. Clown courtesy kept him safe from the harsh and swift justice of clown law. If Lucy was dead, the clowns were coming after him, and Rita's message was meant to serve him notice.

The bar room suddenly turned cold and uncomfortable for Mike. Another customer entered and sat three stools down from him. Jim started chatting with the new customer about work (or was he hardly working?) and the man ordered a Coors Light.

The jukebox started up and the first song was Bob Seger singing about heading west because a change would do him good. See some old friends. Good for the soul.

The Guinness that Mike was drinking tasted flat and wrong. The light level was off. Jim was clearly only interested in Jim. The whole damn bar was fake. It looked old but it it said established 2002 above the door. All these local history pictures and artifacts hanging on the walls were complete garbage, bought in bulk from a giant warehouse in Mexico. Mike got Jim's attention.

"Jim, this one tastes off. I can't drink any more of it. Can I get another one of whatever that other beer was?"

"Not a problem, Boss," Jim said.

"Hang on—actually, I can't let good beer go to waste—even if it tastes like shit."

Mike poured the remaining half of his Guinness down his throat, shook his head to clear it, and let out a belch, forgetting that there were now two other people in the bar. They both laughed at the belch.

"You still want the other beer, Mike?"

"Oh hell ya," said Mike.

Jim poured Mike another pint, and Mike took a sip to try and clear the strange metallic taste. This beer tasted even worse, and Mike spat it out into the glass. The room was starting to get fuzzy and Mike started sweating.

That's strange, he thought. I need to slow down and get back to the gym. I should only drink on weekends. This Rita thing has me weirded out and my body is reacting to the stress. Mike asked Jim for a glass of water.

"You ok, Mike?" asked Jim.

The two other guys at the bar were looking at Mike too.

"Hey, bud. You should take it easy. You're not looking so hot," said one of them.

"You're not looking so hot, mutherfucker. This is how I always look," said Mike, "Fuck you!"

Mike tilted his head back and tried to keep it level with the spinning room, but he lost his balance and fell off his barstool and just missed hitting his head on the stool next to him as he plunged to the floor, knocking his beer off the bar as he fell.

Jim ran to the antique phone at the other end of the bar and dialed 9-1-1. Other bartenders might first see if the person could be helped to their feet and whether there was a serious injury before calling, but Jim's policy was to call for the ambulance first. Rush hour was about to start. Happy hour was about to start.

"9-1-1. What is your emergency?"

"Yeah. Hi. This is Jim at McDougal's on 3rd. A customer fell off the bar and is unconscious on the floor."

"Is he breathing?"

"Yes."

"Was he drinking heavily?"

"No more than usual."

"Did he complain about chest pain?"

"No."

"Was he acting strangely prior to falling?"

"He seemed agitated and he complained that his beer tasted bad."

"Is there any reason to think he may have been poisoned?"

"Yes! Oh shit, yes! Please come quick. And send the police too."

"Help is on the way," said the operator.

Jim hung up the phone and placed his hand on his forehead. The police will want something with her fingerprints. Did she even touch her drink? The glass was still in the bus tray, of course. Anything else? He could point them to where she sat—briefly—and they could dust the table where Mike and she were last night. But, what good would that do? The scene of the crime was at the bar and it revolved around that highball glass, that pint glass, that shin she kicked, whatever she slipped into his beer that would match the contents of his blood, and the words she said as she was kicking him. What was it she said? Something about "That's for my mom, pussy face?"

CHAPTER 47

In which Mike has a most disturbing dream

In the hospital bed, Mike dreamed about how things could have gone 20 years ago. He was talking with Applesauce the Clown, at the entrance to the big tent. Princess was there, with her arms around his knees, and she was kissing Andy. Mike felt jealous, but tried to talk normally with Applesauce, who didn't seem to mind or notice the scene going on below.

Applesauce had a business proposition that he wanted to discuss. He wanted to use the circus train to make pencils but he needed to work out the problem of shortages, or something like that. Mike tried to listen but was afraid that Applesauce would figure out that Mike had no idea what he was talking about, and meanwhile he was trying to keep an eye on Andy's increasingly sexual kissing of Princess. The crowd was starting to file into the tent and they were all dressed in Hamburgler costumes. Of course, thought Mike, Easter is tomorrow.

How had he not realized? They'd need more seating to fit the costumes. Was the formula 2.2 times as many or 1.6? He couldn't remember. He was screwed if he was wrong either way. Pauline walked up and mussed his hair.

"Come on, Mikey. Let's get a drink."

Mikey and Pauline walked to a bar that sort of resembled McDougal's except it also made Chicago-style pizza. A band made up of Mike's teachers from high school came on stage and started playing. Rita was singing and wearing a red velvet dress.

After an introduction where she thanked Mike for being there, she started singing. The crowd watching her numbered fifty to a hundred people. Rita sang a slow and sexy song about birds who wanted to be astronauts.

"Feather-nauts, don't give up.
So wild, so free.
Feather-nauts, you will win.
So hot, so far.
Feather-nauts, reach for your nest in the stars."

The song made both Pauline and Mike laugh at how dumb it was. Sitting at the empty bar, they imitated Rita's blank stare that she was trying to pass for sexy and exaggerated her swaying dance, which ended up just looking a bit awkward because of her height. It was more like a zombie, less like Marilyn Monroe.

The band made up of teachers from Kennedy High, wearing the same shirts and sweaters Mike knew from freshman year, made the scene even more comical. Yet, the audience was into it—hanging on to her every word, swaying along with the laconic beat, entranced by her self-aware swaying and tone-deaf singing.

Mike couldn't look away. The song was repetitive and long. He became aware that he was dreaming the song and the band, and he wanted it to be better—he was impressed with his sleep songwriting, and with this pop music symbolism he'd come up with for the band that he wanted to exist just so he could feel something other than fear towards Rita. As the song went on, Mike's straddling of the two worlds became more difficult to manage and he let himself slip back into dream-reality-mode without trying to control or observe it. Rita finished the song and walked over to where Mike and Pauline were sitting, only now Pauline wasn't there but Jim was. Jim handed them both special keys and told them to go to the room below the stage.

Mike had the feeling he had been at the bar hundreds of times but had no idea there was a room under the stage. Rita knew, and Mike felt jealous and a bit afraid of her. She started walking away, with her key in her hand, and told him to follow, which he did. They went down a hallway and got to a door with no sign or number on it. Rita put her key in the lock, and motioned for Mike to put his in. She opened the door. Inside the room was a couch, a TV, a desk, a king-sized bed, a sink, and small tables on either side of the bed. It was an exact replica of every 2-star motel Mike had ever been in, but half a star lower for not having a window.

Rita entered the room and started getting undressed. She wasn't doing it in a sexy way. It was matter of fact. In Mike's dream world, Rita's strip tease looked like she just came home from a day working at Arby's and she just wanted to take a bath, except that as she undressed, she was looking at Mike expectantly, or so he thought.

Rita had pulled off her dress and hung it up in the closet. She took of her bra and set it on the dresser, to the left of the TV, above the minibar. She unbuckled her boots while sitting on the couch in her panties and stockings and pulled them off, all the time staring at Mike. Maybe she thought this sad face was sexy too?

She crossed each leg over the other and removed her stockings, then got up and put them next to her bra and put her boots in the closet.

Rita stood outside the closet, wearing only panties. Her panties were the type of panties you'd expect a clown to wear, Mike thought. They were white and simple. They weren't the panties of someone who expected anyone to see her panties. But, they seemed to change as she moved towards him. In the different light and shadows between the closet and the desk where Mike was standing, her panties sparkled, and polka dots formed. Rita's face maintained the constant, sad look of someone who was trying to be sexy, but her panties were putting on a show like Mike had never seen. He had to be near those panties, to embrace them, to kiss them, to touch them.

But they were attached to Rita, and she appeared to him to be lifeless and she had just played in a band with three of Mike's high school teachers and she had most likely burned down his workplace, and she was Lucy the Clown's daughter who was hell-bent on revenge and was that the look on her face? Was this anti-strip-tease part of her way of getting back at him?

He knew at that moment that there was some combination, some code, that he needed to punch into the remote control for the TV, but he couldn't remember what it was, and the numbers on the remote registered slowly as asterisks on the TV so he wasn't sure he'd put in the right code. He tried several different combinations. Rita sat down on the couch and started doing a crossword puzzle in a book of crossword puzzles she took out of her purse. Mike kept trying different combinations and nothing was working.

Rita was getting impatient and took out her phone and started typing on it. Mike breathed hard and Rita slammed her phone down on the couch next to her.

"What?" she said.

"I just can't get this combination. It's not working."

"OH - it's the remote? You sure it's the remote, Mikey?"

"Ya. I'm pretty sure, actually."

Mike, frustrated and humiliated, needed a drink. Fuck the code, he thought as he opened the minibar. It contained several small bottles of cheap Scotch, a few beers, and a half-finished bottle of soda water. It had better not be flat, he thought. He turned the screw cap on the soda water bottle and heard a hiss as pressure escaped. Great, this'll do.

He went into the bathroom and grabbed one of the glasses from behind the sink, rinsed it out, and filled it with ice and dumped the water, just to be sure. He then went back out to the bar and poured one of the little bottles of Scotch over the ice, then filled the glass with soda water. He put the soda water back into the fridge and stirred the drink with his finger. He tasted it and it was cool, earthy, sharp, fizzy, and fragrant. The alcohol in the Scotch took no time at all to hit his head and he sat on the desk chair and lit a cigarette. The magical combination of Scotch, soda, and nicotine was his only thought at that moment.

But then Rita and her panties forced themselves into his attention. She was giggling and he could hear her phone making chirping noises followed by her typing on it, followed by chirping noises, followed by giggles and typing. Mike tried to ignore her—she wanted his attention but he knew it would turn out bad and with her trying to kill him again.

Just then, Mike remembered that the circus was about to start. He rushed out the door without saying goodbye to Rita and he drove back to the Wayne County Fairgrounds where Princess was waiting and not happy at all.

"Where have you been?" she asked.

"Sorry I'm late," he said.

"You didn't answer my question. That's fine. I see how it is."

"Aw, Princess. I'm sorry. I was getting a drink with Pauline. How's everything look for the show?"

"Fine," said Princess. She walked away.

Mike walked past the ticket collector. He was a tall thin local with a Tigers cap who knew Mike but who Mike didn't know. Mike walked to the ring, turned around, and looked at the crowd. It was huge. He panicked and shook with fear as he walked to the backstage.

When he got backstage, he found that no one had changed into costumes, none of the clowns had put on their makeup, the place was a mess, and the animals were wandering around free as the performers all sat around a campfire singing and drinking.

"What the hell are you doing?!" screamed Mike.

"Hey boss," said Lil' Lizzy, stumbling towards him with a wine cooler, "I tried to get 'em in line, but they wanted to wait for you."

"The show starts in 10 minutes!" said Mike, as he grabbed his hair and looked around at the chaos, trying to figure out what to do about it. He ran around in a panic, trying to get the animals back in cages, and he didn't see a log lying on the ground and he tripped and fell.

Mike opened his eyes with a start and a woman he'd never met before was standing next to him.

"Good morning, Michael."

"Where am I?"

"Holy Cross Hospital. Looks like you had a bit of a scare down at McDoug's."

CHAPTER 48

*In which Mike receives a visitor
and a letter at the hospital*

As Mike lay in his hospital bed for the first few minutes after waking up, he sorted through his memories and came to a reconciling of what was a dream and what was his actual memory of the previous two days. Or was it still the same day? How long was he out?

The nurse brought a tray of food—a muffin, orange juice, and ice water—and placed it on the table next to his bed.

"How are you feeling?" she asked.

"Like I had one hell of a good time last night," Mike said.

The nurse chuckled.

"Well, you were out cold for eighteen hours. I'd say whatever you were drinking, your body didn't much like it."

Mike did the math. He'd met Rita at 3:00 and she drugged him. Eighteen hours later would put him at near lunchtime the next day.

"Do you think you can stand up?" she asked, "I imagine you'd like to use the restroom and wash up before breakfast."

"Yes, I think so."

Mike's body was stiff, and his head throbbed as he struggled to pull himself up. He noticed that he was wearing a hospital gown, and he wondered how that got on him and whether this nurse had anything to do with it. Had she seen his penis? Had he puked or shat while she was around? He was embarrassed no matter what.

A wheelchair was sitting next to the bed, and the nurse offered to help him get into it. He accepted the offer. He was sure that he could walk just fine, but he was ok with her pushing him around too.

The nurse pushed him down the hall and stopped outside the bathroom. She gave him a small plastic bag containing a toothbrush, toothpaste, and some other items.

"I'll wait right here," she said, "Take your time."

Mike stood up, with some assistance, and went into the bathroom. He inspected himself in the mirror. Except for the hospital gown, being unshaven, and his messy and greasy hair, he looked like his forty-year-old self and he sighed and went into the stall to take a dump.

Mike shat every morning after breakfast for his entire adult life. He stayed on the toilet for as long as he could stand it and he started to feel better as more of the poisons left his body.

When he finished, he wiped his ass and exited the stall, noticing the strong odor. He washed his hands thoroughly, taking his time and breathing in the mix of shit smell and soap smell.

Mike brushed his teeth and washed his face. There was no razor in the plastic bag, and he wondered if that was on purpose to prevent additional injuries, or if it was the unisex goodie bag and there was another one that contained a razor and shaving cream.

When he was ready, he combed his hair with his fingers as best he could, and was conscious of how he'd like to appear handsome and put together for the nurse who was waiting for him outside the door. She seemed nice, and about his age, and Mike appreciated the feeling of someone caring for him at that moment.

Outside the bathroom, the nurse was waiting and talking with a male doctor. Mike felt jealous as he sat in the wheelchair and regained her attention.

She pushed him to his room, and they talked about what he did for a living (he lied and said he was on sabbatical) and where he lived and how he liked it. When they got to the room, he sat on his bed and ate the muffin as the nurse talked with someone in the hall.

She came back into the room and, with a big smile on her face, told Mike, "One of your friends is here to see you!"

A woman he didn't know, dressed in a clown costume and holding three balloons came in through the door and started singing a song by The Smiths. Mike remembered that Pauline used to play it on repeat when he was a kid. It's a song about a "jumped-up pantry boy" (whatever that is) who didn't know his place. Mike used to annoy his older sister by fake ballet dancing when she played it.

Mike knew this was another warning. He hated this song. He wondered why the nurse and the other patients who were standing around watching weren't horrified and throwing this imposter clown out. The nurse was dancing a little bit in place, and was excited that the clown was singing something she liked.

Mike looked around the room and saw that his wallet, his phone, his cigarettes, and his lighter were in a bag on a chair, along with his shoes. They must have cut his pants and shirt off. He wondered how he'd get out of here and what he'd wear.

The clown's makeup was clearly the work of a circus clown. Circus clowns apply their makeup with putty knives. The features need to be obvious, even from the back of the stands.

Hospital clown and birthday clown makeup, on the other hand, has more fine detail. The singing clown didn't look at Mike or anyone else in the room, but at the spot where the wall met the ceiling, and she projected her voice to that spot, much too loudly for a hospital.

When she finished singing, the clown tied her balloons to Mike's bed and handed him a card. The card was in a black envelope and it had a red wax seal on it. The seal had an embossed circus clown face. Mike recognized it as the logo of the international clown court, which oversaw clown licensing and setting clown standards and regulations worldwide.

The clown left without saying a word, and the other patients all went back to where they came from.

Mike's nurse said, "Well, that was one of the more unusual clown visits I've seen. The one that still takes the cake is the stripper clown, though. We had to put an end to that one."

She picked up Mike's chart and then looked at Mike. "I'm going to let the doctor know that you're ready to be seen, and hopefully we can get you out of here soon."

"OK, thanks."

When the nurse left, Mike opened the letter from the clown court and read it.

In the matter of Michael O'Malley be it here known, on this 23rd day of August in the year . . .

Mike skipped over the paragraphs of introductions and formal announcements and pronouncements of the date, the place, the particulars about the makers and enforcers of statutes, the countries and municipalities and other phony legal talk. The clown court had no more legal standing anywhere in the world than a Toastmasters meeting. But, Mike was starting to feel that they could be a whole lot more dangerous.

. . . be it here known, for all eternity, shall be hereby cast out and found to be an enemy of the clown community.

Mike put the letter back into the envelope and set it on the bedside table. He'd never considered being afraid of clowns before—they seemed harmless and, frankly, awkward and incompetent in the real world. But now he had to wonder, considering that one had already tried to kill him, whether he should rethink this.

CHAPTER 49

In which Mike calls his sister

Mike was worried. The clowns were out to get him, and they knew where he was. That damn Smiths song. Mike went over the lyrics in his head. He'd never thought about them much before. Some pretentious British shit, he'd always thought, without ever trying to figure them out. Now these stupid British shit lyrics seemed like they were about him. Whatever. Pretentious bullshit clowns trying to be deep or poetic. But, if Mike knew clowns, they would be back—this wasn't the only thing they had up their stupid clown sleeves.

Mike looked for an opportunity to get out of the hospital. He made a plan to wait until the nurses weren't looking or until late at night and then climb out the window, run to his apartment in a hospital gown, and hope nobody saw him.

But, as it turned out, he didn't have to sneak out or jump out the window or distract the staff. When he told the nurse that he didn't have insurance, that was the end of his stay, and he left through the front door, with his hospital gown on and his wallet and phone in hand. He walked outside and lit the second to last cigarette in his pack and started walking towards his apartment in a hospital gown at 3:00 in the afternoon.

Mike caught the bus that went by his building and stood holding onto the bar until the bus got to his stop. He got off and walked up the stairs to the 2nd floor and entered his apartment, expecting to find his apartment ransacked or even currently occupied by clowns. He was surprised to find that everything was as he remembered leaving it. Rita knew where he lived, so he certainly wasn't safe at his apartment, but he could at least take the time to get dressed and come up with a plan.

The first order of business was a beer and a shower. Mike was happy to find two cans of Tecate in the back of the fridge. He had no idea how long they'd been there, but he grabbed them both and drank them in the shower.

When he was clean and buzzed, Mike got out of the shower and took a clean towel out of the closet and dried himself off. Then he sat on the floor and wept.

The stress had built up over the years. He always knew that they were pissed off, and that he was blamed for ruining clown lives, and that someday he could face his judgment. But, it was always just a vague fear. He didn't think they'd track him down. Now it was real. How real, and how much danger he was in, he had no idea. But, he knew what the clowns were capable of and he knew now that he couldn't ignore them any longer.

With no job, no friends, and no family, Mike had nothing to lose but his life and his sanity. But his life and sanity were plenty to keep him frightened.

He hadn't talked to his sister in a decade, but she was his only hope. The last time he'd heard, she was living in Sacramento, California, and she had a husband and a daughter. If she would take him in or help him out until this passed, maybe he could find his way to a clown-free zone. Legend was that

Belize had outlawed clowns and there was such clown hostility in the whole country that clowns feared for their lives to even walk around out of make up because someone might find out who they were.

Sacramento seemed like it should be closer to Belize, and it didn't seem like a bad place to hide out in the meantime. If he could get there, it would take the clown council at least a couple weeks to find him and send people out there. But it all depended on where Pauline's alliances fell. They hadn't parted on the best terms, but Pauline quit the circus and clowning years ago, and hopefully her loyalty to her brother would outweigh her loyalty to the clown council.

Feeling like he had the beginnings of a plan, he got dressed, made coffee, and called the last number he had in his phone for Pauline.

It rang three times and then she answered.

"Hello?"

"Hi Pauline, it's Mike."

"Mikey? It's been for fucking ever. Where are you? How are you? Are you ok?"

"Ya, it has been. I'm still in Michigan, and I've been better. How are you?"

"Oh, you know. It never stops. Listen, I'm so glad you called. I didn't know how to get in touch with you, but I heard through the grapevine that some bad shit is going down."

"It is."

"Are you safe?"

"That depends on your definition."

It occurred to Mike that Rita may have bugged his apartment. "I can't talk right now. Can I call you back in an hour?"

"Uh, sure. Are you really ok, Mike? Do you need anything?"

"I need to get to Belize or to Aberdeen."

"It's that serious? OK. Call me later."

CHAPTER 50

*In which Mike gets out of town and pulls a
switcheroo*

Aside from his liquor, Mike didn't own much. It was, he supposed, a side effect of feeling like he was living in hiding. He
never started a collection, took up a hobby, or invested in expensive furniture. He had some boxes, and he had a suitcase.
He filled these with the things that were vital to his survival,
along with a few things that were just nice to have.

He packed his clothes, the good Bourbon, his shoes, coats,
and his laptop. That filled three boxes. He packed a box of
books too.

Skipping out on his apartment never seemed like an option before, and he wasn't sure of the right way to do it, but it
was now the middle of the month and he could give two weeks'
notice once he hits the road, leave the door unlocked when he
leaves, and just call some charity to clean it out and lock the
door behind them. This plan seemed reasonable enough,
given the circumstances.

Mike loaded his suitcase into his car. About halfway down
the block, he saw a head of bright orange hair standing outside

a house. Was it just a coincidence that a neighbor picked today to have a clown at their kid's party?

Mike couldn't tell whether he was spotted, but he didn't want to take any chances. He could load the rest of the things into the car using the back entrance. He got into his car and drove around the block, avoiding driving by the scene of the clown.

He parked in the handicap spot closest to the door and ran up the back stairs to his floor. He grabbed two of his boxes and started down the stairs. As he exited the building he saw a different orange head turning the corner to the side of the building. This was getting far too creepy.

Chances were that they wouldn't do anything overt. But, it was their sneakiness that Mike had to watch out for. He decided not to risk it to go back upstairs for the rest of his clothes. He had books and booze, and a small suitcase of clothes. That would have to be enough. He threw the boxes into the back seat, got into the car, and drove through the alleys until he reached the main road.

By now, he figured they were either inside his apartment or following him, or both. If they were in his apartment, would they find anything that would tell them where he was headed?

If they had half a wit among them, they'd already know he was going to Sacramento. He'd need to take a different route to throw them off, and he wouldn't stay for long. But, that's what everyone who isn't on the run says too, and it's certainly what he said when he got to Grand Rapids.

In his rearview mirror, Mike saw a brightly painted Volkswagen Beetle turn into the alley two blocks back. He turned onto the highway. The good thing about being chased by clowns is that fifty-year-old Beetles and busses don't move that fast. Mike's 2005 Pontiac Bonneville was plenty fast and comfortable, and it was more than a match for any car owned by any clown he'd ever seen. The downfall of many clown-owned vehicles is that clowns can't help having shit cars with decorations all over them that fall off when they drive over fifty miles per hour. But, like a zombie apocalypse, it wasn't their speed that Mike was afraid of, it was that there are so many of them and that they're single-mindedly set on one goal—brains. Fuckin' clowns.

Other than the fact that he had to be looking over his shoulder and making sure that he was one step ahead of his pursuers, he was looking forward to a long drive alone.

Mike got on I-96 towards Detroit. He was going the wrong way—a detour through Detroit would add five hours to his journey, he estimated. But, driving down to Detroit might throw them off his trail for a while. He'd make them think he was going east but then do a switcheroo late at night and he could be past Chicago before anyone noticed. How the hell else do you lose someone when there are only three roads that a person can take from Michigan to California? He sure as shit wasn't going to spend any time on Route 12, aka clown highway.

Several hours later, he was in Dearborn, just outside Detroit, and he stopped for gas and to use a pay phone to call Pauline. He no longer trusted his cellphone for making important and confidential calls, and he kept it turned off. By now, most people have forgotten how to make long distance calls on payphones, but Mike took pride in knowing such things. He deposited the necessary change, and Pauline picked up on the first ring.

"Mike! We've been worried. Where are you?"

Mike thought it was suspicious that the first thing she asked was where he was and that she said "we."

"Uh - ya, I'm fine. Thanks for asking. I'm gonna go stay with some friends in New York. Maybe the big city will be safer for me?"

"Do you think you can talk to them? Or see what it is that they want from you or if there's anything you can do to satisfy them? Why don't you come stay with us?"

"Pauline, I really don't think so. I'm going to head east, and I'll let you know where I am when I get there."

"OK. I'm sorry about this, Mike. Some people just won't let it go. I'm sure once you talk to them and explain everything they'll be reasonable. The last thing a clown wants is to hurt someone. You know that, Mikey."

"I have proof that there's at least one clown out there who doesn't feel that way."

"But if you just contact the council, I'm sure they can call off any vigilante clowns."

"I don't think so. It seems to me like the council has put them up to this, and I'll be in in New York."

He wanted to make it crystal clear to her that he was going to New York. She'd assume he was going to stay with Princess, who moved there after the circus closed to try and get into TV or independent film acting. They would find her, and she would say she had no idea where he was, which was true, and by then he would be in Aberdeen or Belize, but he hadn't yet decided which.

He only knew that he sure as hell wasn't going east, and Detroit wasn't safe for him now that he'd told Pauline he was headed in that direction.

Mike hadn't eaten since the hospital, and he decided he'd have time to stop and eat before he started west. He was on the edge of Dearborn, and he found a Big Boy and stopped. If the clowns were coming, he had at least two hours before they could make their way down from Grand Rapids or from the clown capital of Michigan, Ann Arbor.

Big Boy, Mike reflected, was a strange place to stop while hiding out from clowns. The decor, and that fat boy wearing the tablecloth, was a little too close to circus clown-themed, and that was the style that was popular for restaurants when Big Boy was a popular family restaurant for the same kind of people who used to go to the circus.

Nowadays, the young middle-class families like he grew up in go to Olive Garden, leaving Big Boy and Bob Evans for the elderly, the homeless, the ironic hipsters, and people hiding out from vengeful clowns.

Here he was thirty-some miles down the road from Ypsilanti and the Wolverine Grill, which, he imagined, was still standing and in business with Little Greg running things and his beautiful girlfriend, now wife, running the cash register and greeting people as they entered and left and handing them menus and telling them to slap their buns down anywhere and getting back to her word search game or whatever the modern equivalent on the cellphone was.

At Big Boy, Mike waited for a hostess to seat him in the near-empty restaurant. He ordered coffee and a burger right away.

It was eight o'clock and it was starting to get dark outside. He could eat quickly and slip out of town in the dark and get several days on his pursuers.

As Mike sat eating, he thought about his time as the manager of the circus and he remembered a piece of advice that Misty the bookkeeper had given him when he first started working in the business trailer.

She said to never tell anyone how you do your job, or you'll become replaceable. Mike thought this advice was paranoid and old fashioned at the time and he ignored it as he went around telling everyone every thought and idea that came into his head as if he were safe in the circus. He should have known better. Everyone in the circus was scared all the time.

CHAPTER 51

In which Mike stops at a gas station

Mike stopped outside of Chicago just after midnight for gas and to take a leak. As he was pumping the gas, a car full of college-age kids—two guys and two girls—pulled up on the other side of the pumps.

The girls ran inside to use the bathroom, and the guys stood outside by the car. The driver started pumping gas. The other one, clearly drunk off his ass, leaned against the side of the car—a white Honda Civic—and let out a groan. The driver laughed.

"How's it going, buddy," the driver asked the other guy.

"Dude. Fuck! This girl is making me crazy. She's a fucking basket case."

The driver laughed.

Mike, desperate for any normal human interaction, chuckled. The drunk non-driver noticed.

"You wanna take her? I can't handle it any longer?"

Mike laughed, out loud this time. "Sure, yeah, whatever."

"No, I'm serious, dude. She's been riding my ass for weeks. My slightest misstep causes her to launch into a tirade and threaten to walk out. "

The driver spoke up. "So, why do you keep her around?"

"She's gorgeous, for one. And, when she's not threatening me or criticizing me, she's pretty fun. But, yeah, you're right. Seriously dude. She'd get in your car if you offered to buy her a beer. She'll do it just to piss me off, and that's fine with me. I just wanna go home and sleep tonight instead of fighting with her until she passes out again."

Mike, assuming he was joking, pretended to be thinking about it and then said, "Nah. I'm on the run from some evil clowns who want to kill me, and so I don't think I'd be good company and she'd probably just slow me down."

Both guys laughed, and the girls came out of the gas station.

One of them, a fit and fashionable Asian woman in her early twenties, wearing leather boots, black jeans, a black t-shirt with some Kanji characters and a jean jacket, shouted in a shrill drunk girl voice "What's so fucking funny? You're probably talking about me."

The other girl, who was a less fit blond woman of about the same age, followed behind holding two purses. The drunk Asian woman walked up to her boyfriend then looked at Mike. "Is this your new friend? Who the fuck is the old guy? What's up gramps?"

Mike pretended not to hear her, as if she were a beggar or crazy street person. He finished pumping the gas, locked his car doors, then walked away to use the bathroom and buy some more smokes.

As he walked away, she yelled at him, "Hey Aaron's new best friend! Don't you fucking talk? Where are you going?"

Aaron tried to calm her down. "Hey baby, let him go. He's just a guy pumping gas."

"Ya, well, I'm gonna pump him!"

"OK, let's go home now, huh babe?"

"No! I'm waiting here for grandpa."

Mike bought his cigarettes. He glanced outside as he paid and saw the driver and his girlfriend sitting in the front seat, while drunk girl shook her head and pushed Aaron away as he tried to get her into the car. She walked away, and Aaron yelled, "Fine, suit yourself!" and he got into the car and it drove away.

Mike hoped that she'd be gone or that they would come back and pick her up before he got out of the bathroom.

Mike lingered in the bathroom. It was filthy, and he did his best to avoid the biggest puddle of piss as he stood at the urinal. He zipped up his pants and walked to the sink to wash his hands. Looking at himself in the mirror, he thought about the drunk girl out there. She called him grandpa. Is that how he looks to her? He was going gray a little, and he had gained weight since he was her age, and he had some wrinkles, true— he was tired.

But, grandpa? Would he have considered someone who was forty to be old when he was twenty? Yes, most likely. Hell, he thought, people who are fifty now that he's forty are old. None of us has ever done this aging thing before. If we had, we'd be less stupid about it. That girl is going to be forty before she knows what happened and she'll think that Mike, at sixty, is ancient, and he'll think she's so young. That's the way it is and will be until we can figure out how to get out of this whole shitty born-live-die contract.

Mike smoothed his hair and adjusted his pants. He thought about what he'd do if she's still out there. What if she insists on getting in his car? What if she doesn't but is out there alone and in need of help?

A detour from his journey to help someone in need might be good karma if he believed in such a thing.

Mike left the bathroom, careful not to touch the door with his skin, then went out to the parking lot. She was sitting on the hood of his car, lying back and looking at the sky.

CHAPTER 52

In which Mike picks up a passenger

The girl sitting on the hood of Mike's car was half his age. For someone who was furious, drunk off her ass, and abandoned by her friends, she seemed calm.

"Excuse me," said Mike, "You're sitting on my car."

She laughed. "Is that the best thing you can fucking come up with?"

"I don't know what you mean. It's factually correct and implies that I'd like you not to be sitting on my car."

"You're a real robot, aren't you Grandpa?"

"Mike."

"You're a real robot, aren't you grandpa Mike? Boop beep car. Drunk girl does not compute." She leaned back further until her arms holding her body up collapsed behind her and she tried to make it look like that's what she meant to do as she turned her head to look at Mike in a way that may have been meant to look cool, but just looked immature. She could vomit at any moment, thought Mike. Then she did. Mike put his arm under hers to help her off the hood as she continued to vomit and cough.

She finished puking with her head above the garbage can next to the gas pumps, but it was too late then. Most of the puke was on the hood of Mike's car, and it slid downward towards the headlights and radiator. Mike thought about how best to clean it before turning his attention back to the girl who was wiping off her face and shoes with a paper towel.

The gas station owner came out of the store.

"Hey, you can't use my gas station for your puking! Get out of here or I'll call the police!"

"Can I clean this up?" said Mike. "Can she use the bathroom? Do you have a hose?"

The gas station owner pointed to the hose on the side of the gas station, then went back inside.

Mike hosed down his car and the area around the pump, while the girl went inside to the bathroom. When she came out, she was still stumbling, but she was doing her best to appear steady.

"Can I give you a ride home?" Mike asked. Mike had already wasted enough time and he needed to get back on the road.

"I don't have a home," she mumbled, "Take me to yours."

"That's not possible," said Mike.

"Wherever the shit you're going, then," she said.

"I'm going to California. Or Washington. I don't know."

"OK, Mr. President. Take me with you. I'll pay."

She opened her purse and pulled out a roll of bills and handed it to Mike, who considered his situation for a moment before taking it and telling her, "Get in."

PART 3
Adventure On!

CHAPTER 53

In which Jordan finds herself in Mike's car,
headed towards Nebraska

Jordan's sore throat and the ache in her side told her she'd been drinking the night before. She didn't know where she was or how she got there — again. She could smell that she had puked — again. "Keepin' it classy," as her father used to say whenever her mom got blackout drunk.

Jordan was proud to resemble her mom in more than just being classy. Men often told her she looked exotic, and if exotic was half French Canadian from Milwaukee and half Thai from Albany Park, that was her. She tugged her jean jacket tight against her thin chest and buried her face in it to enjoy the smell of her own skin and the warmth of her captured breath for a moment.

She was in a parked car. The man next to her wasn't Aaron. She wasn't in Chicago. She reached between her ankles for her purse, unzipped it, and flipped her thumb along the edge of the rubber-banded roll of cash. It felt like five grand.

She looked at her hands in the dim morning light. Three dots above the first knuckle on her right pinky, five under the band of her watch. That told her everything she needed to remember. She'd planned to cause a scene, dump Aaron, and get out of town before he noticed she'd robbed him blind. She knew from the Sharpie marks there should be another five grand. She felt around her purse. There was a bottle of Pedialyte. She opened and drank it in one gulp. Did she have to get so drunk?

Jordan's braid was pushing into her back, and she flipped it over her shoulder while she inspected her surroundings.

The car was a 2005 Pontiac Bonneville — she recognized the hood. The man next to her, she couldn't identify. He was asleep, with his seat reclined and his mouth hanging open. He wasn't bad looking, but he was older—early 40s, and he was sagging a bit in the middle and around the eyes the way middle-aged men do.

The paper coffee cup from a gas station in the center console cup holder didn't have lipstick on it and was about a quarter full. She took a small sip. The coffee was black and cold, but not bad, so she drank the rest of it.

Jordan loosened the laces of her boots and massaged her ankles while searching her memory for who this guy was and scanning the environment for where she might be. A car drove by—Iowa plates. Another—same. Suburban street, upscale, she guessed the west side of Des Moines. She didn't know anyone in Des Moines, at least not anyone who would still talk to her. She took a Sharpie from her purse and drew a triangle on her right palm to mark her approximate location.

It was coming back to her. The guy was just an unlucky shmoe who was there at the right time for her blowup. He'd have the other roll.

She looked him up and down for the lump. No obvious bulge. She opened the glove box. Not there.

"Looks like I'm stuck with this guy for a minute," she thought.

Jordan zipped up her purse, checked her face in the visor mirror, and reclined her seat to pretend to be asleep until he woke up. Better to find out what he does when he thinks she's still out. Let's get a sense of this guy.

CHAPTER 54

*In which Mike reveals that he's being chased
by clowns*

As the sun rose, Mike shifted his position behind the steering wheel. Jordan closed her eyes and imagined that she looked innocent and sweet. Mike awoke with a grunt and then a gasp and saw Jordan sleeping next to him in his car. Jordan heard him put his seat back up, blow his nose, and try to take a drink from the now empty coffee cup in the center cup holder.

She ran through what his thoughts and actions would be—he'd clear his eyes, check his phone for messages, and then he might realize that there's at least a possibility that the girl in the passenger seat was dead. He'd look for signs of life.

At that exact moment, she would whimper like she was having a bad dream and adjust her hand under her head. Satisfied that she was OK, and charmed by her sweetness, he would wait for her to wake up and then he would reassure her that everything was fine, and he would offer to do anything she needed to get her back home. Or he'd offer to buy her breakfast or get her a room somewhere, so she could take a shower.

All of this assumed that he was a normal nice guy. But, she was also prepared for him to be a creep. If he tried to touch her cheek, or said anything that he thought she couldn't hear, or made a phone call to his wife to lie about where he'd been, or if she heard any sounds like he was jacking off while watching her sleep, she was prepared to run or defend herself.

What she wasn't prepared for was that he would start the car, turn on the radio, and pull onto the freeway—which is what he did.

Change of plans. Jordan opened her eyes and put her seat up.

"Who are you? Why am I in your car? Where's my money?" she demanded.

"Mike O'Malley. Pleased to meet you again. You insisted, and I didn't have time to talk you out of it. Your money's in the paper bag in the glove box. You didn't look hard enough."

Jordan opened the glove box and took out the paper bag. She opened it, removed the roll of cash, and inspected it.

"There's nothing missing," she said.

"No, of course not."

Jordan looked out the window at the passing cars, and the landscape, and the signs: thirty-five miles to Omaha.

"Fuckin' Omaha! Why are we in Omaha?"

"You weren't waking up. I've been driving two-hour stretches at a time since Chicago."

"What's the rush?"

"Are you hungry? Let's stop for breakfast. I'll explain, and we can figure out what to do now."

Jordan was pleased with herself for getting a free anonymous getaway ride out of town, but she knew that her advantage was in outrage right now.

"Yeah, you'd better explain why you kidnapped me and it had better be good, mister!"

Mike wasn't fazed by Jordan's outburst. He pulled off at the next exit and headed for a gas station café and parked out of view of the freeway. Jordan recognized the move. He's on the run, she thought. But from whom? Did she have the dumb luck to get into a car with another con? An addict? Car thief? She looked behind her at the boxes in the back seat. Books? She narrowed it down to car thief or a bad break-up. She looked around the car for blood or a weapon. No, if he packed books after killing his wife, he was a first-class psycho and he wouldn't have left a trace in the house or the car.

"We both know I didn't kidnap you. I told you when we met that I was on the run from clowns. I'm not joking. I wish I were."

"Fuck you, you fucking lying piece of shit. If you don't want to tell me the truth, whatever. You're not going to find out a damn thing about me either. And you'd better not try anything, and don't think I won't give you up to the cops the minute it's in my interest to do so. And, uh, yes, technically you did kidnap me and who do you think they're going to side with?"

"Fine. I'm starving. Let's go inside."

"Fine. I'm buying."

"That's ok with me. I'm broke, frankly, as I told you last night when you got in the car and after you handed me your wad of cash."

"The broke story I believe. The clown story, I don't."

CHAPTER 55

In which they stop for breakfast and Jordan
goes to the bathroom

The Flying J Cafe was a typical I-80 gas station greasy spoon. At 8:00 A.M. on a Sunday, there were a handful of elderly people from the nearby town, a couple truck drivers, and a young Midwestern family making their way westward.

Jordan plowed past the "Please Wait to be Seated" sign and took a seat at the corner booth in the back, flipping over a coffee mug as she sat down. Mike looked a bit flustered and he stopped to ask the waitress if it was OK before joining her.

"I'll have coffee, two eggs over medium, wheat toast, bacon, and hash browns." Jordan got up, swung her purse over her shoulder and headed for the bathroom.

The bathroom had a tampon and sex toy dispenser, a gritty pink hand soap dispenser, and the stall door was bent but could be forced closed and latched. She got out her Sharpie and wrote her phone number on the stall wall along with the generic promise of a good time. She left this in every gas station restroom, like a trail of breadcrumbs, and sometimes it led to her next mark calling.

It wasn't hard to figure out when someone who called her got her number from a bathroom stall. Men trying to be sexy on the phone all sound like bad imitations of late night college radio DJs—breathy-mumbly. Jordan would raise her voice an octave and sometimes do a bad southern belle accent to respond. "A good time? Huh, I don't know where you got that idea, but I could use a little money to buy a bus ticket or a tank of gas to get me back home to my poor mother."

Road trips made her constipated. Hangovers loosened everything up. She didn't usually puke, or so she told herself. This was the second time in the last twelve hours, so maybe she did usually puke. The moment before puking is like the moment before an orgasm plus the moment before a car crash. Her mouth watered, and she knew enough to not even try to hold it back when that happened. She got off the toilet and threw up while making little noise beyond the sound of the puke hitting water, followed by a single cough. She prided herself on her discipline in puking and sometimes imagined herself as an elite Navy Seal puker or a puking ninja. She blew her nose and wiped her mouth with toilet paper, added a smiley face to her stall message, and exited the stall to brush her hair and teeth and put on some lipstick.

She looked at herself in the mirror and smirked. Not half bad, considering. Pretty good if she counted the ten grand she made last night.

Mike was sipping coffee and facing the window and staring at the cars going by. "Amateur," Jordan thought. "Has this guy really never been on the run before?"

She sat down and pointed at him with both hands and yelled to everyone in the restaurant, "Here he is, everyone! Here's Mike!"

"Funny," said Mike, "Yell all you want in here. You'll damn well know who the ones are who are chasing me the minute you see them. Believe me."

"Yeah, right. They'll have big red noses and giant shoes? Is that it?"

"Yes. Most likely, they will be Auguste clowns. Most goons are."

"Auguste? You have nothing to worry about then, right? It's October."

Their breakfasts arrived. Mike made a crosshatch pattern on his stack of pancakes with the syrup and devoured a giant wedge cut from the whole stack. "No. Auguste is a clown character. This is your typical American buffoon or anarchist clown with big shoes. The Bozo-type circus clown. They aren't the smart ones or the evil ones, but they do the bidding of the master clowns and they're tenacious."

"You know a lot about clowns."

Jordan didn't know shit about clowns. She knew men, though. And, she knew that this guy seemed honest enough and was frightened and naive. He'd make a perfect mark, except that he's broke. But, what's with his clown obsession? She had heard of people who have such a deep fear of something that they get mixed up and believe that the thing they fear is the direct cause of problems in their lives that have nothing to do with the thing they're afraid of. A simple example might be someone who has a fear of spiders. If this person gets sick, the first thing they might think to blame is a spider they saw. Some people blame homosexuals for tornados. Maybe this guy has a clown phobia and he's on the run from something. People are fucked up everywhere you go, and sometimes you just play along with their fictions to get what you need out of them. His being broke is probably a fiction too. There's no way a guy can get to be as old as he is and not have a chunk of money stashed away. No skin off her back if he wants to believe in killer clowns.

"OK, let's say there are clowns out to get you. What do they want?"

"Revenge."

"What for?"

"Twenty years ago, I pissed them off big time. I broke the clown code."

"Ah yes. Of course. The clown code. What is this, some kind of secret language?"

"No. Code as in laws," said Mike. "Clown law. They have their own system of laws, their own courts, their own punishments, their own judges and clown juries, and if you're one of them and you violate the code the punishments can range from temporary suspension of your clowning license all the way to . . . well, I don't even know what the worst they'll do is, and I don't want to find out."

"How did you piss them off?" Jordan asked.

Mike stared out the window. "It's a long story. But, the short version is that I pitted them against the dwarfs and I took the side of the dwarfs."

Jordan couldn't control her laughter. She nearly spit out her coffee but managed to swallow it before she cackled and pointed at Mike with both hands.

"Holy shit, Mike! Really?"

Mike wasn't laughing. Jordan composed herself. She almost felt bad for what she was about to do to this mentally ill man, but he wasn't any more mentally ill than the guys who tried to assault her or the alcoholics or the narcissists she'd swindled. Well, except this guy never hurt anyone else—except the clowns, it sounds like! She laughed again imagining him leading an army of midgets against an army of clowns.

CHAPTER 56

In which we learn about Jordan's systems

When Jordan was in high school, she developed a system of marks she could make on her arms and hands with a Sharpie to remind herself of things she had to do, which classes had homework, which friends she had told what secret, and what her story was when her parents or the police asked. She called her system Sharfu.

As Sharfu became more elaborate, Jordan relied on it and trusted in it more. Her dependency on Sharfu was the reason that Jordan quit the swim team. Under normal circumstances, the rate at which Sharpie marks wear off the skin coincides with a teenage girl's attention span. When the marks are fresh, it's time for action. When the marks are faded, it's time for moving on. A daily chlorine bath accelerated the rate of Sharfu decay past what Jordan was comfortable with, so she joined the marching band instead.

As an adult, Jordan used Sharfu to plan how she was going to swindle strangers out of their money, and for getting her bearings when she woke up in a strange place—which seemed to happen more and more often these days.

Jordan had discovered the secret of the universe and it was this: we live in a nostalgia videogame. Most people over a certain age—let's say twenty—inhabit a world that's not as good as the one they remember. Jordan would listen to their stories of past glory and she learned to recognize the patterns. Like a rock climber, she could find the right little crack to grab onto. She could use that to pull herself up, or she could twist it, or open it up just a hair and lodge a new idea into it.

Even people whose past was nothing but suffering would hang onto the suffering like a badge of honor and would talk about how it made them who they are or would brag about their exploits when they used to drink or what a nightmare their ex was.

Jordan was in search of people who opted out of playing the game. They were on her team, and she wanted so badly for them to see it that way with her and to join her in playing the game rather than just being a character in it. What kept Jordan restless was that she could identify the people who weren't in the game when she saw them, but she didn't know what to do with them.

She called the game that everyone else was playing "Nostalgia Galactica."

To opt out of the Nostalgia Galactica was to recognize that everyone's childhood was either the best or the worst, everyone's parents were saints or abusive, everyone's high school experience was a nightmare of bullying or it was the best damn four years of their lives, the music was better back then or it sucked, the food tasted horrible or it was the freshest peach you've ever tasted. Inside the videogame, new experiences are warped by the past and can never measure up—for good or for bad. Outside of the game, new experiences are new.

The moment when you recognize that the stories other people tell keep them moving in a determined path like a ghost in Pac-Man is when you first become aware of the game.

When you recognize that the stories you tell yourself keep you moving in the same path is when you start to move outside of it.

Jordan developed her theory of Nostalgia Galactica while drunk at a classic arcade in Chicago. It became the useful paradigm that shaped her worldview.

Sharfu—the maps and codes she drew on her hands—was her instruction manual and her scoreboard. She didn't track high scores, because having a high score encourages the exact behavior she found so annoying but useful in others.

Her system was simple. Her right hand tracked where she was currently playing the game. She could play anywhere, and so she mapped the entire globe to different lines, bumps, dots, and edges on her right hand.

Her left hand and wrist were how she figured out what she intended to do: it was like pre-programming next moves. The language of the left hand was flexible and ever-changing depending on the people she was around and their patterns, but it generally centered around the symbols of classic videogame controllers. Up Up Down Down Left Right Left Right B A Start. Arrows and dots indicated to her what and how much of it she intended to do. Once she was programmed she could count on her system to move her to the next phase, or to the next level.

CHAPTER 57

*In which we learn about how Jordan's heists
usually play out*

Jordan didn't consider herself to be clever enough to be a con artist. But here she was again—having just pulled off another successful heist. She was $10,000 richer, no one was hurt, and the guy even had a good time before she got blackout drunk and made him so angry and embarrassed by her that he didn't mind that she stole his life savings, as long as she went away.

For a con artist, Jordan didn't have many secrets. She always used her real name: Jordan LeBlanc. Middle name: none. She was twenty-six and had lived in Chicago, Detroit, New York, Los Angeles, and London. She left all her belongings at guys' houses when she fled, which gave her a good excuse to go on regular shopping sprees.

All Internet accounts of her activities stop after she graduated from high school. She was careful to avoid leaving a trace and she would monitor the web for news stories or missing person filings or social media posts from classmates or anything that mentioned her name. It was becoming more difficult to clean these up, and she would often just find ways to contradict or confuse them. If a classmate posted on her high school alumni group trying to find Jojo LeBlanc, she'd email them and tell them she was fine and ask them to remove the post.

The one time a guy filed a missing person report, that was a little more difficult to clean up. She went into the station to talk personally with an officer. By the end of their conversation, she'd convinced the police that she was not missing and asked them to relay a message to the mark that she was fine and that he should trust that she's doing what's best for her. It was always best to make up stories that were vague and to make it sound like she had secrets that she didn't want to talk about right now. Avoid too many specifics.

Aaron was the most recent guy's name. There had been others before him. She could meet them, make them fall in love, get the money, and split in a month—sometimes less— and they'd blame themselves for being so naive in the end and they'd never tell anyone out of embarrassment.

Jordan played the standard sweetheart con, but with her own twist that perfected it. The first step was to find a plausible nice guy loser. The guy had to be someone that someone like her might be interested in if he were lucky. The next step was to be horrible to him, but in a self-destructive way. This is why her penchant for getting blackout drunk was so effective—the mark would get to thinking that he could save her and that she would stop being so crazy if he were just patient enough. After all, he would believe, she did so much for him, and he was better off with her—even if she was abusive and would go into a rage and disappear for days at the slightest provocation like when he left his socks on the bed.

Before her, the guy didn't know how to dress, he was eating junk food all the time, and he had no idea how to manage his money. She had been raised right, he'd think. She knew about home economics, how to cook, she could play violin, and she even understood financial planning. So, yeah, of course it was way better if she just handled that crap. She'd say there was a ten percent chance that they could lose it all, but there was a twenty percent chance that they could triple it. Those sounded like incredibly good odds and she was so confident. Plus, she was beautiful, and she was a lot of fun to be with. She could drink like one of the guys, and she was down for anything. He had always dreamed of dating an Asian woman. Here she was, in his apartment, and she had different ways, but it was her culture and he would have to learn. And of course she didn't have a job—the woman wasn't expected to pay for anything in her culture. And besides, she was getting ready to go to medical school.

After just a few months of free living, Jordan would take off. The guy had been conditioned to accept that she did this every so often when she was mad. She probably went and stayed with her mom—Asian families are so tight. By the time he got worried, she was at least 2000 miles away. She'd send a note. Something like:

"This isn't working, I'm going back to the old country to work for my aunt."

No mention of his life savings. The guy knew she would blow up if he asked about it, and that she'd say his lack of ability to trust anyone was why she was breaking up with him. She's not the kind that would just skip town with his money, he'd think. Holding on to it was her way of leaving a connection—like the girl who moves out but leaves her sunglasses behind and returns a week later to get them and then you end up having make-up sex and everything is back to normal.

But, by the time he tried to check back in with her to see if she was still mad, she had changed her number and he didn't even know what the "old country" was. He never even asked, but he assumed it was "somewhere in Asia." The truth was, she was born in Bridgeview, Illinois, near Midway Airport. Her grandmother came over from Thailand in the '50s and met her grandpa (who was an older all-American whitebread Irish Catholic podiatrist) at the College of Medicine at the University of Illinois.

Jordan never felt bad for her victims. They got what they wanted. They didn't need that money. They were better off without it now that they had some decent clothes and they had lived their dreams of dating a younger Asian woman.

Jordan's mom was adventurous too. Her father was still a doctor in Chicago.

Her parents split up after Jordan, their only child, graduated from high school. Jordan didn't move out so much as there just stopped being a place for her to live after the divorce. Mom decided she'd had enough and moved back to Thailand to be near her mom, who had moved back to die ten years earlier. Dad moved into a hotel closer to the hospital. Jordan was there alone. He told Jordan she'd have to get a place of her own because he didn't want to keep paying for the house. So, Jordan moved in with a horn player named Freddy who she knew from school and who also wasn't going to college. She wasn't interested in him, he just happened to be a guy she knew who seemed OK and was looking for a place to live.

Jordan and Freddy found an apartment downtown—in the loop, which was crazy—a one-bedroom for $1250. Jordan took the bedroom and Freddy turned the living room into his room. There was no need for a living room or dining room when they lived downtown and neither of them expected to be spending much time at home unless they were asleep.

Being downtown put them in in the perfect spot for Freddy to check out every swing band that came through town and to sit in with the regulars. Jordan got fired from her job at the pool but didn't tell Freddy—there was no need to worry him. She knew she'd be OK and that she'd find a way to make money. The lifeguard job was early morning, and Jordan was having too much late-night fun. She always made it to the pool on time, but she sometimes would doze off while watching the early morning lap swimmers.

When her boss, Lacy, caught her sleeping one morning, she called her into the office after the shift. "Well, I don't have to tell you how bad this looks, and how big of a disaster it would be if there was an incident while you were asleep. I'm sorry, Jordan, but we're going to have to terminate you."

"Me?"

"Effective immediately, you no longer work for the pool."

Jordan took the L from Midway back to the apartment, sat on her bed, and cried. She'd never been fired before. Hell, this was the first job she'd ever had. She thought about the words that Lacy used—"terminated." She meant that her employment was terminated, of course, but to use the word terminated about another human, and then to disguise something as important as taking away someone's income—how they pay for food and shelter—with cliché business phrases like "effective immediately" just seemed callous and cold beyond anything Jordan could imagine. Anything she could imagine before her dad sold the house she grew up in, that is. Within a month of graduating, Jordan had been homeless and unemployed. What was next?

That day, in her journal, she vowed to herself to never become dependent on anyone again, or have a boss, or be in a situation she couldn't leave on a moment's notice. She would find a way to survive—thrive even—that was outside of the system and where business speak and sucking up and apologies and alarm clocks and not sleeping when you're tired didn't exist.

CHAPTER 58

In which Jordan tries to hustle Mike

Jordan gave Mike the silent treatment for most of the rest of breakfast. She was exhausted, but she played it off like she was pissed at him. He bought it. She hadn't known him for twenty-four hours, but already he was eating out of her hand and trying to impress her and keep her entertained. Men are easy. She was just glad that they were fifty percent of the population. To try and con a woman would be so much more difficult.

Mike made some sounds while he ate. Little grunts and sniffles and ughs and hmms. She knew these sounds. He was uncomfortable, and he thought these passed for conversation and might get her to break the silence with an apology or question or invitation for him to say something that wouldn't piss her off. Yeah right. When it's going so well? Not a chance.

The food wasn't bad. The eggs were a bit overcooked, but in plenty of butter. The hash browns had some good crispiness and the toast was the right amount of brown. The bacon . . . well, fuck the bacon. It was just bad. But, three out of four was adequate, and she planned to use the bacon to win his heart anyway.

Mike had finished his pancakes minutes ago and was eying the sugar packets.

"You want my bacon? I can't eat another thing," she said.

"Hell yes," said Mike, "But I'm vegan."

"Really?" said Jordan.

"No, just kidding," said Mike, grabbing the bacon off her plate with a fork and his thumb, but not sure why he was bothering with a fork and a thumb instead of his index finger and a thumb.

Jordan watched as he slid the bacon onto his plate and rubbed it around in the leftover syrup and then ate three slices of bacon at once, then downed the rest of his coffee and the rest of his ice water.

"Thank you again. I needed that. You know what they say about bacon."

"No, I don't," said Jordan.

"Yeah. Me neither. People seem to like it a lot, though," said Mike.

The waitress came over and poured more coffee. Jordan saw the look in Mike's eyes as he was picking up the last scraps of bacon and she asked if there was anything else she could get them. Mike shook his head and slurped his coffee.

"No, we'll just take the check," said Jordan.

Mike was trying to pretend it was normal for Jordan to be buying him breakfast. Jordan would have been uncomfortable in this situation too, if she hadn't been training herself for the last three years to be good with it and to be an expert in making this situation even more uncomfortable. Right now, she held absolute power over him. She had the money. A jury of his peers would consider him a kidnapper, and who knows what else could be pinned on this guy who was twice her age and had just driven hundreds of miles with her while she was blacked out. He might even be afraid that she could claim that he drugged her. This was too easy.

Mike smiled a good-hearted smile, but he was looking out the window then at her, then out the window.

"I gotta hit the road. Do you want to come along?" he said.

"I don't know," said Jordan, "exactly where are you headed?"

"Washington, probably," said Mike, "I was thinking Aberdeen."

"What's there?"

"It's the birthplace of Kurt Cobain," said Mike, "It's also the end of Route 12."

"And so, what's that mean?"

"Route 12 is known as Clown Highway in the circus business. It starts in Detroit and goes through the upper Midwest all way to Aberdeen. It takes you through every circus-friendly town west of Ohio."

"But, aren't you trying to avoid clowns?"

"Yes, but here's the thing. Circuses, and therefore clowns, don't go to Aberdeen. It doesn't make sense for them to. Think about it. If you're a traveling circus, and the only towns where a circus can make a profit are lined up along Route 12 from Detroit to the Rockies, but there's nothing once you get over the Rockies, and there's certainly nothing in Nevada, and California is hostile to clowns. It doesn't make any sense to go all the way to the coast and then to backtrack through the towns where you just were when you've got animals to feed, midgets to pay attention to, and all the rest. Plus, it's cold up there, and chances are good that it'll be raining, and everyone will stay in their damn houses even if they cared one damn bit about the circus. So, if you can get to Aberdeen, you're safe from clowns."

"That's really interesting," said Jordan, "Have you ever been to Aberdeen?"

"No."

Mike stared out the window, pretending to be thinking about Aberdeen, but he was really thinking about how he'd like to get away from Jordan for a bit so that he could take a dump, and how they needed to hit the road.

Jordan was wondering how long she'd have to put up with this nonsense. What if he really is on the run and he really is broke? Is it possible that she had the dumb luck to run across the biggest loser she's ever met? She needed to think these things through better. She should only go for guys she knows are going through divorces or guys who just retired or purchased their sports car or have landed that new job. A guy who is legitimately insane, or legitimately running from someone—clowns or not—is about as shitty a mark as she could have run across. But, now she needed a ride, and Aberdeen was more than 2000 miles from Chicago. So, she was stuck with Mike.

"I love Nirvana," cooed Jordan, "Have you ever met Kurt Cobain?"

"No. I'm pretty sure he's dead. But, I feel a special kind of a connection to him, because I spent a good part of my childhood traveling Route 12."

"That's really interesting," said Jordan, "what was it like?"

"We really don't have time to talk right now. We need to get going."

"Come on. If I'm going to be riding with you, I should know who it is I'm riding with."

CHAPTER 59

In which Mike tells his story and lies a bit

"I grew up in Detroit," began Mike.

This wasn't true. While it was true that he was born in Detroit, he grew up a few miles north of Detroit, in Warren, Michigan. This distinction made all the difference in the world to someone who grew up within the city limits, and Jordan knew it, because she grew up in Bridgeview, Illinois.

"My parents were super religious and super strict."

This wasn't true. Mike's dad was a butcher who believed in God but didn't go to church or ever mention it except before dinner, and his mom was a drunk who believed in the pharmacist at the corner drug store who she had a secret crush on.

"My sister and I ran away to the circus when we were kids."

The truth was that Mike's sister, Pauline, was a bad ballerina and a brat and their parents couldn't deal with her, so they sent her to a circus camp one summer and when she wanted to stay on, they said OK but only as long as she brought her younger brother, Mike, along to keep an eye on her. What they were going for was an early escape hatch from parenthood, and this seemed like the perfect out—until the truancy officer came around in the fall and Mike had to come home to finish eighth grade.

"The circus traveled back and forth from New Jersey to Omaha all summer, doing shows all along Route 12 until we ran out of money or until it got too cold to sleep outside. Then, we'd head south to Oklahoma for the winter."

The truth was that Mike never went to Oklahoma—he went back to school. Only the "real" circus performers went to Hugo, Oklahoma, aka Circus City, USA.

Mike rarely told the actual truth about anything. It wasn't that he had bad intentions. He was concerned with being as brief as he could so that he wouldn't bore his listener with a story that had too much detail or too many ordinary parts. This resulted in him telling a lot of lies and then having to remember them later if the listener even remembered that he had said anything to them in the first place, which he was pretty sure they wouldn't, so he never worried about the true story.

"But then you pissed off the clowns?" asked Jordan.

"Yes, big time."

"Is your sister still in the circus? What did she do? Oh wait, and were you a clown?"

"No, the circus closed down and she got married and had some kids. She was a clown. She was one of the best clowns in the country at one point. A real artist."

"Is she out to get you too?"

"I didn't think so until yesterday, but now I'm not so sure," said Mike, "Hey, we'd better get going. I can tell you more in the car. OK?"

"OK, but what did you do in the circus?"

"I was the circus boss," Mike said.

Again, this was a lie. Mike had been the circus business manager, but the job was more like the office manager at a small business who's in charge of making sure the fax machine doesn't run out of paper and the chairs are ergonomic and the breakroom has enough water and yogurt. The real boss of the circus was Mr. Schmid. Mike ruined Mr. Schmid's livelihood when he ruined the circus, and he had often wondered over the last twenty years whether Mr. Schmid was still alive. Whenever he had these thoughts, he'd change the subject in his own head so as not to think about it too much. He folded up his napkin and stood up to leave.

Jordan opened her purse and removed the rubber band from one of her rolls of bills, without removing the roll from her purse, and slid a twenty from the middle of the roll and left it on the table. They went out to the car and drove to the other side of the freeway to fill up the gas tank. Jordan paid cash for that too.

Mike was feeling bad that she was paying for everything and he almost insisted that she let him pay for the gas, but then he remembered the sorry shape that she was in last night and that he was giving her a ride, not the other way around, and he resolved to be a bit more relaxed with letting her and her big rolls of cash pay the way. He wasn't asking her why she had the rolls of cash. He wasn't an idiot. He knew from the circus that you never ask someone how they got rich unless it becomes clear that they want you to ask them how they got rich. It was rule number one of showmanship: the ones with the money will only give you their money if they think you don't care about their money. If you don't care about the money, you need to be made aware of all the great things that can be done with the money if some of the money becomes yours so that you know how important the ones with the money are. It was the same as the midgets who shared their booze with Mike when he was a kid. It wasn't that they had too much booze or that they were so generous that they couldn't help but give away their booze. What they wanted was to show Mike just how much fun it was to drink booze so that they could remind themselves of how much fun they have when they drink booze and feel better about everything. All his business school book learning boiled down to this one lesson and even though he'd forgotten everything he learned in school, he hadn't forgotten the insecurity of wealth.

He'd met her while pumping gas, and now they were pumping the gas together. He chuckled a little. She looked at him while sitting in the passenger seat checking her lipstick, smiled in the corner of her mouth and said "What?"

CHAPTER 60

In which Mike's circus experience gives him
enough sharps to avoid getting hustled by
Jordan

"Did you get a load of the hippie bus? I never expected to see a fuckin' hippie in Omaha," said Jordan.

"Oh shit, where?" said Mike, checking his mirrors and clenching the steering wheel as they pulled onto I-80.

"Back at the gas station. One of those old VW busses went by and it was painted with flowers, rainbows, you name it. Must be on the way to San Francisco."

"Shit. You didn't get a look at the driver?"

"No. You didn't see it? Oh, what, you think it's the ones who are chasing you? You're being chased by hippies now? This isn't doing much to impress me, Mike, if you're scared of some hippies—clowns or not."

"I don't know. There's a lot of overlap." Mike sped up and was going just under 90 mph now. "If it is them, we can at least put some good miles between us. Those busses aren't even freeway legal at this point. I knew we shouldn't have stopped for so long."

"Look Mike, I don't know what sort of problems you've got, but you'd better just take me back to Chicago."

"What? Are you joking? No way I'm going back there. I'll let you out at the next exit, but I'm not turning around."

"You're gonna take me back to Chicago, or you're going to be in big trouble."

"Fine, whatever. I can let you out at the next exit."

"No. It's fine." Jordan turned to look out the window. "You don't have a phone charger in this wreck?"

"No."

Jordan smiled as she looked out the window. That he didn't agree to turn around was a good sign. She might have been wrong about him—he might have a little bit of a spine, or else he was telling the truth about being in trouble.

"Can't you just pay them off? What do they want?"

"They don't want money. They want justice."

"What's that supposed to mean?"

"These are no normal clowns. There's a secret clown world that you don't know. They have a parallel universe of extreme laws, extreme punishments, and, well, extreme everything that no one but clowns knows about. Why do you think anyone becomes a clown?"

"I don't know. They like kids?"

"Yeah, right. People just go and dress and act like lunatics because they like kids? No, most clowns are true believers—fundamentalists—they were recruited—most when they were young—because of specific skills that they have that can be helpful to the secret clown society. They see themselves as a great charitable organization, but their means and the things they do in pursuit of ever greater power are ruthless and horrible. I didn't know the full extent when I was in the circus. It was only after I got out and started doing research on my own and infiltrating their world that I learned about all the horrible things they do."

"Sounds like my kind of people!" said Jordan.

"If your kind of people perform operations on children to stitch dog and rabbit legs onto them, then ya, clowns are your kind of people."

"What?"

"I saw it. A laboratory. It was horrible. They said they were trying to make faster clowns."

"You didn't tell the FBI?"

"I told the police. I told the FBI. I told Scotland Yard. I told everyone. But, you point to a circus clown dressed as a lovable goofball hobo who give balloons to kids with cancer and marches in the city Labor Day parade and you tell them that this clown is trying to create super-human dog boys and is involved with one of the largest criminal enterprises that the world has ever seen, and who do you think they're going to believe? A middle-aged man with no evidence, or the lovable tramp clown? I'm lucky that I didn't get put in jail for suggesting that the head of the Elk's Lodge was also a prosecutor in the International Court of Clowns."

"What did you do then?" asked Jordan.

"What could I do? I tried to disappear. I got a job working at a fucking shipping supply store. I didn't have friends. I didn't tell my own sister where I was living or working. I cut myself off and kept my head down."

"What changed?"

"They found me. They probably knew where I was the whole damn time, but then their leadership changed and they came after me and poisoned me. I got out of the hospital yesterday morning. Fuck. I need to figure out if they're behind us and how far. Can you drive for a while?"

"Sure. No problem."

Mike pulled off at the next exit. He got out of the car, got his binoculars out of his backpack in the back seat and went around to the passenger side. Jordan was out of the car, stretching her legs with her hand out for the keys."

Mike put the keys into Jordan's hand. "I know this sounds like a bunch of B.S., but I'm glad to have some company. If it gets too weird or you don't feel safe, let me know and I'll drop you off anywhere you want along the way."

Jordan adjusted the mirrors and they pulled back out onto the freeway. Mike turned around and put his leg up on the seat so he could face backwards and look out over the long flat straight road behind them with the binoculars.

"Do you see anything?" asked Jordan.

"No. Not right now. It may have just been hippies, and they may have just been going the other way."

"Mind if I turn on some music?" asked Jordan.

"No. Not at all."

Jordan turned on the radio and switched it to a classic rock station.

"So, what's your story? Do you remember anything about last night?"

Jordan laughed. "I don't remember much, that's for sure. I don't remember how I got into your car. You tell me."

"I saw you at the gas station, having a fight with your boyfriend. You told him to leave and he did. When I came out, you were sitting on my car, then you puked on my hood. I offered to give you a ride home and you told me you didn't have a home and that you were going wherever I was going. You gave me your roll of cash and here we are. Does any of that ring a bell?"

"Uhhhhh. No, not really," said Jordan.

"Do you think you should call your boyfriend and tell him you're ok?"

"No way! Fuck that guy." Jordan started to cry.

"Oh shit, I'm sorry," said Mike, "Is there anyone you can call? I think my phone might still have power. It's been off since I left Michigan."

"No," said Jordan wiping her face with her sleeve and turning her head so Mike could get better view of the tears on her face. "I don't have anyone. That guy brought me here from Thailand, years ago. He was my first boyfriend. I didn't have any other options. I worked and saved everything I earned and sent it back home but then I stopped hearing from my parents. It was a gas leak. Killed them in their sleep. My boyfriend convinced me not to go back. He said we'd be over if I did and that I wouldn't be able to come back. He was trying to get to my money."

"Oh shit, I'm sorry," said Mike.

"Is that all you fucking say? 'oooo shit I'm sorry?' You say that a lot, Mike. Do you know that?"

"Oh shit, I'm sorry," said Mike, a bit less convincingly.

What a weirdo, thought Jordan. She didn't understand guys who didn't seem to have hearts and who were so self-obsessed they wouldn't ask her for more details about her heart-wrenching story. They certainly made her job more difficult. Guys who genuinely care about people were easier to con, because they'd want to get involved. Once you have them involved, you have them on the hook. Once you have them on the hook, you have them by the wallet. What would she have to do to get this old guy to care? There was something about people his age, she thought. Generation X. She hadn't known many of them, and she was glad. They seemed to not care as much about her as people her own age or baby boomers. Jordan knew that she was smarter than Mike and she knew that she cared about people more and that she was more real than he was, and she knew that if they were in real danger she could get him arrested or use his phone to post something on social media that would get half the population of the lower forty-eight states to be on the lookout for him. If he thinks he's in trouble and being chased now, just wait until his picture is plastered all over Facebook and he can't walk into a 7-11 without it being reported. It would be better, and this trip would be way more tolerable if she had a phone charger, she thought. She should have picked up a charger at that last gas station.

"I can't believe you don't have a fucking phone charger in your car, gramps," said Jordan.

"Ya, ok whatever. Jordan, look, I'm sorry to burst your bubble, but your story doesn't make any sense. I've been in the circus. I've lived with masters of deception, pick-pocket midgets, pervert clowns, animal trainers who could make an entire audience think that a stuffed lion was deadly, carnival barkers who were half man and half heroin, and ride operators who were experts at knowing which customers' pockets would release a little change and at which point in the ride. I know actual snake oil salesmen," said Mike. "Your game is worse than the most amateur of them. You might be able to trick a couple suburban boys out of a couple dollars by using your sad sweetheart story, but you're in a different universe now. I gave you a chance to get out, but if we're going to be traveling together, we're going to need to get a few things straight. First: you are going to be paying your way, which also means that you're going to be paying my way. That's just the way it is. Consider it an extra fee for my trying to keep you safe and teaching you something about how to be a real con, rather than just a high school imitation of one. Next, you don't have to tell me a thing about yourself, and I'd prefer if you didn't, but if I want any more of your phony stories, I'll ask you for them," said Mike.

Jordan's first instinct was to take out her phone and check for messages and pretend she didn't hear him, but since she already told him she didn't have a charge, and now that she knows he's not as clueless as she thought, she guessed that wouldn't work. She turned her body slightly in the driver's seat and held the wheel at 12 with her right hand.

"I know you're listening, and I don't expect any verbal response, but just sit quietly if this is agreeable to you."

Jordan didn't say anything.

A thump noise came from the back of the car.

"Did you hear that?" said Jordan, grabbing the wheel with both hands and leaning forward.

"Yes. Did it sound like a tire going out?"

"It sounds like something in the trunk."

The noise happened again, and then again, and then it repeated in a rhythm with the music. Sweet Home Alabama. Bump bump bump a bump-bump.

Mike lowered his voice to a whisper not quite loud enough for Jordan to hear, but he turned his head to make sure she could read his lips. "They got into the trunk while we were stopped."

"Who?" Jordan mouthed.

"The fucking clowns."

Jordan covered her mouth as the beating in the trunk became more intense.

Mike reached over and grabbed the steering wheel. He jerked it hard to the right and then back and they heard a sound like several bodies slamming into the wall of the trunk.

Jordan wanted to cry for real. Mike was sweating.

Jordan still wasn't convinced that there were clowns in the trunk. But if it wasn't clowns, what the fuck else could it be? It didn't sound like just one person. Each beat sounded like at least 3 different fists knocking on metal at different tempos with the music, and she thought she heard a low chuckle over the engine and road noise. She didn't know much about clowns, but she had seen old movies where a crowd of clowns all get out of the same tiny car. If they can fit that many clowns in a tiny old little jalopy, how many could fit in the trunk of this boat?

She thought about what she would do in this same situation. Dump the car? Stop at the gas station, buy a fire hydrant or a gun, and then open the trunk? This car doesn't have a keyless remote. He's going to have to use the key, or . . .

Mike looked behind them and then turned to Jordan. "Pop the trunk."

Jordan pulled the lever below and to the left of the steering wheel to release the trunk latch. She looked in the rearview mirror and saw it come open and a mass of orange hair and polka dots appeared and then disappeared as the trunk slammed shut again.

"Holy fuck!" screamed Jordan. She was shaking, the car was shaking, and she felt like she might puke again. "What do we do?"

"We keep going," said Mike, "If we stop, they'll open the trunk from inside."

"That's the plan?" said Jordan. "Just keep going?"

"Well, ya. We have a full tank, and we just ate and peed, so we're good for a while. We can at least buy a little time to figure out something better."

Jordan turned up the radio to try and drain out the noise, and the thumping in the trunk got louder.

"Let's try this," said Mike as his turned the dial to another radio station. "They fucking hate jazz. I just hope there's a jazz station out here."

Jordan couldn't help but laugh. Well, there was something she had in common with clowns.

Mike found a smooth jazz show towards the left of the dial and kept going.

"Wait, why not that?" said Jordan.

"Ya, that was smooth jazz. There are some things that even I won't stand for. Well, there are two things—smooth jazz and

Sting. And, besides, those fucking trunk weirdos would probably like it."

A little further down the dial, Mike found a college station that was playing Miles Davis' Kind of Blue. He let out a sigh and the trunk became quiet.

"Wow, that really works," said Jordan.

"Ya, they're probably in physical pain right now and covering their ears."

"I know how they feel," said Jordan.

"You're joking, right?"

"No," said Jordan, "The sound of those trumpets and saxophones bothers me."

"That's bullshit. This is the second-best record of all time."

"The second?"

"Yes. First is Thelonious Monk's Live at the It Club"

"Oooo," said Jordan. "Swepswonium Mump finger snaps."

Moaning sounds like injured cows or zombies came from the trunk.

CHAPTER 61

In which they both wind up in clown court,
threatened with punishment of death

"I can't take it. What the hell is going on?"

Jordan's hands were clenching the steering wheel, Miles Davis blasted as loud as the stereo of Mike's 1998 Pontiac Bonneville could blast, clown fists from who knows how many clowns pounded inside the trunk while moans of pain rumbled through the seats.

Mike sat tense in the passenger seat staring forward deep in thought, trying to figure out a plan to get out of this.

"Why don't we go to the police?" said Jordan.

"There we go again. Who are they going to believe? Who are we to go to the police? You're probably wanted for who knows what. I'm probably under investigation related to the circumstances under which I left town yesterday. We're both the ones with clowns stuffed in the trunk and no good explanation for how they got there. And, if I'm right, there are a lot more clowns following us and even more who are going to be plenty angry if we make any moves to expose them or to try and stop them. At some point, we'll need to stop, and at that point, I don't see how we're not completely fucked."

"Well, fuck," said Jordan, "I'm not afraid of a dumb clown, and the way things are going now, we're going to run straight back into them if we turn around, or we're going to run out of gas in the middle of nowheres Nebraska. So, let's do this now and try to make a break for it."

Jordan pulled off the freeway and pulled into a gas station and before Mike could convince her that it was a terrible plan. Four clowns jumped out of the trunk. Mike and Jordan tried to run, but the clowns were too fast. They caught Mike and Jordan and carried them inside the gas station store. Three of the clowns tied up Mike and Jordan, while the other clown tackled the gas station attendant, gagged him, and tied him up behind the counter.

The clowns disabled the security cameras, and then they each chose a single bag of potato chips and sat on the counter in a line and waited without talking.

Fifteen minutes later, a VW bus pulled up in front of the gas station, followed closely by a van with balloons and the words "Clown-rific's Party Supplies" painted on the sides and back. The driver of the bus was some sort of guard or police clown. He wore a keystone cop uniform with an oversized billy club hanging from his belt. The van held another four clowns—the driver, who looked like all the other clowns, and three more who were unlike any clowns Mike or Jordan had ever seen. These were somber clowns who wore powdered wigs and white faces and black judge robes. They entered the gas station and ordered the other clowns to move the shelves to create a larger central space. The cop clown from the VW bus brought in a folding table and draped it with a black tablecloth. The judge clowns placed a large red-leather bound book and a gavel on the table as their driver set up three folding chairs for them.

The gas station interior was small, and Mike and Jordan sat on the floor, leaning against a wall. They could see the preparations that were taking place, and Mike could clearly see that the book on the table was the Minneapolis Edition of L'Art Du Clown.

Within five minutes, the gas station was a makeshift courtroom. The judges sat behind the table on the western wall, Mike and Jordan sat in chairs facing the judge table, and the other clowns stood with their backs to the large window panes against which cans of oil, tires, and bags of charcoal were stacked in pyramids and columns of different heights.

The judge on the left banged his gavel against the plastic folding table hard enough to crack it, and the room fell silent. The cop clown approached Mike and Jordan and removed Mike's gag, then Jordan's.

Jordan screamed, and the center judge motioned for the cop clown to re-gag her. She struggled and attempted to protest. The judge clown motioned again for Jordan to be un-gagged, and she screamed again, so the gag was placed on her again. She became quiet again and the cop clown removed the gag once more. Jordan didn't scream this time, but whispered to Mike, "What the fuck is going on? What is this?"

Mike didn't say anything. The next person to speak was the center judge.

"In the matter of Michael O'Malley, of the Great Western Circus of the Americas, the heretofore assembled representatives of the International Clown Court, Minneapolis Chapter, by the powers granted to us from the Cour le International de Paris charter of 1955 do hereby find the defendant guilty of treason and of taking active measures to subvert and undermine the work and mission of the global clown order, etc. By the powers given to us by the Court we sentence Michael O'Malley to indefinite imprisonment at a suitable location, followed by death, which shall begin immediately forthwith."

The center judge then turned his head to face Jordan and spoke to her.

"In the matter of the defendant's accomplice, state your name:"

Jordan remained silent, and the judge waited for a moment before continuing.

"The defendant's accomplice appears to be not a clown and thus by the rules of the clown court, I hereby invoke my privilege to give her a clown name for the purposes of her trial. Defendant's accomplice shall hereby be known to all the clowning world as 'Plucky'."

The clowns gathered along the window all applauded in unison and smiled. Mike recognized this formal clap as the same applause that would be given to anyone when they were officially given a clown name or when the name they had been using as a clown was officially recognized and recorded by the International Clown Court. Mike had received this same applause when he became an honorary clown by a court led by Lucy the Loon, also known as Lucy the Clown, the cook and former manager of the Great Western Circus of the Americas. The laws of the International Clown Court state that no clown may accept orders from any non-clown. So it was the tradition of circus clowns that the manager of the circus must either be a clown or must be made an honorary clown by an official panel of clowns. Mike could juggle, and he possessed some rudimentary clowning skills that he had picked up from a childhood of living and traveling with clowns. At the time, he was well-liked by the clowns of the Great Western Circus of the Americas. They gave him the name "O'Clowny the Hobo". This name was stripped from Mike years ago, when he became clown enemy number one.

Having officially given Jordan her clown name, the head judge continued.

"In the matter of Plucky the Clown, the court hereby finds the defendant guilty of conspiring and assisting in the evasion of clown justice. In the laws of the clown court, conspiring or

aiding in the undermining of clown culture and traditions car-
ries a punishment equal to the sentence given to the aided."

"Shut up already!" screamed Jordan. "Let me the fuck go
you fucking creeps."

The clown with the gag stepped behind Jordan. The head
judge waved his hand and one of the trunk clowns gagged her
again.

Jordan struggled with trying to get out of the duct tape
that was binding her hands together and her ankles to the legs
of the chair. The clowns against the wall stood silent and the
head judge spoke.

"Both defendants having waived their rights to speak in
their own defense, the punishment shall commence immediately."

The head clown banged his gavel, and two clowns lifted
Mike and Jordan and carried them to the van. The judges got
into the VW bus while the remaining clowns put the aisles
back where they were and removed the folding table, the red-
bound book, the gavel, and the chairs and loaded everything
into the bus and the van. They left the gas station attendant
bound up behind the counter and shut the trunk and doors of
Mike's 1998 Pontiac Bonneville before heading back east on I-
80.

CHAPTER 62

In which they devise a plan to hoodwink the clowns

The cop clown blindfolded and handcuffed Mike and Jordan to the interior walls of the van on opposite sides, with their feet facing each other. Jordan heard balloons being blown up with a helium tank and streamers being hung around them. The clowns giggled as they worked. Classic rock played on a small radio hanging from the roof of the van.

Mike and Jordan were both still gagged. With their feet facing each other, they devised a simple system of communicating. Mike applied pressure to Jordan's feet and spelled out words using Morse code. Mike had learned it when he was the assistant to the circus magician, and he guessed that a girl who wanted to grow up to be a spy or a con woman would have learned Morse code.

Morse code is a reliable way to communicate about cards and for giving tips for any other trick that involved audience participation—such as the one where the magician asked an audience member to tie the best knot they can tie to hold the magician's wrists together before he gets tossed into the tank of water. As soon as the magician is inside the tank, his assistant taps out the type of knot that was tied using his foot and any other information that might be helpful to the magician. After a couple months of practice, Mike could tap out detailed information with his foot while simultaneously talking about how dangerous the trick was and giving a detailed history of the trick and how many magicians had died while doing it and so forth.

Now in the van, hurtling down I-80, headed east as fast as an old van and a VW Bus could go, Mike tapped his foot against the bottom of Jordan's to ask her if there was any chance of her slipping out of her handcuffs and to tell her that when he said so, they were both going to attempt to escape at the same time. Jordan said that, yes, she would be able to get out of the cuffs. Mike's were tighter, and he knew there was no way he could get out of them. The plan they came up with was that Jordan would start groaning and when one of the clowns asked her what she wanted and removed her gag, she would ask for water. If the clown brought her water (which wasn't guaranteed in clown confinement) she would knee him in the groin and get his keys and uncuff Mike and they would escape by jumping out of the van while moving at fifty-five miles per hour down the freeway. It was a terrible plan, and Jordan told Mike so.

She had a better idea. She liked the part about asking for a glass of water. But, when they brought it and ungagged her she would make fun of the clown and ask if he was too afraid of a little girl to uncuff her and let her drink by herself. Next, she would figure out which clown was in charge and she would seduce him somehow and steal his keys and then pound on the wall behind the van's driver until he pulled over and opened the back, thinking that his comrades needed help and Mike and Jordan would be waiting there to swing helium tanks at the driver and run to the front of the van and escape.

Mike complemented her on this genius bit of psychology. Clowns, Mike explained (using Morse code) are insecure, and it wouldn't be hard to use that against them and to convince them that there was no risk in unbinding her hands and taking off her blindfold since the van was in motion and she was just a small girl and there were four of them. Jordan told Mike to shut up. This conversation was taking much longer than a normal conversation would have taken, because both Mike and Jordan were rusty with Morse code and they had to keep asking each other to repeat letters and words.

Mike told Jordan that he had to admit that her plan was better than what he had come up with, but it still relied on a whole lot of luck. Jordan told him to shut up again. Mike said "make me." They both laughed a bit under their gags and Jordan kept going and changed her gagged laugh to a gagged moan of agony.

The van clowns gathered around her and prodded her with their feet as she squirmed and moaned. One of the clowns started to remove her gag before another one of the clowns yelled at him, "What are you doing, Bonko?"

"What? She's in pain. I can't let a creature suffer. It ain't right," said Bonko.

"She's not a creature, she's a prisoner, and a bad one," said the other clown.

"She's just a little girl," said Bonko, "and besides, she's tied up. Let's find out what she wants. I'll wear gloves."

Another clown, this one a woman, spoke up, "I agree with Bonko. We're clowns, not torturers. It's the mission of the clown to be caring and compassionate. If we don't treat our prisoners with respect, we don't deserve respect."

"That's a very touching speech," said the reluctant clown, "go ahead and loosen her gag and find out what she wants, Bonko, but if something goes wrong, don't say I didn't tell you so."

"Ya. Ya. Whatever, boss," said Bonko.

Bonko reached behind Jordan's head and untied her gag.

Jordan stopped moaning and spit out bits of cloth that had come off the gag. "Water, please. May I have some water," she gasped.

Bonko tore open the plastic around a thirty pack of shrink-wrapped plastic bottles of water and pulled hard at one of them until it squeaked out of the plastic. The other bottles in the 30-pack loosened once the one was gone, and they flopped around in what remained of the cardboard and plastic packaging.

Bonko groaned a bit as he twisted the cap off the bottle of water. He held it up to Jordan's lips, and she made as big of a scene as she could while trying to drink—or rather, while trying to not drink—from the bottle. She spilled most of it, hit her face against the bottle, cursed and cried, and finally stopped and pointed her face in the direction where Bonko was standing.

"Can you please just remove my blindfold and one hand and let me drink the water myself. This is humiliating."

Bonko looked at the other two clowns and shrugged.

Jordan pleaded. "I can't escape. I'm tied up. I can't see where we're going. There are no windows. I can't overpower you—there's just one of me. Please, please, have some decency to a fellow human and clown."

"You're no clown," shrieked the woman clown.

"But I am," said Jordan, "Have you already forgotten that I was just given my clown name. I must have some rights according to the clown court."

Bonko scratched his head. He wasn't sure whether she had rights or not. It wasn't his job to know L'Art Du Clown inside out, unlike the smart clowns and the judges. But, it certainly sounded legitimate to him.

"What will happen to you if you're all found to be violating my clown rights?" said Jordan. "Maybe you'll be punished. Maybe they'll suspend your clowning license. Do you know? Do you want to take that risk?"

The clowns moved off to the other end of the van and conferred with each other. The truth was, none of them had any idea how clown law worked. They just did as they were told, and what they were told to do today was to get Mike. Jordan had just been in the way. The judges were able to come up with a justification for capturing her too, but they all knew that the case against Jordan was much weaker than the case against Mike.

After several minutes of conferring with each other, they decided to release one of Jordan's hands and to unblindfold her, but they warned her that if she tried anything they would not only tie her up again, they would also knock her out for the rest of the trip and that they'd hurt Mike as well.

"I don't care about this guy," Jordan said, nodding her head towards Mike. "I barely know him. I heard, though, that there was a reward out for his capture, and so I figured I'd help capture his traitorous ass."

Jordan turned her face to Mike and snarled, and then turned back to the clowns. "Ya, that's right. Why do you think we stopped at that gas station when you were parked right around the corner? Why do you think I left the trunk unlocked when I went inside to pay for the gas? Why do you think I stopped the car just a few miles later even though we had a full tank of gas? I'm on your fucking side, comrades, and we fucking got him! How long has it been? Twenty years since he betrayed the clown world by siding with the midgets? How long have we suffered this humiliation? This calls for a drink, my fellow clowns! This is truly a momentous occasion!"

The clowns howled with laughs of joy.

"Untie me, comrades, and let's finish decorating this place. It's time to party!"

CHAPTER 63

In which Jordan drinks too much at an
underground clown party

Bonko the Clown, Monty the Magical Moron, and Cindy, as Jordan and Mike would later find out their clown names were, were gleeful when Jordan told them that she had tricked Mike. They bounced around and clapped while dancing. "What a devious girl! What a plan! Plucky the clown is the pluckiest clown around!"

Bonko stopped the celebration for a moment by raising up his hands into the air and shushing the other clowns.

"But, if you really did bring Mike to us as you say, and if you really are on our side, and if you really don't know this guy, then why did you say those things about us during the trial and why did you try to get away?" said Bonko.

"Bonko. Bonko, Bonko, Bonko. Leave the thinking to the boss clowns, will ya, huh?" said Monty, "Let's party! She's not going anywhere!"

Bonko agreed that now wasn't the time for thinking—it was the time to party—and he untied Jordan's hands, but left her feet tied to Mike's because she was still a prisoner until they could tell the judge clowns about the mix-up once they got back to Minnesota or wherever they were going. Cindy opened a cooler and took out two beers with each of her hands and handed them around to the other clowns and to Jordan.

Jordan estimated that the ride would take at least six hours, based on how long she and Mike had been traveling in the opposite direction. There would need to be a stop in there somewhere to use the bathroom, considering that the clowns were all drinking now. Her job between now and the bathroom stop would be to conspire with Mike using their foot Morse code while carrying on with the clowns and becoming their friend while also not getting too drunk. The cooler, like a clown car, seemed to hold more beer than was possible, and the clowns got funnier, louder, and more talkative as they got drunker.

Poor Mike sat blindfolded and gagged against the other wall as the festivities went on. Jordan considered whether she should ask them to have some mercy on him and give the poor guy a beer, but it was evident by the way they talk about him that he was their public enemy number one and she would only betray her real motives if she said anything.

"Hey, so just how much scratch am I gonna get for helping you capture this weirdo?" she asked Cindy.

"Oh, I don't know! But, I imagine it will be a lot! You saved us a lot of trouble, and once the clown court hears how you tricked him and we captured him so quick, we're all going to get bonuses!"

"We'll be rollin' in patches!" said Monty.

"What does he mean patches?" asked Jordan.

"Oh, that's right, you're a new clown! We don't earn money for good deeds we do for the Clown Court, we get patches! You see this one here, I got that for helping to rebuild the event center after the 2008 fire. This one right here," she said, pointing to her left elbow, "I got for going to Mexico City to help recruit new junior clowns. This one here, I got for . . .

oh, well, that was a very special mission—and very secret. I don't know if I'm supposed to tell anyone about that one."

Jordan gestured with her beer for Cindy to sit next to her. The other clowns were standing around Mike and talking about him like he was the new barbeque grill.

Cindy sat down next to Jordan. Jordan leaned over and whispered, "Come on, you know you wanna tell me! What did you get that patch for?"

Cindy blushed and put her hands on her cheeks. "Oh, I sure do wanna tell you. I feel like I can trust you. I know Bonko isn't sure yet, but he's always been a little bit of a stick in the mud."

"Of course you can tell me," said Jordan, "Come on!" Jordan poked her elbow into Cindy's side and made the corniest face she could make while winking.

"Oh all right! What's the harm in telling! You see, there's one place in the United States where clowns don't go. Well, where clowns used to not go, that is! It's Aberdeen, Washington. We stayed away for decades, and the town became a sort of a safe place for anyone who was trying to escape from the clowns."

She lowered her voice to a whisper and put her mouth close to Jordan's ear. "We suspect that this guy here was trying to get to Aberdeen. We don't care, though. You know why?"

"Why?" said Jordan.

"Because this patch right here," said Cindy, pointing to the patch on her left knee, "this ol' patch right here, I got for helping to build and staff the first and only secret clown social center, library, and Clown Law Enforcement Center anywhere in the world. We are in Aberdeen, and we're taking notes and getting ready to round up all the fugitive clowns in one swoop. Swoop! Justice will be done. If your boy here had made it to Aberdeen, we would have gotten him along with all the others. And, believe me, there are some who are worse than him. Not many, but the ones who are worse than him are going to be a lot more difficult to capture. The only thing that made this guy hard to capture was that we had to wait until a very powerful clown who was protecting him died, and then we had to find him. Finding him wasn't that easy, but there are always ways, right?"

"How did you do it?" asked Jordan.

"We went through his sister. She's been a clown even longer than him. She's one of our best. We never asked her for his whereabouts before because we didn't want to arouse suspicion before we were able to do anything about it. If we had, he might have gone even further into hiding. This patch right here," Cindy said, pointing to a patch on her other knee, "I got for going to Sacramento and getting Mike's sister, Pauline, to tell me where Mike lives."

"How did you get her to tell?" asked Jordan.

"It turned out to be very easy," said Cindy, "Pauline is not very bright. She's a genius when it comes to clowning, but as a person, she's dumb as a stump. Funny thing was, Pauline only knew the state, but that was enough info for our super-secret agent to track him down!"

Cindy clinked her bottle against Jordan's and the two of them drank. Jordan looked at Mike, with a gag and blindfold, and couldn't tell whether he had heard any of what Cindy had just said. Morse code tapping on his foot at this moment would be too risky, with Cindy sitting right next to her, but she and Mike would have to change their plans.

Jordan tried to crawl over to the cooler to get another beer.

"Oh hey, darlin', don't strain yourself. I'll get us fresh ones." said Cindy.

"Ha, it'd be helpful if I weren't tied down!" laughed Jordan.

"Ya, I know. But, the boss says we gotta do this so we don't get in trouble with the judges when we stop. It's nothing personal, mind you." said Cindy.

"When are we gonna stop?" asked Jordan.

"Great question," said Cindy, "I gots to take a leak, and I'm sure you do too! I'll find out."

Monty was still standing over Mike and admiring and talking about their catch. Cindy kicked at his ankle. Monty turned around and smiled at Cindy with his giant clown smile.

"Yes, darlin'? How are you doin'?"

"I'm fine as frog's hair," said Cindy, "but us ladies wanna know when we're gonna take a pisser break!"

"An excellent question," said Monty, "I'll find out."

Monty moved to the front of the van and picked up a walkie talkie from a tool bin and spoke into it. After a minute, he came back and stood next to Cindy.

"The judges say there's a Big Boy about fifteen miles up the road. Can you hold out until then?"

"Can do!" said Cindy, while making a gee-whiz arm motion and winking at Monty.

"I hope you like Big Boy!" Cindy asked Jordan. "It's pretty much all we eat when we're on missions."

"Oh gosh, I sure do! It's pretty much my favorite place to eat when I'm drunk!" said Jordan.

"Whoohoo!" Both Jordan and Cindy shouted as they clinked their bottles together again and then competed for who could finish theirs first.

"You know what, Plucky, I think that's a perfect name for you," said Cindy.

Fifteen minutes later, the van pulled up behind the Big Boy, and the cop clown opened the doors from the outside. The clowns who had ridden in the van and who had been wearing white judge wigs at the gas station were now wearing orange clown wigs and looked much less somber. The clowns all gathered around the back of the van and Monty and Bonko carried a cooler from the van and set it on the ground. They opened it and handed beers around to all the other clowns, who opened and chugged them.

Bonko handed one to Jordan.

"What the hell are you doing giving our beer to a prisoner, Bonko?" said one of the bus clowns.

"She's one of us. How do you think we were able to capture the traitor so easily? She hoodwinked him!"

"Hoodwink! Hoodwink! Hoodwink! Hoodwink!" chanted several other clowns.

A gruff-faced elder hobo clown, who Jordan recognized as one of the judge clowns, even now that he had changed his costume, climbed up in to the van and brought his face close enough to hers that she could smell his beer and cigar breath. "She betrayed the traitor, you say," pondered the elder clown.

"That's right, boss. She hoodwinked him!"

"I do love a good hoodwinking," said the elder clown, "but how do we know that we're not being hoodwinked right now?"

The elder clown squinted while looking into Jordan's eyes, as if he was trying to see into her soul.

"Why the hell would I want to hoodwink you?" said Jordan, "I care about one thing only: getting that reward money. Now, untie me and let's get some Big Boy!"

Mike squirmed and tried to escape his cuffs and gag on the other side of the van. The elder clown stood up and kicked Mike in the shin. Mike winced and fell to the side in pain as the elder clown said through his teeth, "There you go, pussy-face. We finally got you." He then turned to the clowns who were watching from outside the van and yelled, "Well, clowns! This is a momentous occasion indeed! Let's party!"

The clowns cheered and one of them let loose a net containing a dozen helium balloons from the van and then pushed them towards the open cargo doors, over the heads of Mike and Jordan. The balloons floated above the Big Boy parking lot and all the clowns watched and drank their beers until they could no longer make out the balloons against the late afternoon sky above somewhere in Wisconsin.

The elder clown broke the silence and asked, "Is everyone ready?"

The other clowns cheered.

"Well then, let the shooooooww begin!"

The elder clown took out a large key ring from his pocket and squinted his eyes at each key until he found the right one, which he used to open an unmarked door on the back of the Big Boy. He propped the door open and the clowns lined up to file through it. Monty the clown led Jordan through the door, and Bonko the clown was leading Mike, who was still blindfolded and cuffed, but no longer gagged.

Through the door was a staircase, lit by strings of multicolored Christmas tree lights on the handrails on both sides. The stairs went down two flights and ended in a lobby or waiting room decorated with circus posters, brass and wood on the walls, ornate mirrors, and a circus-themed chandelier. A clown dressed like the Big Boy statue, with checkered pants and suspenders, welcomed everyone and offered to take any coats or bags. When Big Boy saw Mike, he squealed, "Is this him? Is this the traitor? Is this the famous Mike O'Malley?"

The elder clown put his hands on his hips and nodded. "That's him alright."

Before the elder clown could finish confirming that it was Mike O'Malley, Big Boy had wound up his foot and he kicked Mike as hard as he could in the shin. "I've been waiting for a long time to do that." Then, turning to the other clowns, he said, "It is an honor to have you at the North Milwaukee Big Boy! Drinks are on me tonight, comrades!"

The double doors on the opposite side of the lobby from the stairs they came down swung open, revealing a night club that resembled the Circus Circus casino, but in miniature. The dance floor lit up as the clowns entered. Either this was a private party, or we're early, thought Jordan, seeing that no one else was in the room and that there was no music playing.

Jordan headed for the bar. The clowns all raced to get their favorite booths around the dance floor. The music started up: classic rock, of course. Jordan recognized the first song—Smoke on the Water—and she rolled her eyes at the bartender who seemed to be about her age and wasn't wearing a clown costume. She thought she detected the slightest crack in his professional appearance as he asked her what she'll have. "I'll have a gin and tonic," said Jordan.

As night approached, food was brought in from the local Polish restaurant. Stuffed cabbage, potato pancakes, kielbasa, pierogi, and much more was set up on two folding tables against one wall of the bar. More clowns arrived at dinner time too and they lined up to fill their plates. The clowns had been drinking for a few hours at this point and were looser. They removed Mike's blindfold and allowed him to eat, but not to use his hands. They put a plate of steaming hot stuffed cabbage and potato pancakes and a Milwaukee's Best in front of him and laughed as he struggled to eat and drink without using his hands.

In the meantime, Jordan was working on a plan and flirting with the bartender. Three drinks in, she was using her finger like a Sharpie to draw lines, dots, and circles on her hands and wrists while trying to remember the positions of the ones she had imagined drawing a moment ago.

"Nervous?" asked the bartender.

"No, are you nervous? What kind of bartender talk is that?"

"Sorry, you just keep fidgeting with your hands and doing things like you're taking notes. Do you want to borrow a pen?"

"Yes, please! That would be tits. Gimme another G&T too."

The bartender chuckled and handed her the pen from his shirt pocket, then made a gin and tonic and placed it in front of her before taking away her empty glass. As he was placing it on the bar, he leaned in closer to her and whispered.

"What are you doing hanging around these clowns?"

"Hah, that's funny. Clowns, because they are," said Jordan, while trying to draw a line along one the lines on her palm (the one that represented I-80 and I-94) with the ballpoint pen.

"Well, I could ask you the same thing, now couldn't I?" said Jordan.

"I work here," said the bartender, pointing to his name tag, "call me Joe. What's your excuse?"

"I'm working too."

"Oh." said the bartender, "Sorry. I should mind my own business."

"Fuck you, fuckface! Not like that!"

Jordan drank half of her gin and tonic and then wiped her mouth with her sleeve. She pointed with her index finger and glass towards Mike.

"See that guy over there? The one trying to eat without his hands?"

"Ya, of course."

"I helped bring him in and I'm waiting for my reward."

"I'm sorry, but exactly what kind of reward are you expecting to receive?"

"Cash money, bro. I'll get it from the clowns, spring the guy anyway because he's my ride, and then probably spend a couple months pretending to be his girl until he gives me his life savings, then I split."

"There's a pretty big hole in your plan," whispered Joe.

"You have a big hole in YOUR plan, buddy," said Jordan, slurping at her gin and tonic, "OK, and what's that?"

"There's no way these guys are going to pay anyone for anything. See all that food over there? They don't pay for it. It was donated for the Milwaukee Children's Hospital fundraiser that was held last month. The clowns put it in the freezer rather than serve it at the benefit, and then they thaw it for these parties. I'm only getting paid because there are families who still eat at Big Boy upstairs. Believe me, I'd rather be up there. At least the people up there tip once in a while. But, you know who owns this place?"

Jordan looked around, trying to figure out who was the boss.

"The old hobo clown. He built this club forty years ago and then built a Big Boy on top of it. He's the landlord, so when he says to send down a couple servers to tend bar and serve food, the Big Boy manager has to obey. Did they tell you they were going to pay a reward?"

"They mentioned something about patches. I don't give a fuck about patches, but I was thinking that was in addition to the cash."

"Fuck no. Patches is what you'll get. See that lady clown? They call her Punky the Clown, but her name's Cindy. She runs a t-shirt shop in old town. She makes all the patches too. She's never been paid for a single one, but she can't stop making them now."

"Why not?"

"As goofball as it sounds, they run the clowns like the mob. Every business in town pitches in something for the fundraisers the clowns put on, but the donations never get to the children. The money, food, blankets, school supplies, canned goods, toys—all of it—go straight into the clowns' pockets or they sell the shit on eBay. Everyone knows that's what happens. The children's hospital is fine. They have corporate sponsors and giant trusts and foundations that give them more than enough funding for whatever they need. They know that the fundraisers are a sham, just like everyone else. But, there's an unspoken threat of some sort of consequences if you don't comply with the clown demands when they come around."

"Does anyone ever refuse?" asked Jordan.

"Oh yeah, sure. Cindy did when she started up her business five years ago. She was new in town, from Chicago. She was in a band—that's where her name came from. Frankly, I don't think she could have afforded the donation if she'd wanted to make it. But, the next thing you knew, she was one of them. She joined the Rotary Club, and we started seeing her on the other side of the table at the fundraisers and church carnivals. She changed. We don't know what happens, but the people who start out refusing the clowns always end up becoming one of them."

"What the fuuuuck," slurred Jordan, as she made a hand gesture indicating to Joe that she wanted another drink.

Joe made her another drink, placed it in front of her, and took away the empty glass.

Jordan turned away from the bar on her stool, and was looking at the table where Mike was seated, with the clowns gathered around him laughing and smoking cigars.

"Well, shit. If I'm not gonna get paid, I'm sure as hell not gonna sit around this creepy-assed joint," said Jordan.

She stood up, steadying herself on the bar a bit. "Don't worry. I'm a pro," she told Joe, as she picked up her drink and stumbled to the booth where Mike was being held.

"Hey," she yelled to the booth in general, "Are you gonna let this guy use the crapper, or are you gonna have him shitting and pissing all over the back of your van the rest of the drive? I don't know about the rest of you ass clowns . . . " Jordan barely held in her laughter after she called them ass clowns. "But, smelling some dude's shit ain't my idea of a party."

"Plucky the Clown!" howled Monty the Clown. Monty waved a sausage in front of Mike's face while singing to him in a low voice, "Plucky the Clown is a very very very bad clown."

Then, pointing the sausage at Jordan, he said, "You, darling, need to mind your own business. We'll mind ours. You mind yours."

"OK, about my business," said Jordan, "why don't you give me my fucking reward for bringing this guy in and I'll get the hell out of your hair and I hope I never see you again."

"Oh, there will be a reward, little Plucky," said the elder clown, "but you have to wait until we get to where we're going."

"How do I know you're not lying?"

The elder clown pretended to look offended, then he pretended to cry, then he threw his head back and started laughing. All of this through his horrible clown make-up and with a paper plate of Polish sausage and mustard with cabbage on the table in front of him. The four other clowns at the table laughed along with him.

As they were laughing, Jordan pulled on the table, which moved away from the booth chairs, and she threw it to the ground. The drinks and plates scattered on the floor and the clowns' laughter turned to anger.

Jordan put up her hand in a "talk to the hand" gesture to the whole table and looped her arm through Mike's arm, which was handcuffed still behind his back. She helped him up as the other clowns were trying, from their seats still, to hold him back.

Arm in arm, they ran to the door they had entered the underground Big Boy clown club through and Jordan tried the knob. It was locked.

The music stopped, and the clowns were gathering around them.

"Fuckin' locked? You keep him in handcuffs and won't even let him use the pisser and the whole time you know there's no way he's getting out? What the fuck kind of people are you?"

CHAPTER 64

The adventures of Peter Lundelhart

The only written account of clown jail was in a book by the famous American adventurer (and exaggerator) Peter Lundelhart. Lundelhart's book, first published in 1980, contained chapters about his most well-known adventures, along with some adventures that were less publicized and less believable. The book got less than great reviews when it came out and many people accused him of lying to fluff up the book. Later in his life, Peter would admit during an interview with a college newspaper that he had lied about some of the adventures he wrote about in his book, but he wouldn't say which. It didn't matter at that point because no one was paying any attention to Peter Lundelhart.

No one except for Mike O'Malley, that is. Mike paid attention to everything that Peter Lundelhart said and did, and he read every interview and every account of his public performances at county fairs and high school gyms around the country.

Mike needed to know what he was in for. He read and re-read Peter Lundelhart's account of clown jail to look for clues as to how to avoid it and, if he were unlucky enough to wind up there, how to get out.

Of all the stories in Lundelhart's book, the clown story was the most ridiculed. The other stories in the book dealt with situations that seemed more plausible, or that other people had reported doing at some point—dining with cannibals, his memories of being brought up by apes, swimming across the Great Lakes while towing barges, and the (pretty boring) story of how he learned to walk across hot coals while he was living in India and how that experience helped him to survive working in an office in Ohio during the early part of his career.

After Mike left the circus, someone mailed him a copy of Lundelhart's book, with a note scribbled in the inside front cover:

"Hey pussyface. You're gonna find this book very interesting. Study it well, and don't neglect to floss!"

Mike has a pretty good idea who sent him the book—there was only one person in the world who would both call him pussyface AND remind him to floss—Lucy the Clown, aka Lucy the Loon. She retired after Mike destroyed the circus for all future clowns. Maybe she felt she didn't have anything to lose and so she'd try to help Mike. Or maybe she was taunting him. Was Peter Lundelhart's account of the clown jail meant to be taken at face value, or was Lucy the Clown trying to tell him that there was a secret meaning or hint inside the book?

For the first year after he went into hiding from the circus clowns, Mike studied the book like others study the bible. He memorized the clown jail chapter. It wasn't a long chapter, but the details contained within it were horrifying if they were true.

The good news, however, was that Peter Lundelhart managed to escape and he described his escape in some detail in his book.

He would later say that his tale of escaping from clown jail should serve as a warning to anyone who might be less than nice to clowns: reform your ways—the clowns are watching and keeping a list of who's naughty and nice. Clowns are slow to anger, and clown jail is reserved for only the worst offenders of clown law, but it's best to play it safe. Lundelhart had offended and hurt many different groups: cannibals, the KKK, religious fanatics of all stripes, and members of the Republican party. In his book, speeches, and a short-lived TV show, he'd tell the tale of each experience and at the end of the story he'd conclude that facing his fear of the evil thing made him no longer afraid of that thing and that there was no reason for him to be afraid in the first place. Reading his book, Mike wondered if Lundelhart would ever learn his own lesson.

It was a speech that Lundelhart gave about facing your fears head-on that caused him to fall out of favor with the American public and to become the butt of jokes and the object of scorn by animal rights activists and suburban mothers.

"Evil is stupid." he started. "The only weapon evil has against men of principle is fear. If you're not afraid of the evil, it wilts and becomes as harmless as a puppy. But, do not confuse harmless with not evil. Evil must be stamped out. We must not allow these evil puppies to thrive and procreate. For even a pack of evil puppies can do real harm. Be vigilant. Do not allow even the cutest puppy to survive. Stamp them out! Stamp them out! Stamp them out! Stamp them out!

After this speech, the phrase "stamping out puppies" was used by the media as shorthand for any proposal to deal with looming problems before they become imminent dangers. If a politician would propose trying to implement an earthquake warning system or warn about the dangers of artificial intelligence, it would be dismissed with "well, this sounds a bit like 'stamping out puppies!' don't you think?"

Reprinted here is the entire text of Lundelhart's account of clown jail.

How I Was Imprisoned, and Nearly Met My End, In Clown Jail
by Peter Lundelhart, IV

It was May of '78, and I was exploring the great American Northwest Regions. While trudging through the deepest wilderness, I spotted some strange tracks, the likes of which I had never before seen. These tracks—which I estimated to be the tracks of a dozen two-legged creatures or six four-legged ones—were spaced out like human footfalls, but the imprints were of a size and shape I couldn't explain. They were too small to be snowshoes (and this was made even more unlikely because of the fact that it was June in the forest), and they were far too large to be the shoes of human feet. I contemplated whether they might be the footprints of the fabled beast known as Sasquatch in these regions.

I followed these tracks for several miles. As will happen, day turned into dusk, and I had still not found the strange creatures who had made the tracks. I set up camp in a lovely clearing near a stream. I gathered firewood and set to making my fire. That being done, I pitched my tent and cooked a wonderful meal of wildflowers and pinecones that I had gathered on the day's hike.

As I was preparing to eat, I heard a rustling in the nearby brush. Beavers and critters of all kinds and stripes are plentiful in these woods, but so are bears and less-friendly species. I switched on my flashlight and stood up to shine it in the direction from whence I heard the rustle.

Through the trees, perhaps a quarter mile away, I could see the light from another campfire. Strange, thought I, for I wouldn't think that another party would venture so far into these woods. Unclipping my binoculars from my belt and holding them to my eyes, I spotted around the campfire the most bizarre and repulsive scene I have ever had the misfortune to lay my eyes upon. I won't describe this scene in these pages, for reasons that will become apparent, but it involved about a dozen circus clowns, dressed and made-up in their circus finest. I didn't know whether they had seen me, but I didn't want to take any chances. If they had spent any amount of time in the woods at all—and judging by how far into the wilderness and the horrible things they were doing, they had—they surely would have seen me by now. Did they not care who saw what they were doing? No. It turned out that I was already ensnared in their devious clutches.

Wanting to get out of the woods and to safety, I left the fire burning—something you should never do, by the way, except in the direst of circumstances—and I left my tent and sleeping bag—not to mention my delicious supper—behind. I took with me only my canteen and my small duffel which contained a pair of dry socks, a sweatshirt, a rainproof hat, and a tube of snakebite cream.

I hadn't ventured twenty feet from my encampment when I was assaulted by perhaps four of the worst-smelling clowns I'd ever had the displeasure of running into. They captured me, in the complete darkness, by the ankles and wrists, and they carried me to their camp.

These clowns threw me into a tent filled with pamphlets and books. It appeared that I had stumbled upon some meeting of a governing body of the clowns. Before this day, I had not the slightest notion that such a thing would exist. However, it has been my experience that anywhere you have a group of people greater in number than ten, you'll have at least one among their number that feels the need to organize and legislate—and clowns are no different. Legislation and organizing bodies often result in rules and laws, and in the case of the clowns, it seems that they ended up with more rules than they knew what to do with. These rules had been distributed to the clown populace through a series of pamphlets and brochures over the decades, and now this conference in the woods was being held, from what I could gather, to form more laws or to better organize the ones that they already had.

Being that I am strictly opposed to the formation of laws and governing bodies, owing to their propensity to restrict individual liberties and freedoms, I found their legislating and debating (what I could hear of it from my position tied up in the library tent) to be more offensive than the opening ceremony that I had earlier stumbled upon.

I was forced to sit, tied up, for several hours, listening to the insipient noises of men and women who had heretofore been fully capable of operating as clowns and doing the things that clowns do as they gave away their rights to an organization which they called the

International Clown Court. The entire scene made my blood boil.

The last order of business was for them to decide what they should do with me. I was carried out to the place near the fire that was serving as the pulpit or dais for the event and a clown wearing a tall, curly, white wig came out of a tent and stood next to me.

During the next 15 minutes, I was tried and sentenced for the crime of trespassing on a top-secret meeting of the International Clown Court for the Northwest Region. I have to hand it to these clowns, they don't waste time with namby-pamby notions like human rights and due process in their judicial system. It seems to me that if you must have a system of laws, it should have only the most basic of laws, and justice should be swift and certain—as it is in the natural kingdom and in the Lord's kingdom. It was unfortunate for me that I had wound up on the wrong side of such swift and certain justice, however.

I was sentenced to one year of imprisonment. At the time, I had no idea how miserable a place clown jail was, but I resolved to escape by any means necessary.

Over the next 24 hours, I was transported in the back of an unmarked van to a location that I now know was in the suburbs of Minneapolis, Minnesota. Clown jail was located underneath a warehouse in an unsavory part of town. Upon arrival, I heard the sound of a large warehouse door open and then close as we entered. I was then carried out of the van and brought to an elevator, inside of which my blindfold was removed. It appeared to be a normal freight elevator with a dim lightbulb in the roof.

Upon exiting the elevator, we entered a small lobby with cinderblock walls, three chairs, and a receptionist window and security door in the opposite wall from the elevator and which the chairs were facing.

The two guards on either side of me sat in two of the chairs, and I was made to sit in the middle chair. Handcuffs bound me to these two guards. Now un-blindfolded, I could see that both of the guards were dressed up in cheerful clown costumes, but with the only difference between them and your typical circus clown being that they wore a sad face with exaggerated frowns and giant tears painted on their cheeks.

We sat, silent, for what must have been thirty minutes, before the receptionist—also in full clown make up—appeared in the window. She motioned for us to approach, and the guard clowns brought me to the window. I was asked to hand over my personal belongings, which the guards stripped from me and handed through the window. Included in my belongings was my patented Adventurers Pocket Knife, which can be obtained via mail order using the form in the back of this book.

My clothing and possessions stripped from me, I was uncuffed and pushed through the door to the left of the receptionist window, where I was given a prison uniform. The uniform consisted of giant shoes, baggy pants, and a blouse. Each item was orange, but with white polka dots of varying sizes. I put on the uniform, and then another door opened. I walked forward into a central courtyard surrounded on all sides with cages. Each cage was eight feet by ten feet in size and held as many as fourteen clown prisoners. Although it didn't appear possible for that many adults to fit in to such small spaces, somehow they did it. The noise level and smell of the place was something that no one should ever have to endure.

Two new guards, who stood next to the door through which I had just walked, escorted me to a cage on the far wall that already contained eight other prisoners. The door was unlocked, and I was pushed in with a mighty shove and I fell upon the floor. The other clown in the cage approached me and began to lick my skin. I later discovered that prisoners in clown jail are deprived of many of the essential nutrients that a person needs to survive, such as salt and magnesium, and they can get some of their required nutrition by licking the skin of new inmates who had not yet been starved of nutrition.

My good reader, I urge you to not allow yourself to become so deprived and depraved. For your own good, please refer to the order form in the back of this book to order my scientifically-formulated Adventurer Nutritional Vitamins, which contain everything needed to keep even the most active adventurer healthy in even the most adverse circumstances. I only wish that I had these vitamins during the horrible ordeal that was to follow my initial introduction to the God-forsaken world of clown jail.

After an hour of constant licking, my skin was red and raw, and the other clown prisoners had extracted every possible nutrient they could get from me. I was left naked and cold on the floor, where I fell unconscious.

When I awoke, the other clowns were pacing around the room in a line while I laid in the center. I was informed that this pacing was the only exercise permitted to clown prisoners, and they would partake in it for one of every three hours during the day and night.

The food served in clown prison is atrocious. I hesitate to even describe it as food. Paste would be more accurate. It resembles a food that was eaten by the natives of the pacific islands, called poi, but lacking the color, charm and taste (such as it is) of that basic porridge. The gruel served to clown prisoners resembles tile grout in color and texture. The taste, also, is not unlike what one would expect grout to taste like. In fact, it may have been grout that I was dining on during my stay in the clown jail. The only redeeming quality of the clown jail meals was that each clown was given his own bowl of the foul grout-food and his own spoon with which to eat it, rather than being served from a communal trough.

After three days of eating this grout, sleeping on a dirt floor with no sleeping bag, and my only exercise being walking in a four-foot diameter circle, my vitality was sapped. Sitting on the bare floor of the cell, with my seven cellmates and wearing my now filthy clown pajamas uniform, I knew only that I had to find a way to escape or I'd soon be dead.

The easiest course of action seemed to me to be to convince my cellmates to help me overpower one of the guards during feeding time and then make a dash for the exit and to the elevator. But the subject had to be broached carefully, for it is my experience that some men place more value on avoiding punishment by their captors than they do on their freedom. If I told the wrong clown, that clown may have alerted the prison guards that I was planning an escape, which would surely lessen my chances of ever getting out.

During exercise periods, I would strike up conversations with the other clowns. I asked them about their families, about their particular brand of clowning—for I found this to be a topic of considerable pride among clowns—and I inquired about their feelings on life in the clown jail. Only one clown out of my cellmates expressed that he was happy and deserved to be in clown jail and wouldn't trade it for anything. This was the clown I would need to stay away from, for such men are the bane of conspirators everywhere—the dreaded happily tortured soul. The downfall of clown jail would represent an end to this clown's hope of ever absolving himself of whatever crimes he had committed. More than likely than not, if he were ever released from his hellish cage, he would find another cage—be it in alcohol, gambling, or loose women—in which to wallow away his time.

Once it became apparent to the other clowns in my cell that I was planning an escape, we implemented a devious trick for ridding us of our meddlesome happy prisoner. During meal time one day, my cellmates began to talk about how the food tasted better, and how it wouldn't be long before they were dining on first-class airplane food, they had heard. There was a grout shortage, they said, and so the grout would be saved solely for those in solitary confinement. As predicted, this news upset our merry tortured clown so much that the very next day, when food was being served, he acted out in a way so vile (and which I will not describe here) as to cause him to be moved post-haste to the lower and more cruel section of clown jail known as solitary confinement.

In solitary confinement, I heard told, clowns had their clown uniforms and makeup stripped from them and replaced with business suits. This may have only been a rumor because I never saw a single person in a business suit during my brief stay in clown jail, but I like to believe that it is true and that the business suit represents the worst torture that the International Clown Court could conceive of.

With the meddlesome clown gone, the remaining clowns in my cell and I were free to openly discuss our plan for escape—as long as we did so when the guards were otherwise occupied—which was most of the time; the smell and noise level in the jail were so horrible the guards would spend as little time as possible guarding anything, and instead would sit in the lobby or even in the warehouse above the jail.

Our plan was simple and ended up being quite similar to how I had originally envisioned it, but with some important improvements made by those who were more experienced with clown jail. It turned out that my original plan would never have worked, because the elevator required a code to operate and that code was changed (or was supposed to be changed) on a weekly basis.

Fortunately, one of the clowns in my group happened to arrive in clown jail on a day when the elevator was broken. This clown arrived in clown jail via a ladder that's accessible through a hatch in the ceiling of the receptionist's office. To escape using the ladder, we'd need to overpower the receptionist, pull down the telescoping ladder from the ceiling, and climb up. With any luck the access door in the warehouse wouldn't have a lock on it, and we'd be able to simply climb out, get past any guards who were inside the warehouse, and exit to the outside world.

We picked the following Thursday to implement our plan. Thursday was garbage day at the warehouse above, and we knew to expect several large garbage trucks to rumble the jail in the early morning. If trucks were in the warehouse, the warehouse door might be left unlocked, so our thinking went. This would be our chance to escape, and perhaps even to sneak ourselves into the garbage truck if we were extremely lucky, to make our escape.

Our plan was by no means water-tight. It relied, in great deal, on luck. But, it's the best that we could come up with given our circumstances. As it turned out, it didn't require luck at all and we shortly discovered that the guards and staff of clown jail are among the laziest and sloppiest administrators of any punitary institution we had ever heretofore heard of.

When Thursday came, we did our best to act normal. The guards rolled the carts of warm grout through the central courtyard and began ladling bowls of the foul mush to each prisoner; opening each prison cell for just long enough to serve its inhabitants and then locking the door again before moving on to the next.

When the guards opened our cell, we pushed together against the cell door and forced it open with a force so great as to knock both guards and the cart filled with warm grout to the floor. A great cheer went up in the clown jail. At that point, we knew that we had to make a change to our plan to attempt to free as many of the other prisoners in the jail as we could. Each of us dashed to one of the other cells and opened the doors, which were similar to common house door locks in that they could be opened from the inside but not from the outside—except in this case, they were reversed as to only be openable from the outside.

With perhaps hundreds of clowns released from their cells, our plan to escape up a small ladder in the ceiling looked more unlikely. However, the guards were no longer an issue, because the sheer number of clown prisoners overpowered them and locked them inside one of the cells, along with the receptionist and the grout cart.

One of the escaped clowns had a peculiar specialty. He was a wizard with many different electrical and electronical devices. By disassembling the access panel to the elevator, he was able to decipher the particular code that was in use and render the elevator operable. The elevator held perhaps ten normal people at a time, and may have been capable of holding twenty clowns, but because of the weight limit and the known poor repair of the elevator, we went up to the surface in groups of ten. I remained behind and ascended the elevator with the final group of escapees.

My dear reader, what I have described in the previous pages is true, no matter how fanciful it seems. The situations and events described are not the imaginings of a depraved mind, as some of my critics will surely claim. These events happened to me. I do not know what became of clown jail after I helped to release all of its prisoners. Whether any of the prisoners were recaptured, and what they were held prisoner for in the first place, I do not know.

Upon escape, I reported my experience to the local police—as it is any adventurer's responsibility to do when he comes upon any illegal or suspicious activity. I have never returned to that spot nor sought to determine what became of this horrendous underworld of clowns. Perhaps someday one of my readers will seek to find out whether this secret clown society and jail still exists. I highly advise against this. Sometimes, it is best to leave the unknown as it is. If you should ignore my warnings and you should find out some bit of information about this clown underworld, I do not care to know anything more than what I already have firsthand knowledge of.

Adventure On!

CHAPTER 65

*In which Mike and Jordan are captured
and held in clown jail*

After Mike and Jordan tried to escape from the Big Boy, the
clowns tied them up and carried them outside and locked
them in the back of the van. Twenty minutes later, Monty,
Cindy, and Bonko came back to the van and got in the back.

All three of them were drunk and scowling at Mike and
Jordan.

"You little pricks," said Monty, shaking his fist, "you tried
to trick us, and we don't appreciate that at all."

"Ruined the party, too," said Cindy while lighting a cigarette. "You're lucky you got out of there at all after that mess
you caused, you little slut whore."

"Who the fuck are you calling 'slut whore'? Let me out of
here right now," said Jordan.

"You're not going anywhere but straight to jail, which is
where we should have gone first anyway," said Monty.

"Ooooo, I'm fuckin' scared," said Jordan. "You're taking
me to your bullshit clown jail. Whatever. Mike, why the fuck
aren't you saying anything?"

Mike was terrified. He'd been trying to avoid this moment for twenty years and he didn't see any way out now. His best hope was that clown jail had changed or that Lundelhart was exaggerating. If Lundelhart wasn't exaggerating, Mike hoped that the jail was in the same place and hadn't been upgraded. Mike went through the possible escape routes Lundelhart had described: the ladder in the ceiling of the receptionist office, the cheap door locks, the elevator code panel. What were the chances, though, that they continued to use the same jail after everyone escaped and a detailed description of the escape was published in a popular book? If they did use the same place for the jail, what were the chances that they didn't upgrade the security?

Mike looked at Jordan and did his best to smile a reassuring smile. She's just a girl, he thought. If I'd had kids, she might be my daughter. She seems tough. She does do a shitty job as a con or whatever it is she's trying to be. Her goofball sweetheart gag isn't going to get them out of clown jail unless she can get one of the clowns to fall in love with her. If she can do that, she deserves to win best actress—and she's already shown how bad she is at acting. No, Mike was going to need to figure this out.

"And this guy! Am I right?" said Jordan. "He never fuckin' says anything. Just all the time in his head. I have no idea what he's thinking about. Were you a mime, Mike? Because I think you'd make a pretty good one."

The other clowns were ignoring Jordan, but she continued.

"Seriously, clowns. Ha! Seriously clowns, get it? No, really, you can just let me out here and I'll walk home. I used to dress like a clown for Halloween. They said I was a cute one too at that. I think I'm gonna fuckin' puke."

Mike moved away from Jordan as far as the ropes around his wrists would let him. The other clowns were still ignoring her. She puked into Monty's lap and he stood up, but then fell over as the van turned a corner, hitting his head against a toolbox on the way down.

"Oh fuck! Oh fuck!" yelled Bonko.

Cindy picked up a towel and held it against Monty's head, then pulled it away, looking for blood. It was clean. The smell of the puke caused Bonko to puke.

"Goddamn it, why are there no fucking windows in this thing," said Cindy.

"We gotta stop, I can't take this smell," said Bonko, between heaves.

"No, we're not stopping," said Monty, who was awake but not moving from where he fell on the floor of the van, "we're almost there."

Jordan was wiping her mouth on her sleeve and seemed to be doing much better. Mike was pressing his face into his shirtsleeve, trying to breathe and avoid getting sick. He had the advantage of being the only on in the van who wasn't drunk, but it didn't do him much good given the circumstances.

Jordan eyed the situation. "Bunch of amateurs. It's like you've never seen some puke before," she said. She worked up as much spit as she could in her mouth and then swallowed. She'd done this a million times. Some water would be helpful to make things right again, but she was a little more sober now, and she remembered to look at her hands.

There was nothing there of much use. The intersecting lines on her palm said that they were outside of Milwaukee, but she knew that even when she was drunk. The pattern of dots on her wrist reminded her that the bartender might fall in love with her if she needed him to. Jordan had a special symbol for bartender in her code—two dots with eyebrows. The symbol was a tribute to the bartender with the unibrow at the Green Mill, where she'd practice her small cons on tourists and he'd take half the cut for playing dumb. Bartenders are always watching and listening and are harder to con and harder to seduce. If the bartender was a newb or seemed gullible, she'd draw the bartender dots with eyebrows and a plus symbol to the right of it. It's rarely ideal to make the bartender fall in love with you—it pretty much ruins that bar forever—but she knew she wasn't ever going back to the Big Boy and he seemed the most likely candidate to help her escape. That wasn't going to happen now.

She checked her other hand. She lifted her watchband with the thumb of her right hand. Nothing new there. Some old marks that were wearing off. Those were useless now too.

Monty was still on the floor. Cindy was still holding a towel against his head. Bonko was holding his stomach and staring hard at the floor. Mike held his nose against his arm pit. Jordan was annoyed. The van slowed down and stopped. A few seconds later, Jordan heard a large warehouse door open, the driver of the van got back in, and the van pulled forward slowly.

The van stopped inside the warehouse and Jordan heard the warehouse door close. As soon as it did, Bonko banged his fist on the rear doors of the van and yelled for someone to open them.

A muffled voice from outside responded, "Don't get your panties in a bunch, nitwit, I'm coming."

The door opened, and a man dressed in a gray jumpsuit stood for a moment, taking in the scene in the back of the van before covering his mouth and nose with his hand.

"Holy mother of fuck! What did you do to my van? I'm gonna have to hose it out with bleach!"

Bonko climbed out of the van as fast as he could and doubled over to puke on the warehouse floor, but nothing was coming out. Cindy remained in the van with Monty.

"Get the prisoners out of here and to processing NOW and fetch the med techs with a stretcher for Monty."

The man in the jump suit signaled to someone else and three large men in identical jumpsuits came over. He detached his walkie talkie from his belt and spoke into it.

"This is Joe at the van. Send a couple med techs up here with a stretcher right away. Monty got hurt."

Then, turning to the three men in jumpsuits he said, "Get the prisoners into the elevator."

The three men in jumpsuits heaved themselves up into the van. One of them untied Mike while the other two held each of his arms. Once untied, the one who had untied the rope picked up Mike's feet and they all lifted. The one on the feet put Mike down momentarily while he climbed out, then the ones on the arms did the same. Once on the ground, they carried Mike away.

A moment later, two medical technicians arrived with a stretcher. They climbed into the van, slid Monty onto the stretcher and fastened him to it. He was awake and protesting that he didn't need to be lifted out and could walk just fine.

"It's just a precaution, darling," Cindy reassured him. "Thanks Joe. Take good care of him."

"We sure will, ma'am." Then, looking to the other Med Tech, the one Cindy just called Joe said, "OK, Joe, you heard the lady. Lift with your knees."

As Jordan watched, she was catching on. Everyone in the clown world who wasn't a clown was called Joe.

The med techs lifted Monty out and Cindy and Joe followed to help.

Jordan was alone in the back of the van, with no one watching. She stretched the rope tying her to the side of the van as far as it would go and searched the van for something she might be able to use to cut herself free. Looking along the side of the van where she was tied, she found a tire iron, a large box of (empty) balloons, spools of string, more rope, and, buried in vomit, a small notebook like a cop would use, with a spiral binding on the top. Picking it up with her bound hands, she read the cover:

Property of Monty the Clown

If found, return to Clown City, 10 B Street Apt 1, Sacramento, CA 95814.

Jordan flipped the cover open and read the first page:

October 1

Breakfast: muffin, coffee (black)

Lunch: ham sandwich with cheese, Vernors ginger ale, cotton candy

Dinner: corn nuts, 2 corn dogs, churro

Day one of the diet is going great. I'm just saying no to temptations and I feel better already. I passed by the elephant ear stand today and just waved. They probably think I'm broke. Would I take a free one if they wanted to give me charity? That will be the test, right? I have to be strong. I'm doing this for Cindy.

Jordan turned the page.

October 2

Breakfast: muffin, coffee (black), orange

Lunch: Sub sandwich (1 ft), chocolate chip cookie, Vernors

Dinner: Red vines, rum

Day two! I barely had time for dinner today. We've been called out for an emergency mission. It's an all hands on deck chase to get some guy who I guess really pissed off someone a long time ago. I'd heard of him, but never met him. The way they talk, he sounds dangerous. Cindy and I are headed out in the van tomorrow and have been prepping it. Rumor has it they're bringing judges and everything. They must want this guy bad. I can't say I'm not nervous. The diet may have to be on hold for a few days. These trips, and the nerves, always do a number on my good eating habits. At least I'll be away from the churro vendor for a couple days, though, right?

That moron Bonko is coming with us too. I couldn't say no—he's like a stupid child. Let's just hope he doesn't fuck it up too much this time. We've got a couple guys from the warehouse who'll be driving the van—that was Cindy's idea. Good for us if someone else does the driving because A) we can drink all we want, and B) when we get away from home, we still get hassled for D.W.C., driving while clown.

Jordan heard footsteps and the talking of Joes approaching the van. She wiped the notebook off on her pants and stuck it under the strap of her bra for safe keeping. She returned to where she was when the van stopped and listened.

"Well, they seem pretty excited about having that guy, huh?" said the first Joe.

"Yeah. Somehow, I expected him to be a bit more badass. The way they described him was way better than the real deal."

They both laughed.

"Hey, she's not going anywhere. Let's have a smoke before we haul her."

"Damn right."

Jordan heard them light cigarettes.

"You got one for me?" Jordan yelled to them from the van.

The men, surprised to hear her talk, and by the casual sound of her voice, laughed and came around to the back of the van.

"It fucking smells in here, sweetheart," said the first Joe.

"Tell me about it."

Joe climbed into the van, took a cigarette out of his pack and put it between Jordan's lips, then lit it for her.

"Thanks, man," said Jordan, taking a long drag and then leaving the cigarette hanging out of her mouth.

"We aren't supposed to be doing this," said Joe #1.

"Ya, but they'll be busy downstairs for a while," said Joe #2.

"I can't fuckin' believe how bad they messed up the van. How far did you have to ride in all this puke with them?" asked Joe #1.

"Ash my smoke," said Jordan out of the side of her mouth.

"Oh shit, sorry about that," said Joe #1, taking the cigarette out of Jordan's mouth, flicking the ashes off it, and then putting it back.

"Just fuckin' untie my arm. I'm not going anywhere," said Jordan.

Joe #1 looked at Joe #2 and then nodded. Joe #2 leaned into the van to untie Jordan's wrists.

He seemed like a nice guy to Jordan. They both seemed nice. "What are nice guys like you doing mixed up with these clowns?" asked Jordan.

"Fuck if I know," said Joe #2, "No, seriously, we work in the warehouse—party supplies and shit—the boss rents the basement and the vans to the creeps. I don't have any idea what they do down there, but we help put 'em into the elevator and we get a bonus. Works for me. I don't ask questions. Damn this knot is tough."

"Shit, I hear the elevator coming back up," said Joe #1, "I'll be right back."

Joe #1 left the back of the van to greet the elevator. Joe #2 finally got the rope untied. Jordan kissed him on the cheek once he got it, and at the same time leaned far enough over to grab the tire iron. She swung it as hard as she could, the cigarette still hanging out of the side of her mouth. The tire iron connected with the side of Joe #2's head and he collapsed to the side, and then slid off the back of the van to the warehouse floor.

"What the fuck was that?" yelled Joe #1. He came running towards the back of the van. Jordan was standing inside it and swung at his head and missed. He rushed towards her with his arms stretched out to the sides to block any additional swings of the tire iron. Jordan dropped it and crawled under the van. At the same time, Jordan saw three pairs of clown shoes approach the van. Joe #1 dragged Joe #2 behind some boxes and then walked to the side of the van to greet the clowns.

"Let's get the girl down there now, Joe," said one of the clowns.

"Sure thing. I'm just waiting for my partner to get back from the shitter. She's tied up pretty good in there, so no worries. We'll send her down in a couple."

"Good. After you do that, clean up the back of the van and get it ready for deliveries."

"Will do, boss," said Joe #1.

The clowns walked away from the van, towards the warehouse office.

"You fuckin' bitch," whispered Joe #1 under his breath. "I'm going to kill you."

Jordan looked around under the van for anything that might be useful. She felt a handle of some sort underneath her side. She crawled back to get a better look. It was a trap door. She tried turning the handle—it turned. She opened it as far as she could under the van. There wasn't enough space under the van to open it enough to get in, though.

"As soon as they're out of sight, you're dead," said Joe #1.

Jordan watched the clowns. They were at the other end of the warehouse and she could see that one of them was the guy they were calling Elder Clown. She didn't recognize the other two. They went into the glass-enclosed warehouse office and shut door. Two of them had their backs to the window facing the van, and the Elder Clown was talking to them as he lit a cigar.

Joe #1 got his keyring out of his pocket and walked around the van to the drivers' side. He started it up and Jordan flattened herself against the ground under it. The van pulled forward. As soon as it was clear of Jordan and the hatch, Jordan opened the hatch. She saw a metal ladder inside it and she climbed in and shut the hatch behind her. Once in the hatch, she saw a lever for locking it, which she slid across and banged into place.

Joe #1 pulled at the handle on the outside of the door, but it wouldn't budge.

The ladder was in a tube not much wider than Jordan's shoulders. She could look down between herself and the ladder and see that it seemed to go down quite a way, but she couldn't see what was at the bottom. Just darkness. She started down before realizing that the lit cigarette in such a small space wasn't a great idea. She pressed it out against the wall of the tube and dropped it. When it hit the ground, she could see the faintest red glow from a still-burning ember and she judged that the ground was two stories down.

She knew that she was going to the same place that the Joes would have brought her if she had cooperated. But, she had no choice at this point. She climbed down slowly. The ladder was coming loose from the wall of the tube in places and the whole thing was rusty and filled with spider webs. As she got closer to the bottom of the tube, she heard voices, but couldn't make out what they were saying.

Just as Jordan reached the bottom, a door opened on the side of the tube next to her and light came in. Four white-gloved hands attached to polka-dotted sleeves grabbed her legs and yanked Jordan from the ladder and through the door.

Smooth jazz played through the ancient ceiling speakers. The clowns who pulled her off the ladder circled around her while she lay on the floor. They seemed to be waiting for something or someone, and they were just guarding their catch to make sure she didn't get away.

Someone slid a pair of handcuffs through the door and one of the clowns grabbed them. One of the clowns grabbed Jordan under her arms and picked her up while the other handcuffed her.

Jordan was in an office with a single desk, beige cubical walls, a four-drawer file cabinet, a typewriter, and a window facing towards an empty waiting room.

"We don't have time for any more tricks, Plucky."

"The more you misbehave, the longer your sentence."

"Ah fuck. This girl isn't worth our trouble. Let's just get her into a cell."

One of the clowns pressed a button on the wall near the door and it buzzed as the door unlocked. They carried Jordan through the door.

She was in a square room with mostly empty cells lining the walls. One cell held four people, including Mike. They carried her to the cell just to the left of Mike's and threw her in, closing the door behind her.

There was a metal door in the wall between Jordan's cell and the cell that held the other four prisoners. There was a plexiglass window near the top of the door and she could see through it to the other cell. The door locked on her side like a room-to-room door in a motel.

The jail had a dirt floor, and smelled of mold. Everyone in Mike's cell was wearing identical clown outfits—orange with polka dots. One clown, in particular, stood out. He was an elderly dwarf. The sleeves and legs of his baggy uniform were rolled and pinned to fit his body. He was walking around the cell and mumbling to himself.

Mike came to the room-to-room door after the guards left and pressed his face against it to whisper.

"Are you ok?"

"What do you think, numbskull? Oh yeah, this is exactly how I wanted to spend my Saturday. Great. Thanks a lot."

"They let you keep your own clothes, at least."

"Ya. I must be more trouble than most prisoners. Or maybe they ran out of costumes. Either way, I'd almost prefer to have one of those get ups. I've been puking in this for three days now, and it's pretty ripe."

Jordan looked down at her clothes, which she'd selected for a night at the pub two nights ago, but also for practicality and comfort because she knew she'd be waking up who knows where and with who knows who. She had on leather boots, her black jeans with pockets (they were skinny men's jeans, but they were the best she'd found), a white t-shirt with some kanji characters on it that read (she'd been told) "Fuck you. No, I'm not Japanese," her jean jacket, and her lucky locket on a chain around her neck, containing a picture of her mother.

Her purse was in Mike's car at a gas station somewhere, along with most of her money. She was smart enough to put a few hundreds in the inside zipper pocket of her jacket.

Jordan retrieved Monty's clown diet notebook and journal from her bra and handed it to Mike.

"Here, I found this," she said. "It might be useful in some way."

Mike read the cover and then turned over the notebook in his hands as if he'd never seen a notebook before and wasn't sure how to open it. He flipped through it until he got to the last page that had writing on it. He flipped backwards from that spot to the start of the last entry.

October 5

Breakfast:Cheetos, coffee

Lunch:Cheetos, Pepsi

Dinner:

gas station hot dogs (2), slurpee

Being on the road fucking sucks. It's not like it used to be. The clown court used to pay for rooms and food, but not anymore. My diet always goes to hell on the road. I'm not even recording all the snacks anymore, because it's just too much work. He may not be good for much else, but Bonko sure knows how to pack snacks. He's got Twinkies, Circus Peanuts (I still hate those things), Fruit Rollups, jerky, and the aforementioned Cheetos. Lots of Cheetos. I'm eating mostly Cheetos—I forgot how much I like them.

Anyway, we drove down I-94 yesterday to intersect with the Detroit clowns. I can't stand those guys. They bring better food than we do, though, so I can't knock that.

Our timing was perfect. It turned out that the fugitive had been seen outside of Chicago and they figured he was only a couple hours ahead of them. The plan was to keep driving as fast as they could and take shifts to catch up with him when he took a break. They mentioned that he had someone with him too and it looked like a girl. Did he kidnap someone? I wouldn't put it past him, from what I've heard about this guy . . .

Anyway, we ended up being ahead of the Detroit clowns when we got down to the 80 and we're in "hot pursuit" now. As missions go, this one has been pretty easy so far, and let's hope it ends quickly and we can catch this guy and get him back to Hawthorne.

That was the end of the last entry. Mike flipped through a few more of the pages but didn't stop long enough to read anything.

"So, anything useful?" asked Jordan.

"Well, I know that these clowns are malnourished, but that's nothing new and they're used to it. I also know where we are, exactly."

Jordan looked down at her hands at the mention of location. She was glad Mike knew, because she hated not knowing.

"Where?"

"He says Hawthorne in the book. That makes sense. It's a neighborhood in north Minneapolis. Fun fact: they named it after Nathaniel Hawthorne. It's a pretty beat-up place now, but it was a hot spot for circus people to move to fifty or sixty years ago, so it makes sense that they chose it for the clown jail."

CHAPTER 66

In which breakfast is served

Jordan was exhausted. It was 4:00 A.M., and the only sleep she'd gotten since leaving her boyfriend in Chicago was when she was blacked out in Mike's car. She laid down on the cot on the opposite side of the cell from the door to Mike's. She'd be able to think up a plan to somehow get out of this mess tomorrow. But, she had to sleep. Food would be nice too.

The clowns that Mike shared his cell with were all asleep. The little one had a strange snore. It started as a high-pitch squeal and ended as a little grumble. Jordan had never heard anything like it before—and she'd heard a lot of snorers in her time. It was like "eeeee-ooo-um-ugg eeeee-ooo-um-ugg." This little guy is going to drive me insane, she thought.

Jordan was wishing she had stayed with Aaron. He was a dope, it's true, and his friends weren't any better, and he'll never leave Chicago—but he was nice, and he gave her space and didn't ask a lot of questions. He wouldn't have ended up in clown jail, she thought.

What Jordan wanted more than anything—well, besides to be out of clown jail, a cheeseburger, a good night's sleep on a bed, to talk to her mother again, and a peach pie—what she wanted less than any of these things but more than anything else was to have enough light and a Sharpie and a pencil and a notebook, so she could make a real plan and figure out what the hell to do next and how.

She went over some facts about the day in her head. They were in north Minneapolis, underneath some sort of party supply rental company warehouse. Mike wasn't making shit up when he said he was being chased by clowns. What the fuck did this guy do? How can he be asleep on this cot, with all this noise, and with the smell? Jordan resolved to do some sort of background check on future targets before getting into their cars. Apparently, her instincts weren't as good as she thought they were.

Jordan suspected that in a day or two, Aaron would start wondering whether she was ok. He may contact the police. They may start looking for her and even put out a bulletin. Minneapolis isn't all that far from Chicago—not as far as she usually goes, anyway. It's possible that someone might have seen her somewhere who might see a flyer at the post office and tell the police. Maybe the bartender at the Big Boy? It was likely that Mike's car would get towed from the gas station. Would someone at the roadside diner identify her and link her with the car? Would the police find her purse under the front seat? Would they wonder why she was carrying so much cash? Aaron would tell them that was his money. Or, would he? She was supposed to have invested it for him with her brother-in-law. Would Aaron suspect at that point that he'd been conned? The investigation could turn at that point from a missing persons case to a criminal case. Jordan needed to get out, so she could set things straight and organize her life again. What if the police somehow tracked her to this warehouse and to clown jail? That seemed unlikely. But, that would be her ideal situation. She'd be out of here, the clowns would be shut down, she'd have the perfect (extremely odd, but perfect) alibi for why she disappeared. And, she could claim that the money was demanded by them and there was nothing she could do. She didn't know why they didn't take the money. Maybe because they're clowns, that's why. How could the police track her to this spot? No one has seen her since the Big Boy, except for the guys in the warehouse, and they'd be happy if she were dead and they had no idea what was going on beneath them. Didn't they ever get suspicious? Did anyone ever suspect that the clowns were this creepy? The more Jordan thought about it, the more she realized that they had the perfect cover for committing any crime they wanted. They were clowns! "Hey, we're just clowns! We love the kids! We're all about fun!" But, they were the worst criminals she had ever heard of. They weren't interested in money and they didn't seem to have any other demands that she could figure out.

Her mother once told her to think hard about what someone wanted but that they weren't telling you.

"If you want to know how to make someone happy, or how to avoid a bad situation before it becomes bad, or how to get what you want, you need to figure out what other people aren't saying."

Jordan thought it was rather cryptic advice at the time, but she thought about it a lot. She assumed that her mother was talking about sex, because it was the closest thing that her parents ever gave her to a birds and bees talk.

Jordan did her best to follow this advice, and she found that she was able to seduce anyone she wanted by just anticipating what they weren't saying. In high school, she got a bad reputation among the other girls because she wouldn't play hard to get. If she wanted something and a boy wanted something, what more was there to discuss? The same went for breakups—if the boy was losing interest or she was, she called it off. She didn't suffer broken hearts. The boys may have, but they'd have to learn that it was pointless and that they got what they wanted but didn't know it yet.

As she got older, Jordan figured out that her mom's advice applied elsewhere. Getting an apartment in downtown Chicago wasn't hard if you knew what the landlord wanted and could give that to him. She told him she had a job with a software firm, that she was engaged to be married, and she was sure this would be the hippest corner in the loop in a few years and she couldn't wait to be at the center of it.

She may have gone a little bit beyond believability in making herself sound perfect, but she'd never gotten an apartment before and no one was going to rent to a recent high school graduate with a part time job, no credit, and parents who wouldn't help her.

Jordan said she'd bring by the proof of income after she gets her first paycheck, but did he want to talk with her new boss to make sure that she's telling the truth. The landlord didn't want her to think he thought she was a liar. He said that wouldn't be necessary. His building was a little run down, he knew, but if it was so close to her job where she says she'll spend most of her time—he heard that about these software jobs—then, ya, it makes sense that this is the perfect place for her. He asked when they could move in and Jordan asked if tomorrow would be too soon. She understood that this wouldn't give him time to get it cleaned, but she would take care of that. She loves cleaning, after all. Now the landlord was almost as excited as Jordan and he couldn't even wait to give her the keys until she finished writing the check for the deposit and first month.

The clowns weren't easy to figure out at all. Mike believed they wanted power. Jordan was starting to think that what they wanted most of all was respect. Maybe respect was the way to get on their good side and get out of this mess.

Jordan looked around her cell. The walls were made of cinderblocks and looked as if they had been clawed on for years by a wild animal. The paint was old and peeling away. The front of the cell was metal bars like the jails you see in old westerns. She could see through the plexiglass on the top of the door between her cell and Mike's, and she could hear everything that went on in Mike's cell because the wall didn't go all the way to the ceiling.

In her cell were a toilet, a large plastic utility sink, a cot with a thin pillow and a scratchy orange wool blanket, a dim lightbulb hanging from the ceiling, and a wooden chair that was painted bright colors—like the kind that might be hanging on the wall in a Mexican restaurant.

Jordan had had one previous jail experience—just that one night in county—and it was nothing like this. The clowns clearly knew nothing about running a jail. For one—the place was filthy. The county jail, and every other jail she'd ever heard of, smelled like bleach. Disease is a real concern when you keep unhappy criminals in close proximity. Proper ventilation, cleaning, nutrition, exercise, and sleep are parts of what keeps the place from turning into a warzone and are just as important as the locks on the cells.

By the looks of this place, it had been some kind of underground holding area for large animals at one point. Maybe it was the county animal control, or maybe it was the basement of a research lab for hair products. It clearly wasn't built to hold humans.

With just the dim light of her single bulb, it was difficult for Jordan to analyze the whole situation, but the locks on the cages confirmed it all for her. They were standard cheap household door locks—lions and bears wouldn't be able to open them, but a human with a little knowledge about lock picking would have no problem. Jordan didn't have any knowledge of lock picking, but from what she had picked up in her reading and obsessive watching of heist movies, this one should be a snap. She just hoped that someone else in here knew how to pick it.

Jordan sat on the chair to wait for morning and she fell asleep.

In the morning, a clown walked past her cell and the cell next door and banged a metal spoon on the bars while yelling, "Wake up time! Wake up time you scumbags!"

The courtyard outside the cages was lit up with four florescent light fixtures. Another clown was pushing a food cart into the room. The cart had three metal dishes warmed from below by Sterno cans. The clown pushing the cart stopped it between the two occupied cells and removed the covers from the food trays.

It looked like the remnants from the complimentary breakfast at the airport hotel. The first dish was half full (the back half) with a thick mass of scrambled eggs. The second dish held baby potatoes, cut into quarters, with rosemary—over-cooked of course. The third tray held gray pork sausages, about the size of Jordan's middle finger.

One of the clowns picked up a large metal spoon and dipped it into the scrambled eggs and came out with a large spoonful of steaming egg, which he took a bite from.

"Breakfast time! Ye should all consider yerselves lucky. We didn' always 'ave fancy cuisine like this in here!"

Both clowns cackled and then stopped at the same time.

The jail was quiet, and Jordan could hear heavy breathing from the little person in the cell next door. It sounded like an old dog with a cold.

The breakfast clown spooned eggs, potatoes, and three sausages onto a plate, opened a door in the bars on Jordan's cell and put the dish through. Jordan grabbed it and went to the back of her cell. She turned her chair to face the wall and sat on it to eat.

Behind her, the clowns were feeding the other prisoners. Mike spoke up and demanded to speak to a lawyer. This made the clowns laugh again. Mike also demanded that they put him in touch with his sister. The clowns found this hilarious too.

Jordan finished eating before the other prisoners, and she brought her plate to the front of her cell.

"Excuse me, sirs. Will you be so kind as to take my plate?"

The two clowns were sitting on folding chairs nearby and smoking. One of them grumbled and put down his cigarette and walked to Jordan's cell. He opened the door a crack and took her plate and then slammed the cell door shut and locked it.

"Listen, guys—I know that this isn't the number one thing you'd like to be doing today," Jordan said to both clowns, in the nicest voice she could muster. "But, I can make it much more pleasant for you if I didn't smell so bad. Can I get a bar of soap in here and a towel, please?"

The clowns looked to each other to decide. After a moment, the guard clown said, "Well, since you said please, we'll consider it." An hour later the guard clown returned with a clean towel and a bar of soap and he handed them to Jordan though the bars.

Jordan spent the next two hours removing her clothes one piece at a time and using the bar of soap and the sink to wash herself and her clothing, which she then wrung out as best she could and put back on. She was wearing damp clothes, but she felt like a human again and could think.

She wrapped the bar of soap in a paper towel and put it on the side of the sink.

"Excuse me," she said to the guard who had been watching her wash herself and her clothes, "can I get a toilet brush and some Pine-Sol?"

CHAPTER 67

The tale of Lucky the guard clown

The guard clown seemed pleased that Jordan was talking to him like a person, and he was pleased that someone in the clown jail was doing something about the smell. To prisoners, he was known as "guard clown," but to the other clowns, he was known as Lucky. He was lucky at one point, he guessed.

Lucky was an alcoholic retired lawyer. It wasn't his idea to retire at 54, but when he missed too many court appearances, told the judge to fuck off, and mooned the jury, the law firm's partners "strongly recommended" that he retire.

Lucky hated the corporate speak lack of accountability that "strongly recommending" represented. Lucky hated being a lawyer. He hated the games and fine lines that lawyers had to walk—between telling a judge or jury that "the following section deserves further inspection" and screaming at them "listen up you dumb fucks!"

After the senior partners told him they "strongly recommended he retire," Lucky did what any alcoholic lawyer with a chip on his shoulder would do.

The problem with torching a law firm is that someone is almost always there. The junior partners were in their offices more often than they were home, and they weren't the types to go along with a drunken revenge torching of the office.

The law firm bosses gave Lucky (his real name was William McThurdle) a day to decide whether he would quit or get fired. Why the hell did they give him a day? This seemed like professional malfeasance or willful malpractice or malbrain-thinkythinky or just a plain fuck-up, which should be enough to convince the jury that William "Lucky" McThurdle was innocent of all charges for the actions which he was about to undertake. It's not his fault he torched the place—they fucked up by letting him back in!

Lucky figured that 3:00 A.M. was as good a time as any to do it. The bars were closed, the junior partners and interns were gone or asleep, and the security guard at 1 Lawyerville Road wouldn't bat an eye at a lawyer deciding to sleep in his office after a marathon happy hour rather than risking another DUI.

Lucky stumbled past the security guard carrying a full gas can. The security guard waved and said "you take care now, Mr. McThurdle"— he was busy watching Die Hard.

Lucky took the elevator to the penthouse, used his keycard to enter, uncapped the gas can, and held it at his side, tilted just enough to pour a constant stream of gasoline as he walked. Lucky inspected the copy room, he checked out the break room, he walked by the (locked) boss' office, he circled the conference room a couple times, and he paced his own office and took the picture of his kids from his desk and put it in his coat pocket. As the gas can was getting down to the last cup, he drizzled his way back to the receptionist's desk and drew a straight line from the curved glass brick wall to the opaque white glass double doors with the law firm's initials on them. He tossed the gas can back into the office as he stepped out, then he found his Zippo along with a wad of singles and change in his pocket. The lighter burned steady and slow—he could always count on his zippo and he didn't want to let it go. He fished out some of the dollar bills from his pocket and lit them, then snapped the lighter closed and put it back in his pocket.

Lucky dropped the flaming dollars onto the carpet and the flames grew as they hit the trail of gasoline. He figured that ought to be enough, and he pressed the elevator button. The elevator was still there, and he didn't have to wait. He got in and rode it to the ground floor. The guard nodded as he exited.

What he didn't know is that the flame never made it under the frosted double doors and into the lobby. The hallway burned up a little, but the carpet was flame resistant and the fire went out after the gasoline was spent.

A couple hours later, Jenny from HR sent an email addressed to All Staff.

"Attention: It is apparent that someone broke into the office last night and attempted to cause a fire, or else there was some other gross maladjustment to the building's systems. I cannot be sure of the exact nature and cause of the odor, but it does resemble gasoline and fire. I notified the fire department and they are presently investigating. I strongly advise all staff to work from home or a suitable off-site location today until the situation can be appropriately and satisfactorily resolved."

Lucky knew it was just a matter of time until the police showed up at his door, so he threw his bowling trophies into a duffel bag and walked out. The kids lived with their mom. They'd be fine. He'd miss them, of course. But he was a fugitive from corporate life now. He drove as far as he could from New York, then left his car on the side of the road near a bus station in upstate New York and bought a Greyhound ticket to Minneapolis.

CHAPTER 68

The Song of the Breakfast Clown

I skiddled my poop through all seven seas
I sailed on ol' Ahab's ship
I've seen the white whale and now here's me tale
tis a rare derriere that I've kicked!

Me papa he was a sailor
Me mother she was one too
Me aunts and me uncles, from helles to dunkles
We eat only fish guttings stew.

But there was a young miss, who became me old wife
She toiled and troubled with landlubber life
T'wasn't hooks in me sleeves or wood in me pants
which saved this poor clown from the hempen jig dance

They say the way to a sailor's heart
taint with lovin' or leather or lace
but a hot cup o' coffee, and pancakes or wafflee
served by a friendly lass face

I docked me boat one wet April morn
in a port city whose name I forget
I buckled the hatches and heave-hoed my catches
to see what alls I could get

The fish monger man was a burly brusk rogue
a more churlish chap never has been
he offered me seven when he knew it was eight
and now with the fishes he swims

I sloshed me old bones and me deck stomper boots
into a little cafe by the pier
and I when I saw her I says maybe she would be me lady
then she grabs me by the ear

I spent near a moon in her cellar
'twas dank and dungeonous too
when the coast was all clear, she poured me a beer
and I shanghai'd myself for that brew

She brought me to ol Minnesota
where her mama and pappy resides
I'm a sea skipper snake in the land o the lakes
now I gets no salt waters and tides

CHAPTER 69

In which Lucky and Skipper are just happy to have someone to talk to

"But, what happened?" asked Jordan. "Why are you working in a secret clown jail?"

The breakfast clown and the guard clown both took drags of their cigarettes. They seemed to Jordan to be like an old married couple who both thought at the same time, ate and smoked at the same pace, and finished each other's sentences. Skipper, the old sailor, let Lucky do most of the talking. He interjected every once in a while with a grunt or to add a detail.

"We were both new in town," started Lucky, "In those days, it was even harder than now to meet new people and to find your tribe. You find yourself going to places you'd never go to back home—like pancake breakfasts and strawberry festivals. Free or cheap food, bingo, entertainment, other people. I tell ya—when you're broke and hiding, having a few good friends comes in mighty handy."

"Arr. The Oddfellers looked mighty odd, but they were good in a pinch."

"Arr indeed," said Lucky, "So, we started running into each other at these breakfasts and at the A.A. meetings and at bingo. Pretty soon, we discovered each other's situations. Me—escaped from trying to blow up my law firm, and him—" Lucky pointed his thumb at Skipper.

"A barnacle-covered scallywag with a liver full of bilge water and a list of offenses longer than the Nile."

"This guy," said Lucky, "This is why I love him. He's so colorful."

"Shut yer pie hole, yer makin' me blush."

"Anyway, the point is: we couldn't be more different, but we were both doing the same thing—laying low. The Oddfellows Club chairman took notice of us and how many pancakes we ate, and we started to become known and trusted in the neighborhood. That's when we got the invitation."

"'Ahoy,' it says. Came in a fancy enverlope. I never seen such a fancy enverlope before. 'Come to the Clowns Anonermis circus buffet in the basement of the V.F.Doublyer.'"

"I never even knew the hall had a basement, did you?"

"Nope."

"So, we both got these invitations. Thick paper. With wax seals. And we follow the directions and use the password to get into the basement. And, well, you're a clown, right? So, you know how it works. And we go in and everyone's dressed up and they welcome us and it turns out that it's a party for us!"

"Real nice un too."

"They threw us a 'welcome to town' party. After that, we started getting invitations to more official clown events. And, after a few of these, they ask if you want to be a clown. You get benefits, food, great parties, what's not to love right?"

"Arr."

"And so we join up at the same time and they have the induction ceremony. This was, what, June '98?"

"Arr."

"We learned to clown and we went on the road with the circus. Ah, the memories! Ah, those days! But, little did we know, there were some F.B.I. informants who had infiltrated the group and after a time, me and Skipper are in hot water again. We're getting subpoenaed and threatened. The head clown offered us a way out. Work in clown jail and it'll be like you don't exist. So, what are we gonna do? We say sure and here we are, what is it now? Decades later?"

"Arr."

"It's not so bad, most of the time."

"Now that we got the vittles figur'd out."

"Ya, the food here was atrocious when we first arrived. They fed the prisoners actual real grout—like ceramic tile grout! What they fed the staff wasn't much better. I had a buddy who worked at the business traveler hotel up the street, though, and we cut a deal to handle their leftovers. That was the first order of business, right Skipper?"

"Arr. Ya can't skiddle if ya ain't got yer viddles, says I!"

"I'm still not sure what he means by that," said Lucky, "Did you enjoy the breakfast?"

"I'm not enjoying much about this experience, I have to tell you," said Jordan, "but the breakfast has been the most pleasant part of it so far."

"Arr. Ya seems like a nice lass. What are ya in for, if'n ya don't mind my askin'?"

"No, I don't mind at all. That's just the thing. I don't know. I guess because I was with that guy. But, I only met him yesterday and I don't even know what he did and why he's here."

"That guy," said Lucky, "that guy committed the worst offense you can commit against a clown. He made us look like fools."

"Isn't that the point of clowns?"

"No! Certainly not, and I would be careful about what I say further along those lines if I were you. You may end up incriminating yourself if the wrong clowns hear you talk like that.

"Clowns aren't fools. This was established long ago, when we first started writing down clown law in L'Art Du Clown in the 1940s. Article two of the clown code reads as follows:

'Let it hereby be established that, given our unique status, our specific expertise, our role as prime instigators of fun, and our history of persecution and mistreatment, that no clown shall be made a complete fool of against his will. Any person or entity that causes a clown or clownhood in total to be made a fool shall be in violation of the spirit and the letter of clown law and shall suffer accordingly with loss of both property and freedom.'

"The way I read this section," said Lucky, "is that if you do something that embarrasses a clown or makes him look stupid, you need to be locked up."

"Doesn't that seem a bit harsh?"

"Consider the history. For thousands of years, or whatever, clowns were court jesters. They sat by the king's side and many of them acquired great wealth. The court jester was a person of great power—who else could make the king laugh or had the opportunity to sway the leader's opinion through humor? No one. Jesters were the root of the modern free press. They could speak truth to power and not risk beheading.

Years later, clowns in France were seen as a threat to the Nazis, who banned clowning because they were afraid of ridicule. This shows just how evil the Nazis were—even the most hideous and heartless leaders prior to Hitler acknowledged the unique position of the clown. Nazis can't survive humor.

Since the war, and because of L'Art Du Clown, we've restored our pride and our culture and our place in the world. When Mike, as the manager of one of the premier circuses in the U.S., staged an illegal drunken midget rebellion—against the wishes of his senior clown, and in spite of all the warning signs—he not only put the Great Western Circus of the Americas out of business, he also embarrassed and made a fool of clownkind. He meddled with things he knew nothing about. He stuck his nose into traditions and gave us all the finger because he thought he could improve upon the circus by upsetting the balance between clowns and dwarfs. When he pulled his little people stunt, some say it was because he was in love with a midget and he was angry with his sister. Speaking as a lawyer, or former lawyer, it's when you're feeling love or anger that you're least likely to make good decisions. He screwed up big time. Did he think he was going to impress the midgets by ruining the circus? Did he think he was going to get back at his sister for whatever she did? Did he just feel like he didn't get enough attention because she was a Master Clown and he was a clown in name only? I wish they'd have a real trial, with witnesses and testimony, so that we could call everyone in here and get some answers. But, L'Art Du Clown is light on the details when it comes to how trials run, except to say that if it seems like someone has made a fool of clowns, that person is guilty and should be locked up. That's why he's here. I'm not real clear still why you'd be here, but I'm sure we'll find out eventually."

Skipper had been sitting and listening while packing his pipe. When Lucky finished talking, Skipper looked up at Jordan and winked. "Ahoy, but long as yer in here, we aim to have some fun with ya."

"Look guys, I don't want any trouble. I just want to get out. I promise if you let me out that you'll never see me or hear from me again. I won't say anything bad about clowns or go to the police or anything. So, I don't know what kind of sick and perverted "fun" you're talking about, but if you try anything, deal's off and I will get out of here on my own and I will go straight to the police and have this thing shut down."

"Aww. Relax, lassy. We just want to know if ya wants to play some tiddlywinks?"

"Tiddlywinks? What the fuck is that?"

"Ya know, tiddlywinks! Arr!"

Lucky opened a cell across the courtyard from Jordan's and brought out a folding card table and a third folding chair. He set up the chairs around the table. In the meantime, Skipper took a folded piece of black felt out of his large coat pocket and unfolded it onto the table. He pulled out a small leather bag and poured its contents onto the table. He dumped the contents of the ashtray onto the ground and wiped it out with a corner of his shirt before setting it in the center of the piece of felt.

"Have you ever played tiddlywinks?" asked Lucky.

"No . . . not really. You flip the little things, right?"

Lucky opened the door to Jordan's cell and invited her to have a seat on one of the folding chairs.

"Yes, that's right. You just flip the little things."

Lucky looked at Skipper and rolled his eyes.

"Seems you've got a lot to learn, little miss," said Lucky.

"Arr ye ready fer 'winks?" said Skipper, heaving his hook into the air above his head and winking aggressively in Jordan's direction.

"Yes. Please. I want to learn to play tiddlywinks," said Jordan.

"OK. This here is the 'squidger'," said Lucky.

Skipper and Lucky each held up pieces of plastic that were larger and thicker than the small multi-colored disks scattered on the piece of felt.

"Squidger? That's a strange name." said Jordan.

"Ahoy! The squidger it is and don't ya question it or you'll be walkin' the plank!"

"OK, ok! Got it. Squidger."

"The table here is the field. Those "little things" are the winks, and that there is the pot. The goal is to flick the most winks into the pot. We'll go around the table, and we'll all flip as many as we can until we miss. We're starting with a big pot, but once you get better at it, we'll switch to a shot glass, which is closer to regulation size."

"OK. I've got it so far. Go on."

"Go on? What the hell do you mean? That's it. That's the game. Go on. You think there's more?"

Lucky was getting fidgety and irritated.

"It's goddamn tiddlywinks! What do you want? You think it's gonna have lights and buzzers and balls and whirring sounds and a VCR? This ain't yer video arcade super-rama blamo blamo blamo bot with your 'joystick' and your 'tokens' and your prizes. You use the fucking squidger to flip the winks into the pot. You pot the most winks, you win. You don't pot the most winks, you lose. There's no consolation prize and there's no extra life. You got it? Do we have a tiddly or what?"

Skipper sat packing his pipe while Lucky was ranting.

"Yes, sir. We have a tiddly," said Jordan.

"Well, it's about damn time. Let's go. Since you're new here, you'll go last. Sorry, them's the rules."

CHAPTER 70

In which Mike and Jordan befriend the son of the famous Russian clown

After breakfast, Mike sat on the floor of the cell, against the back wall, wedged between an old dwarf and a hippie clown who smelled like elephant shit. He no longer had to wonder what rock bottom would feel like. After two days of being chased by the clowns, he'd been captured, and it was just as bad as he had feared—except for the food. That turned out to be tolerable.

This was the same jail that Peter Lundelhart had been kept in, and few improvements seemed to have been made to it. Mike was surprised that there were only five prisoners, though. Of course, they had to stuff us all into one cage, Mike thought. Fucking clowns.

The cage locks were as Lundelhart described—flimsy household doorknobs. It was a safe bet that the hatch was still in the receptionist's office, and that the elevator code panel could be smashed to bypass it.

Mike needed a drink—something to clear his head and help him to relax and figure out how to get out. Lundelhart had only mentioned the grout—nothing about what he drank while in jail. It may have been rubbing alcohol, which Mike would welcome at this point as a last binge and a certain escape.

If he was going to make it, he needed to think like Lundelhart. The first step would be to figure out who he shared a cell with and what kind of people they are.

Mike looked at each of his cellmates. The hippie clown had fallen asleep with his chin resting on the top of his gut. The old dwarf was carving small chips off a piece of wood with his thumbnail.

"I could use a drink," Mike said to the old dwarf.

The old dwarf leaned over and reached behind the toilet. "Is a little too early for me, but have at it, friend," he said with a Russian accent, while handing Mike a jar containing a urine-colored liquid. "My name is Victor. Victor Karandash."

"I'm Mike. Mike O'Malley."

Mike smiled and lifted the lid on the jar. It smelled sweet and musty, with an unmistakable note of ethanol.

"I call it Victor's Sucker Punch. I save ze jam and fruit cocktail and make it out of zat. Give me yours and I can up the production, da?"

Mike tasted the hooch. It wasn't bad. It was raw and unfiltered and reminded him of an English farmhouse hard cider, with extra farmhouse. He smiled at Victor and nodded approvingly.

"Nice job, Victor."

"Thank you, Mr. Mike."

"Karandash. There's a famous name. You're not related to THE Karandash, are you?"

"He vas father of me. Not zat he knew it."

"Wow. That's amazing. What was it like to have him as a father—I mean, he was the most famous Russian clown ever, right? He was a big deal."

"Huge. He vas more famous than any movie star or rock star today. Karandash vas the pride of Russia. He vas the people's artist. He performed to packed houses every night—for fifty years! Not only vas he best, he trained za generation zat came after him."

"Karandash was a stage name, though, right?"

"Oh yaaah. His real name vas Rumyantsev."

"And yours too, right?"

"Well, no. As I vas saying, Karandash traveled all over Soviet Union. He may have zousands of children for all I know. My mother vas single and she named me Victor Karandash ven she found out zat I'd be a little person too. It vas in honor of the great Karandash, but she vas also preparing me to succeed in vorld. And look at me now, huh?"

"Did you ever meet your dad?"

"Da. I did. When my son vas born, and ven it was clear zat he too vas going to be a little person, I wrote letter to Karandash and introduced myself. I said, 'My name is Victor Karandash. You don't know me, but I am your son. My mother, now deceased, told me about the humor and light in your eyes and your generosity. I trained as clown as boy and I've always striven to live up to your example. Now I have son, who is also little person, and who will also grow up being told stories about you. I intend to name him Andrew Karandash, and it is my dream zat he will someday meet grandfather of him.'

Month later, I receive letter back from Karandash. He said zat he vould be in our town zat fall and zat he vould like to visit me and grandson. He sent two tickets to circus in letter and said to show za letter to ticket taker.

Ticket taker vas his daughter—half-sister to me. To zink of it give me chills. I didn't dare introduce myself as her half-brother. I didn't know if she knew of her father's other children. I vas afraid and ashamed.

I held out letter to her, and my hand vas shaking. My other hand held onto my vife's hand and she held our son, Andy, in her other arm. Ven Karandash daughter read za letter, she smiled and kissed my cheeks and exclaimed 'Velcome, brother!' She zen kissed my vife and little Andy and led us to Karandash's tent. It vas greatest day. He vas so full of life. He vas sixty years old at za time, but he moved like twenty-year-old. He vas so full of joy. He told me how proud he vas zat I named son after him and zen he tell me: "But, good sir, if I may be so presumptive. Ve no longer live in old country. Soviet Union is not much longer. For za future of son may I suggest zat you give him name Americans will understand, and not name of an old and soon to be dead Russian.

'Vat do you suggest?' I asked.

'How about Andy Pencils?' he told me. 'Karandash' is Russian vord for pencil, you see.

'My vife, Lolly, and I loved name and from zat day on our son vas known as Andy Pencils.'

"You're Andy Pencils' father?"

"You know him?"

"Of course I do. Everyone knows Andy. I'm so pleased to meet you, sir."

If Victor was Andy Pencils' father, Victor must be at least 80 years old. That's unheard of for a dwarf.

"How long have you been in here," Mike asked.

"Nearly forty years. I'll tell ya, I've seen a lot of clowns come and go through here. I could tell you stories."

"Well, it seems like I've got time. I'd love to hear them."

"How do you know Andy? How is he doing?"

"The last time I saw Andy was about twenty years ago. I was managing the Great Western Circus, and we did a week in Ypsi. Andy was doing great at that time."

"But vat happened?"

"I don't know what Andy's up to today. At the time, he helped me put together the event that led to me being here with you now. He didn't know. I didn't know."

"Vat do you mean?"

"I've done a lot of thinking about what happened. I'm still not totally clear on how or why it happened like it did, and it's been a long time, but the short story is that I fucked up by sticking my nose where it didn't belong."

"Ah yes, za old 'Nasensteckinwoesnichthingehört'."

"Pardon?"

"Is German for putting your nose somewhere vere it doesn't belong or something to effect. My German is bit rusty, but I'll never forget zat vord."

"That's a good one," said Mike.

"Sorry, please go on. You were schticken za nasen."

"Yes . . . sticken the nasen, and so much more."

Mike took another sip of the Sucker Punch and continued.

"Looking back, I was the most insecure circus punk kid there ever was. My sister was a great clown. I looked up to her. I wanted to be her. But, I didn't want to put in the work, and I didn't have her 'Jee Nee Says Quey', as she would say.

Instead, I went to college. I got a degree in marketing—specifically entertainment and circus marketing. I learned everything there is to know about the modern circus, about Vegas circuses, about modernizing classic art forms, and about staging events for a television audience. I came back to the Great Western Circus, and they put me in charge of marketing. I was supposed to be the circus's savior. Well, it didn't quite work out that way."

"I'll bet you butted up against some pretty big butts vith your business school ideas, am I right?"

"Yes, but the problem wasn't the nay-sayers. The problem was me."

"Da, but what were they thinking putting a kid in zat position?"

"You can't blame them for trying. They tried everything else. We had lions to feed. Do you have any idea how expensive it is to feed lions?"

"I know how expensive it vas in 1950s Russia, that's for sure, and I'm lucky zey didn't eat me a couple times. It's amazing zat circus lasted as long as it did with all its expenses and risks."

"That's true, but the clowns blame me for putting the last nail in the coffin and for the clown recession."

"But, what was za act Andy helped with? I can't believe Andy vould go along with something zat would harm anyone or zat would make people lose jobs."

"I wanted to right the wrongs. I wanted to be the savior of the dwarfs. I thought I was going to come in with my genius idea that no one had ever had before and make the world appreciate the dwarfs again by holding a grand event that would catapult them back into their rightful positions as the leaders of the circus."

"And . . . za clowns weren't happy about zat at all," said Victor.

"Exactly. But, how could they be? I threw out the balance of power, the circus traditions, any shred of predictability, the unspoken and spoken rules of the circus that I didn't even know. I threw all of that out the window because I was in such a rush to make an impression and to fix everything."

"And so vat happened?" asked Victor.

"We had a party like you wouldn't believe. Hundreds of littles came from all over the Midwest. The place was packed. I hadn't taken the time to plan or establish a structure, or to lay the groundwork, or to prepare anyone for the event. I just had them show up, and what do you think happened?"

"FUBAR."

"Exactly. And guess who wasn't so happy about the resulting mess?"

"Zese guys?" said Victor, pointing his thumb towards the door.

"Exactly."

"And, Andy helped you organize zis event?" asked Victor.

"Yes. He never wanted to hurt anyone. He saw it like a family reunion. I don't think he even realized how badly the clowns would take it."

"How could he?" said Victor, "He never joined circus. He didn't want to be any part of zat, except in stands watching me. Did he ever mention me to you?"

"No. He didn't."

"Promise me zat if you ever get out of here zat you'll find Andy and tell him story of me. Tell him I didn't mean for it to be like zis. Tell him I love him, and zat I've always loved him."

Mike teared up as he watched Victor wipe his head with a filthy towel and hold back his own tears. His tiny wrinkled face distorted in a grimace of anguish and pleading.

"Yes. When I get out, I'll find him, and I'll tell him anything. What happened?"

CHAPTER 71

In which Victor Karandash tells his story

"You see, Mike," said Victor, "There are times in a man's life when he has to make a choice. There are times when a man says to himself, 'I can go this way, or I can go that way.'"

"These are truly the times that try men's souls. But, these are the things we must go through. The ups and the downs, the zigs and the zags, the ramparts red glare."

"Yes, true." Mike was buzzed and didn't mind all the dramatic build-up. But, he did notice that Victor's Russian accent had disappeared.

"Well, it's like this, Mikey. You don't mind if I call you Mikey, do you? You look like a Mikey to me."

"No, don't mind."

"It was a dark and stormy night, from sea to shining sea. I was three sheets to the wind, and ah you wanna know what I did, I'll tell ya."

Victor gestured for Mike to bring his ear closer, and so Mike did. "I shit in Master Clown Claude de Boom's soup." Victor slapped his knee and rolled onto his back laughing.

"What? I mean, what? You've been locked up for forty years for that?"

"Yes, that's the unfunny part of it, isn't it?"

"Indeed. How did it happen? Why? Where?"

"It was 1970. The circus revival was in full swing around here. I was touring with one of the big companies. Claude was too. He was a big deal, Mikey. You know who he is right?"

"Yes, of course. My sister studied with him."

"Ah, then you know. I take it your sister was deflowered by M. de Boom?"

"Well, no, she hadn't been flowered for a long time before she met him."

Victor rolled onto his back laughing again. When he recovered, he continued.

"So, this guy . . . he doesn't give a fuck, right? He uses his French accent and his position of power and his shriveled old pecker like they're Halloween candy. He's giving it out to everyone and the women line up at his door. So, long story short, he made it with my wife, and I took a shit in his soup."

"And you were put in here for that?"

"No. I wasn't locked up until years later. We had a good laugh at the time, M. Claude de Boom apologized for screwing my wife and said he couldn't help it because she's so beautiful. I apologized for shitting in his soup and said I couldn't help it. We were friends again and the show went on.

"But then, I don't know how many years later—do you remember that guy Peter Musselhead Funlefuck whatever his name? I tell ya, Mikey, getting old sucks."

"Lundelhart," said Mike. "Yes, I know of him and I've read his story."

"OK, so you know how he planned and executed a brave escape from this place and how he was the only person in the history of clown jail to ever escape and it only took him a matter of days to plan and execute his daring escape and how he was a hero?"

"Right. Wait, are you going to tell me that's not exactly how it happened?"

"Bingo."

"Once you get to a certain level in the clown hierarchy, you're expected to take a shift at running the prison. It's like an initiation, and it's how the clowns make sure that there's always someone competent running the show, without them having to pay anyone. Well, it was my turn when they brought Lundelhart in. This guy was a crier. All night long, he was sobbing and moaning. I'd stop in and the guard would beg me to just let him kill this Lundelhart because he couldn't take the moaning and the crying any longer. I said we couldn't kill him because word would get out and then we'd all be in trouble.

I had a better plan. We started leaving Lundelhart's cell unlocked. It took the dummy three weeks to figure it out. We'd drop hints too. We'd tell him—'Don't you wish you could just walk out of your cage, climb up that ladder in the hatch in the back of the receptionist's office, and be free?' He'd moan and cry, moan and cry, moan and cry. Finally, I did a magic trick to cheer him up, and at the end of the trick, I let a dove out of my sleeve and Lundelhart was so hungry he started grabbing for it and the door opened as he was reaching through the bars. I said, 'Oops!' and walked out of the room. Twenty minutes later, the jail was empty."

"So, you let everyone out, but you're in jail for shitting in Claude's soup? How does that work?"

"There's nothing in L'Art Du Clown about clown jail, so there are no laws governing what to do to someone who helps people escape from it. Curiously enough, there are laws about what to do with someone who shits in another clown's soup. I was tried and convicted for soup shitting and sentenced to life. The escape was a major embarrassment and they needed to put these cells to use again, so there was a time there where they were sentencing everyone to life. For the last decade or so, it's been just the three of us in here, until you and the lady came along, that is. I gotta say, it's good to have some new company, but I wish it weren't under these circumstances."

"But you must have tried to escape in all the years you've been in here, haven't you? What happened?"

"My roommates here aren't the brightest bulbs," said Victor, nodding towards the sleeping hippie clown, and the obese clown sitting on the toilet who Mike had failed to notice before. "The way out of here is to have one prisoner distract the guards while another jimmies the lock, goes through the lobby door, gets the code for the elevator from under the reception-ist's keyboard, and holds the elevator for the rest of us after we somehow incapacitate the guard. Easy peasy, right? Well, not for these guys. They've been trying to get their heads around it for years. We tried once, when we were all in separate cells. I was the distractor, they were supposed to get out of their cell, go through the lobby, and get the elevator. But, they bungled the lock pick and the guard heard and asked them what they were doing. They told the whole thing—about how I was distracting them, and how they were picking the lock so they could get the elevator, and how then we'd all be free. After that, they put us all in the same cage. The plan doesn't work so well if everyone's in the same cage."

"Ah, I can see that. It's more difficult to cause a distraction, right?"

"Exactly. And, even when there are people locked in who have more than half a brain, the plan won't work: first, because of the distraction element, and second, because we have to assume that after my pea brained friends blabbed the whole thing, they might have changed something. Like not having the elevator combination under the keyboard."

"I'm curious," said Mike, "how do you even know that the elevator code was under the keyboard in the first place?"

"Well, that's the easy part. The receptionist and I had a thing going on for a while. We'd have these conjugal visits, if you know what I mean. All that stopped when they put us in the same cell, of course."

"It's still the same receptionist?"

"Oh yeah! That's the best job in here. You don't have to deal with the smell much. You don't have to work much. You have your own office. It's a dream job for a lazy clown, and that's what Rebecca is. She's been in that job for twenty-some years now.

"Besides being a cry-baby, what was Peter Lundelhart like?" Mike still couldn't wrap his head around Lundelhart not being a brave adventurer, and he wanted some shred of greatness to hold onto to inspire him to persist.

"My memory is a little fuzzy, Mikey, but it's starting to come back to me now. Yes. Yes. We called him Dunderfart. He didn't like when we did that. We captured him while he was spying on a clown convention and picnic in Eden Prairie. He was in the bushes—I don't know why. Maybe he had some kind of fetish and was watching us go to the bathroom. Strange guy. Anyway, everyone was there—Master clowns, Master-Master clowns, Master-Elder Clowns—the whole gang. We held the elections of the board, reviewed the budget, that kind of thing. One of the Master Elder clowns went to the bushes to take a leak and nearly pissed all over Lundelhart, but he doesn't let on that he sees him. Lundelhart was squatting and holding up a couple branches like it camouflaged him. The way this Elder Master Clown tells it, it was all he could do to keep from laughing."

"So, he wasn't deep in the forest surviving on bugs and berries?"

"Not even close. He was swiping hotdogs when he thought we weren't looking and peeking in the bathroom window at the lady clowns sitting on the shitter."

Victor stood up and put his hands above his head and stretched from side to side in a calisthenics type of movement. "You gotta stay active in here, Mikey, it's the only way to keep from going crazy. I do some of this." He stretched to the right twice, then to the left twice, then to the right twice. "And I do some of this." He ran in place for a few seconds, then put his hands on his knees and wheezed for a few seconds.

"I've never been much of one for exercise," said Mike.

"Well, I commend it to you," said Victor.

"It seems to be keeping you youthful, so I'll consider it. So . . . that's odd about Lundelhart. How did you capture him?"

"Ah yes. We planned it out that four of the biggest clowns would gather near the bushes where Lundelhart was hiding and they'd talk about basketball or something. When one of them said the word "catapult" they'd all rush Lundelhart at the same time and carry him to the garage, where there was a large animal cage that was sometimes used for moving donkeys and ponies to birthday parties and whatnot. It worked like a charm, and pretty soon we were all gathered around the cage drinking beers and watching Lundelhart in his cage. Giving him a taste of his own medicine."

"So, it was all made up?" Mike still couldn't get used to the idea of his hero being a fraud.

"All of it. One hundred percent—except that we did give him the same sort of trial that you got, and we did bring him here. When we got him here, you wouldn't believe the trinkets and nonsense that we found in his backpack. He had this cheap plastic pocket knife—the blade was plastic! He had at least six bottles of vitamins with his face on them. He had a magnifying glass, a compass, two cups with a few feet of string between them, and binoculars. All of it was cheap plastic like you used to get from a cereal box. So, anyway, we brought him in and we gave him the clown suit, and we found a cell to squeeze him into. I tell ya, Mikey, the laws were enforced back in the 8os. No one took any shit and even the slightest harassment of a member of the clown union would land someone in clown jail for way too long. These days, they don't have the funding or the interest in keeping people for lesser crimes."

"But they do still have those crimes, right? Do they enforce the lesser crimes at all?"

"When necessary. But, it's much more likely that you'll receive some other form of punishment on a first offense."

"Like what?"

"Oh, like forced labor for a short time. Maybe they'll shame you into helping to clean up after the party where you heckled the clown. Or, maybe they'll get you to carry the equipment back to the truck under threat of them calling the cops—which they'd never do, by the way."

"It all seems pretty benign."

"Except for clown jail, right?"

"Right."

"If there's one thing that clowns have learned in the last forty years or so, it's how to use punishments that are appropriate to the crime without inconveniencing themselves too much."

CHAPTER 72

In which Jordan demonstrates her skill with Tiddlywinks

Jordan was starting to get the hang of tiddlywinks.

"Arr, so yous say yous never played the tiddlywinks, eh?"

"No sir, never in my life have I ever played the tiddlywinks."

"I think ya be pullin' my stump, lass. Yer as good with the winks as I've seen 'em."

"Yes, indeed. A real goddamn natural," said Lucky.

"Awesome. So, what do you say I teach you everything I know about tiddlywinks and you let me out of here?" said Jordan.

"Now, that's the one thing we can't do. You see that little guy over there? That's exactly how he ended up in here forty goddamn years ago."

Jordan knew this already because she'd been listening to Victor's story while she was talking and playing tiddlywinks with Lucky and Skipper. She had a bad habit of always wanting to know what everyone around her was talking about.

"What? He used to be a guard?"

"Nah, m'lady, he used to be the boss here for a spell. And, he didn't just help people escape, he let 'em all go. Looked the other way while they waltzed out the door. Waltzing waltzing waltzing Matilda!"

"Damn sonofabitch is a little senile now. He's ninety damn years old. He thinks they locked him up for shitting in a guy's soup. No, I'm pretty sure it was for letting all the prisoners go," said Lucky, "I'll tell ya. That's some big brass balls for such a small guy."

"Who's the boss of the prison now?" asked Jordan.

"Har! Har! Har! Don't cha be thinking yer getting outta here like that! The boss they got here now be the meanest god-damn landlubber ever lubbed the land!"

"Besides, back then this place was packed. They had four to a cell in every cell. It must have been the smelliest place on earth. If they hadn't let all the prisoners out the neighbors would have sent the health inspectors or some damn shit down to investigate sooner or later. It was sort of a blessing actually!"

Jordan concentrated hard on the game. She rubbed the edge of the squidger. If only it was sharp and she were more of a badass like Michelle Yeoh, she could use it to slice both of their necks and run for the exit.

"Arr ya gonna shoot or are ya gonna just fiddle with the squidger?" said Skipper.

"Ah, yes. Sorry."

Jordan made quick work of the five remaining winks, shooting them one by one into the pot. When she was done, she leaned over the table with her palms flat on the felt and her arms straight and looked from Skipper to Lucky.

"Play again?"

Lucky laughed and threw back his head. His orange wig almost came off as he did so.

"Well I'll be damned. That was the finest winking I've ever seen. Either you're a hustler, or they ought to call you 'Lucky'!"

"Arr. Maybe later, Lass. You'll be seein' an awful lot of us in the next years!"

Skipper dumped the winks from the ashtray into his leather pouch, then folded up the felt. He put the felt and the bag of winks back into his coat pocket. Lucky folded up the table and chairs and then put them back into the cell. Now that Jordan was on the outside of the cells, she could see that the cell next to hers was being used as a storage closet. It held the folding table, folding chairs, a popcorn cart, helium tanks, and several rolling clothing racks with clown costumes hanging from them. Wigs, shirts, pants, and suspenders hung from the racks, while shoes were organized along the far wall of the cell from smallest to largest.

Once Lucky and Skipper had finished putting away the tiddlywinks table, Lucky put his hands on his hips and exhaled while looking at Jordan.

"Now, we just have one more thing to put away. I almost forgot!" He laughed as he grabbed Jordan by the wrist and pulled her towards her cell. Jordan didn't resist.

"That's right. Just don't cause any trouble for us and your stay will be as pleasant as can be," said Lucky.

"Arr. You sure got the touch with the winks!"

"Thanks, Skipper," said Jordan as she walked into her cage, "I'm going to tiddle my winks right out of here before long, though. You'll see."

Skipper and Lucky both laughed.

"I'd watch what I be sayin' if I were you," said Skipper.

"Especially when the boss comes around," said Lucky.

"You never did tell me who the boss was," said Jordan. "What's his name? What makes him so bad?"

"His name," said Lucky, "is Schmid. He's a German. I don't think I need to say anything else."

"Arr. Besides, lady, you'll be gettin' to meet him here to-night. He's got a special treat planned for you and yer boyfriend over there! Har har har!"

"And don't go thinking you're special and you don't have to follow the rules just because we let you play a little tiddly-winks. As soon as the laundry truck comes back today, we're getting you into the uniform just like yer boyfriend over there!"

"Arr. Yer boyfriend!"

"Ya, that's your boyfriend."

Jordan raised her eyebrow. These clowns really wanted her to confirm or deny that Mike was her boyfriend. That seemed a little bit strange.

CHAPTER 73

In which Mr. Schmid visits the jail

The current boss of the clown jail was Heronimus Schmid, also known as Mr. Schmid. He was a German. He was also the former owner of the Great Western Circus of the Americas.

Lucky and Skipper warned Jordan about Schmid. When they left the jail after the tiddlywinks, Jordan talked to Mike through the door separating their cells and told him what she had found out.

"Hey Mike, how's it going in there, pal?"

"Fuckin' awesome. How are you holdin' up? I see you have some new friends."

"Strange guys. But, I've been thinking about what you told me about clowns and how they just want to be loved. I think that's our ticket out of here."

"You may be right," said Mike.

"They said the boss of the jail is coming by tonight. Some guy named Schmid?"

"Holy shit. Did they say anything else about Schmid? His first name or anything?"

"His first name may be Mr. They said he's German."

"I can't fuckin' believe it."

"You know this guy?"

"Yes. He was my boss at the circus. I ruined his circus and probably wrecked his retirement too. I wouldn't be surprised if he hates me and has been planning his revenge for all these years. He must be . . . shit . . . he must be pretty damn old now."

"What do you think they mean by a special treat?"

"Huh?"

"They said Schmid is going to have a 'special treat' for us?"

"I have no idea. The last special treat I got from Schmid was a glass of whiskey and a cigar. I'm guessing this time's not going to be the same."

"Sorry I doubted you about the clowns."

"I don't blame you. It's some weird fuckin' bullshit."

"Sorry I got so drunk."

"That's your thing, isn't it?"

"Yeah, kinda. It usually gets me where I wanna go."

"Is this where you wanna go?"

"Shut up, you goddamn sonofabitch."

Jordan pounded her fist on the door. Mike pounded back.

Mike's cellmates had been watching and listening to the whole conversation. When Mike turned around, the hippie clown spoke.

"Looks like someone is in looooove."

Victor cackled and his whole tiny and old dwarf body shook like it was coming apart.

"Dudes. Shut the fuck up. Have you ever seen Schmid?"

"Have we ever seen Schmid?" said Victor. "Why yes. Only about every Tuesday night. 'Tuesday night fun,' he says. I'm sorry, Mikey. I don't know how you survived working for that guy."

"What do you mean? He was pretty OK when I worked for him. He kept to himself, but he shared his booze and taught me a few things about how to run a circus. Or, he tried to at least."

"Well. I don't know what happened to him, but that's not the Schmid we know."

"Nope. Not by a long shot," said the hippie clown.

The obese clown just sat on the toilet, with his pants on, and shook his head back and forth while making clicking noises with his mouth.

"What do they mean by a special treat?"

Victor scratched his head and appeared to be thinking.

"No idea. That's a new one. It must be pretty special."

"Are you going to tell me anything at all? I know Schmid. If there's any info you can give me that might help me deal with him or survive whatever this treat is or anything, please tell me."

"No, sorry Mikey. You're on your own with this one," said Victor.

For the next seven hours, Mike and Jordan sat on opposite sides of the door and communicated by tapping on the door in Morse code with their fingernails.

They talked about themselves. Mike told Jordan about his sister, Pauline, who was now retired and living in Sacramento with two children and a husband. He told her about his parents who still lived in Michigan and who never had anything to do with the circus and had never even been to the circus until Pauline started hanging around with clowns when she was a teenager.

Jordan told Mike about how she grew up trying to make money any way that she could. It wasn't that she needed money or that her family wasn't well-off, but she was obsessed with earning money. She sold newspapers and flowers on the street and had lemonade stands when she was little. When she got old enough to take the L by herself, she cleaned the kitchen of her aunt's bakery every night after school so that her aunt could go home and take care of her dogs and get some sleep. When she was old enough to have a job, she started working at an ice cream shop downtown and worked her way up to assistant manager. She'd bring home the ice cream that was going to be thrown out every night and she'd melt it and use it to make soap that she wrapped in plastic wrap and sold to her friends at school. "It only takes a little bit of lye to melt a body," she'd tell people when they asked about why she makes soap.

Mike and Jordan passed the hours like this; telling stories about their lives through dots and dashes tapped on the door.

When they heard noises in the receptionist area of the jail, Mike and Jordan knew that Mr. Schmid would be entering. The other clowns woke up too, and they waited for the inevitable opening of the jail door and the entrance of Schmid.

The door opened, and Lucky entered first. He looked around, as if he was doing a security sweep of the area. But, in an orange wig, red nose, giant shoes, and a white jumpsuit with multi-colored polka dots, he looked like the clown who used to prep the crowd for the official start of the circus.

After Lucky finished his sweep of the area, Mr. Schmid entered. He had a cane—that was new, thought Mike. He had more wrinkles, and was fatter and stooped over now too, but overall, he looked like Mike remembered him.

Mr. Schmid walked in a straight line to Mike's cell, with his eyes locked on Mike's as he neared. He had a slight smile on his face. He stood, sizing up the situation for a full minute before he spoke. When he spoke, Mr. Schmid had the same voice that Mike remembered from twenty years ago. His was a deep, Tennessee Williams New Orleans voice with the gravel of a five-cigar-a-day habit. His speech still held a trace of the curiosity and passion of the man who, at thirty, bought into the circus with every dime he could muster. But, his passion was tempered by the weariness of the man who had supported the circus through far more bad times than good and who had been betrayed and abandoned by Mike, the man he once thought of as a son.

"Well, if it ain't Wonder Boy himself. I've been waiting for a long time to see you again, Mikey. You never wrote. You never called. It wasn't like I was hard to find. I've been right here, Mike. You were damn hard to find. Damn hard. You didn't even tell your sister where you were living. You're not on the Internet. What if you won the Publisher's Clearinghouse Sweepstakes or some shit? What if they wanted to give you a Tony for that fuckin' midget festival you staged?"

"Ya, I know I kinda just disappeared," said Mike. "And I want to apologize for how things fell apart and for how I handled it—or didn't, I guess."

"You know, Mikey, it would have been a lot better if you had said that twenty years ago instead of pretending like everything was running according to plan and then going into hiding when it all turned to shit."

"That's not how I remember it, sir."

"Oh, really? Well, please. Tell me what it is that you remember, Mikey."

"The Festival of the Littles was poorly organized and a bit of a mess," said Mike, trying to put the best possible face on an event that he knew was a disaster. He'd hoped that Mr. Schmid wouldn't remember it being as bad as Mike had remembered.

"We had midgets puking on the crowd, Mikey," said Mr. Schmid. "That's just one of the unwritten rules of the circus, you know? It's one of those things that you just shouldn't have to say, because it should be common sense that you don't puke on the crowd you're trying to entertain."

"I know. But, the few shows we did after the Little Festival went well, right?"

Mr. Schmid shook his head and cut Mike off. "We had a packed house, yeah, but it was all rubberneckers hoping that we'd crash and burn again. That's not sustainable as a business model. You should know that."

Mike felt like it was twenty years ago and Mr. Schmid was mentoring him again—teaching him the value of the circus traditions, the significance of whiskey to the American circus traditions, and how to read an audience. Mike's brief day-dream reminiscence ended when Mr. Schmid swung his cane against the bars of Mike's cell and it made a clang like a gong. His voice raised to a yell, as if Mike were running away and Schmid needed to tell him one more thing—something so important he'd been practicing it in his head for the last twenty years, and he wanted to make damn sure that the message got through for this, his one chance to say it to Mike's face.

"And then you just up and left when the rubberneckers stopped coming. Do you even know what we went through after that? Did you think that was the end? Did you think that you could just leave us all high and dry, wipe your hands, put on your top hat and sail off to the Keys for the winter?"

"I guess I was ashamed and embarrassed," said Mike.

Mr. Schmid lowered his voice. "Do you think that no one else is ever ashamed and embarrassed? Do you think that we expected you to be perfect? Do you think that we thought that a kid straight out of college was the solution to all our problems and that we were counting on your dumb ass? You think you're that important?"

"But you have been hunting me for twenty years?"

"No, kid. We weren't fucking hunting you. You made that shit up. We tried to contact you for a while so we could give you your final paycheck, and we could have used your help with making calls and selling off the assets. The clowns wanted to come after you, but Lucy called them off. 'He'll come back when he's ready,' she said."

"So, then, why did you come after me now?"

"Your opportunity to make good was closing up, Mikey. I'm almost ninety now. Lucy was ninety-eight when she died. You're not a kid anymore. If you were going to get this off your chest and make things right and apologize to the people who you hurt so that we could all have some damn closure, a good time to do it would have been before the fucking people who you hurt were dead, don't you think?"

"Yeah."

"Lucy couldn't order the hunt. She had lung cancer. One of the last things she said was that her one regret was not getting you in front of her and hearing you say that you're sorry for not listening and for destroying the circus. It was her life's work, Mikey. You destroyed her life's work when you fucked around with the circus and refused to listen to her."

"I know. I'm sorry."

"Well, it's a bit too late for that now. You're here. She's not. Do you know how they found you, Mikey?"

"No, I don't."

"Lucy's crazy-ass daughter spent six months looking in phone books, looking through public records, and visiting every city where she thought you might have ended up and drinking in every bar in those cities, until she found two bars where her description of you rang a bell with someone. Then she followed you for weeks. She knew where you lived, where you worked, where you drank, where you shopped, the whole thing, Mikey."

"Wow. Was she responsible for the fire at the store too?"

"That was a bit of what you might call 'unauthorized improvisation', but yes."

"I thought so."

"She thinks she did you a favor with getting you away from that job," said Schmid.

"She's probably right," said Mike.

"She says 'hi,' by the way."

"Um. OK. So, what do we do now?"

"I'm going to sit here and make you feel uncomfortable for a while I rest and smoke a cigar. You're going to sit in jail until

I determine that you've been in there for long enough. How does that sound?"

"Fine."

Lucky brought a wicker chair with a red cushion into the jail and placed it behind Mr. Schmid. Schmid handed Lucky his cane and sat down. Schmid took a cigar from his shirt pocket and used a knife from his coat pocket to cut off the end. Lucky lit it for him. and Mr. Schmid took several large puffs and blew the smoke towards Mike.

The other clowns in Mike's cell put their hands over their ears and closed their eyes. Victor turned around to face the wall and hung his head. Mike and Jordan watched Mr. Schmid and he watched them back.

After about five minutes, Mr. Schmid turned to Lucky and whispered, "Now."

Lucky brought out the card table from the storage cell and set it up in front of Mr. Schmid. He draped a table cloth over it and put the ashtray in the center, and Mr. Schmid ashed and then extinguished his cigar. Lucky opened the door to the jail reception area and Skipper pushed in the food cart and stopped it just to the left of Mr. Schmid. Lucky returned from the reception area carrying two elaborate silver candle sticks, which he placed on the table. Skipper came around to Mr. Schmid's right side and set up Mr. Schmid's salad fork, his dinner fork, his bread plate and butter knife, his dinner knife, his soup spoon, and his other spoon in an approximation of the proper way to set a place setting, as done by an old sailor who had been around the world enough to learn such things but never had a chance to put them into practice. Lucky folded Mr. Schmid's napkin into a swan.

Throughout this elaborate setup, Mr. Schmid sat motionless and stone-faced, staring at Mike.

Skipper went to the storage cell and retrieved two bottles of wine—one white and one red and an ice bucket. He opened both bottles and poured a glass of the white wine into the skinnier of Mr. Schmid's wine glasses before nestling the bottle into the ice in the bucket and finding a spot for the bucket and both bottles of wine on the cart.

When the table was set and the preparations were complete, Skipper took the lid off the trays on the cart one by one and handed them to Lucky. As Skipper removed each lid and as the smells reached their noses, the clowns in Mike's cell wept. Lucky called out the contents of each tray.

"Here we have freshly baked French bread smothered with garlic butter."

He paused for dramatic effect before unveiling the next tray.

"Here we have the Caesar salad with extra anchovies."

Another pause.

"Here we have the soup. Cream of broccoli."

"Here we have Brussels sprouts roasted in olive oil with bacon and balsamic vinegar."

"Here we have southern fried chicken, extra crispy."

Once all the dishes had been announced, Lucky went to work serving Mr. Schmid generous portions of the salad, bread, and soup. The soup and salad served, Mr. Schmid unfolded his napkin and placed it on his lap. He then spoke.

"Someone is going to die tonight," he said. "It could be any one of you, or it could be me. Here's what's going to happen. I'm going to start eating and drinking now. I'm going to be doing that for several hours. And, you're going to watch. As I eat, you're going to think about your crimes. Each of you, but especially my wonder boy, Mikey. You're going to think about what you did and what you should have done. I'm going to eat so much that I'm going to be sick. And you're going to watch and not say anything. If you speak, you'll die. If I eat and drink as much as I feel like I just may eat and drink, I may die. This is the game and those are the rules. Now, if you'll excuse me, I'm going to eat."

Lucky pressed play on a tape recorder on the lower level of the cart. Soft music began to play.

Mr. Schmid smiled and then his smile changed to a frown. He squinted his eyes at Mike as if trying to see something beyond him.

"Do you know what this is, Mikey? Go ahead, answer."

"Um. Blue Danube?"

"Correct. An der schönen blauen Donau. Strauss."

Mr. Schmid picked up his fork and took a bite of his salad. He put his fork down after the first bite, put his napkin on the table and stood up. Holding his wine glass, he waltzed around the room with an invisible partner, humming along with Blue Danube.

"Supper, my boy, is meant to be enjoyed at a leisurely pace. When Lucy was still alive, we'd dine together every night. We'd dance. We'd drink several bottles of wine. We employed several of the midgets from the old circus to cater to our whims as household servants. I don't have to tell you about the extraordinary skills of the little people, right Mikey? Ah yes. Da da da da da. bump bump. bump bump."

He sang and danced and sipped his white wine until the song was done. Another waltz came on, and Mr. Schmid sat down and took another bite of his salad. He chewed slowly and then speared another forkful of salad and an anchovy. He held this forkful of salad in front of his face, not eating it for a moment, appearing to consider it. He then spoke again, all the time with the fork full of salad hovering just below his face as if framing him.

"Here's the thing, Mikey. I have regrets too. I do. My biggest regret is that I never married Lucy. I had my ideas about what was right and what was wrong, and she was a woman who was stronger, meaner, and better than me in just about every way. I was intimidated. She didn't care whether we were married or not—she was going to just keep on doing what she was doing. She asked me if I wanted to marry her, and she said that was OK with her if it would make me feel better. I told her no and that I liked it the way it was and that we didn't need to be married. But, I did need that, Mikey. I never told her until she was on her death bed. She called me a sissy."

Mr. Schmid lifted the fork to his mouth and bit it off as if he was a shark—as if he were trying to show how much he wasn't a sissy.

"Ah but she was a hell of a woman, and she could cook. Not just for me—she could cook for sixty-some circus folk—the acrobats, the thin man, the midgets, the fat man, the animal trainers, and the clowns. You remember that, Mikey?"

Mike didn't talk.

"Well, do you?" Mr. Schmid said, spearing another forkful of salad.

"Yes, sir."

"Don't gimme that 'sir' crap, son. What was the best thing you ever ate that she cooked?"

"Corned beef."

"Ah yes, Lucy's corned beef. She only did that once a year, and always the day after St. Patrick's Day. She knew a good deal, and she knew a bad deal too."

Mr. Schmid turned to look at Jordan for the first time. She was holding onto the bars of her cell, entranced by the food, but also trying to act calm and cool.

"I never knew Lucy," said Jordan.

"You're a circus clown, though, right? What was the best food you ate in the circus?"

"I'm not a circus clown. I was just with Mike when they caught him."

"Ah yes. Rules is rules. Right, Skipper?"

"Arr," said Skipper.

"Are you married, er, what's your name?" asked Mr. Schmid.

"Jordan. No."

"Where are you from, Jordan?"

"Chicago."

"Well, what was the best thing your mother cooked you?"

Mr. Schmid pushed his salad away, and Lucky picked it up, along with the salad fork, and he replaced it with a bowl of soup. He filled up Mr. Schmid's wine glass just before Mr. Schmid took a sip.

"Frog soup."

"Ah, frog soup, eh? Where do you get frogs in Chicago?"

"I don't know."

"You're Thai?"

"My mother is."

"And dad?"

"Irish."

Mr. Schmid got the faraway look in his eyes while staring at Jordan.

"Lucy was Irish. You are too. Right, Mike O'Malley?"

"Yes," said Mike.

"What was it Yeats said about the Irish? 'An abiding sense of tragedy which sustains him through temporary periods of joy,' or some goddamn thing. You've got it in spades, son. Lucy had it too."

Schmid slurped a spoonful of soup and took another sip of wine.

Jordan was starving. They hadn't eaten since the hotel breakfast that morning.

"Mr. Schmid?" she said in her sweetest little girl voice, "May I have a piece of your bread please?"

Mr. Schmid put his hand out flat above his shoulder and Lucky placed a thick slice of the French bread into it. Mr. Schmid pushed his chair back and walked the bread over to

Jordan's cell and handed it to her through the bars. Jordan took it and waited until Mr. Schmid turned around before she devoured it.

The clowns in Mike's cage were still turned around with their hands over their ears. Mike saw Mr. Schmid's generosity and figured he had nothing to lose.

"As long as you're handing things out," he started.

"Fuck you! Fuck you, Mike O'Malley! You'll get nothing from me for the rest of my goddamn life except pain. And you should be thankful that you get that much. I ought to flay you! I ought to personally rip out your arms from your body and roast them! I ought to cut out your eyeballs! I ought to force feed you grout until your insides become as hard and heavy as mine!"

Mr. Schmid sat down and looked at his food as if to say, "Now, where was I?" He picked up his spoon and slurped his soup. It was as if he were eating his soup at Mike—slurping against him.

"I won't do those things," he continued, "Instead, I'm going to enjoy this meal. I'm going to enjoy the hell out of this meal. I'm going to enjoy this meal for hours—for days if I want to. And, it's going to destroy you. I'm going to eat until it destroys you. I'm going to eat until I puke. I'm going to eat until well past when I'm full. You're going to hate me more and more as I eat more and more. I'm going to tell you every detail about how Lucy wasted away. I'm going to tell you how the circus wasted away. I'm going to tell you how the midgets had to find jobs and how it crushed their souls. I'm going to tell you about how the clowns had to become independent operators and their total lack of any business sense meant that they had to spend most of their time fishing through dumpsters for scraps and filling out paperwork to get food stamps. I'm going to tell you about what happened to your little girlfriend,

Princess. Did you even keep in touch with Princess, you god-damn worthless piece of shit?"

"No," said Mike, his face in his hands.

"Damn right you didn't," said Mr. Schmid, "Well, she moved to New York. She got some gigs working on commercials. She lived in a shithole with six other little people. All her possessions were sold or stolen. When she thought she was finally getting her big break—a part on a sitcom—she showed up on set and was used as a sex toy and discarded by the producer of the show. Say what you will about the circus, Mike, but it was a safe place. It was a hell of a lot safer than the corporate world or the TV world or the movie world or any of these other places that everyone thinks are safe just because they don't have trampolines or wild animals. Fuck 'em, Mike! Fuck you, Mike! You did this! You brought your goddamn business school into the circus and your corporate-political sense of justice to the circus and you changed it from a living, breathing thing that was fading into its senior years and was going to die for a time before coming back as it has over and over. You changed it into a goddamn profit center with employees worried about their pensions and whether the poster from the government was hung in the right place."

For the next six hours, Mr. Schmid ate and berated Mike. No one died. When he finished eating, Lucky and Skipper each held one of his arms and walked him to the exit. He threw his cane at Mike's cell and Lucky ran back to retrieve it before leaving the jail and punching the code into the elevator to return Mr. Schmid to the surface.

CHAPTER 74

In which Victor helps Mike and Jordan
devise a brilliant scheme to escape

In the windowless underground clown jail, day and night merged and the only way Jordan could keep track of the days was by when the only meal of the day, breakfast, was brought in.

The breakfast was whatever was the leftovers from a business hotel nearby and those breakfasts run until 10:00, so breakfast was somewhere between 10:00 and 11:00. Unless they reheat the eggs to the perfect lukewarm temperature, breakfast was the only time marker that was certain since they took Jordan's watch away and made her wear the orange clown jumpsuit like the other prisoners.

After a few weeks, Jordan could tell the day of the week by the contents of breakfast. Monday was the scrambled eggs, potatoes with rosemary, and sausage links. Tuesday was the French toast, sausage and hash browns. Wednesday was the scrambled eggs, sausage patties, and tater tots. Thursday was the cheese omelet, bacon, and potatoes with rosemary. Friday was scrambled eggs, sausage links, and tater tots again. The hotel didn't serve breakfast on the weekend, which is how Jordan knew it was the weekend. On Saturday, they had day-old pastries and bagels. On Sunday, they had two-day-old pastries and bagels.

After the second week of being in clown jail, Mike and Jordan figured out that they could unlock and open the door between the two cells. Jordan wasn't happy about this because now they all had a larger cell, but Jordan was sharing her space with four other people. When the guards were present or when Jordan needed privacy, she would lock her side of the door.

Mike and Victor Karandash came over for frequent talks about people they both knew from the circus and about the outside world and about how to escape. Jordan, as the only one of the three of them who had ever been in a real jail, pointed out that if they were in a "real" jail, escape would be almost impossible. But, their imprisonment was more like a hostage situation and there were plenty of ways they could get out that might just happen and that they needed to look for opportunities and take advantage of them rather than planning an elaborate escape that would require circumstances to be a certain way.

"You play it fast and loose, don't you, darling?" said Victor.

"I guess," said Jordan.

"Circumstances aren't just going to happen the right vay all your life, and you're not going to be able to rely on luck and taking advantage of people's veakness for your youth and bangs."

"Whatever, grampa."

"You like calling people that, don't you?" said Mike.

"Ha. Ya, whatever, grampa."

Jordan knew she was being a brat and that she had no right to be talking the way she was talking to her elders, but what Victor was saying wasn't going to happen was, in fact, what was going to happen. Jordan knew that they'd come over to her way of thinking if she were difficult enough.

"So, what exactly do you propose?" said Mike.

"How much of that hooch have you got?"

"I have couple pints now, and another on the vay," said Victor.

"Do the clowns know about that?"

"Sure. They taste it once and vant no part of it. So, they look other way as long as I pretend to hide it."

"I'm going to get wasted and offer Lucky and Skipper some of it next time we play tiddlywinks. They'll take it, because they will. Do you have a batch that's stronger than the others?"

"Da, fer sure! The one I made from grape jellies."

"Great. I'll give that one to them, and I'll sip from the less strong one."

"Ah ha. I see where you are going vith this. It could work. Drunk clowns are some of the biggest pushovers in world and they vill just let us walk out," said Victor.

Mike was fidgeting and looking agitated.

"Mike, did you want to say something?" said Jordan.

"Yes. Is this the only trick you have? Are you that uncreative that the only thing you can think of for how we're going to get out of here is the exact same trick you use to break up with boyfriends?"

"Yes, that's exactly right," said Jordan, "I'll keep using it as long as it works. If it ain't broke, don't change it, right gramps?"

"The saying is 'If it ain't broke, don't fix it'," said Mike.

"Robot."

"I can't wait any longer, and I can't stand to drink that goddamn lukewarm coffee and eat those fucking greasy eggs again. I say we do this tonight," said Jordan.

"But, don't you think we should consider Victor's plan," asked Mike, "Victor, who's been in here for forty years and knows every crack and crevice in the place and who's been thinking about this for longer than you've been alive?" said Mike.

"Well, no. No offense, Victor, but I don't think you want to get out. I think you stay in here because it's easy and because you've gotten used to it. I don't want to grow old in here. I'm getting the fuck out the way I know how and you're both welcome to join me—but not those two weirdos you share your cell with."

"Well, if that's the way it's going to be, that's the way it's going to be. We might as well try," said Mike.

"You mean that I might as well try. Your old asses aren't going to be doing anything. I'm the one who's going to be doing all the work."

"Right. Sorry," said Mike.

"Whatever."

"What? It was your idea. I'm supposed to feel bad for you now that I agree with you and we're going to do your idea?"

"No. But, give me some respect and some room and leave me alone. You're damn right it was my idea. You're making me crazy," said Jordan.

"Let's keep it together," said Victor, "I don't want to be around you two anymore zan you two want to be in here. Ze plan sounds fine, and it can't hurt to try it. The worst that can happen is that I'll be out of hooch and guards will put on a show for us or sometzing and Jordan will have a nasty hangover. When are you going to do it?"

"Today."

"I'll get hooch ready and make sure I know vich jar is vich."

Mike and Victor went back to their cell and Jordan was finally alone again. She felt nervous, but she reminded herself that this would be easier than any escape she's ever done, because she hasn't had sex with the either of the guards. She thought Skipper was kind of funny in a Popeye the Sailorman way. There wouldn't be any risk of them trying to force one last hookup before she leaves for good. But, perhaps the lack of a sexual aspect to this escape would make it more difficult to pull off. She was committed now, and she knew that her plan would work because it always did.

CHAPTER 75

In which they execute the plan

"Winks, winks, winks, winks! It's time to play some winks! Winks, winks, winks, winks! It's time to play some winks."

Skipper and Lucky were dancing and singing as they entered the jail. Jordan estimated that it had been three hours since breakfast. Jordan got up off her cot. Everything was ready and in place for her plan. The hooch was tucked under her mattress, she made sure to eat as much as she could for breakfast, so she wouldn't get blackout drunk this time, and here they were—right on time for the daily tiddlywinks match.

"Well, aren't you two chipper this afternoon," said Jordan. "Did you get laid?"

"Ooooh, good afternoon, little feisty one," said Lucky. "For your information, today happens to be our Friday, not that you would know or care. Tomorrow we can sleep in, go to the lake, do some laundry, buy some groceries . . . "

Skipper interrupted. "Drink grog and watch Price be Right! Arr."

"Just three more hours, and then we're gone," said Lucky.

"Well, let's get the party started early with some winks!" said Jordan, doing her best to sound excited for them. She had a pretty good sense of who these clowns were by now. They weren't different from the college boys she'd dated. They talk and care only about themselves, they expect other people to be excited when they talk about themselves, and their self-worth is tied up in whether girls are interested when they talk about themselves. In short: they were easy to manipulate.

"Huzzah!" said Lucky.

Lucky got the table out of the storage cell, and Skipper placed the felt and poured the winks out onto it while Lucky was getting the chairs and unfolding them in their usual positions. Skipper used the corner of his shirt to wipe out the ash tray, then he examined it, spit in it, and wiped it out again with the other (cleaner) corner of his shirt.

When the table and chairs were set up, Lucky unlocked Jordan's cell. At this point, it would have been easy on any day for the inhabitants of the other cell to burst though the dividing door and run through Jordan's open cell door and make a break for it. Jordan knew that this approach was the more traditional way to break out of a jail. But, she still felt like her approach was better and, furthermore, she wanted to prove to the rest of them that she was right. Besides, if her plan didn't work, it's like the little guy said: there's no harm done, and they can always try the little guy's plan later on.

As Lucky was opening Jordan's cell, she reached under her mattress and took out the pillow case that she had packed the two jars of hooch in.

"Woah woah woah. What are you doing? What have you got there?" said Lucky.

"I thought I might like to celebrate your Friday with you," said Jordan as she reached into the pillow case and gave Lucky a peek at the top of one of the jars. "Would you join me for a drink?"

"Ah! I never touch the Sucker Punch. That stuff'll make you go blind, I swear," said Lucky.

"Come on! I hate to drink alone, but don't think I won't if it comes down to it," said Jordan.

Before Lucky could react or say anything else, Jordan had slipped out of her cell and was unpacking both jars of Sucker Punch onto the table.

"Ahoy, lassy! I sees ya brought the grog!" Skipper threw back his head and laughed.

"Damn right," said Jordan. She opened one of the jars, took a sip, and passed it to Skipper.

"Don't mind if I do," said Skipper while taking a swig.

"You know, this is totally against protocol," said Lucky.

"Right sure, dude. I'm willing to keep it hush-hush if you are," said Jordan, winking.

"Shiver me timbers! That stuff ain't half bad. I gotta hand it to you Victor, yer gettin' better," said Skipper, taking another swig.

"OK, fine. Let's wink," said Lucky.

They sat down and flipped winks to see who would go first. Jordan let Lucky win.

"I'm feeling lucky today," said Lucky.

Jordan laughed. "Give me much more of this hooch and I'll be feeling Lucky today too, right guys?" She grabbed a jar and pretended to swallow two gulps.

Skipper and Lucky both laughed. "Watch out fer this one!"

The tiddlywinks game commenced, and they passed around the two jars. Jordan forgot which jar was the stronger one, but she was pretty sure that they were feeling the effects more than she was. She continued flirting and encouraging Lucky and Skipper to drink more. This was the easy part, she thought.

After an hour of playing, both jars were empty.

"Hey Victor, you got any more of this stuff," slurred Lucky.

"Oooh yeah," said Victor. He stood up off his cot and then crawled underneath it. When he emerged, he had two more jars: one was pink and the other was yellowish brown. "This one here," he said, holding up the pink one, "this one was made from the Thanksgiving cranberry leftovers last year. This other one, well I think it's from applesauce. Don't mind the color -- that just means it's aged."

Victor handed the two jars through the bars of his cell and Lucky stumbled out of his chair and took them eagerly. Lucky started drinking the pink one before he even sat back down. He no longer cared about passing the jars around, and Skipper had to ask Lucky to pass the other jar to him.

"Say, guys, you must be pretty good at clowning after how long you've been clowns, huh?" said Jordan.

"Well . . . you could say that. I think you should say that, in fact," said Lucky, who was increasingly resembling a very drunken Dean Martin.

"Why don't you give us all a little show? I think we're all curious what kinds of things you know how to do."

"Oh gosh, I don't know. What do you think, Skipper? Do you think she's been a good girl? Does she deserve a show?"

"Arr. Flbbbdfkj grdaghddff."

"You'll have to excuse my colleague. He gets somewhat incoherent when he gets tipsy," said Lucky.

"OK, twist my arm!" Lucky stood up and pantomimed his arm being twisted by some unseen force.

Jordan laughed and clapped.

Lucky tugged at Skippers arm, and then seeing that Skipper wasn't in the mood to get up, he started the show without him.

"It's October in Minnesota and the leaves outside are starting to turn and the air is chilly, but the sky is clear. Now, picture a cornfield, picked and mowed clean near where the highway and the train tracks cross. Picture the biggest big tent you've ever seen on that cornfield. Five thousand seats, all filled. Outside the tent, people are pulling up and parking their cars in the roped-off parking area and the cheerleaders from North Woods high school are directing them and asking for donations for the homecoming parade.

Inside the tent, you can smell and feel the heat from the portable hot air blowers mixing with the smell of the straw on the floor. But, most of all, it's the smell of the elephants, the horses, the lions. It's a wet, warm animal smell and it feels just right.

Picture the families in the stands. Mom and dad, Bobby and Cindy, all wearing blue jeans. Some in overalls. Some moms have strollers, some dads brought coolers filled with Bud Light, or they packed a flask in their inside coat pocket. They're waiting for the show to start and trying to get the attention of the cotton candy guy or the peanut lady or they're looking at the other families and recognizing someone they haven't seen since spring and waving. Over there is that little girl from Cindy's class that had the birthday sleepover last year, and when I picked them up Cindy asked what a "hussy" is.

It's getting close to show time. We wait. It's showtime. We wait juuuust a little longer. It's thirty seconds past show time and those thirty seconds have felt like forever to the families. NOW!"

By muffling his voice with his hand, Lucky was able to achieve an "off the stage announcer voice" and he began. "Ladies and gents, kids, dogs, cats, parrots! I present to you Lucky the Clown!"

Lucky threw up his hands and took in the wild applause while making whooshing noises with his mouth to simulate the wild applause.

"Now, I come out to center stage. The spotlight is on me. I look to my left—expectant crowd. I look to my right—expectant crowd. I look forward—expectant crowd getting just a tad impatient. A little wave and 'peekaboo' to the baby in the front row, but it's really for the mother, you understand. I raise up my left arm and the big tent goes quiet. I wiggle my little finger and the music starts playing—it's Mozart. I reach up with my other hand and start pulling long, colorful ribbons out of my sleeve. They keep coming. They keep coming. And then, birds! I act surprised. The crowd loves it. Then I go into my dance routine. It starts like this. I listen to the music. There's a little trill. I smile. My foot taps, then it's like I can't control it. My whole leg is stomping along to Mozart in a totally inappropriate way and it shows on my face that I can't stop it. I try, but I can't and the dance spreads like this."

By now, Lucky was doing a wild dance, flailing his arms and legs, and he was drunk, which made the dance even more unpredictable than it otherwise would have been. Skipper was sipping at the Sucker Punch. Jordan was clapping out a beat for Lucky to dance to. Mike and Victor were watching and waiting for their opportunity—they had both put on their shoes and made sure they were tied. The fat clown sat on the toilet. The hippie clown was rolling a piece of newspaper into a cigar.

The more Jordan clapped and hollered, the crazier Lucky danced. Finally, he indicated that the dance was about to wrap up and Jordan stopped clapping the beat and just started clapping and Lucky waved his arms to the crowd and smiled and mouthed the words "Thank you, thank you so much" to his audience in the stands.

Lucky put his hands on his knees and exhaled a few times to catch his breath. "I've still got it," he said.

"Damn right you do!" yelled Jordan, with glee.

"Arr," said Skipper as he took another drink and stirred around the little plastic disks on the table with his finger.

"What happens next?" asked Jordan.

"Next, I run backstage and a man in a suit comes out. Suddenly it's like the high school principal just walked into the room. This guy . . . this guy is all business. He has a briefcase and he opens it up and takes out a clipboard and starts looking around at different things in the ring as if he's taking an inventory. Then he starts mumbling to himself. 'No No No. This won't do.' He says, 'this chair is too expensive. This rope is the finest rope I've ever seen. What sort of a madman put this show together. Let me taste that cotton candy! Why, this is the finest Egyptian cotton! This is too good for a common circus. And those benches! Those are the most comfortable benches. No. I'm going to have to shut this circus down, it's not cost effective and it can't possibly be profitable.'

"That's my cue to run back out. I beg. I plead. The audience is on my side, and they're begging and pleading right along with me. The accountant isn't giving an inch. I put my hands on my hips and face the audience, then I make the universal sign for 'I have an idea!' I put my finger into the air, then I look over to the accountant, who is bent over inspecting a light fixture. I get behind him, and I yank his pants down. Underneath, he has pink polka dot underwear. He runs off stage and the crowd goes wild.

"As soon as the laughter stops, a voice booms out over the big tent, announcing the ring master, and then the ring master runs into the center of the center ring.

"He has a three-foot-tall top hat, coat, tails, the whole getup. What a sight! Oh I love the circus! For ten years after I became a clown, this is what I did, with small variations and improvements year to year—sometimes it would be the accountant who tries to shut down the circus, sometimes it would be the fun police, and once we tried having it be my wife who wanted me to take out the garbage, but that gag didn't play well, even in the 8os. Those were the glory days, am I right, Skipper?"

"Arr. mrfal burrrp."

Lucky sat down in his chair and took the last jar of hooch out of Skipper's hand and took a swig. Then he put his head in his hands and started crying.

"Best damn time of my life. Why the hell did I waste so much time trying to be a lawyer. I was a shitty lawyer. If only I had known what I know now about how we waste time when we try to be who we aren't. Oh, my mother tried to teach me! I'm sorry mama!"

Jordan put her hand on Lucky's arm. "You've done well, Lucky. Sometimes you need to go through the bad parts so you can appreciate the good parts when you find them." Jordan had read something like that on Facebook once and it stuck with her as something she could use at some point, rather than as something that she believed or had any experience with herself.

"You got that right," said Lucky. "I've seen so much shit. I've seen shit upon shit. I shat a lot of it. Now, I look back at it and I think, 'Yup, that's shit.' And then I had my days in the circus. It all seems so brief. And then you retire from the circus, or the real accountant or fun police come along, and the circus shuts down and I can't pull anyone's pants down to save it, and I have ta rely on the generosity of the Foundation for Retired Clowns plus the free food I get from volunteering down here. And it's just not the same, you know?"

"Yes, I can see that. You must have been quite a sight there in that big tent with all those people and your magnificent clean costume and your fresh makeup and in the air that smells like a farm. There must still be a circus somewhere for you. Who says you can't go out there right now and find the circus and don't leave until they hire you. Even if they can't pay you—how much worse would it be to work for the circus and get free food and no pay, rather than being in a hole under a warehouse and not getting paid."

Lucky sniffled and wiped his nose on his sleeve.

"Yeah. Yeah. You're right. But, who would watch the jail? Who would make sure that you get fed? Who would play tiddlywinks with you? I've been doing this job so long that I know every nook and cranny. I know how to mix the flour into the eggs when there aren't enough leftovers. I know how to clean the costumes so the vinyl spots don't fall off. Who's going to do all this? Who would want to?"

"It's not your job to worry about all that, Lucky," said Jordan. "You have to look out for yourself for once. You're such a kind and caring person, but it seems like maybe you don't spend enough time taking care of you. Besides, there are only a few of us in here. Is it really worth your precious time to be the guard of so few people? And, you know that none of us is all that bad. We're just like you. We had bad things happen to us and some of us did bad things that we're sorry for, but our time is precious too."

Lucky looked thoughtful drunk, as if he were weighing the relative sins of each prisoner. As he scanned their faces, which were all looking at him now, he couldn't even remember why some of them were in the jail.

"You're right. The world would be a better place if no one were locked up in clown jail. But, that's not a call for me to make. If you let everyone out of jail, you end up in there yourself, like little Victor K there."

"This is your time now, Lucky! Go out there and show them that you're not some washed up old drunk clown! Make your mark! Do it now!"

Lucky stood up and danced and stumbled and weaved around the room, tried to skip, but then reconsidered and got a look of determination on his face as he made fists with both his hands and looked intensely at Jordan.

"I'm going to do it. I'm going to put in my two-week notice in the morning."

"Is that how you roll, Lucky? Don't you want to burn it down? Don't you hate this place for the years it's taken from you? Don't you want to tip over that breakfast cart, just once?"

"Holy shit." Lucky put his face into his hands. "I've never thought about it like that before. What's happened to me? I've gotten fat, lazy, complacent, and evil. I used to have such values. I became a lawyer to fight the system, and I quit being a lawyer to fight the system. Now I am the system. Fucking hell."

Jordan pressed his button a little harder. "You need to do it now, Lucky. If you give notice, they're going to try and talk you out of it or they're going to force you to stay. Who knows what they'll do. Here's what you do: leave the keys here with Skipper, Mr. Schmid will get them tomorrow. Then, you go right out the door. If anyone asks us where you went, we don't know anything."

"Dammit," said Lucky, "that's exactly what I'm going to do. And, I'm going to tip over that damn breakfast cart."

Lucky unhooked the jail keyring from his belt and placed it on the table in front of Skipper. He took one last look around the jail, waved goodbye, and then ran for the exit. On his way out, he raised his foot up and pressed it solidly against the breakfast cart and gave it a shove. It rocked back and forth a little but didn't turn over.

Jordan grabbed the keys as soon as Lucky was out of the room and unlocked Mike and Victor's cell. Mike and Victor dragged Skipper into the storage cell and locked him in. Jordan, Mike, and Victor waited a couple minutes after Lucky was gone and then headed for the exit themselves.

Jordan flipped on the light in the reception area and saw cubby holes on the wall with clown names and clothes in them, as if it was a day care center. Jordan found her cubby hole, next to Mike's. She dumped out the trash can next to the receptionist desk and dumped the contents of both cubby holes into the garbage bag, tied a knot in it and handed it to Mike.

"Here you go, Santa. Don't fuckin' lose it."

Jordan looked for a cubby for Victor.

"You're not going to find anything. I was captured in these clothes," Victor said.

When Jordan looked back as they were getting in the elevator, the hippie clown and the fat clown were still sitting in the cell.

The elevator climbed up to the warehouse. The door opened, and everything was calm at first, but then three workers in coveralls rushed out of the warehouse office and ran towards Mike, Jordan, and Victor. Victor's little old legs couldn't carry him fast enough. He tripped as soon as he started trying to run. Mike and Jordan were well ahead of him and they looked back to see the men in the coveralls picking him up by his feet and hands.

Victor shouted to Mike and Jordan, "Don't vorry bout me! I'll be OK. You get out now! Remember vat I told you!"

Mike had forgotten that he promised to find Victor's son, Andy Pencils, and, frankly, he had hoped that Victor would escape too so that he could find him himself and Mike wouldn't have to. But, as he was running toward the warehouse exit, and as Victor was being dragged screaming back into the elevator, Mike was thinking about where and how he might find Andy in the quickest possible way, so he could just get it over with and get back to some sort of a normal life and a normal routine. But, the first thing after he got out of the warehouse would be to take a shower and get a beer.

The door to the left of the rollup door was unlocked, and Mike and Jordan went through it. Mike closed the door behind himself as if no one had noticed their exit. They were in an industrial neighborhood in the suburbs of Minneapolis. It was a dark and chilly October night, and they were wearing clown suits and hadn't showered in at least a week but they'd both lost count of exactly how many days it had been.

"OK, let's find somewhere to hide out until morning," said Jordan. "I hope my phone is with my clothes. There must be a shelter or something. Or let's find a payphone and call the police."

Mike was looking around in a panic and breathing heavily. "No! The last thing you want to do in a town like this is to call the police on the clowns. They're one and the same. If we were on the west coast, sure, calling the police would be OK. But, here, the police are more likely to take us back down there. And, dressed like this, we're sitting ducks for any vigilante clowns to recapture us. Let's find a place to change and then figure out how to get back to my car and get the fuck away from here."

They ran a couple blocks toward the freeway, which they could see in the distance. No cars drove by, and the streets were empty of people.

"I can't wear this getup anymore. Give me the bag. I'm going to change in that doorway," said Jordan.

"I won't look," said Mike.

"I don't fucking care. What are we, ten?"

Mike followed Jordan to the doorway of the SureWay Air Compressor factory showroom. They were likely being recorded by the security camera, Jordan thought, which might or might not help them at some point, but more likely no one will ever see the video and it doesn't matter.

They tore into the garbage bag and found their clothes intermingled inside. Mike untangled his jeans from Jordan's and pulled off his clown pants to put them on.

"Eww. You're going to keep wearing your clown underwear?"

"Oh shit, I guess not," said Mike.

"You're pretty weird, gramps."

Mike dug around in the bag until he found his boxer shorts—the red ones. He liked those. He pulled off his pants and his clown underwear together and then put on the red boxer shorts.

Jordan was taking off her clown top, facing not quite away from Mike—maybe three-quarters. She threw the clown top into the flat-topped hedges, and Mike did the same with his clown underwear, clown pants, and clown shoes.

Jordan started laughing. "Someone is going to find this when they open the shop tomorrow."

Mike laughed along with her. Soon, they were both laughing uncontrollably as they changed into their clothes. They tried to make the discarded clown clothes be as obviously strewn over the bushes and the walkway as possible.

"Clown orgy!" screamed Jordan.

"Holy shit, I never thought my own clothes would feel so good," said Mike.

"You got that right, mister," said Jordan.

Mike finished dressing first and he checked the contents of his jacket pockets while watching Jordan lace up her boots. "I still have my keys, but the cash is missing," he said. He checked in his wallet. "My driver's license is gone too, but I still have a library card."

"That'll come in handy for sure," said Jordan.

When Jordan looked up from tying her boots, she saw the headlights of a Volkswagen bus headed towards them.

"Oh fuck, it's a damn VW Bus," she said.

"Huh? Oh shit. Let's go."

Mike took Jordan's hand and she didn't protest as he guided them around the side of the building, to the road behind it. They ran toward the freeway. If they could make it there, Mike thought, a trucker might give them a ride. Which direction did they need to go? I-35 South would get them close to the gas station and, if they were lucky, the car hadn't been towed or stripped.

They alternated between running, jogging, and walking as fast as they could with their stiff legs toward the freeway. When they were almost underneath it, Mike pointed out that the entrance was a block away and he again reached for Jordan's hand to redirect her. Again, she didn't protest. Maybe they could be friends after this, Jordan thought. Mike thought that maybe if she hung around he wouldn't be so lonely after this. He thought about how it's not true what they say about how all you can think about is survival when you're in a life and death situation. His thoughts were racing everywhere as they ran hand-in-hand to the freeway entrance.

Mike was thinking about how Jordan's fingers were soft and small. He was thinking about how he must smell terrible and he hoped that wouldn't be a deal breaker for any trucker that stopped for them. He was thinking he should hide while Jordan tries to flag down a truck and then come out once the truck stopped. He was thinking that it was sad, but a sad truth, that there was almost no chance that he would be picked up hitchhiking, but that there was almost no chance that Jordan wouldn't be picked up hitchhiking. He was thinking about that shower and that beer, and how he could have both if they could get back to the car. He was thinking about how he hoped the car would still be there somehow and he was trying to remember whether he had locked the doors. He was thinking about Victor and how he promised to find Andy Pencils. And he was thinking about Rita the clown who thought she was doing him a favor by finding him and forcing a reckoning.

When they got to the freeway entrance ramp, Mike told Jordan about his plan to hide in the bushes while she flagged down a ride.

"No, you fucking pervert," she said, "we're going to hitch-hike together and you're not putting me in some rapey guy's cab, even if you're there too. Sorry, but I don't think you're much in the way of insurance."

"Fine by me," said Mike, "but no one's going to stop for us on I-35. Let's head to the gas station and try talking our way into a ride. We can use the bathroom to clean up too."

"Now you're thinking," said Jordan.

At the gas station, they took turns using the bathroom. It was the first time in weeks that Jordan had looked at herself in a mirror. She looked like hell. To start with, her face was filthy. Her bangs were too long, and her eyebrows needed to be plucked. She had bags under her eyes, and her lips were chapped. In jail, she washed herself as best she could with what she had every few days, and she brushed her teeth more often in the jail than she ever did when she wasn't locked up, but even the best hygiene in that hole wouldn't keep her together. Her clothes though, were, surprisingly, not covered with puke. Someone at the jail must have gotten sick of the smell and washed them.

She washed her face and hands in the sink and spent a little extra time on cleaning under her fingernails. It was the first time in as long as she could remember that she didn't have a plan or even some faded marks or at least a phone number written on her hands.

When she was clean, she went outside and found Mike sitting on the curb outside the gas station store. The sun was starting to come up, and the warmth on her skin felt good. She walked into the store and smiled at the cashier. He smiled back. He didn't recoil in terror at her ugliness, so she must have done at least an adequate job in the bathroom. She browsed the shelves for a few minutes, and she struck up a conversation with the cashier about the weather and the neighborhood and where he grew up as she pocketed a couple candy bars and a Sharpie.

She said goodbye to the cashier and went outside, where she found Mike in conversation with a truck driver. Both of their eyes turned to her as she approached, and she slapped the driver on the back when she was close enough.

"So," she said, "can you give us a ride or what?"

Mike laughed a little, uncomfortably. The driver smiled at Jordan like she was a spunky kid. "Well, I was just telling this guy that the company has a strict no rides policy and I'll catch hell if anyone found out."

"We won't tell," said Jordan, winking at him and playing with her hair.

"Aw hell. It sounds like you two have had quite a time, from what this feller is telling me," said the driver, "the damn tweakers robbed me once too. I'll never forget those teeth. I could have taken him easy, but he said he was packin' and I didn't want to find out if he was lyin'. He was probably lyin'."

"Thank you so much, mister," said Jordan, "my brother and I will behave, we promise."

"Well, now, I hadn't said yes yet." The driver fidgeted a bit and fished a cigarette out of his pack. Jordan held out her hand. The driver smiled and gave her one and a light.

"Aw hell, ok. You want a smoke too, bro?" he said to Mike.

Mike nodded and smiled and the driver held out his pack for Mike.

"Say, you two are brother and sister? How does that work?"

"Adoption," said Jordan.

"Oh. Yeah. Right." said the driver.

Mike asked for a light and the man flipped his lighter and Mike lit his cigarette over it. The driver's attention was on Jordan, and she was working it.

"So, where are you headed?" Jordan flipped her hair and played with the strands around her ear.

"Clear on out to Denver," said the driver, "You?"

"Our car is near Omaha, we hope. At a truck stop."

"Hell, I can take you right there."

"We've got money in the car. Can you lend us twenty bucks to get some food until we get there?"

"Shit. OK. Here you go." The driver opened his wallet and gave Jordan a twenty. She stroked his arm. Rewarding good behavior made that behavior more likely, and there was no behavior she liked better than someone handing over their money to her.

"Thank you so much," said Jordan, as she jogged to the store. "Mikey, come on, this one's on me."

Mike smiled and thanked the truck driver. "I didn't get your name."

"Sonny," said the driver. "I'll meet you two back here in fifteen."

"Ten-four," said Mike. As he was walking towards the store, he thought about what an ass he was to be using trucker slang.

CHAPTER 76

In which our heroes endure the journey of four hundred miles

Jordan sat by the window and Mike sat in the middle in the cab of the semi-truck. On the way out of Minneapolis and every chance he got, Sonny, the driver, hinted that he'd rather that Jordan were sitting in the middle.

"It ain't safe to have the bigger person sitting in the middle, you know?"

Jordan wasn't buying it. "We'll take our chances, sir."

Mike was trying to gauge whether Sonny wanted to talk or whether he was a silent driver. He attempted small talk, but Sonny kept turning the topic back to reasons that Jordan should sit in the middle.

"No offense, Mike. Seriously. But, it would be much easier for me with the shifting if I had more room, which is why I think you should swap places with your sister there."

After Jordan rejected his request a few times, Mike got in on it too. "No offense, but she'd really like to sit by the window. If it's that difficult for you, you can just let us out."

"No, no. That's fine. I'm a pro. I've been doing this for thirty years," said Sonny.

When it was clear that Jordan didn't want to sit next to him, he tried to impress her with his driving skill, and then he tried talking to her in a quieter voice than she'd be able to hear from all the way over by the window and told her that if she switched places with Mike she'd be able to hear him better. When they stopped to buy a soda and smoke, Sonny opened the driver's side door for her to get in, thinking that Mike might get in on the other side and then Jordan would be in the middle. Jordan climbed up into the cab and slid over to the window. Mike got in on the driver's side too and slid over.

And so it went for the first two hours of the six-hour drive to Omaha. After two hours, Jordan fell asleep with her head against the window, and Mike tried to talk with Sonny about sports.

"What do you think of the Vikings' chances this year?" said Sonny.

"Oh boy. If we get rid of the other team, maybe this year they'll finally go all the way, right?"

Sonny laughed and slapped Mike on the knee. "That's the way, son. Skol, Vikings!"

"Skol Vikings!" Sonny honked his horn and pumped his fist while cheering. "Seriously, though, I think Brzezinski knows what he's doing."

"Totally," said Mike.

"Best team money can buy, right kid?"

"Totally," said Mike, "are they playing today?"

"Haha! Good one. They should make 'em play during the off season for the salaries they get, am I right?"

"Exactly. We want our money's worth. We pay their salaries," said Mike.

"Right. And then they kneel during the national anthem? It's a disgrace."

Mike was starving, dehydrated, and exhausted. But, this guy was nice enough or crazy enough to give them a ride, so he tried as best he could to play along. The conversation was getting too far down the road into unfamiliar territory, so Mike changed the subject.

"So, you don't usually pick up hitchhikers?" said Mike.

"Well, I'm an independent operator, so I don't have a company telling me what I can and can't do and who I can and can't pick up. But, the DOT doesn't like long haulers picking up rides, that's for sure. There are exceptions for emergencies, of course, but you'd damn well better believe that I gotta report when that happens. The problem, you see, is liability. If we got in a wreck up there around that next turn, and I had unauthorized riders, whose neck is on the line do you think?"

"Yours?"

"Exactly. So, I shouldn't be doing this. But, I come from the old school. I didn't become a trucker so I could follow someone's rules and be safe. I became a trucker to make some money, live free, take drugs, and see the country. I'm from Nashville, Tennessee. When I dropped out of high school in 1975, there was a truckin' school just down the street and I worked for the man for twenty years. Back in the day, it didn't matter whether you worked for a company or you had your own truck—we were all picking up hitchhikers, talking on the CBs, driving eighteen-hour days, and hooking up at the truck stop. But, they put on all kinds of rules over the years and now it's just like any job, except I don't have to go to an office and I can see what people in their cars are doing with their hands. I've seen some things, let me tell you. But, after twenty years, I had enough saved to put a down payment on this truck. I told the company to shove it, and I was free again. Do you know that I'm supposed to have government posters hung up in here?"

"Really," said Mike, "that seems pretty strange. For what?"

"OSHA. DOT. DMV. DOE. All of 'em. They want me to plaster over the windshield with papers telling me what I can and can't do. Well, fuck 'em. I gotta get an inspection every year to make sure I have the posters. You know what I do?"

"What?"

"I have a piece of 3/8 inch plywood I keep under the seat with all the posters glued to it. I can take that out and put it on the dash there any time I need. It meets their requirements, but I don't have to look at it day-in and day-out. Fuck 'em."

"That's a good idea," said Mike.

Mike and Sonny talked for several hours more. Jordan pretended to be asleep.

They stopped for breakfast and then again a few hours later for lunch. When they finally neared Omaha, Mike recognized the truck stop where he and Jordan had eaten breakfast. "Ours is the next exit," he said.

"Ah, the old 'Pop-n-Drop'," said Sonny.

"Pardon?"

"That's what we used to call it back in the day. 'Pop-n-Drop'. It's where you pop your pills and drop your pants."

"Awesome. I'll have to remember that one," said Mike.

Jordan pretended to wake up, and she stared out the window. She thought if she hoped enough and looked hard enough, it would affect whether the car—with her purse in it—was still where they'd left it.

"Well! Look who finally joined us again!" said Sonny. "Did you have a nice nappy nap?"

"Stop the truck!" screamed Jordan. "Just fuckin' stop! Pull over! Now!"

"Whoa! What's the matter, girly?" said Sonny. "What's got her panties in a bunch?"

"I think you'd better stop now," said Mike.

"OK fine! Jeez!"

Sonny put on his hazard lights and pulled onto the shoulder of the freeway. Jordan jumped out just before the truck came to a stop. She hopped over the guardrail and ran perpendicular to the freeway until she was out of sight. Mike got out of the truck at a more leisurely place, hopped the guardrail, waved to Sonny and walked parallel to the freeway to the next exit.

It took Mike an hour to walk to the gas station where the clowns had kidnapped them. His car had been towed to a parking space behind the garage, but it was still there. The passenger side door was unlocked. Jordan's purse was gone. He opened the glove box and felt around in it. The money was gone. His boxes of shit were still in the back seat though, so at least he had his first edition signed copy of Geek Love, for what it's worth.

"Fuck." Mike unlocked the driver's side door, got in, put the key into the ignition and turned. It started. Mike put his forearms over the steering wheel and looked hard at the back of the gas station, trying to figure out what to do next.

Mike put the car in reverse and looked over his shoulder. Standing behind the car, wearing a clean black shirt with "Visit Omaha" written on it in pink letters and holding several large plastic shopping bags and with her purse slung over her shoulder was Jordan.

Mike slammed the shifter back into park and jumped out. He threw his arms around Jordan, and she dropped her shopping bags.

"I'm glad to see you," said Jordan.

"Me too," said Mike.

"I got some things. Can you open the trunk?"

Mike opened the trunk and Jordan lifted her bags and put them on top of Mike's boxes. "By the way, the owner was cool. He never called the cops, which is super-strange. But, maybe he's got something shady going on. Or is he on the clown payroll too? I don't know. Anyway, I gave him a couple Benjamins for his trouble and it's all good."

Jordan opened the first bag and pulled out each item and inspected it before presenting it. "Here we have an amazing Omaha shirt, men's large. Here's an Air and Space Museum hat. It looked like something you'd wear. Here's some sunglasses. Here's a new phone charger. Here's a pack of smokes. Here's a Pepsi." She opened the 2nd bag. "Here's all the candy and chips."

"This is incredible. Thank you."

"Let's get out of here."

"Fine with me. I'm going to Aberdeen. You with me?"

"Yes," said Jordan, "and I want to apologize for not believing you about the clowns. Turns out they are real. You did hear what that clown said in the van, right? About the secret clown headquarters in Aberdeen?"

"Yes," said Mike, "and I'm pretty sure I still have friends there. I have to warn them."

Aberdeen is almost a thirty-hour drive from Omaha. The quickest route is to go north on I-29 to Sioux Falls and then take I-90 until it dead-ends into Route 12. I-90 through South Dakota, through Billings, through Bozeman, is what ruined the old West. It stopped being the land of the educated rancher or the independent cowboy, or the land of motorcycle repairing pilgrims studying maps, and it became the land of the entitled baby boomer survivalists who never would have made it as far as Rapid City if they couldn't stop for a soft serve cone at Wall.

For the first few hours, they were both looking in the rearview mirror for old VWs and scanning rest areas as they passed, looking for flashes of orange hair.

At some point in South Dakota, they both felt safe that they weren't being chased. Jordan slept for four hours while Mike drove and then Mike slept for four hours while Jordan drove. In the morning, they were a good twelve hours from

Omaha and they stopped for breakfast at the truck stop in Billings, Montana.

The radio in the truck stop was on a classic rock station. "Glory Days" by Bruce Springsteen was playing.

"Fucking hell. I hate this song," said Jordan.

"Ya. Me too. When it starts, I think it's a good song for drinking, because he keeps talking about having a few drinks, but then you realize that it's the same old trash my parents' generation has been shoveling at us since the moment they first got jobs. Yes, of course you're going to sit around talking about the old days, Bruce, because that's all you've ever done. Fuck you, Bruce!"

"Do you think we should get drunk?" said Jordan.

"Yes," said Mike.

It was 10 A.M. in Billings, Montana. Mike and Jordan ate their breakfasts while Jordan used her phone to read reviews of Billings bars that were open in the late morning. Billings, being a college town, has a good number of bars.

"Hey Mike," said Jordan.

"Yes, Jordy," said Mike.

"There's a bar called Hooligans. Is that Irish enough for you? Or will you only drink at a bar called O'Malley's?"

"Is there a bar called O'Malley's? That would be appropriate."

"No. Just a Hooligans."

"That'll do," said Mike, "How are the reviews?"

"Um. Let's see. The service was kind of crappy. The best brew pub in Montana. Best place to watch the big game."

"Oh, fuck. Sold. It doesn't mention anything about lunch buffet or an 80s D.J., does it?"

"No, nothing like that."

"Okay, cool. We should be safe from clowns there."

They finished breakfast, Jordan paid, and they drove into downtown Billings.

Hooligans is like most sports bars. They have TVs, they have video poker, they have beer signs on the walls and hanging from the ceiling, they have deep fried food and a decent burger. At 11:00 A.M., they're like most bars—pretty dead. Mike and Jordan sat at the middle of the bar. Jordan ordered a greyhound. Mike ordered a whiskey highball with Jameson and Vernors ginger ale.

"I've heard that there are thirty-six questions that you can ask someone and by the end of it they'll be in love with you," said Jordan.

"That's handy," said Mike, "do you know what they are?"

"No. That's all I remember."

"When I was a kid there was supposed to be a sound that would make people shit their pants. They called it the brown note," said Mike.

"Same sort of thing, I guess. What do you think the questions are?" asked Jordan.

"It's probably not 'Will you fall in love with me?' thirty-six times."

"No. Definitely not, or else I'd still be in the truck with Sonny."

"The first one is probably 'Would you like another drink?'"

"Yes, I would," said Jordan.

"The second one probably isn't 'Will you buy it, because I'm broke.'" said Mike.

"No, but ya," said Jordan. Jordan handed Mike $300 and then shooed him away to fetch more drinks. When he walked away, Jordan checked her phone. She had several text messages from Aaron, the guy she dumped back in Chicago:

"Hey babe. Just checking on how you are and how my investment is doing. I hope ur ok."

and

"Look. I know I screwed up. I suck."

and

"Where are you?"

She also had two messages from her mother in Thailand:

"A man just told me there's a Thai proverb: 'bad seven times, good seven times.'"

and the message from a few hours later:

"The man was lying."

Jordan laughed out loud.

Mike returned a few minutes later with two more drinks—a greyhound and a mimosa.

"Oooo. Mimosa, huh? That's fresh. Watch out, though. I'm a brunch whore."

"What does that mean?" asked Mike.

"I don't know. I heard someone say it once." Jordan sipped her mimosa and, looking Mike in the eyes the whole time, drank the rest in a single sip. "So, what are we going to do now that we've escaped the lousy evil clowns? Who's in Aberdeen?"

"I think Princess is there. And Andy Pencils too."

"Victor's dad."

"Yeah."

"Who's Princess?"

"She's from the circus."

"She's from the circus and you want to see her?"

"And she was my friend."

"Ah ha. Okay."

"It's not like that."

"I don't give a fuck, Michael."

"Right. Okay. Maybe it was like that."

"Of course it fucking was like that. Do you think I'm your girl now just because I give you money and we were locked up in a clown jail, and we're getting drunk together?"

"No."

"Okay, good. Because you're still pretty gross to me."

"I know it. Want another?"

"Yeah. Isn't this one bottomless?"

"No. The mimosas aren't bottomless here. Hooligan's is a class joint."

A man wearing a fur hat and a military-style jacket walked into Hooligans and started shouting. "You have to get out of here. Everyone has to leave this building now. This building has been condemned upon my authority as God's messenger."

The bartender came out from behind the bar with a shotgun and pointed it at the man. "Sir, I need to ask you to leave."

Mike sunk his head low to the bar and turned towards Jordan. "I think that must be the Hooligan," he said. Jordan laughed and put her hand up to shush Mike.

"I will not leave," said the man with the fur hat. "I am the lord thy god, and ye who shall come before me shall feel my wrath for the insultations you have lain before me forever eternal condemnation!"

"Sir, you need to leave now!" The bartender raised his voice to a shout so that he could be heard over the shouting of the man with the fur cap.

Mike stood up and touched Jordan's arm to signal to her that they should leave.

"I shall not be moved!" shouted the man as he reached under his jacket and pulled two pistols out of holsters. He pointed one at the bartender and one at Mike and fired. The bartender fired his rifle. Mike and the man with the fur hat both collapsed to the floor and Jordan and the bartender ducked under the bar.

Chapter 77

In which Jordan goes to Aberdeen

Jordan contacted Mike's sister, Pauline. She and her husband came out the next day. Because Pauline was Mike's only surviving family member, his car and the contents of it became her property.

"We already have a much nicer car," Pauline said, "so I don't have any use for it. If you want the car, it's yours. You can drop off the books at a Goodwill or something."

"Thank you. I'll take it. I think I'll hang onto the books, though," said Jordan.

Jordan explained to Pauline that it was a closed casket deal due to the nature of his death, and Pauline decided against having any sort of ceremony. "He didn't have any friends as far as I know, and we haven't spoken in years," she told Jordan.

"I was his friend," said Jordan.

"It's so sad what happened. It makes you think," said Pauline. "Please come visit us in Sacramento any time. A friend of Mike's is a friend of ours."

"Thank you, I will. I have to finish something for him first," said Jordan.

Pauline hugged Jordan in the lobby of the hospital. Pauline's husband stood by the door with his arms folded and his chin tucked down. Jordan cried on Pauline's shoulder, and after a few minutes, Pauline's husband walked over to them.

"We have to get the airport," he said. "I'm really sorry. This is just horrible. Let us know if there's anything we can do. And, please do come visit us if you're ever in Sacramento."

"Thank you so much," said Jordan.

Pauline let go of Jordan and walked out the revolving hospital doors. Her husband stayed behind for a minute. Once Pauline was outside, he spoke in a hushed voice to Jordan. "Do you have enough money to get where you're going?"

Jordan shrugged and wiped tears from her face.

Pauline's husband took out a checkbook and wrote a check for $5,000 and handed it to Jordan.

"I can't take that," said Jordan.

"No, please. I insist."

"This is too nice. You don't have to do this."

"We want to. It's the least we can do. Please use this to settle his affairs and to take care of yourself too. I never met Mike, but I heard good things about him and if he's anything like his sister, he must have really been something special."

"He was." Jordan wiped her face on her sleeve again and took the check.

"Well, it was nice to meet you. I'm sorry it wasn't under better circumstances. We really do have to catch that flight."

"Thank you. I'll be ok. I will come visit."

Jordan left the hospital and got on the freeway headed west. Five grand was more than she expected. Mike's sister must be loaded. If she was the reason the clowns were able to find him—as he suspected—then Jordan was sure that she hadn't gotten enough money out of her. From the way Mike talked about his sister, it seemed to her like he wouldn't care if she took advantage of the situation and did visit them in

Sacramento down the line. There would be time for that later. The first thing Jordan wanted to do was to get to Aberdeen. She owed it to Andy Pencils to tell him about his dad and to warn him about the secret clown center. She wasn't sure how she felt about Princess. She sounded like kind of a bitch. But, Jordan hated owing people anything, and so she planned to take care of her debt to Andy first.

The drive across Montana was long, but uneventful and beautiful. In Spokane, she stopped and found the nicest hotel in town and paid cash to stay in their nicest room. She spent the next day buying new clothes and eating whatever she felt like. She took Mike's books to a used bookstore, and they offered her a couple hundred bucks for the signed copy of Fight Club and the first edition of Breakfast of Champions. She kept those two and sold the rest—four boxes full. Another box contained several half full bottles of bourbon.

She bought a small suitcase with good locks and she packed her new clothes and her two books into it, got the car detailed, got a haircut and manicure while she waited for the car, and then stayed another day in the ritzy Spokane hotel and read Breakfast of Champions while getting shitfaced by herself on the liquor part of her inheritance from Mike.

The next afternoon, Jordan packed her suitcase and the remaining booze into the car, bought a muffin and a large coffee in the hotel lobby, and headed west again. The straight roads of eastern Washington glided beneath her and the warm fall air felt like a pillow after the coldness of the mountains as she cruised at fifty-five miles per hour in the right lane with the windows down.

She turned on the radio and found not much but 80s music, country, and the kind of news radio station that you know is going to start and end with a denture commercial. Jordan chose the 80s station and she sang along with a John

Mellencamp song as she remembered the words from her mom singing it around the house while they cleaned up the evening slop.

Ain't we America

You and Me?

Ain't we America

We're something to see, baby!

Jordan was getting nostalgic and she embraced it for a moment. It felt good. Her hot coffee, her muffin, the old music, the empty highway across the open plain with the big sky and no one was after her and she didn't need to talk to or trick anyone. Plus, she knew she looked good. She had new sunglasses, she'd made up her face, she had on a new black jacket with a red top under it and even new underwear and shoes. Plus, she'd lost a little weight in clown jail.

She felt bad about leaving Mike—but she didn't know him. He had some strange stuff going on in his head and in his life and she was better off without him.

She hoped that the clowns would leave her alone now that he was gone. They had no reason to be mad at her—except that she escaped from their jail that she shouldn't have been in in the first place. Mike told her that Aberdeen is the one place where clowns won't go, but then it turns out that it's the worst place in the world if you're trying to get away from clowns. Whatever. It was time to put the past behind and enjoy listening to John Mellencamp. It must have been his birthday or something because the next song was by him too.

Little ditty, bout Jack and Diane!

Jordan shouted along with the song and beat the rhythm on the steering wheel.

Hours later, Jordan rolled into Aberdeen.

Aberdeen, Washington is a small town containing people who were born in a small town, lived a life with little opportunity in the small town, and would probably die in a small town. Aberdeen used to be a logging town. But now its biggest industry is meth, followed by remembering Kurt Cobain, who was born there and who didn't die there.

Jordan drove up and down the streets of the downtown area, trying to find a place where the local little people might hang out. But, store after store was closed and boarded up. The main street had some "walk of fame" stars that stretched for several blocks, spaced out far enough that you forgot about the last one each time.

The signs of attempted downtown revival were there—the new brewery and a coffee shop. But, the decay was everywhere and was maintaining a firm grasp. The suburbs would be aglow with car dealers and mattress stores, Jordan thought.

She parked the car near the VFW hall. If it's true that clowns control such organizations in the rest of the country, it stands to reason that in Aberdeen, where there are supposed to be no clowns, the VFW hall might be a good place to at least find out something about the local circus underground. Jordan couldn't believe that she'd fallen into such a stupid world and that now she was trying to make sense of it.

It was evening and there was an A.A. meeting just letting out at the hall. Several men in flannel shirts were standing outside smoking and drinking coffee from paper cups. Inside, the lights were on and there he was—a little person—standing on a chair next to a plastic folding table and wiping out the inside of the coffee pot with a dish towel. Jordan felt the eyes of the men by the door piercing through her as she walked into the hall and stood next to the little person.

"Hi, can I ask you a question?"

"Fer sure! Fer sure! That's what I'm here for," said the little person.

"Do you know where I might find Andy Pencils?"

A woman, this one normal height, approached from the side and said, "Eww. What do you want to find that guy for?" Then she started laughing.

"You found him," said Andy.

"Oh thank goodness. Can I buy you a drink, er, oh sorry. I need to talk to you about something," said Jordan.

"Sure thing." Andy put the dish towel down and slapped his hands together and shook them a few times to dry them. He bent over to grab the edge of the table as he stepped down from the chair, then he motioned for Jordan to sit on the chair.

"Welcome to my office. Have a seat, please," he said.

Andy Pencils was old. He was the oldest midget he knew. For being so old, he didn't seem worn out. He had little difficulty climbing onto and off chairs, he still ran a mile every morning, and he enjoyed a laugh and a good meal as much as the next guy. When he was in his prime, getting out of control at midget orgies was fun and he was always sure that he'd wake up in the morning—albeit sometimes in unexpected places like in the washing machine or hanging on a coat rack. But, as he got older, he had too many scares and so he joined A.A.

When Andy first started going to A.A. meetings, he was surprised to discover that the main attraction of Aberdeen's A.A. meetings is that they provided the perfect cover for people who don't want to be sober. At the A.A. meetings, drunks learned better ways to disguise their drinking—mostly by pouring their liquor into coffee. As long as Andy kept going to meetings and as long as he only drank at the meetings and talked about A.A. and his buddies in A.A. at every chance he got, no one suspected that he was still a drunk.

Jordan sat down in the folding metal chair. Andy stood in front of her with his thumbs through his suspenders.

"What can I do ya for?" he asked.

"Oh shit. Where to start?"

"At the beginning might be a good place," said Andy.

"No. I think I need to start at the end with this. Mike O'Malley is dead."

"Oh my. Oh my indeed," said Andy. "What happened?"

"It was a random madman at a bar in Billings. He just shot. From just a few feet away. Mike died on the way to the hospital."

"I'm so sorry for your loss. He was a good guy. He had a tough time as a kid, and he made some bad decisions, but I was always rooting for him, you know? Are you OK?"

"Me? Yeah, I'm fine. I barely knew him . . . well, except that we were locked up together."

"Oh fuck. They got to him?"

"Yeah. They got him. My one regret is that I didn't believe him. It sounds so crazy—clown jail? No one would have believed that. Right?"

"Fer sure. I thought it was a circus myth myself. But, I never worked in the circus, at least not in any official capacity, you see. But, you got out of clown jail? How?"

"Clowns aren't that smart," said Jordan.

"Indeed. Fer sure," said Andy, "Thank you for coming here to tell me about Mike. What a shame. What a horrible terrible shame. Dammit."

"There's one more thing."

"Hang on. Do you want some coffee? I could make a new pot. Or we could go to the diner?"

"I think I need to tell you the other thing then you can decide if you want to drink coffee with me."

"OK. Fair enough. Spill it."

"Your father is in clown jail in Minnesota. He told us to find you."

"Old Vic? That sonofabitch must be ancient by now. How can that be possible?"

"He almost escaped with us. But, he was too slow, and we couldn't stop to go back for him. I wanted to. But . . ." Jordan sniffed and wiped her eyes.

"Now, now." said Andy, "It's a miracle that he's still alive. I hate him being in there, but he's been away most of my life and when he was around, we didn't have much of a relationship. Did he say anything else?"

Jordan couldn't remember whether Victor had said anything else. It wasn't her job to remember what Victor wanted to say—that was Mike's job. Jordan felt like a responsibility she never asked for was given to her and she resented it and wanted to get out of it with as little hassle as possible, so she made something up.

"He said to tell you that he loves you."

"Don't lie to me, please. He didn't say any such thing."

"No, he didn't. But, I can't remember what he said. That was Mike's job. I'm sorry."

Andy walked closer to Jordan and put his arm over her shoulder to hug and comfort her.

"Well, whatever will be will be, right?" said Andy, "The old bastard never gave a shit about me and I returned the favor. Mike's passing hurts me much more. There's someone else we need to tell, and she's not going to take it well."

"Princess?" asked Jordan.

"Yes. I guess Mike mentioned her."

"Once or twice."

"She'll be home by now. Do you have some time? Can you come along?"

"Yes. Believe me, I don't have any plans. And, I feel like I should be there."

"It's just a few blocks away."

Andy Pencils led Jordan to his apartment, on 2nd Street in Aberdeen. Andy shared the apartment with Princess. Princess took care of him, fed him, made sure that he made it to his doctor appointments, and kept him company. Andy had a pension from Ford that, along with his Social Security payment, provided them both with enough to live on.

Andy and Jordan climbed the three flights of stairs up to the apartment, above a vacant store front. When they entered, they found Princess sitting on a love seat, wearing an apron, watching Jeopardy, holding an icepack against the top of her head.

Princess was forty-nine. After the circus shut down, Princess spent a few years in New York. She had parts in some independent films, a music video, and the odd off-Broadway play. But, her acting career never took off. When she started having the usual midget aches and pains, and after the incident with the sit-com producer, she knew that her hope of being an actress was gone. She contacted some of the old circus folks looking for a safe roommate anywhere in the world. When she heard that Andy Pencils needed a caregiver and companion, she packed her bags and set out for Aberdeen.

Little people distrust normals to be their caregivers, and with good reason. Normal people have a long history of cruelty toward little people. The horrible truth—and one that Mike had worked to bring to light during his time in the circus—was that it was almost certain that a norm living with midgets would take advantage of them in subtle ways like putting the cookies on the top shelf. When adults do this to children, it's understandable. But, when adults treat other adults like children, it's flat-out abuse. Other forms of abuse that midgets living with norms endure include: the non-stop sit-com-style jokes ("Don't make me hurl you into the sun, little man.") and—much worse—lack of accommodations for their shortness. In his time, Andy had lived through having several roommates who refused to even have ladders and step stools in the apartment, because it was inconvenient to move them out of the way when using the stove.

Andy and Princess's had shared their apartment for the last 18 years. They had adapted it to their height challenges, but (upon the landlord's insistence) they didn't make any structural or permanent changes. They used custom small furniture, cinder blocks, and 2x8 boards to create runways in front of counters and sinks. They had special door lever attachments installed on all the doors to make opening and closing them more convenient—and safer. They installed motion detecting light switches to turn on the lights when they entered rooms.

Being Andy's helper gave Princess a sense of purpose and she embraced it with gusto. But, in the years since she left New York, Princess had neglected or ignored her own failing health. She had a persistent headache, joint and back pain, and type two diabetes as a result of her obesity. If she stayed hopped up on the pain pills, she could function normally for most of the day. But, when evening came around these days, she just wanted to go to bed and try to sleep.

Princess stood up and brushed off the front of her apron and turned off the TV.

"Ah shit, Andy, if I knew we were going to have company, I would have cleaned up a little."

Jordan stood in the doorway as Andy took Princess's hand and kissed her cheek. "Princess, this is Jordan. She was Mike's friend."

"Was?" Princess whispered.

"Yes. Mike's dead."

"Was it them?"

"Yes and no," said Jordan.

"Ah shit," said Princess, "I don't want to know anymore right now. I need a drink and a smoke and I'm starving. Will you stay for dinner?"

"I'm sorry," said Jordan.

"Well, will you stay for dinner? It's not much. I didn't know we were having company. Here, have a seat."

Princess removed the board that served as her make-shift TV dinner tray from between two normal-sized chairs that sat in front of her small love seat. She brushed off one of the chairs with her hand and then slapped it a couple times.

Jordan hung her purse over the back of the chair and sat down. Princess went to the kitchen, where she had cinder blocks and boards that she walked around on so that she could cook.

Andy sat down in Princess's love seat and shouted to Princess. "You know, we could just go out. You don't have to cook. Do you want to talk about Mike?"

"I don't want to talk or think right now," said Princess, "I told you I'm starving. Do you want a drink, Jordan?"

"Yes, please."

"A beer or a gin and tonic?"

"G and T, please."

"G and T? Oh, yes, gin and tonic."

"I can get it."

"Oh please, no. I'm not handicapped. I'm just short and fat."

Princess filled two glasses with ice from the refrigerator door, then walked along her planks to the corner of the kitchen where she kept the gin on the counter and filled the glasses half full. She walked back to the refrigerator and got out the tonic water and topped off the glasses. "I don't have any limes," she said, "Mike wouldn't consider it a real gin and tonic. G and T." Princess took a sip from one of the glasses. "But, it'll do."

"Thank you," said Jordan, standing up and taking the glass from Princess. They tapped their glasses together and then both drank. "Andy—you want me to make some coffee?"

"That would be swell. Thanks."

Princess stretched to reach the cabinet with the coffee and filters. Jordan stepped in to help and Princess swatted her away.

"I can do it," she said, and then added, "Sorry. I'm not used to having normal people in the apartment. You're always trying to help. I know you mean well, but I'm an adult."

"Understood," said Jordan.

Princess talked as she went through the routine of making the coffee. "Mike and I were friends. I might have been his only friend in the circus. But, he wasn't around for long. He was always in a hurry to be somewhere else or to be someone else. I think his sister did a real number on his head, to tell you the truth."

"He was a good kid, though," said Andy.

"Yes, of course he was a good kid," said Princess, "but that's beside the point. He was a fucking mess in the head. But, aren't we all? But you've known him more recently than me. I'm just babbling."

"No, no. Please go on. I only met him a few weeks ago and we spent most of that time in jail."

"Oh shit. Clown jail?"

"Yes."

"Mike's worst fear. Was it as bad as he imagined? Is that where he died?"

"Clown jail was horrible. But, it was horrible because it was so poorly run. I think Mike imagined it would be organized and evil, but it was evil and a mess, which is how we got out."

Princess nodded. "I can see that. You don't get into clowning because you're good at life." Princess finished preparing the coffee maker and turned it on. She watched for a minute as the first brown drops of coffee dripped into the carafe. "I guess you'd better tell me how he died so that I stop making up things in my head."

"We escaped the jail and started driving here. We stopped in Billings, Montana and a crazy man shot and killed him."

"Just random?"

"Yes."

"Are you sure it wasn't a vigilante clown?"

"This guy wasn't a clown."

Princess lit a cigarette and put a pot in the sink and turned on the water to fill it. "Andy, did you hear this? That's so horrible."

Andy didn't respond. He was asleep on the couch.

"Fuck. I mean . . . Fuck. Well, he did always say that someday he wanted to see Montana. I think he said that. Or, maybe that was someone else. Ah, fuck. Getting old sucks."

Princess heaved the full pot out of the sink and placed it on the stove and turned it on. "Do you like spaghetti?"

"Yes. Doesn't everyone?"

Andy woke up and waddled over to between where Jordan and Princess were standing. "We do it a little different here," he said.

"How's that?" said Jordan.

"We do it East Detroit-style. Do you know what that is?"

"No. I've never heard of that."

"It's Prego with tuna fish. You'll love it."

"Sounds a lot like North Bangkok-style spaghetti," said Jordan.

"For reals?" asked Andy.

"I have no idea, honestly."

"Huh. I've never thought about it, but now that you mention it, that's interesting to think about. Where did East

Detroit Spaghetti come from? Could be Bangkok. Could just be. Maybe so. Princess, what do you think about this?"

Princess stood with her cigarette hanging from between her lips, watching the pot of water for signs of life.

Chapter 78

*In which we find out something important
about Mike.*

From their brief interaction, it was clear to Jordan that Princess's heart and body were broken years ago—her acting dreams were dashed, she was addicted to pain pills, and she had outlived her dwarf family and friends. Mike's death didn't affect her much.

Andy Pencils cared in the way that an old man can care about someone else's death. That is—not much.

Jordan took another sip of her gin and tonic and glanced at the markings she'd made on her hand. She checked them off in her head as she finished the rest of the drink. Money— she was only expecting to get a couple grand out of Mike's sister, so she came away better than expected there. Check. Car— Mike's car wasn't bad. It was luxurious in that 1990 country club way. Check. Got rid of the guy—sure, he wanted to get rid of her as much as she wanted to ditch him, but that's what you call a "win-win". Check. Escape to Aberdeen—the line on her right palm traced from just under her middle finger to just above the first knuckle of her pinky, just below Seattle and to the northwest of Portland. Check.

Jordan was impressed with herself that the plan she cooked up worked. Mike got rid of the clowns for good, she earned a little money, and she didn't even have to get blackout drunk to do it.

Mike wasn't dead. The closed casket, the 'on the way to the hospital' death, and the weepy conversations in the lobby of the hospital were all a story made up for Pauline. As lies go, Jordan was sure they were among the flimsiest and most easily disproved she'd ever told. Pauline and her husband bought it all. It turned out Mike was right about there being nothing that people won't believe when it confirms their world view.

The crazy man at the bar didn't have guns. He shouted for a while, the bartender asked him to leave a few times, and he left on his own after he had said what he needed to say. Mike ordered another round of drinks and they watched a commercial for a car dealership on TV.

Mike leaned back on his bar stool and took in the atmosphere of the bar, the taxidermy animal heads, and the taste of his whiskey. "I've always wanted to see Montana."

www.ingramcontent.com/pod-product-compliance
Lightning Source LLC
Chambersburg PA
CBHW070906260626
47162CB00007B/2572